Hugh MacLennan

Hugh MacLennan was the winner of a record
five Governor General's Awards for his work.
The New Press Canadian Classics series also
includes three of his other novels, *Each
Man's Son*, *The Watch That Ends the Night*,
and *Two Solitudes*.

*From - Santa
1993*

Marian Mildred Dale Scott

Painter Marian Mildred Dale Scott was born
in Montreal in 1906. Her work is in many
public and private collections in Canada and
has appeared on the covers of previous New
Press Canadian Classics.

New Press Canadian Classics

New Press Canadian Classics, featuring works
by Canadian artists on the covers, is an inno-
vative series of high quality, reasonably
priced editions of the very best Canadian fic-
tion, nonfiction, and poetry.

W9-CIA-058

Press Canadian Classics

newpress CANADIAN CLASSICS

Hugh MacLennan
Voices in Time

Stoddart

Published in 1993 by
Stoddart Publishing Co. Limited
34 Lesmill Road
Toronto, Canada
M3B 2T6
(416) 445-3333

Canadian Cataloguing in Publication Data

MacLennan, Hugh, 1907-1990
Voices in time

New Press Canadian Classics
ISBN 0-7736-7393-8

I. Title

PS8525.L45V6   C813'.54   C93-093140-8
PR9199.3.M23V6 1993

Originally published in hardcover in 1980 by
Macmillan of Canada

Published by arrangement with Macmillan Canada
A division of Canada Publishing Corporation

Printed and bound in the United States of America

Contents

To Tota and Frances

Ihr naht euch wieder, schwankende Gestalten,
Die früh sich einst dem trüben Blick gezeigt.
Goethe

PART ONE

John Wellfleet's Story

A WARM MORNING IN JUNE, not a cloud in the sky, another winter and a long cold spring gone over at last and the lilac was in bloom again. The scent of it entering the open window of his room was so intoxicating it brought a mist to the eyes of the elderly man standing beside it. During his illness the past February he had wondered if he would ever smell lilac again. But now the sun was warming his veins and one more summer at least seemed assured to him, his seventy-fifth.

The buzzer stabbed the silence and made him start, for it had been more than three months since anyone had called him. He went to the instrument eagerly, wondering who it might be who had remembered he was still alive. What he heard was an unfamiliar and apparently youthful voice announcing itself as André Gervais and asking if this was Mr. John Wellfleet.

"Yes, I'm Wellfleet."

The man Gervais then informed him that he had in his possession some papers and had good reason to believe that they were concerned with Wellfleet's family. The old man's eagerness vanished.

"Mr. Gervais, did you say? I don't think I know you. Did I hear you say something about my family?"

"Yes, that's what I said. Your family."

"Well, I have no family."

"But you must have had a family once. Let me explain. These papers aren't new. They're so old I can hardly believe they're real. There could be quite a situation here. I can't understand much about these papers, but they might turn out to be very important."

The stranger spoke fluent English, but there was an intonation of French in his voice and Wellfleet, thinking he was an official, replied in that language.

"Je le répète, Monsieur. Ma famille n'existe plus."

Gervais went on in English, "I don't think you understand me. These papers are very old."

Oh, for God's sake, the old man thought, another of them! Papers and questionnaires, this form and that form and that form and this form, his life had been turned into a bog by them. He said nothing and the stranger went on.

"I went to the Bureau of Records, of course, before I called you."

"What good did that do you?"

"It's certainly unreliable, the Bureau. There are many gaps."

"Did I hear you say gaps? You must be very young if you've just discovered that."

"Yes, I'm young, but there *is* a Bureau. They've been trying to restore the data for quite a while now. You must have known that."

"I did not know it."

"The Bureau can't be entirely useless. I certainly found the information that there were people called Wellfleet living in Metro a long time ago. So my question is – were you one of them?"

What's he after? Wellfleet thought. Then he remembered how vulnerable he was.

"Yes," he said bleakly, "I may have been one of them. But when I was young the city I lived in wasn't called Metro, and what difference does it make where anyone lived that long ago?"

He was on the point of breaking the connection when he heard Gervais say eagerly, "I have a name here – Stephanie Wellfleet. Does that name mean anything to you?"

It was so sudden the old man's throat seized up and for several seconds he could not articulate. When finally he spoke his voice was asthmatic.

"She was – she – she was my mother."

The man called Gervais became excited: "I had hoped she was, but in a case like this I had to be absolutely sure. This is wonderful."

Wellfleet felt as though someone had torn stitches from a wound in his soul. Over the years a hard-tested instinct of self-preservation had drilled him to control a naturally impulsive character, but now the control broke.

"Who the hell are you?" His voice rose almost to a scream. "Why can't you people leave me alone? My mother? How do you know she even existed? How do you know her name? And what business is this of yours anyway?"

He was breathing thickly, noisily, because his pulmonary tract was congested. Gervais was talking, his voice was kind, he was trying to soothe the old man, but Wellfleet was hearing nothing. His mother! He had been told that all the records had been destroyed long ago. Completely obliterated. And since then the volume of disappointment, fear, humiliation, and loneliness had been what it had been. This young man, whoever he was, could know nothing of that. He could know very little about anything that had mattered.

Occasionally his mother returned to him in his sleep and was so real he could hear the caress of her voice. But it was a cold thing, a cruel thing. So often when he tried to remember those he had loved in his youth and younger manhood, tried to remember them when he was awake, they had no more life in them than the faded photographs you find in a drawer when you are looking for something else. And what could this mean but that those we have loved so vastly that they have been translated into the memory cells and the mystery of our minds, and have been so woven into our own lives that they were our reason for existing – after they have been dead long enough we can recover them only when we are asleep.

"No!" he shouted, and broke the connection.

When he stumbled to his feet the beauty of the morning was gone and the walls of his room were weaving as though he were drunk or seasick. He blundered outside and collapsed onto a bleached wooden chair on a patch of fresh grass. For several minutes his lungs rasped to his breathing, but gradually his blood pressure subsided and he was still.

Three other old men were taking the sun but they had no interest in him nor he in them. He watched a robin fly into the lilac bush with a worm in its bill. The sun heated his limbs and stirred a little color into his long, pale face. The sky was enormous this morning, deep blue over the fields and trees. Summer was certainly coming; on a day like this it was almost here. Even the hum of a mosquito was soothing.

But there was no way this solitary old man could soothe his mind. He went inside again among his books. The walls of his room were double-lined with them and if he still felt human it was they that had kept him so. In his youth he had been lazy and irregular but he had always enjoyed reading. Only when he had been discarded as inoperative had he become a student. These books out of a lost and marvellous past were his only friends. He had collected many before the Destructions and had found many more afterwards in out-of-the-way places where they had been lost or forgotten, but none of his books helped him now. He picked up one he had been reading with pleasure the night before but now the words refused to come alive for him. He sat still and cursed himself for the fool of fools for having cut off this André Gervais, or whoever he was, without having learned a single thing except that somehow he knew his mother's name. He had no idea how to recover him.

Wellfleet had drilled himself to accept almost everything after his own world had vanished, but he had been isolated too long to know what had been happening in the last two decades. Vaguely he was aware that a new generation was coming alive again, but he had never met any members of it. Years ago the Third Bureaucracy had relegated him to this compound where he was allowed a small room and enough food and clothing to keep him alive.

The rest of his day passed in a slow tension and in the early twilight he went to bed hearing the birds singing until the last oboe-throb of an oriole ceased and it was dark.

Lying in the dark he sank slowly down into the sea of his own past. So long ago the morning of his life; so long ago even his middle years when the marvellous, tragic structure they had called civilization had shattered itself.

Inevitably, after a pause, a raw new bureaucracy had emerged out of the wreckage and this was the one that had ordered the past to be ciphered out as though it had never been. But how could this André Gervais have discovered his mother's name? It unnerved him to know that he had. Then he remembered something he had not taken in when Gervais had been talking to him. The young man's voice had been kind.

As drowsiness seeped through him there welled up the images of some girls and women he had known, and he had known many. A few of them were the only treasures he had left, apart from his books. Now it was Joanne. He dozed, came awake a short time later, saw light from a risen moon washing the spines of his books, then faded off into the depths of sleep. How long he slept he did not know but it must have been several hours, for when he woke the moonlight was gone and the room was dark.

Once more he was a man in his prime, for in a long dream Joanne had returned to him in the full reality of her living flesh and spirit. Small, so near-sighted she was almost blind without her glasses, surely she had been as valiant as anyone he had ever known. She had been absolutely honest. With herself first of all, for her essence had always been private. Only those who had been truly loved by her had discovered how rarely beautiful she was, for only they had seen the wonder of her love-smile. He lay still. She had returned to him with uncanny accuracy – her eyes when she loved, her lips when she loved, the body of a profound human being as supple as the muscles of sea tides when all of her moved and rippled in a whiteness of love – where was she now? *What* was she now? Her body had been dust for years but she had never been more real than she had been a few minutes ago.

His eyes closed and after a while he slept dreamless until the morning.

TWO

A GROUND MIST VEILING THE TREES, the sun seeping through it, the feeling of a hot day coming, a true summer day after the long cold in this cold land. He had eaten a light breakfast when the instrument stabbed the silence and he went to it as fast as his stiff knee could move. It was André Gervais again.

"How kind of you to call me! I never thought you would. I'm so ashamed about yesterday. I don't think there's anything serious the matter with my brain but it was so sudden. Your mentioning my mother's name, I mean. She vanished so long ago. I'm forgetful, I suppose, but I think it's because I've been alone so long. I see it in the others here where I live. We try to like each other, but we don't really find each other interesting. My best friend is a chipmunk. I save crumbs from my meals and when I go outside he comes to me and eats off the palm of my hand."

Gervais spoke quietly, carefully. "I'm the one who should apologize, Mr. Wellfleet. I was far too eager. Now I'd like to explain why I called you. When I called I was only taking a chance on your name. I mean, I was astonished to find you were real. But when you told me that this lady – this lady Stephanie Wellfleet – that she was your mother, it was such marvellous luck I could hardly believe it and

I suppose I became excited. You see, this proved that what I had found was genuine, and if it's genuine it's absolutely priceless."

The old man was as bewildered as ever. "I'm afraid I don't know what you're talking about, so perhaps you could explain."

Gervais, still speaking quietly, told him that he was a young man, twenty-five years old, and that he was calling from the ruins of the old Metro where he worked. A few years ago a group of men had formed a small company to commence the building of a new city on a section of the ruins because, so said Gervais, they had been told by several travellers that this was one of the great natural sites in the world. From some old books they had learned that in the far distant past many famous cities had been destroyed and new ones built on top of their ruins. In the central part of the wrecked Metro they had found a wall standing and had blown it down to level the place. While the debris was being cleared away, Gervais himself had found two large cast-iron boxes, each one weighing about twelve kilograms without the contents. On each box was engraved the name "James Wellfleet" and the number 1872.

Wellfleet listened in a daze. Then he sat down.

"Give me time to think," he said. "It was so long ago. James Wellfleet was my great-great-grandfather and he died long before I was born. I suppose 1872 was a date under the old system." A memory blazed up in his mind. "This is incredible. Yes, suddenly I remember. It was after my stepfather's death. His name was Dr. Dehmel. He was a German."

"A man called Dehmel has left a lot of record in these boxes, but I can't understand much of anything I found in them. Do you know about the boxes themselves?"

Wellfleet began to tremble and his voice was unsteady. "Yes, I do remember."

"You saw those boxes?"

"No. No, I never saw them, but I knew they had been lost. It was the only time I heard my mother cry. She'd had a hard life and she had terrific control. All our lives were in those boxes, I remember her saying. All our lives. I was only a boy and I thought she meant money."

The young man's voice became eager again: "Something far more valuable than money was in them. They had heavy padlocks and they were so corroded I had to burn them off. When I opened the lid I found hundreds of papers and photographs and rolls called tapes, whatever that means. The boxes had been perfectly airtight and the contents were as fresh as yesterday."

The old man was silent, trying to remember. Yes, those boxes must have been stored in the basement of the house where she and Uncle Conrad had lived. A year after her husband's death she had gone to England to spend half a year with a sister who lived there. While she was away a developer had bought the property, smashed the houses down, and dug a hole thirty meters deep and a block long. His mother's furniture had been taken out and put into storage but there was no sign of the boxes.

He told Gervais this and added, "All this happened on top of what had happened to her before." His breathing became asthmatic again. "This is unbelievable. Did I hear you say that some of that building was still standing?"

"Only a wall and a half. It was an empty shell."

"It was one of those crate-shaped buildings we had everywhere. It was forty floors high."

He sat in a daze, motionless, lost in a confusion of memories. Then he heard Gervais speaking.

"We want to know where the truth is. We've heard all sorts of stories about the past, but how true were they? In school they gave us the Diagram, but you were a teacher once and you know what that was worth."

"So you've checked out my record since you last called me? Well, why not? What was the Diagram worth? It was their chief instrument in obliterating the Past. It was supposed to be history, but it omitted nearly all the history of the human race before the Third Bureaucracy. Do you know what the word 'history' means?"

"I know what it means, but I don't know what it *was*. We've found many books, but very little from the time when you were young. Everyone knows the Destructions happened, but we weren't told why. Do you know why?"

"Oh, Mr. Gervais, how can I answer a question like that? *What* happened—yes, I know that. What happened was that hundreds of millions of human beings and animals were obliterated within a few hours and the metros turned into graveyards. For years we'd known there was a chance of this happening, but we never believed it would. Afterwards the Bureaucracy—I've already called it the Third

Bureaucracy–the people in it now were babies when the Destructions came. Their parents had survived because they didn't live in the metros. They were on farms and in small towns and pockets outside the action." He paused. "I wonder if I can possibly make you understand. The metros had become the central nervous system of the entire world. Communications–and they were marvellous–the bureaucrats, the organizers, the planners, the headquarters of everything–they were all in the metros. Nobody could be independent of them. When they were destroyed, the whole system ceased to exist. Those who were on the outside were in horror, just as I was myself. The first few years were so terrible that I can't bring myself to remember them. There was no control at all. It was every man for himself. It was as though the whole world had been thrown back six or seven hundred years without having the organizations those ancient people had." He paused, breathing heavily. "Of course, there were many survivors who understood small skills. Some of them could repair small engines, but they couldn't manufacture them. They couldn't refine fuels. Fortunately a good many doctors who had practised in small towns and in the country survived. They had their medical books, but they could no longer get the drugs they needed. Anyway, medicine survived after a fashion. Then gradually little patterns of order began to appear and another Bureaucracy came into being.

"This Bureaucracy couldn't have been anything else but bad. One of their leaders was a maniac who went around preaching 'They brought the wrath of God upon themselves and upon us all. So let their names and deeds be obliterated forevermore.' That's why they concocted the Diagram, and for a while anyone who tried to tell young people about the past was in danger of his life."

Again he stopped, waiting for Gervais to speak, but Gervais said nothing.

"This part of the world," he went on, "was probably luckier than most others because one of the hydro dams survived. Well, of course you know all about that. At least we had electricity and there were men who understood how to use it."

"Quite a few factories have been built lately," Gervais said quietly. "We're learning. We know how to manufacture wires and repair turbines. We're learning very quickly."

"Of course, I always knew there were survivors who had enough skills to restore a little of what was lost, but there was no will for it. The Bureaucracy was hopelessly ignorant. They couldn't endure their memories or face their future. They also had power, and were crafty enough to know that if the intelligent survivors became organized, they would lose that power."

Wellfleet's breathing had become congested and he felt weakness coming over him. It was the old trouble. He had been sitting with his head down and his neck bent forward and the calcium deposits along the back of his neck had been restricting the flow of blood to his brain. He lifted his head and breathed rhythmically and heard Gervais speaking again. Gervais was saying that he wanted to turn the papers over to the old man. He was saying he longed to meet him and talk with him. Wellfleet shook his head.

"If these papers are personal, I can't understand who would care about them today. If my mother is in them they must be at least fifty years old."

"I'm not sure, but I think some are much older than that."

What was the use? Wellfleet was thinking. How could anyone explain to a man of Gervais's age, brought up on the Diagram, what the world had been like before the Destructions came? He said it aloud.

"I think I might understand if I had a chance," Gervais said.

"It would be too dangerous even to try."

Gervais was surprised. He felt pity, even sorrow, for this old man he had never seen or heard of until yesterday. Where had they been keeping him?

"Mr. Wellfleet," he said quietly, "believe me, there's no danger any more. The Bureaucracy has changed. There's a new mentality. It's the books we've been finding. Some with pictures of cities long before Metro. They're very beautiful. Those metros – we've collected many photographs of them and they all look the same. I can't understand why people wanted to live in places like that."

Wellfleet gave a sad laugh. "Most of them didn't have a choice. I'm sorry, Mr. Gervais, it's not your fault. I understand that. But what you don't know must be just about everything there ever was. Let me ask you a simple question. Do you know how many people are in the world now?"

"We're trying to find out. Would you know?"

"How could I possibly know? I'd guess the population might be what it was three or four hundred years ago, but it's only a guess, and a wild one. When I was your age there were hundreds of millions more people than there are now. None of my friends survived. Lately the faces of a few of them have been coming to me like photographs printed one on top of the other. Some of them were beautiful. Some were gentle and some were even happy. It was nothing in their characters that killed them. It just happened. So perhaps this damned Bureaucracy is right after all. Maybe it's just as well that you should be prevented from knowing what was lost. Your parents would understand what I'm trying to say."

There was another silence, then Gervais said, "I love my parents, but they refuse to say anything about what it was like when they were young."

"I can believe it."

Again buried emotions surged up and the old man was unable to speak. The young man told him he had made a list of names connected with the papers and he began to read them off a paper he had before him – Stephanie Wellfleet, Dr. Conrad Dehmel, many more whose names John Wellfleet had never heard. Finally Gervais asked him if he had been named after his grandfather, John Wellfleet, and was he old enough to remember him?

When he heard this, the old man went out of control. It was too much and it was coming at him too fast. For years that had become a long blur of empty time he had tried to lock away the meaning of everything he had been, known, and valued. For the next few minutes young Gervais wondered if Wellfleet had gone out of his mind, for he was sobbing and crying.

"You don't know! You can't know! Nobody ever will know for ever and ever. They obliterated their lives and then they obliterated their names. Every remaining record they found they deliberately destroyed. It wasn't like that ever before. My grandfather knew the names of his family going back for more than two hundred years into the Old Country and now he might never have been. People like him and my mother and Valerie and Joanne and everyone I knew and loved – even famous men we all knew – where are they? Only in my memory and sometimes I'm not even sure they're there. My memory is a blur."

The young man felt fear. He listened to Wellfleet's breathing grow steady and a moment later he heard his voice come out strong and firm.

"Mr. Gervais, it so happens that I never knew the name of my real father. My mother, I think, was the purest soul I ever knew in my life. When I was sixteen, she told me that my actual father was a distinguished Englishman who hadn't informed her that he was married to somebody else until she discovered she was pregnant. Previously she had believed she was engaged to him."

Gervais said nothing.

"But when I was a child," the old man went on, "this did not matter because of Grandfather. His own children were grown up and married and his wife – my grandmother – she had died a few years before. That's what Mother told me. Mother used to keep his house and look after him and he was the kindest man you could imagine. He'd lost his money in business. There were some very smart business operators around then, but at least he wasn't classified inoperative as the Bureaucracy classified me. Nobody was then. Grandfather loved all young and growing things. You'd never believe this, but in those days in the pre-Metro city there were wild animals on the mountain. You should have seen the squirrels. Somebody called it the City of Squirrels. And the wildflowers! There were all kinds of them on the mountain and Mother and Grandfather knew the names of them all. Just think of that. They knew the names of the flowers."

He stopped abruptly and with an effort he quieted his breathing again.

"I'm sorry, Mr. Gervais, I talked too much and couldn't stop. Talking to somebody real is like eating after you've been nearly starved to death."

After a short silence, Gervais said, "Of course, we've all heard stories. And the Diagram. Was there any truth in it?"

"Oh, that! Yes, I suppose there was some. If you want to make a good lie stick, you've got to put at least a little truth into it."

"Then let me ask you another question. Was it when you were a child that the old System began to fall apart?"

"I've often thought you could make a case for that idea. But let me tell you, there was a long, long trail a-winding before the final Destructions came. Am I confusing you? Of course I am."

"There's another name here – Timothy Wellfleet. Do you think he's alive still?"

The old man passed a long-fingered hand over a long, narrow forehead.

"For God's sake, what next? Timothy, did you say? He was an older cousin of mine but I never met him. When I was a schoolboy he was famous for a while. He was a star on what we called the networks. I won't waste your time trying to explain it, but it was a picture system we called television. It went everywhere. He was what we called a star for a short time and then he disappeared. I never knew what happened to him. I can't believe he's alive. If he is, he's in his nineties. I know Mother knew him well. She was his first cousin and a good many years older. I have a vague idea that for a short while she helped bring him up. Otherwise I never thought he had anything to do with any of us."

The young man hesitated, then asked carefully, "How long is it, sir, since you were in Metro?"

The shock of it returned and brought a buzzing to Wellfleet's ears. He had gone into Metro shortly after it was destroyed. He had gone in with the impossible hope of finding his mother and Joanne. After a short time among the ruins he had lost his way and had vomited from the stench of the decomposing bodies. He had never gone near the place again.

Gervais's voice now became urgent. "It might make problems if I went out to see you, but you can certainly see me. There's a transporter service into Metro and it passes the place where you've been located. You know that, I suppose?"

"Somebody told me about it."

"You must come in to look at these papers. I told you I'm lost in them, but I've made a kind of catalogue. There are nearly a thousand personal letters. All kinds of photographs. Diaries and journals. And the narratives! I've never seen anything like them. Some by Timothy Wellfleet. Many by Dr. Dehmel – many diaries from him. Not much from your mother." He paused. "There are a lot of items called tapes. Would you know what they are?"

"Yes. I won't try to explain it to you, but I even have two machines and possibly those tapes would fit them."

"I think they were planning a book," Gervais said, "but I'm very confused. Much of the language I don't understand very well, and some is in a language I don't even recognize. Timothy seems to have been the one who was to put the book together. He writes in a wild kind of way and I can't understand much of it."

"From what I've heard of him I'm not surprised you can't understand him. I never knew him personally. But Conrad Dehmel! He married my mother when my sister and I were seven years old. We were twins. I called him Uncle Conrad. He was what was called an historian. He was even an archaeologist for a time."

"A what?"

"They used to dig up lost cities. Something like you seem to be doing now. He spent a long time studying the records of one of them. I can't remember the name of the place but it was in the Sahara Desert somewhere."

"What happened to it?"

"I was only a schoolboy when Uncle Conrad died and I can't answer that question. I suppose there was another time when the cities broke down and the people abandoned them. There might have been a war. There were always wars. Uncle Conrad spoke and wrote in five different languages. All I know about his earlier life is that it was a miracle he was not liquidated in one of our own wars. He knew a lot. He knew an enormous lot."

"Were there many people like him when you were young?"

"In Europe there were quite a few."

"But if there were men with all that knowledge, why couldn't they stop what happened?"

Wellfleet gave a rueful laugh. "I used to hear Uncle Conrad say those very words himself. He belonged to something called the Club of Rome. The members were afraid of what was coming and made plans to avert it, but it made no difference at all. When everyone's having a ball, who wants to stop the music?"

He knew that Gervais did not understand him but he made no attempt to explain further. It would do no good if he tried. Then Gervais mentioned still another name.

"There's a girl here. Her name is Esther Stahr. Did you know her?"

"I never heard of her."

"She was one of Timothy's girls and she seems to have been his partner for a time in something I can't understand. There's a lot of record about their conversations. She says several times that in those days the real power was hidden. What does that mean – conspiracies in the Bureaucracy?"

Wellfleet broke into a laugh that sounded to Gervais slightly insane.

"It's not your fault, but I can't possibly make you understand what it used to be like in the world. I know the Diagram told you that it was about this time that we cracked up. I can't deny there's some real truth in that. But let me tell you there never was a time in the history of the Galaxy – I don't suppose you even know what that word means – never such a time as when I was young. It was marvellously exciting. Anything could happen. You name it – anything. It was a golden age. The golden age of the Common Man. Nothing like it had ever happened before and nothing like it will ever happen again."

He stopped and after a pause he heard Gervais ask quietly, "But if this was a golden age, why did it destroy itself?"

"Oh, for Christ's sake! Anyway this Esther Stahr, whoever she was, what she said was right. The bureaucracies – we called them governments – it wasn't them that mattered. It was the geniuses. Vehicles out in space with equipment so sophisticated they could photograph gophers sitting in front of their holes. Anything was possible. The efficiency was unbelievable. Of course, there were a few accidents. That spaceship that got away from them – yes, that spaceship. But of course you know about that."

"Spaceship? What do you mean – spaceship?"

"Are you telling me you don't know about that?"

"I never heard that word."

"That God-damned Third Bureaucracy! Yes, that's right. Now I remember. It *was* one of their forbidden words. Do you know what space is?"

"Mr. Wellfleet, of course I know what space is."

"Okay, but this spaceship. It aborted. It got clean out of control. Afterwards, their computers – you don't know what they were but never mind – they buzzed like beehives and still the boys couldn't find out what went wrong. Then they gave up and issued that communiqué, and brother, was it ever beautiful! I remember it word for word. Listen and I'll tell you. 'Exhaustive check-outs on every detail of Mission U.E. 31 – that meant Universe Explorer No. 31 – confirm abort self-inducted. It is therefore assumed that an unknown factor was operative in this abort.' Then they handed out the usual crap about sympathy for the families and about not letting this balls-up interfere with the continuation of the space program. And now you tell me you never even heard the name of it!"

Gervais had not been able to understand more than half of the old man's vocabulary. Wellfleet went on.

"This mission was special because there were two girls aboard. Two guys and two girls. Women were getting into everything then and they organized a big protest against the space program. Why should men get the high of being shot out there and no women? It wasn't fair, they said. By this time the organizers were getting worried because everyone was getting bored by the space trips, so they said okay, this one will be different. The idea took on. Nobody said it officially, but maybe they'd be having sex out there in space and would it be possible when they were weightless? We were all agog and then it aborted." Wellfleet paused. "You know, that thing about the unknown factor bugs me to this day. Those girls and boys still out there wandering through the light years on account of that unknown factor. Of course, they may have sailed into the sun and been burned to death."

There was a long silence until Gervais said, "Is this really true?"

"I told you, didn't I?"

"But are you sure it happened just as you said?"

"Oh, for God's sake!" The old voice became querulous. "You came to me, I didn't come to you. I've been badly treated. Everyone my age has been shucked off into nowhere. Well, let me tell you there are still a few of us left and we've seen things you can't even imagine. And let me tell you something else. We were young too, once."

In another silence Gervais heard the old man breathing noisily. Then he said shyly, "My friends call me André."

Startled, Wellfleet asked if he rated as one of his friends.

"If you'll permit me."

The old man almost choked up. "If I'll permit you! Thank you, André. Thank you very much for that. It almost makes me feel human again."

"And now," Gervais said, "when will you be coming into Metro to take over these papers?"

Wellfleet hesitated. "I don't know."

"Is your health not good enough?"

"I'm not sure I want to see those papers."

"But why not? I can't understand you."

"André, it was such a long time ago. There is something you'll never understand till you're as old as I am. Everyone I ever knew and cared about was destroyed. After that came the years of virtual slavery teaching lies in the Diagram in order to eat. Then they declared me inoperative and put me out into this compound. I suppose I should be grateful for that, but I'm not."

There was a silence. Then Gervais's voice became almost commanding: "I'm asking you to come back to life again. I want you to make a book out of this. Thousands will read it and you'll be alive again."

"Did you say a *book*!"

"I said a book. Even under the Diagram there were printing presses. Now they can be used for something real. They can be used for the truth."

"It's too late."

The young man's voice became even more commanding. "You can't do this to yourself, Mr. Wellfleet. It will be awful if you back out."

The old man sighed, then he gave an incredulous laugh. "I thought everyone real was dead, and then you appear! For years I've tried to forget I was ever inside Metro." He laughed again. "It's marvellous to hear a young man's voice again after all these years. Okay, André – why not? When do you want me?"

"The sooner the better."

"Tomorrow?"

"I'll be here waiting for you. I want you here because we have a mock-up of the nucleus of a new city and I want you to see it. So tomorrow it is?"

"If I don't go in tomorrow I probably never will. Is it true that Metro's all overgrown now?"

"A lot of it is, but some large fragments of the ruins are jutting up all over the place. There's been a lot of excavating and levelling in the old center – that's where I'm located. I should warn you that it isn't pretty. But in time it will be cleaned up."

Gervais explained in detail how he could be found in Metro, and it was with a feeling of not knowing where or when he was that the old man heard the names of the very streets that had been his haunts when he was young. The streets were no longer thoroughfares but their names had remained. He knew there was nothing new in this. Place names had always been the most permanent things in the short little human story.

THREE

*A*FTER DE-ACTIVATING the instrument, Wellfleet went outside and sat on the chair near the lilac. Yesterday he had been low and used up as though his soul had arthritis, but now beauty was returning to him in waves. Those he had loved in his youth had not vanished after all. Somebody else knew they had existed. Perhaps in time many would know, for André had asked him to write their story.

The lilac candles nodded in a stir of wind. These ones were white, full-bodied, and of a fine original rootstock. He remembered some lines his mother had repeated to him one evening in spring when he was a child and couldn't sleep:

When lilacs last in the dooryard bloom'd,
And the great star early droop'd in the western sky in the night,
I mourn'd, and yet shall mourn with ever-returning spring....

But he was not mourning now, he was feeling almost joyous. He smiled to himself as he remembered those experts who had predicted that a time would soon come when there would be no more animals or birds or lilac trees. As usual, they had been wrong. A later generation of experts explained their survival by proving that they had developed better adaptation techniques. A farmer he had known had put it more simply: "The buggers have learned to hide so well it takes you half a day to find them."

He fell into a reverie. He remembered passages of poetry and surges of music and he was thankful that the period was over when he could not bear to listen to the symphonies in his record collection because they so terribly increased his sense of loss for the great coherent time in which they were born. Even before the Destructions he had felt like this. Finally his thoughts returned to André Gervais, who had been born so many years after the Great Fear; many years even after the Destructions.

Nobody of André's age could imagine what the Great Fear had been like. There had been a few others in the pre-scientific past which psychologists said were caused by sexual hallucinations, but none of them were as uncanny as this one. During it he had even tried to deny its presence, but he had known, like everyone else, that suddenly everything had become unreal. So what could he say to André if the young man asked him to explain the Great Fear? André was sure to ask him some time because this was one of the folk legends the people were conscious of today. Tell him that the planners had planned the people into paralysis? Tell him that every problem the Bureaucracy tried to solve only produced four or five worse ones? Tell him that the metros went out of control? André had seen photographs of those colossal cities, but he could have no idea of what they had really been like. Or simply tell him that the Smiling Bureaucracy reached the end of its rope and was replaced by the Second Bureaucracy which was probably insane?

The mists had lifted and as the sun heated the air he remembered the line about the earth abiding forever. He burst into a gale of laughter as he recalled a famous scientist explaining that it had not abided forever; that it was, as earth, only about eight billion years old, give or take a few billion either way. This was something he would not bother telling André.

A delicious languor spread through him as he watched the parent robins flying in and out of the lilac where their little ones were waiting in the nest for the worms. He rose, stretched, and went inside, and after a light lunch of a composite he lay down to doze. The emotions of the morning had left him happy but fatigued.

Fully dressed he lay on his cot and closed his eyes, and while he was still half asleep and half awake Joanne returned to him again. It was the night they had met in the empty house they had found. He was not promiscuous then, for she was his only woman. Her hips were moving slowly, lovingly, sinuously, with the twilight soft on her head as he lay on his back watching and loving her intense little face and her shoulders the color of mother-of-pearl, and then the peace came and she was curled up beside him as they both fell asleep.

How long he slept he did not know because his watch had stopped, but the position of the sun told him it was late afternoon. Again he went outside and sat in his chair and watched the robins at work in their last shift of the day.

After he had made and eaten his supper he went outside again and watched the sun go down. Twilight darkened away from the corona of burnt-orange in the west, and when finally it was dark the perfume of the lilacs was stronger than ever. The atmosphere was so clear he could imagine himself able to recognize the spaces between the constellations. The stars owned the sky completely, for the moon, still carrying its quota of plastic national flags, was on the other side of the earth in its intimate hideousness and distant beauty.

He thought how pleasant it would be if André and his friends, and their successors and the successors of their successors, actually did manage to create a new city on the ruins of the old one. He could not believe they would, but it was pleasant to think about it. One thing at least was sure: it would be several generations before they could put together the technical equipment to turn it into a metro.

In his childhood in the pre-Metro city the evening star had shone like a pharos over the gap where the great street curved up through the pass in the mountain that was the city's heart. Year after year that star had welcomed the breadwinners home from their daily work. It had been one of the many friendly things that had made his city the most beloved on the continent to those who knew it. They never understood what the star had meant to them until a developer blotted it out with another huge oblong of concrete and glass. Not long afterwards the local bureaucracy renamed the historic old place Metro.

FOUR

NEXT MORNING he waited at the embarkation point for the LIMT — they still called it that, the Linear Induction Motor Transporter. Its principles had been discovered when he was a schoolboy but nobody had done anything about it so long as they still had enough oil.

When the transporter arrived he climbed aboard and noticed that it was cleaner than it had been the last time he had used it. That was seven years ago when he had travelled thirty kilometers east to visit an acquaintance in another compound. He had been allowed three vouchers a year for the transporter but had used hardly any of them. He looked out the window at farmland that seemed more prosperous than the last time he had seen it. They stopped in a number of villages and he saw some horses and wagons on their streets. The transporter continued westward toward the ruins of Metro. In the outer grid, the section originally named the South Shore Development Zone, some buildings seemed at least half intact, but they looked tired and ill-used and reminded him of the faces of men who had spent years in prison. The broken shell of a high oblong building stood alone, but closer to the river the concrete was visible only as a kind of outcropping.

Across the river, nearly five kilometers distant, was a wide tumble of grassy mounds with many fragments of buildings jutting out of it and the contours looking like mountain foothills. The invincible grass, the all-concealing and all-healing grass, had mantled the wreckage of Metro, had made it look soft and green and shadowed in the hollow places. One bridge only was intact and the transporter swept silently across it. The river was violet-colored and shivered in patches of wind. The transporter followed the old curving route into the heart of what once was the Old City. There were thousands of birds. Red-winged blackbirds balanced on shrubs and long stalks of coarse grass, in the softer grass robins hunted for worms, and many seagulls were white against the green of the mounds. He had been told that fish had returned to the river after nearly a century.

The transporter passed through this eerie beauty and entered a hideous area of about four square kilometers. Most of it was bare and acrid-looking and reminded him of the parking lots of his boyhood. He noticed deep, raw cavities and recognized them as the foundation holes dug by the developers who had destroyed the Old City and built a metro on top of it. On the edge of one of these he saw a dusty pile of debris and realized it was composed of human bones and broken skeletons. It might have been on the edge of this very hole that young Gervais had found the boxes with those papers he was so excited about.

In the heart of this empty area the transporter stopped and he and seven other men got out. These others were all young.

Wellfleet stood still, looked around, and felt weird. Metal standards had been erected with the names of the excavated streets, and just as André had told him, they were the same names the streets had borne when he was young. For a moment he felt faint and had to lean against the nearest standard.

It had once been such a wonderful city, even though it had been made ugly many years before the Destructions came. He was standing in front of what once had been the campus of the university. Even during his time as a student the towers of glass and concrete had been built up around it, yet he had been happy there. He remembered walking slowly down the university avenue from a late lecture talking about Plato with his professor. He remembered lying on the grass with friends on warm autumn days. Then it came over him that it was on this very spot that he had first met Joanne. Now it was buried in rubble, for when the Destructions came the glass and concrete of the high buildings had been blasted in all directions.

"I must stop remembering," he whispered. "I didn't come here to remember."

He steadied himself and walked slowly to the address André had given him and finally emerged from the ruins into a cleared area near the river. There he counted twenty-one new buildings set around a square with infant trees growing in front of them. In one of these buildings he found his new friend.

André Gervais was a strongly built, vivacious man, short-haired and clean-shaven, with a pale olive complexion. He was about seven centimeters shorter than Wellfleet and seemed very young. What Gervais saw was a gray-bearded man stooped in the shoulders and gaunt, with loose gray hair receding from a high, rectangular forehead with a prominent vein on the left side. The nose was also long and there was a slight twist in it, as though it once had been broken. The eyes were gray, resigned and watchful and to Gervais unfathomable. He felt awe at what those eyes must have seen, but he also thought that if this pathetic survivor had anyone who cared for him, or for whom he himself might care, he would look distinguished. He held out both his hands and the old man took them gratefully.

FIVE

JOHN WELLFLEET was experiencing a sensation he had seldom known in the past forty years; it was happiness. Gervais had introduced him to a few of his colleagues, had showed him the two heavy cast-iron boxes with the name and the dates cut into their flanks, and had left him alone with them while he went off to work in another room.

He had also left him alone with the mock-up of the nucleus of the new city and Wellfleet had been studying it. The influence of the books they had found on Renaissance architecture was obvious, yet there was a real difference. These buildings, if they were ever made, would give out a suggestion of surprise, of delight, even of wings in the air. And he thought – it could be possible! Yes, it could. One of them might be a genius. Having been pap-fed on lies and bureaucracy, having rejected both, perhaps their native wits were free. Free as no native wits had been for more than a century in his own time, for all of his own contemporaries had had to labor under such a monstrous weight of information and theories that an elephant the size of Mount Everest would not have been able to digest it all.

Looking out the window he was surprised to see some ships at a few docks near by. He had heard in a vague way that trade was reviving farther down the river where the communities had been too small to have been worth destroying. Gervais came in and his face was expectant.

"This could be wonderful," Wellfleet said, pointing to the mock-up.

Gervais smiled. "It *is* wonderful. A wonderful man imagined it. But I don't think you believe it will ever be real."

Wellfleet hesitated. "Pay no attention to anything I say. I've seen everything I valued ruined. I'm not a good witness. However – " he hesitated again, then said, "cities aren't planned, you know. They grow."

"On a site like this a city is sure to grow. Were you ever in Florence?"

"I thought you'd ask me that. The Florence I saw was a museum."

"But this I can't understand. If your people had examples like Florence, why did they build those metros?"

Wellfleet smiled. "My dear André, they just grew. Nobody planned them. They were the places where the power was, and for most of us life in them was marvellously exciting. The old people never had much of a chance, but who cared about them?"

The young man had not been listening to him. His fine-drawn face was rapt as he talked of his dream.

"What we're going to do isn't new. We've read about it. We don't have to live in these ruins all our lives. A city is born. If it's a beautiful city it grows. Men with wonderful ideas come to it and live there. They meet each other and exchange ideas and the city itself becomes a kind of genius. This could never happen in a metro."

Wellfleet said nothing; did not even permit his face a flicker of expression. Obviously the young man had found some books about ancient Athens and Florence. He did not tell him that the Athens he himself had known had a population seven times larger than the Athens of Pericles and that the traffic jams in Florence had been deafening. He heard Gervais asking if the metros had choked themselves to death, and if that was why they had died. The conversation frustrated him and he shook his head.

"Look, André, they might well have choked themselves to death, but they were blown to pieces before they got around to it. What difference does it make? There's never been anything immortal in a city. Some great ones withered away and were forgotten. Many were destroyed by wars. There were always wars. I saw a city that was destroyed by trees. Once it had been a city of a million people, but when I saw it the only inhabitants were rats and the cobras that crawled into the ruins to eat them. I don't know why the people abandoned it. Maybe a war. Maybe a pestilence. I don't know. But the trees grew up and rived that city apart. I saw it with a lovely girl of the region. Dark eyes and skin the color of old ivory. She was so supple. Even her bones were pliant. A few years later the bomber planes came and after them came the politicians. I'm sure she never survived, but I'd hate to think she was burned alive by napalm. When Florence was the most cultivated city in Europe they used to burn people alive to support the religion, and they did it individually and with great ceremony. In my time the burning was completely technocratic. The bomb-aimers never saw the people they burned to death. However, let's change the subject. Tell me – is the Bureaucracy working with you people in this?"

He listened with some skepticism while André explained that the whole character of the Bureaucracy had changed now that people of his own generation had become a part of it. Wellfleet did not mention that so far as *his* own generation was concerned, the Bureaucracy was behaving the same as ever. Why not? When he had been André's age, the young had never given a thought to the old people. While André continued to talk he was looking out the window to the river.

There it still was, that wonderful stream born in the lake-chain flowing at high water down its channel to the distant sea. Pure and wind-flecked it poured through the green mounds and the outcroppings of mangled steel and concrete. He knew, as he was sure André did not, that this was the youngest of the world's great rivers, yet was much older than the earliest city ever built. In the long story of the earth, it too would probably be mortal.

Gervais stopped talking and Wellfleet said quietly, "I can't believe it was all useless."

"I don't think I follow you."

"All the human energy expended here. All the human love. It was delightful to watch the children on their little skis on the mountain. Tell me, André – are you married?"

"For two years."

"Any children?"

A shy smile. "The first one is on its way. What of your own children?"

"I don't know."

Gervais looked puzzled, and Wellfleet's eyes were steady on his.

"I mean, I don't know whether they're alive or dead. I had two children, and then they went off with their mother when she left me for another man. Don't look so surprised. That happened pretty often in those days. It was almost routine. I may even have had one more child, but I'm not sure."

Wellfleet swayed slightly in his chair and Gervais looked at him anxiously and asked if he was all right.

"It's nothing. It will pass in a moment. I'm not used to luxury any more. For so long a time, emotions have been a luxury I couldn't afford."

Gervais got to his feet. "You're probably hungry and it's lunchtime. I've got a treat for you, I think."

"Yes, lunch would be fine. I'm not hungry – but yes, it would be excellent."

"This time I can promise it will be. One of my friends caught a salmon last night."

"Where did he find the salmon?"

"Out there, of course." He pointed to the river. "Didn't you know there are thousands of salmon in the river now?"

"Good God!" Wellfleet also got to his feet. "When I was your age that river was an open sewer mixed up with every kind of chemical waste you could imagine. If the Destructions brought salmon back to the rivers, maybe they were worth while after all. I haven't tasted salmon for fifty years."

When he joined the others at the table he was ravenous. It had been nearly twenty years since he had tasted any food that had not been processed.

Afterwards Gervais filled a small case with papers from the heavy iron boxes.

"You may as well take these back with you today," he said. "They'll do for a start. The boxes would be far too heavy for you to carry and I wouldn't dare trust them to the public service from Metro to Outside. But don't worry about them. Two of our people are going out in your direction the day after tomorrow and they'll deliver the whole lot to you."

Gervais walked with him to the transporter embarkation point and waved to him after he had got aboard. The transporter moved off and when it was across the river the old man closed his eyes. He could hardly believe what had happened to him today. He had broken a routine as deadening as a prison term and he was at once elated and tired out. "Am I really back in the world again? Am I really?" And a little later he thought, "Are people really becoming kind again?" He was afraid to fall asleep least he sleep on past his compound.

SIX

*T*WO WEEKS LATER his four peony bushes were in bloom and it was pleasant to have still another witness that the invisible time-clocks in the plants and migratory birds had paid no attention to what mankind had been doing to itself. He went into Metro again and this time he discovered something priceless, that he was at least a quarter as valuable to André as André had become to him. After his own children had left, the need of young people had grown in him so that the lack of them had become an ache. Now he was experiencing an intoxicating emotion: the pleasure of an old man when he discovers that a young man wishes to learn from him.

"I want to know where the truth is," André had said in their first conversation, and how could he answer such a question? Could any important truth come out of these papers he had been given?

"There's an enormous quantity of material in those boxes," he said. "I'm not one-tenth through reading it. Yes, they're genuine. There's no possible doubt of that. Your lists were a help, but the whole package is in confusion. It's all got to be sifted and pieced together and some of it is as distant from me as the last pages are from you. There's also the problem of language. Conrad Dehmel has left a long section written in German. I used to speak German fairly well, but I've forgotten so much I'll have to relearn it. Fortunately I've got a dictionary."

"So you think it will take a long time?"

"Two years at least. Perhaps longer. And that's another problem. I'm not young any more. But the worst thing is that I can't believe that anyone alive today will be interested in these people. After hundreds of millions have vanished, why should they be?"

"No, John, you're wrong. Absolutely wrong. Can't you understand what it means that you're the only person I ever met who was alive in those days?"

It was another fine day, the sun was bright on the river and huge white clouds were floating slowly out of the west.

"Yes, I was certainly alive then," Wellfleet said quietly, "but I was too young to be involved in anything these characters were doing. When Timothy was famous I was barely fourteen. By the time I reached college the mood had changed and Timothy was forgotten. Don't get any romantic ideas about me, André. I wasn't a very good example of my generation. Most of the others deserved a better chance, but I'm not sure I deserved anything better than what I got. For a time I was hooked on hash – that was a drug we smoked. I had no ambition and I used to wander around the world. Once in London I met this Welsh girl. Her father had been a miner, but she had education and she sang like an angel. The only job she wanted was to teach small children. Her name was Valerie." He paused, thinking back. "After we'd lived together for a week she said, 'Let's go to India' –just like that. We hadn't anything you could call money but we didn't care. We'd be going to warm climates and we'd sleep in bedrolls on the ground if there were no youth hostels. Maybe we'd be able to get a few short-term jobs. We didn't, of course, but we did get to India. Valerie was so frank and open about everything. 'You won't mind if I love other boys besides you?' she said. 'And of course you must love other girls besides me.' Is it like that now?"

Gervais looked at him almost with pity. "No," he said.

"She was so graceful, André. She was really a joyous girl who lived for every moment. Waking up with her in the mornings was always exciting. Once in the foothills of the mountains I woke up and she wasn't there and I nearly went crazy. I ran around in all directions calling her name and all I heard was my own voice echoed back from the cliffs. Finally I heard her call me and guess where I found her. There was a stream pouring down from a bowl in the rocks where the water was white with foam and there was Valerie stark naked in the pool. This was the highest mountain range in the world. The water came down from the high glaciers to the foothills where the climate was tropical. Pure cold water and blazing sunshine. Is this boring you?"

André just looked at him.

"This was a lyric," the old man went on. "She had golden hair and blue eyes and I'll never forget how she laughed. But the strange thing was that I never really knew her. When we returned to Europe she said good-bye to me and I found out she could be quite hard. I'd never suspected that. She told me to think of it as a lovely holiday but now it was over and she was going to marry someone else. He was an older man with a lot of money. I was devastated, but I knew I had no right to complain."

"Was she the mother of one of your children?"

"No. And she never wrote to me again. I decided to come home and got a job as a teacher in what we called a high school. Then I married a woman I never should have married." He shrugged. "I already told you about that."

There was a long silence and finally Wellfleet nodded towards the pages on which he had assembled a tentative work plan.

"This material seems awfully patchy to me. I'm not sure I can find any real pattern in it. But that's not the main problem. The real problem is to make anyone believe there ever was a world like these people lived in. Sometimes I find it hard to believe it myself."

He got up and cupped his chin in his hand, feeling the bristle of his beard in his palm.

"The problem is where to begin," he said.

"Why not at the beginning?"

"But where *is* the beginning in all this stuff? Conrad Dehmel when he was a boy? That was in another country in a time I knew very little about when I was young. I know much more about it now because I was Outside when the Destructions came and I had a great many books. One priceless one – we called it an encyclopedia." He looked at André steadily. "I'm still confused about these papers. I don't know for sure whether there's a story in them or not, though I think there is. Voices in time, that's what they are, and who cares about any of them now?"

"You care about them yourself, don't you?"

Wellfleet sighed. "I'm beginning to care very much, but in a way you may not be able to understand. They've made me ask so many questions I should have asked when I was young. Questions about myself. I'm involved in this too, and it troubles me."

"Do it, John, and you won't feel alone any more."

"I may feel even more so." He rose to his feet. "There's another problem and it's serious. If I write this I'll have to write it for myself. This will mean there'll be all kinds of things I'll talk about that nobody today can understand. It's going to require a glossary, and you'll have to help me with that. When it's finished – if it ever is – you must read it and note down every item that needs explaining."

"That sounds easy enough."

"Wait and see. I don't think you'll find it so." He paused. "There's one thing more. Those tapes I explained to you. Most of them are what we called audiotapes and by good luck they fit my old machine. But several are videotapes." He explained to Gervais what they were. "From the date on one of them I think it's of vital importance. They'll be useless unless I can have the use of a projector. I'll describe it to you and if you make enquiries you may find one somewhere. I took courses in what we called Communications and if one turns up, I'll be able to use it."

The autumn leaves were falling before Wellfleet began to write. By now he felt he had been living in a vast time-house divided into many separate rooms. The first lines he wrote, believing that he would cut them out later, were these:

"As it is with the individual, so it may be with the whole world. When the individual is wounded in his soul he often wishes to die. But time passes and then, for no reason he understands, he wants to live again. Can it be the same with communities?"

His thoughts returned to Conrad Dehmel. He realized at last that his stepfather had lived through something of a preview of what he had lived through himself, for in the war which had been fought before he was born, nearly every city in Conrad Dehmel's country had been blasted to fragments. He had been too young really to know Conrad Dehmel when he was alive. Now through these papers it seemed that he would have the chance to know him at last. At least Uncle Conrad had been sure of where he was, which was more than he could say for himself. His own youth? What chance did it have, really? Bombarded by pentillions of words, pictures, ideas, explanations, counter-explanations – who could have sorted out a fraction of what had been thrown at them? That was why marijuana had been such a relief.

So, facing a blank sheet of paper one morning and trying to write, he recalled a night from long ago that had no connection with anything in his life before or since. They were smoking and it was like a rocking cradle. Voices from far off, delicious visions so vivid you could reach out and caress them, a girl lying on the floor with her cheek against his thigh while the others were talking distantly, but so wisely and fascinatingly, out of a cloud and he had wondered whether he and the girl were really mating in the depths of the ocean millions of years ago. He could not remember her name or even what she looked like.

He forced the recollection away and concentrated on Timothy, who had been twenty years older than himself and had come out of a luxurious and conforming era before he revolted. At this stage Wellfleet was reasonably sure that Timothy intended to use this material for a book that would make him rich and perhaps even free. And how typical of his mother that she had never told him that she and Timothy were planning a book together.

Wellfleet smiled, thinking that after all these years he could afford to smile at Timothy, who had been one of those men who can write only when the impulse moves them. There were some finished passages in Timothy's unmistakable style, but few of them were linked up. In between were hundreds of sketches and comments of the sort you might find in any writer's notebook, but there was little continuity and this meant it was impossible to let Timothy speak entirely for himself. The more he thought about it, the more complicated his task became. In most parts he would have to weave this divergent material into some kind of form and he doubted if he would be able to do it.

Then panic seized him. What if he did not live long enough to finish it?

"I'll have to begin somewhere," he muttered to himself, "and I'll have to begin now."

He decided to begin with Timothy.

PART TWO

Timothy Wellfleet's Story
as told by
John Wellfleet

WHEN TIMOTHY WELLFLEET was three and a half years old and too young to remember, his father went across the sea to fight in an enormous war and the boy was almost eight before he returned. He was the only child of that marriage and he lived with his mother in the large stone house where my own mother was born. It had been inherited by my grandfather, John Wellfleet, after whom I was named, the gentle old man who had been a father to me when I myself was a child.

Mother often talked of that house because never in her life had she been so happy as when she lived in it. There were gardens in front, and behind were the woods of the mountain with squirrels, ring-necked pheasants, songbirds, and even a few raccoons and harmless snakes. The front windows looked down the long slope of the city, undulating waves of green when the leaves were on the trees, at night a shining wash of electric lights sweeping down to the broad belt of darkness that was the river.

Timothy's father, Colonel Greg Wellfleet, the youngest of my grandfather's brothers – at least twenty years younger than Grand-father – had bought the house after Grandfather had failed in busi-ness and lost his money. Montreal was a sizable city then, but no megalopolis yet, much less a metro. All the families who had lived there for more than three generations knew each other and when older people mentioned Grandfather's name it was always with sympathy. "Dear old John Wellfleet was simply too much of a gentle-man to understand how to do business with the kind of people who've come to the top lately." The man who skinned him was a character whose name I forget. I once heard an older man say that he had come over from Belfast with only one pair of pants.

After Timothy's father returned from the war, my mother went back to the old house to take care of Timothy. She was Timothy's first cousin and twelve years older than he.

During the war years when his father was away – they called it the Second World War – Timothy lived alone with his mother and the servants – there used to be plenty of servants then – and this seems to have been when his troubles began. I mean troubles in his character that showed up later.

It is hard for me to imagine an establishment like that old house when Timothy was a child. Had he not described it so carefully in the papers I would never have guessed that any house was like that. Many nights during the war the downstairs was filled with men in the uniforms of the army, the navy, and the air force, and the noise they made when they talked and drank and sang and danced with their women and girls was like the noise of a riot. There were nights when the little boy did not get to sleep until three in the morning. He grew accustomed to the great walnut tables laid out with whole boiled salmons and delicious cold hams, cold roast beefs, and jellies, to the whiskeys, rums, gins, sherries, and brandies arrayed on the sideboard, to the glasses for red and white wines and the hot rolls and butter pats with ice cubes keeping them stiff and cold. Like a young animal he sensed the throb of greed in the house on nights like these, which was not a greed for money but for life itself, the men for the women and the women for the men, for some of these men were going to be killed, others had already missed death or had returned wounded, and some of them had already killed other men. He grew accustomed to watching these strangers with the candid eyes of a lonely, resentful child. He also grew accustomed to those heavy footsteps, often shambling footsteps, mounting the stairs to the second floor where the bathrooms and lavatories were, mounting even to the top floor where his own room was. Once he heard a different kind of noise and when the door opened a crack, there was a big military officer wrestling with a tall, thin woman who had a long, thin nose and a desperate face. Both of them were panting and the woman was holding him hard and twisting her hips against his. Then the woman pulled away and whispered in a kind of gasp, "No, Harry – no – we can't do it here." After staring at each other with heavy breathing, both of them went back down the stairs without noticing a child's face in the crack of the door.

His father's photograph stood on one of the living-room tables and to Timothy he looked like a hostile intruder, with his officer's face and the uniform Timothy had come to hate without knowing why. Years later he learned that his father was considerably over-age for a combat officer and that he had used influence to get himself posted overseas. His father was ten years older than Timothy's mother, who was a small woman, neatly slim. His father was burly and tall, big all over, and his face in the picture wore the expression of a man who had always been bigger and stronger than other males, even when he was a boy at school.

For Timothy the war was just the war, the biggest thing in the world, and he had no interest in it. When his father came home after the victory with his sirloin face and all the medal ribbons on his chest-stuffed uniform he scared Timothy because he was so huge and full of authority and his big square-fingered hands hurt when he picked up his son and tried to be jolly and affectionate with him. Timothy thought he must be crazy, for how could any full-grown man expect a child to believe he loved him when he had never seen him since he was a baby? What his father really wanted, he thought, was to own him. Then came the time in the last week of August when his father drove down to Maine with him for a week of surf-bathing ("It's time the men in this family had some fun together, Timmie") and when they undressed in the bath-house his father's tool (Timothy's word) was so massive it reminded him of an animal's and scared him so badly he could hardly sleep that night.

They went home again and Timothy was sent to a boarding school for the first time in his life. A year later when he was home the shouting began and his mother's face showed the usual streaks of tears. The boy could not understand it, only that his parents now hated each other. Then he began really to hate his father on account of all this terrible anger that had entered the house with his return to it.

Soon came the morning when his mother packed his things into two suitcases and put them in the trunk of her car, Timothy having been born in the kind of family that could afford two cars. Her own suitcases were there already, and on an early October morning when the leaves were scarlet and the air was the breath of the earth itself they drove down across the border into his mother's country. They drove all day, his mother tight-lipped, and it was twilight when they reached a place called Scarsdale where his mother's father lived.

Her own mother was dead and Timothy stayed more than eight months in the house of his maternal grandfather, who now was a widower. During this time his mother came and went. He was sent to school in Scarsdale while his elders awaited the result of a lawsuit between his parents to decide who would have the custody of Timothy. The court awarded the boy to his father and two days after the verdict his mother descended from Montreal and for Timothy it was terrible. She kissed him with her face wet with tears and though her thin, nervous hands held onto him in nervous spasms he sensed no tenderness in them, only fury because she had lost something that belonged to her. The boy was aghast, for he was thinking of that huge animal-thing of his father's and how awful it must have been for his mother and at the same time he resented her because she had never really looked after him and now she could not protect him. He also sensed fear in her. Later he was to write, "I could smell it."

More days passed and he heard her arguing with his grandfather.

"I'm sorry, Alix," the grandfather said. "Of course I'm sorry for you, but what is the point of all this? You've never paid any respect to my opinions, but I trust I'm at least entitled to them."

"He's cruel," the mother said. "And he's coarse."

"Did you say cruel? Didn't he take care of you? Did he ever strike you? Of course he didn't. Greg was a soldier just as Everett was. He did his duty and I'd like to remind you that his country did its duty before ours did. What's happened is your own fault and you know it and—"

"I suppose you think he was faithful to me all those years he was over there?"

"Can you prove that he wasn't?"

"None of them were."

"Do you know that? If so, how do you know it?"

"Because everybody knows it."

"That, Alix, is a meaningless statement. As a lawyer, I have to tell you that the court's decision was a proper one. As a man, I will tell you something else that isn't popular these days. In affairs like this the woman does not automatically have the right to the child. A male child, believe me, needs a father just as much as he needs a mother. Timothy's been weaned quite a while, Alix."

"What about Timmie? Yes, what about *him*? Did anyone ask *him*?"

"And did you ask Timothy how he would like it to live with this new man of yours? The boy's nine years old and now you're going to marry a man with three sons of his own and all of them are older than Timothy. What chance would the poor boy have with a crew like that? And what chance after your next divorce? All right! All right!" The old gentleman lifted his hands. "It's a bad business all around and you can call me old-fashioned if you wish, but responsibility is responsibility and that's all there is to it."

"Responsibility!" she said, and broke into tears.

"There's another old-fashioned word called honor."

The little boy, crouching on the stairs outside the living room and hearing all this, thought how phony his mother was and how he would tell one of his schoolfriends what she was like. So the whole lot of them were phony except his grandfather, and now he supposed he would be taken away from here and sent back to the man with the terrible tool.

The day after this scene his mother returned to Montreal to pack the rest of her belongings and it was a long time before Timothy saw her again. She had wanted him to attend her second wedding, but her father had circumvented this. He kept the boy with him in Scarsdale. Timothy's schoolwork was going badly and he did not sleep well. Though his grandfather did his best to be a companion to him, the old gentleman always left for the city in the early morning and seldom returned before seven in the evening. When the school term ended, his grandfather told him to begin his packing. His father would arrive in three days and they would all meet in New York.

"It will be fun for you to see New York," his grandfather said, trying to be cheerful, but Timothy wondered why the old man didn't live in New York himself if it was all that terrific. The worst thing was knowing that he would have to return to his father and not see this kind old man again. His grandfather was still handsome with stiff gray hair, very straight in the back and high in the shoulders. He came from what the Americans called "an old family" and Timothy had the impression that he hated what his world was turning into. Years later he still missed his grandfather; he wrote that he wished the old man were still alive now that he himself was grown up so they could talk man to man. He wrote that his grandfather had always been kind to him and had tried his best to give him the security of knowing the difference between right and wrong.

In New York they checked in at the old Plaza Hotel where the doorman knew his grandfather and called him by his name, and that afternoon they went to the zoo together. Timothy had never been in a zoo before and he hated it. A huge tiger stood on his hind feet with his forepaws reaching the top of the wire of his cage and he shook the wire and snarled at the people who were staring at him. There was also a camel that for some reason reminded him of his father.

The next morning Colonel Wellfleet arrived after breakfast. He had driven down the night before and stayed at another hotel. They met in his grandfather's room where both men shook hands silently and were unnaturally dignified with each other. The old man said it would be pleasant to drive north through the Adirondacks on a day like this and his father agreed that it would be very pleasant. The stiff embarrassment of the two older men with each other was devastating to the little boy. Finally his grandfather patted his head, wished him luck, and said it was time for him to leave for the office.

"You may as well stay here, Greg," he added, "till your car is ready."

Timothy's eyes followed the straight back, the high shoulders, and the crisp white hair out of the door and out of his life – a man, so he was to write years later, the like of whom he was never to meet again, "because he was the only man I ever knew who could use words like honor, duty, and responsibility without making me feel like throwing up."

After he left, Timothy's father did his inadequate best to relax the atmosphere. He asked the usual paternal questions about the boy's school, about his sports and his friends, but as he got nothing in return but monosyllables and avoiding eyes, he hunched down behind his newspaper until the desk phoned to say that his car was at the door.

They drove north for most of the day and reached Montreal in the evening with Timothy asleep on the back seat under a rug with a cushion under his head.

TWO

*T*HIS I HAD NEVER KNOWN until I read the papers – Colonel Wellfleet had asked my mother to come to the house to take care of Timothy when he brought him home. Among the many photographs I found in the boxes was one of Mother with Timothy, and if I do say it myself, she was a very beautiful young woman. Timothy looked a normal boy, reasonably robust but not wide in the hips like his father. Most of the Wellfleet men, myself included, had faces that made you think of horses, though thank God none of the women were like that. Timothy's face was somewhat horse-like even when he was a child. Anyway, this is what he himself wrote:

"When I woke up and went into that God-damned house I found my cousin Stephanie waiting for me and after an hour with her I felt better than I ever could remember. I don't know what it was about her. She looked so gentle even though she had one hell of a temper if she felt like it. All the Wellfleets had quick tempers, but when Stephanie got sore she made you feel she had a right to get sore. I mean, she made you feel you deserved it and that it was good for you. And was she ever stubborn! You could no more make her change her mind than a mule. I'd have been scared to death if she'd ever got really sore at me but she never did. The thing was, she was all woman. I mean, she never tried to think like a man the way too God-damned many women do and crap everything up. Everything about Stephanie was very young except her eyes. They were big and brown and sort of washed over with a look that would make anyone feel good. And she was just plain dumb innocent about all sorts of things because her parents were so old-fashioned they'd never told her how babies were born till she was in her teens and by that time she knew anyway. But I can tell you this. She learned all there was to learn about me in the first half-hour even though she was only twelve or thirteen years older than I was.

"There was a hot meal waiting for us that night but I said I wasn't hungry and only wanted some soup. Stephanie paid no attention at all and after the soup she asked my father to cut me a really big slice of the roast beef. I only ate it to please her, but it made me feel better afterwards. All the time we were eating, the Old Man kept telling stories that were very corny; you know, trying to impress Stephanie. I could see he had an eye for her but of course he was very correct. Being correct ran in that family, and Stephanie made a very big thing out of it and always called him Uncle Greg and that stuff. He was really the big deal, my Old Man. He and the rest of his brothers had all started well-heeled, but the Old Man kept heeling himself better all the time and he really creamed the soup. It used to embarrass me how insensitive he was. You'd have thought he'd have been ashamed having Stephanie there in that house where she was born, working like a nanny looking after a snot-nosed kid like me, but he probably thought he was doing her a favor because her parents were poor and she could use a little extra dough. He used to make a very big deal about how he had come to the rescue when old Uncle John went broke. 'Rallied around' was how he put it. I can just hear him. 'Somebody's got to rally around to help old John.' Fuck! At that time money was real and land was dirt cheap. The Old Man knew he was buying a gilt-edged investment for practically nothing. By the time the war was over that house was worth three times what he'd paid for it and ten years later it was worth ten times more."

In some of the other papers, Timothy said that the house declined in value later on account of some political troubles, but everything about money was crazy by the time I'd grown up. Nobody knew from year to year what it was going to be worth. But let Timothy continue:

"After dinner Stephanie put me to bed and told me stories and when I still couldn't sleep she sat beside me and stroked my forehead and the back of my neck with the loving patience Florence Nightingale was supposed to have had but probably didn't. When I woke up next morning she was fully dressed and the first thing I saw was her smile. I haven't got over it yet. Apparently old Stephanie really wanted to see me with my eyes open. I can't remember ever seeing my own mother smile at me like that. Maybe she did sometimes and I've forgotten, but I saw about fifteen times more of Nanny than I ever saw of my mother and Nanny was just an English woman with big red hands who was paid to do a job. But it was really great the way Stephanie made me feel. I didn't want her for a mother because I couldn't stand the idea of a mother just then, but I did think it would be wonderful to wake up next morning and be twenty-five years old.

"But there was one thing the matter with Stephanie that I can tell you was the matter with my whole God-damned family, every one of them. They never told you in words a lot of things you needed to know if it made anyone else in the family look bad in consequence. What I needed to know most of all was how my mother could have stayed married to my Old Man for so long when she couldn't stand him. All I got out of Stephanie was that Mummy and Daddy had decided it was best for everyone if they lived separately and that we weren't to talk about it. I wanted her to admit to me what a bastard the Old Man was and what a bitch my mother was. It would have made me feel a lot better if she had done that. It would have made me feel less alone and peculiar and as if everything was somehow my own fault. All of them were supposed to front for each other like the Three Musketeers. The worst crime you could commit in that family – I mean the whole lot and not just this half-assed little end of it I belonged to – the very worst crime was to say anything even reasonably critical about anyone connected with the family.

"Let me give you an example of what I mean. There was that time when Stephanie brought over one of those dozens of cousins of mine to play with me. He was the same age I was, his name was Algie, and his mother came from some place in England. Now anyone could tell just by looking at him that Algie was a pain in the ass. He was a little red-haired kid and he kept talking all the time in that accent of his about what great people his mother's family in England were, how one of them had been a Lord Warden of the Cinque Ports four or five hundred years ago, so after he went home I told Stephanie that these Cinque Ports couldn't be such a big deal if they'd ended up in a jerk like Algie. There was hell to pay. Stephanie gave me one of those looks she was so good at and I felt I ought to be crawling under stones. Then she really gave it to me about the way I talked. Just like the worst kind of American, she said. 'If you keep on using "big deal" for everything as well as all the other bad language and calling your cousins jerks, you'll soon be known as the most horrible child in Montreal.' It took me a month before I stopped doing it and even then I only stopped when she or the Old Man were around.

"But what I'm trying to say here is that Stephanie was really a lovely person and she had a beautiful speaking voice. The whole town knew the Wellfleets were old-fashioned. I mean, the sons all went to RMC and the girls came out at two or three thousand a throw, but Stephanie was old-fashioned in a nice way. All the women in the family were supposed to have beautiful manners and I guess they really did have them if you liked Jane Austen, but Stephanie's manners were actually kind. I mean, she never tried to produce an effect with them the result of which is only to make the other guy feel lousy. It wasn't Stephanie's fault that her father disapproved so much of the twentieth century that he never could get along in it and got royally screwed in consequence."

When I read this I couldn't help smiling. Whatever else he may not have been, Timothy was a pretty shrewd observer. I knew all about that look Mother could give you and I'm pretty sure Uncle Conrad knew about it, too. Timothy, by the way, wrote this passage when he was sixteen. His style matured somewhat later on.

What happened to him next was bound to have been routine. When that year ended he was sent off to an expensive boarding school in Ontario and my mother returned to the four-room apartment she shared with her parents. By that time her own mother was bedridden and had only two more years left.

Timothy continued to brood over what had gone wrong between his parents and it was at the boarding school that he found out, or thought he found out, why he had no mother any more.

There was a boy a year older called Scrivener whom Timothy admired who told him that much the same thing had happened to himself, the difference being that he was in his mother's custody while Timothy was in his father's. This Scrivener, whom Timothy described as "cool," explained that when the soldiers were overseas they screwed every woman they could lay their hands on (Timothy's words) and Scrivener said he had it all worked out. Say at any given time there were three hundred thousand Canadian soldiers and airmen in England, allow an average of ten different women to each man, and that meant about three million women, which Scrivener said "was a hell of a lot of screwing." He also said it was one of those things that gets to be a habit like booze and cigarettes. His own mother had remained faithful and that was why he was in her custody and now his father was married to a much younger woman. He explained to Timothy that what had happened in his case was that his mother had been screwing around the town while her husband was away and that the Old Man had found out about it. When Timothy asked if this meant that his father had had no women when overseas, he was told to grow up.

"For your Old Man it couldn't have been cozier," Scrivener said. "He looks good and your mother looks bad. Pretty soon, you watch. He'll marry a young girl just like my own Old Man did."

So it was no surprise to Timothy when the housemaster called him out of prep one night and said his father was on the phone from Montreal. As his father had never phoned him before, Timothy was pretty sure of what he would say and he said it. Timothy had a new mother who was very beautiful and, as Timothy put it, "the old bastard began by practically ordering me to love her sight unseen." They were off for a short honeymoon to the Caribbean but would be back in time for the Easter holidays. Then his stepmother came onto the line and told him how wonderful it all was and that she was beginning to love him already. Predictably, Timothy concluded this episode with the observation that he wanted to throw up.

There was an American book called *The Catcher in the Rye* which was a Bible for the kids of Timothy's age and it's impossible for me to know how much of his early vocabulary was derived from it or to what extent it crystallized his attitudes. This novel was one of those universal things for its time and place, but after I lent my own battered old copy to André, he said he couldn't make head or tail out of it.

When Timothy came home for Easter, he found his father and stepmother with their skins as tan as Hindus and according to him it was "God-damned indecent how they behaved in my presence. The old rut couldn't keep his paws off her even with me there in the room." She was twenty-one to his forty-two and Timothy thought it "neat" that he was actually double her age and even neater that she was exactly half of his. She was about the same size as his own mother with the same kind of blonde hair and blue eyes. He noted also that her mouth could be pretty petulant at times if she felt like it, and to this he added that "she had as beautiful a body as any man could hope to get his hands on, but what was the good of that if you had to look at the vacuousness of her face?" Though he did not know it at the time, she was already pregnant.

Looking back on those years from my present place in time, I think I'm right in saying that it was seldom as tense for my age group as it was for Timothy's. Many of our parents had divorces, but there was not so much guilt in the air. Now once more I can let Timothy continue, mentioning that this and anything else he wrote in this story was written when he was much older, indeed after he became famous.

"If there are any historians around in the next century, even if they are only computers, I wonder what they are going to say about those years when we were told we had never had it so good, when the cities grew like cancers and their skies went tan with sulfur dioxide and winter snows looked like coal in March and young people were conned into instant marriages and instant families? The deterioration of my father was all the evidence I needed to understand what the System was doing to everybody. He talked, acted, ate, drank, and took his routine southern holidays like everyone else he knew, and whatever had been unique in him – and now I know that much had been unique – slowly died from spiritual malnutrition. Of course, on the surface he was a success story, which meant that he was a classic failure story. Anyone who began those years with a solid backlog of capital would have had to be a moron if he didn't treble it inside ten years, and in business my father had the instinct. During the first years of his second marriage he and my stepmother produced five children, two boys and three girls, until my stepmother, looking drained but always bright and pert, already dyeing her ash-blonde hair, declared that five were enough.

"I used to wonder if by then she had come to hate him without having the brains to know that she did. When she married him his muscles were iron-hard from the war, his lungs were still cleansed by fresh air, and his dark hair included just enough gray to make him look like the first prize to a girl who thought *South Pacific* was the greatest show on earth. Now his hair was a dull uniform gray, his breath was short, and his waist was getting thick, and what had she to show for the great adventure but the sagging flesh of over-stretched abdominal muscles which had gone soft after doing their work. But can you believe it? That woman never missed a chance to tell her friends how happy she was, even when her face wore that look of blank resentment you see on the faces of women who feel they have been cheated of the best years of their lives. My father was a prime mesomorph, as I am not. I read somewhere that a lot of mesomorphs lose interest and conk out sexually long before some skinny guy is still raring to go.

"This may explain why my father, in my eighteenth year, at last began to take an interest in me. He even tried to talk to me about the war, but it was so much a part of his code to underplay anything connected with bravery that it took all my imagination to translate into even a quarter-reality what he said. He was bursting with life in the war. There was also the time when he reminisced about pre-war Montreal, and when he talked about it he never mentioned the French except to say how much he liked them. He was sincere about that. He was also sincere, in the sense that he believed it, when he said that the French Canadians would far sooner work for an English boss than for one of their own people, and it never crossed his mind how arrogant he was even though quite possibly he was telling the truth.

"But one thing his class certainly had and it was physical courage. They didn't scare worth a damn. Nearly all of them went to the war and it was not from Father but from one of his junior officers that I learned how he won his Military Cross. He stormed across a causeway in the Dutch polders ahead of a platoon of volunteers with the bullets cracking past his ears, all the time bellowing some crazy song in the voice of a berserk bull until at last he drowned it in the roar of his Sten gun when he and his men took the position.

"He was not alive like this any more, though his doctor pronounced his health to be sound. Now that he seemed to have some interest in me I tried to be fair to him and even asked myself whether he had really been faithful to my mother when he was overseas. In the strict technical sense it wouldn't have been practical for him never to have touched a woman all those years he was away. That wouldn't have meant he was unfaithful to her, not in any sense that a sane woman could hold against him. Now I think he quite possibly was faithful to her. Now I think the poor dumb guy really had idealized her. I think he got the shock of his life when he came home and found out what had been going on while he was away. I was pretty crummy when I was a kid and I should have seen one very plain fact. It wasn't Father that kicked her out of his life, it was my mother who kicked him out of hers. And at least he valued me enough to fight for me against her."

Another passage from Timothy may explain why there was at least a little truth in the Diagram; that it actually was about this time that the System began to crack up. Whatever you may think of Timothy's character, he was certainly observant and sensitive. Listen to this:

"Hardly anyone could be alive in those years even if he thought he was with it a hundred percent of the way. The System simply did not let you be a human being unless you were content to live like a bum. How could anyone be a human being in that decade of the spiritual *castrati* programmed by Dr. Spock, interpreted by the interpreters of Dr. Freud, its religion packaged in cellophane by Doctors Peale, Sheen, and Graham, the whole lot of them conned into believing, into really believing, that nobody in the history of this world had had it so good as us? I can see them. Not my father but the ones who came along just after the war – I can see them in their white shirts, their thin ties, their charcoal suits, their crew cuts, playing it cool, oh, but so suave and cool, expressing their rages in calculated smiles and really believing that if they failed to win friends and influence people to put money into their pockets they didn't qualify for the Prosperity Club. A shout of real fury? The explosion of a good old-fashioned belly laugh? It was like farting in Eisenhower's face.

"I was sad for my father, I really was. In those years he tried to do his best for me, but all the time I was watching him grow older, lonelier, and emptier. Perhaps he was too old for those children of his second marriage. Perhaps they were too young for him. Maybe it was even simpler. The poor old bastard who could be so brave in battle and so shrewd in business, who was genuinely good-natured as I later had to admit – did he really believe all the big lies of his time and place? Somehow I don't think he did. Or maybe when he came back from the war and the big boom took over, maybe he just didn't notice what it was leading to and got hooked and couldn't get off the line. In the end I think he was simply worn down by the changes in everything he had known. I can see now that he would have made an excellent father if he had been born fifty years earlier, because fifty years earlier the things he believed in would not have been lies. He was not without honor, and I say this with envy because honor is something I have never had.

"Yes, he was insensitive. He just didn't know any better. As, for example, that carefully studied expression (was it sly or only embarrassed?) when he'd suggest that I take one of the cars and go north 'with some nice girl,' which was his way of letting me know that he accepted the moral shift which allowed that a girl could be a nice girl if she went to bed with a man she hadn't married. Or when he pressed me with handouts of money I hadn't earned so that I felt ashamed when I accepted them. He seemed to be trying to make up to me for things he was quite intelligent enough to know I had missed, but money wasn't the way to do it. Why could he never understand that the last thing I needed from him was any kind of indulgence and the one thing I inwardly craved was the kind of leadership he had given his men at Walcheren? I would look at my stepmother, that cheated child, and at the smallest of the new children playing on the floor, and Father would notice my expression and then he would look down, deep down, into his drink.

"I had no ambition because I honestly did not know where I was, so I accepted a place in the plastic paradise-penitentiary our upper middle class had imported from south of the border and paid for by selling out all those billions of dollars' worth of the national resources. I got my so-called education in it. I got my job in it. I married in it. I sired two children in it, and slowly I was dying in it.

"Then suddenly, when I was thirty years old, I believed I had been reborn. I thought I had become an entirely new kind of man. But how many ex-cons ever get over what the jail has done to them?

"Anyway, it is with this so-called new man that my story proper begins. I try to look back on him as though he were a stranger, as though he were not me at all, for when I recall what I was like in those days my grief and shame are almost more than I can bear. Perhaps if I had possessed the talent to cut absolutely free and to become absolutely poor I would never have done some of the things I did. But instead I became famous for a while and made a lot of money.

"O God, even if You don't exist, or exist and don't give a damn, will You ever answer this question? Why, if I was born into a world that Stephanie showed me could be so lovely, born with such a furious instinct to live, love, and enjoy it, even perhaps to enjoy You, why did so many of us have to be born in a time when You simply closed Your door and locked us out?"

It was at this point that Timothy's climacteric begins, with him "talking, thinking, and acting, when I was flying as high as an astronaut but, unlike an astronaut, did not know who was in control of the module. I wish I could say that what ended this phase of my existence was some wonderful light on the road to a new Damascus, but I was much too modern for anything like that to happen to me. Esther Stahr once told me that I was so modern that I had already made myself obsolete."

THREE

FOR THE NEXT FEW YEARS Timothy was sure that he had it made, and most people would have agreed with him. He had become one of those movers and shakers who build up a dream, live in it, and believe in it, and the seventh decade of that century favored characters like him everywhere. When I was a boy I occasionally saw him in action and thought I knew him well. But what I saw was not a man at all, it was only an image and a voice on the screen of the universal box of the era, a habit in prime time, but one so addictive that for a country with a modest population he had an enormous audience spread out over six time zones from coast to coast with thousands of miles of empty forests, lakes, plains, and mountains in between.

He called himself a television journalist, and the famous and the obscure passed through his studio in droves. The curious thing was that after the show was over, hardly anyone remembered anything anyone had said; they remembered only the impressions Timothy had been able to create. Of all the interviews I saw, there is only one I recall, and only a few seconds of that. Timothy had a famous scientist in his studio; I think he was called a Nobel Laureate. He looked about thirty years older than Timothy, and as usually happened when he had an older or more famous man in front of him, it was compulsive with Timothy to enter into a conspiracy with his unseen audience and insinuate that the older man was covering something up. As often he was.

"Now, Dr. Anderson, you've been telling us how the world began and how brilliant it was of the scientists to be able to find it out." He paused and deployed his most innocent smile. "But of course there were no scientists around when the world began." Another pause, during which Timothy looked thoughtful and innocently sincere. "Now I have a question with which Science – I hope I'm not getting out of my league – may be more humanly involved." Another pause. "How do you think the world will end?"

The scientist measured him and answered, "In an armchair. Staring at electrical vibrations in boxes and listening to fools."

This must have been one of the very few occasions when a guest put Timothy down, for all the advantages were his. Editorial pundits and plain ordinary citizens never tired of Timothy. They ran out of adjectives in their efforts to nail him down – revolutionary, controversial, cheap, brilliant, vulgar, courageous, brash, sincere, abrasive, exhibitionist, irresponsible, fabulous – adjectives were running wild in those years and were quickly worn out into nothing. But to people with a grievance, and there were millions of them, Timothy for a time was a genuine culture hero, and he was probably accurate when he wrote that at the height of his popularity he could have had his choice of hundreds of different girls a night.

Here is a tape I found with his own reflections on himself. He made it several years later after he had vanished from the media:

"What happened was that I had unconsciously made myself one of the safety valves of the very System I was trying to destroy. I was far cheaper than policemen and torture chambers. For what did the System care what happened to its front men so long as nobody was able to change it? What could have been more to its advantage than to have individual human beings hated for what it was doing to everyone? So much the better for it if the public believed the System could be changed by changing its front men. The System was mindless, but it had the unerring instinct of the Law of Gravity. Even while millions of viewers detested me personally, not many of them missed my programs. They got too much of a bang watching me sandpaper the egos of politicians and big shots, me with the image of the People's Champion giving it out that if nobody had the guts to rip those mechanical tooth-smiles off the front men's faces and show up the wolves, foxes, spiders, and jellyfish underneath, this old curiosity shop they had the impertinence to call Our Free Way of Life might just as well close its doors with the final clang."

This was vintage Timothy, and even at this distance in time I can't say he was entirely wrong. For during those very years when he and a few others were the most strident in their abuse of the politicians, the real power men, the unseen ones, were moving quietly in for the final takeover.

A young Jewish girl called Esther Stahr was his coproducer on the show; indeed it was Esther who had made the show possible in the first place. He loved her, he feared her, and he usually went out of control when he lost her approval. She had been born in the Orthodox faith and her father was still a synagogue cantor and a tailor in a two-room shop on the Main with living quarters overhead. His three children were now self-supporting and urged him to let them help him move into a more comfortable district, but he told them he had worked here all his life and was too old to change his ways. He also told them that too many Jews had become too rich too fast for their own good. Timothy wrote that "Esther came naturally by that appalling Jewish conscience that makes more trouble for them than all their deals and politics put together," and he was never sure when her conscience would spring out at himself. On her way through college she had lost her religion and replaced it with Marx, but she abandoned Marx after a few years in his company. "If that damned woman lived to be ninety," Timothy wrote, "she would still be the righteous Jew. She would observe the High Holidays. She would search for the truth. She would make someone like me feel like a flea on a hot stove."

"Truth!" he used to shout at the poor girl. "Who wants it when he can get magic? This medium of ours is pure magic and if it tries to be anything else, it bombs. Oh sure, one of your boys made it, but if I ever had Jesus Christ on our show I'd abort the Sermon on the Mount and turn him into a Freedom Fighter." To this she replied, "One of our boys made Barabbas, too." And his reply to this was, "One of your boys has made everything. You name anything at all and one of them has made it."

Timothy wrote and talked much about the nature of our city in its last pre-Metro days:

"Could any city have been so self-intoxicated? Those were the years when at last the French people exploded. Along with our world championships in hockey and bank robberies, our dream politics and Expo 67, our new-found art that not even the painters themselves could understand, drugs, sex, pornography, Mafia, American corporations and dwindling British survivals, demonstrations, riots, bombings, debt-merchandising, growth disease, and madness, I really believe there was something more and bigger than all this in Montreal. For underneath the surface of this electronically wired Cleopatra whore of a town, its sky arctic blue when the wind came down clean from the north but otherwise reeking of sulfur dioxide, carbon monoxide, and all the subtler perfumes of technology – underneath all of this was a primordial life-wish of uncanny power as the memory-traces imprinted on the collective subconscious of a people who had been taught they were history's outcasts, victims for three centuries of some of history's most adroit con men, were suddenly activated and they claimed the right to be themselves no matter what themselves turned out to be.

"They called it revolution and perhaps that was what it was, though it was like no other revolution I ever read about in a history book. I loved it. I adored the excitement of it. I was sure that omnipotent youth was with me. Protests into demonstrations into riots and bombings, with drugs and sex playing a thunderous obbligato – after the dull correctness of our earlier years, how wonderful it all seemed. But it was not until the kidnappings began that the city felt the true horror-fear that grabs a man's throat when he looks up from his armchair and sees an ape's face pressed against the window pane staring at him.

"Most people recognized the ape instantly. I didn't, and that's why I ignited this story."

Again, vintage Timothy.

FOUR

ON A FINE OCTOBER MORNING Timothy flew down to Washington with his cameraman, and in the afternoon they flew home with a videotape made in a huge and very peculiar building.

A Major General Eli Sprott had agreed to give Timothy an interview because he was the son of Colonel Greg Wellfleet. Timothy did not mention to his father that he had used his name to obtain this interview; had he done so, his father would have been on the phone to the General within five minutes, for General Sprott and Colonel Greg Wellfleet were very special friends "because they had shared a grand climacteric when they met and shook hands on a battlefield carpeted with Nazi dead (so the communiqué put it) after American and Canadian troops had closed the Falaise Gap during the Second World War. When the war was over they kept up their friendship, Sprott fishing for salmon with Father along the Moisie River, Father shooting wild birds with Sprott in North Carolina, their big memory the war, the war the best years of their lives, all those great anecdotes about what the master-sergeant said to General Patton, or how the private from a Newfoundland outport was promoted to corporal because he had farted loud and clear while Monty was strutting past on an inspection. Two old soldiers who never died. Two old soldiers who refused to fade away. Two old soldiers who had never grown up."

Now the massed maples of the Adirondacks nineteen thousand feet below the aircraft were scarlet with autumn and Timothy was tense, excited, proud of himself, and badly wanting a woman to set her seal on his experience. He needed sleep but his brain refused to rest. He was so wound up in those days that it never rested at all, sleep being merely a spell of unconsciousness. He knew about the kidnappings in the city but he had little interest in them. Had he not come from the Pentagon, the first Canadian journalist in five years to have come out of that place with a live, taped interview?

Réjean Roy, his cameraman, was in the aisle seat beside him reading a magazine called *Sports Illustrated* and in profile his sickle jaw reminded Timothy of the prow of an obsolete British cruiser, the photograph of which still hung in the downstairs lavatory of one of his great-uncles who once had served in her. Réjean's lean face was well seamed with hockey scars and there was a permanent dent in his right cheekbone. He was so engrossed in his magazine that he did not look up when Timothy asked him what he really thought of General Sprott.

"Okay I guess, you know, far as he goes, like when I was a kid I used to cut the grass for a guy like him down in Knowlton."

"Ah, but the difference is that General Sprott cuts his own grass."

"It says here Fergy's gonna hang up his skates. That could mean we're outa the playoffs again."

"To hell with the playoffs. Who cares about those bloody play-offs?"

"*Calvaire*, everyone cares about them."

Réjean went on reading his magazine while Timothy pondered how to save the interview from what Sprott had done to it. Here, he thought, was a really quiet American. His aide was a Major Peabody and the sergeant who had conducted him into the General's presence wore a name plate identifying him as Prouty.

"Yes," said Sprott when Timothy asked him if everyone in his section was a New Englander, "this little corner is known locally as the Wasps' Nest."

Nobody's fool, thought Timothy, not in the Pentagon or anywhere else. The General's rimless glasses glinted when the light caught them, there was the smallest hint of chicken skin about his windpipe, but the rest of him was taut, lean, and hard. "Handball at 1730 hours, Lootenant?" "Yes, *sir*! Handball at 1730 hours."

Not even Timothy could imagine Sprott doing anything consciously dishonorable and he decided that this must be the focal point of his treatment of the tape. An hour with Sprott had given him the idea that the truly horrifying thing about the Pentagon was that men like Sprott inhabited it, which meant that it was just another modern office complex where competent salaried men, fewer of them slit-mouthed than you would find in any ordinary megalopolitan highrise, went to work every day from nine to five.

While Réjean was setting up his camera, Sprott had conversed in a low-keyed New England twang "with plenty of those clean cusswords American career officers pepper their conversation with to con people into thinking they're just boys like everyone else." Sprott looked so much like an intelligent version of Calvin Coolidge that Timothy opened the interview by mentioning the fact and asking if there was a family connection.

A canny look appeared on Sprott's lean face. "After I turned fifty a sizable number of people have asked me that very question, Mr. Wellfleet. May I call you Timmie?"

"Well," said Timothy with his best smile, "is there?"

"Could be."

"And how long have you served in the Pentagon, sir?"

"Twenty-two years. Mostly in. Sometimes lucky enough to get out."

"Out in Viet Nam, perhaps?"

"No."

"Korea?"

"Yes."

"A better war than Nam?"

"Hell, Timmie, you know as well as I do no war's a good war."

"So you would say your business here is to prevent war?"

"Right."

That was how how it started, and Timothy knew that if he was going to get anything out of Sprott he would have to work for it. He would also have to be careful how he went about it, for he had the idea that Sprott had decided to have his fun with him. Already his eyes had taken in the character of the office: the usual filing cabinets and maps, the family pictures including three little children who had been identified as granddaughters, Karsh's photograph of General Eisenhower with "To Eli from Ike" written in the bottom right-hand corner, the stuffed salmon mounted on a plain maple plaque with the information beneath it that it had been killed on the Moisie River on

June 12, 1961, and had weighed out at forty-three and a half pounds.

Now in the plane on the way home he was recalling the General's flat, honest voice parrying his questions. Yes, Viet Nam was a problem all right, but mostly a political one. The wrong war in the wrong place? General Ridgeway was on the record as having said that once, yes. And would you agree? The mean fact about any war, Timmie, is that it's always the aggressor who picks the place to fight it. But didn't the United States pick Viet Nam? If you can believe that, you can believe anything. Suppose I do believe it? Then I'd be under the obligation of remarking that you'd be in the company of round about seventy percent of your profession. Are you suggesting, sir, that we journalists will believe anything? No, I just gave you a figure, give or take one or two percent either way. Yes, that was an interesting question but he could not answer it because it touched on classified information. Important classified information? Hard to say, but could be. Timothy tried another question, the General said it was an excellent one and he'd be happy to answer it in detail, which gave Timothy the signal that it was a very bad question because the General talked to it for seven minutes. Now in the aircraft, remembering how the old boy had played with him, suddenly Timothy saw a way "to make this dud interview more lethally informative to my kind of audience than if he had given me the entire battle order of the American Army in Southeast Asia."

He nudged Réjean and said in French, "Once we've put some clothes onto that dummy of a tape it can be out-of-this-world wonderful."

Réjean nodded without lifting his eyes from the magazine. "The Alouettes could be the surprise of the year," he said in English. "They could go all the way."

"Listen, Réjean, I hate to do this to you but I want that tape for the weekend. As it stands now it would stink out any living room inside of two minutes. So this is what we're going to do. First, we play the General straight off the tape all the way through. No cuts. No splices in the sound track. Just take it as it is. You panned his office once. Okay, I want the pan repeated in the middle and once more in the end. Jacques can look after that. But I want a lot more. So can you go to Toronto tonight? Tomorrow at the latest?"

"Why do I have to go to Toronto?"

"Because that's where nearly all the stuff is that I want. The basis of the show will be Sprott himself, but I want his face off the screen for at least three-quarters of the playing time. But I want his voice and my voice on the sound track *all* the time. Now, instead of his face, this is what I want you guys to do. You and Jacques can splice in clips of what we went down to Washington for, which wasn't Sprott but Viet Nam and what it's really all about. So I want corpses, gunships manned by clean-limbed American boys, burning babies, screaming women fading into a lab with short-haired scientists in white coats, fade out into the circular face of a Dow Chemical executive, LBJ quoting Deuteronomy when he began the damned thing. Nixon in, Nixon out – flicker flicker and an over-voice saying, 'The greatest President since L. B. Johnson,' G.I.s lying around stoned, prisoners being murdered, students setting fire to college buildings and cops beating them up – all this I want while underneath Sprott keeps twanging along like Old Man River, and this will be the message – that Viet Nam's not a war at all but a colossal corporate-conglomerate enterprise."

"How am I going to remember all that?" said Réjean.

"You don't have to. In Toronto you go to Jim Cuddiford – he's a smart Englishman and a friend of mine. I'll call him up and tell him what I want."

Timothy recorded that two things he was going to play straight and they were the beginning and the end. According to him, Sprott was perfect in both of them. At the end Timothy gave a friendly but puzzled smile.

" 'Sir, it's been wonderful of you to give us so much of your valuable time but there's just one more question I have to ask.' A pause and another smile. 'How do you sleep in your bed?'

"I underestimated him. You should have seen that lean, shrewd Yankee face deploying the smile of a poker player laying down four kings against a full house.

" 'That's an interesting question, Mr. Wellfleet, to me at least. You know, sleep's never been a problem with me. Only time I ever took a sedative was when a medic shot one into me after my left buttock caught a splinter from an 88 in the Huertgen Forest. No aspirin, even in the middle of the Cuban thing.'

" 'The time you were eyeball to eyeball with the Russians?'

" 'Where did you hear that guff, Timmie?'

" 'Are you suggesting those aren't the exact words of President Kennedy?'

" 'Don't know. Wasn't there.' "

This seems to have ended the tape played to the public, but Timothy in his notes added the following of his own: "And is there a human being alive smarter than an old-line Yankee Wasp and could this explain why our world must come to an end? Beyond Sprott can evolution go any farther? And if it can, will Sprott let it? And will God have mercy on the rest of us if the time ever comes when Sprott finally succeeds in boring Him?"

From the expression on his cameraman's face Timothy sensed that Réjean Roy was not happy about this scenario.

"Okay, Réjean, so you don't like it?"

"You're the boss."

"Well, why don't you like it?"

Réjean shrugged. "The idea could be okay, but back home there's only one thing they're thinking about now."

"Fuck all! Two politicians kidnapped and what the hell? It's happening all over."

"Maybe, but at home they're not used to it yet."

"They soon will be."

"You better walk easy on this one, Timmie."

Timothy said that he and Réjean always got on well together, that Réjean was one of the best cameramen in the whole network, and that he was lucky to get him from the French sector for his two shows a week. Réjean spoke the French of an educated man, or at least of a well-trained one, but he had picked up his English in hockey rinks and ball games and fights in a district ethnically mixed. Timothy claimed to speak better French than Réjean spoke English, but when they were together Réjean usually spoke English even when Timothy was speaking French.

"Sorry, Réjean, but I still want you and Jacques to go to Toronto."

"There could be problems there."

"How do you mean, problems?"

"Some of the guys in Toronto don't like you any too good. And this General today, he don't like you at all."

"He'll like me a hell of a lot less when he finds out what we're going to do to him."

"You go easy, Timmie. That General could be a very big-sized problem for you. Remember what happened to those guys on the other show? I forget its name but I sure heard about it. You know, the guys that got this big American politician and made him look real bad. Those guys were fired."

"Listen, Réjean, those guys asked for it. They frigged around with the sound track. This politician was one of Kennedy's original think-tankers and they really screwed him up. They asked him a question – see. Then they cut out his answer and replaced it with an answer to an entirely different question. They did that four times. As if that wasn't enough, they jazzed up the sound track and handled the cameras so that he not only looked like a crook, he looked like a moron. Well, he got sore. A complaint came to Ottawa straight from the President and out those guys went on their asses. But we're not going to do anything like that. We're going to play the sound track straight all the way. Everything Sprott and I said is going to be repeated word for word and precisely. So now – can you get me the stuff?"

Another shrug, not a contented one. "I can get it, I guess, if you give me a list."

"Then no problem at all."

After which Timothy added the thought that "problem" had become the all-purpose word of the System, like "fuck" in the army.

He closed his eyes and tried to sleep but no sleep came because he was unable to pinpoint the cause of some apprehensions "that were crawling around inside of me like scavenger cells in a damaged brain." Then he began thinking about Esther Stahr and desire for her stabbed him. It was more than six weeks since he been in bed with her and now, after five different women in the interval, she was the only one he craved in the entire world. She was still on his mind when the aircraft blasted itself to a stop on the ramp of the airport.

The moment he entered the terminal building he could feel the tension in it. He recognized the president of a big corporation trying to make himself invisible against a wall with his hat pulled down almost to his eyes. "Uptight," he muttered. "Maybe you're right, Réjean."

When they were going out with their bags and TV equipment they were stopped at a check-point, and it was the first check-point either of them had ever seen in that airport. There was a desk and two men, one in policeman's blue, the other in a nondescript brown suit with a nondescript brown fedora and a red face also nondescript until you looked at his eyes. They were checking the identifications of everyone except the children and the very old people, and when it was Timothy's turn he asked the plainclothesman what the flap was about.

"Haven't you been listening to the newspapers lately, Mr. Wellfleet?"

Timothy acknowledged the choice of words with a professional smile and said cheerfully, "Since you know who I am, officer, may I pass? I'm in the business."

"So you are. In the business."

This reminded Timothy that a year previous he had grilled a high RCMP officer on something connected with an Indian reserve, with the result that questions embarrassing to the Force had been asked in Parliament. Still another area in which he was unpopular. The RCMP man took his time as he searched their bags and when he found Réjean's tape he scrutinized it with such concentration that Timothy grew nervous. He admitted that policemen always made him feel nervous because they reminded him of his father.

"That tape's got nothing to do with anything here," he said. "We made it in Washington this morning. Here – would you like to see our ticket stubs to prove that's where we came from?"

The officer returned the tape to Réjean and said, "Thank you, Mr. Wellfleet, but that won't be necessary."

"May we pass now?"

"Why not?"

"It's like I said," Réjean said as they went out with their gear to the parking lot where Réjean's car was. "This whole town is very uptight. There's only one thing in this town now."

"It's been coming for years. Cool it."

"Yeah, but like I told you, they're not used to it here."

"And like I told you, they soon will be. There's plenty more of the same where this came from."

They drove off "into the tawny pollution of the city's high prosperity with a pale sunlight filtering through it and the leaves on the roadside looking tired and gritty." Half an hour later they drew up in front of the apartment building in the central city where Esther Stahr lived.

FIVE

*T*HE MOMENT HE SAW Esther's face he realized that the change he had been sensing in her for a long time had grown to the point of some kind of decision. When he put his arms around her and kissed her there was no eager surge of her hips, no mouth opening to welcome him, just two stern eyes looking at him in judgment.

"I've missed you, Esther."

"Have you, Timmie?" she said and turned away and sat down.

"Now for Christ's sake what's the matter?"

No answer.

"What have I done?"

She continued the kind of silent treatment that rude ancestors of today's females doubtless gave to hairy and inarticulate males in caves long before the first Ice Age.

"Okay, Esther, what's this all about?"

She watched him steadily and said, "Please stop trying to look so innocent."

"I don't know what you mean."

"As you once remarked to me in another context, that's what the girl said to the sailor."

"Is it this kidnapping flap? Is that it?"

Her eyes continued to scrutinize him. "Our pigeons were sure to come home to roost sooner or later. I should say *your* pigeons, for you haven't paid any attention to an opinion of mine for nearly a year."

"I simply don't know what you're talking about."

"Which is the trouble. Just for the sake of a story you do it. Just for the sake of a story you'll do anything now. You and a few others have been building up the egos of these neurotics till they think they can get away with anything. You make them feel they're the center of the universe. A little more of this and it will bring back the fascists. If you were French it might make a little sense, but you aren't. What's the matter with people like you? Do you want to turn yourselves into the Jews of the future?"

"Now just what do you mean by that one?"

"You Anglo-Saxons. Or Anglo-Saxons like you, would be to put it better. The Wasp is *everyone's* target now. Or didn't you know it?

According to you – or according to what you do on the program – every Wasp is guilty until he's proved innocent. Did you read that last communiqué from these kidnappers, the one they left in the garbage pail?"

"It so happens that I've been in Washington, and preparing for Washington, and in Washington this two-bit crisis isn't the only thing on people's minds. If they printed anything at all about it, they must have put it in the back pages. I never saw a mention of it."

"Here they put it on the front page. The paper is there on the table. You'd better read it."

Timothy read the then-famous (or at least locally famous) message written by a kidnapped cabinet minister to his premier. Deep in the recesses of Timothy's mind this affair was to linger like a half-healed scar for the rest of his life, for reasons I will give you later. Afterwards, of course, there were so many kidnappings, bombings, skyjackings, and assassinations all over the world that even in our city this affair was soon forgotten, but as Réjean Roy said, our people had still to get used to them as something normal.

Timothy looked up from the paper. He admitted later that it had shaken him a little, but he was in no mood to admit this to Esther. He grinned at her and said, "You've got to hand it to them. This is terrific propaganda."

"You make me despair."

He sat down again. He wanted her body, even though there were plenty of other bodies he could have. Which meant, I suppose, that he wanted her body to want his. It would have been beneath his intellectual dignity to admit that he also wanted her soul to like his own soul.

He calmed down and said in a professional voice, "All right, Esther, you know more about this than I do. So tell me what's really happening."

"How can I, when nobody knows anything?"

"Esther dear," he said calmly, "don't forget that I predicted kidnappings six months ago."

"You also predicted that the kidnappers would be students. Well, it doesn't seem that they are."

"How do you know that?"

"Because the police know their identities, and students they are not."

"If the cops are so smart, why don't they go in and get them?"

"Because they've gone underground, of course. Timmie – look at me."

He looked at her.

"Timmie, we Jews have an instinct."

"Well?"

"This thing is not small. It's one of the biggest things that's happened in this city. Queer things are going on under the surface. People you and I know nothing about are operating here."

She turned away and went to the window, standing with her back to him. The window was open and they could hear the deep, asthmatic breathing of a great city.

"The Pentagon is incredible," he said. "Just like a jail. It's even built like a super-maximum-security penitentiary. The inmates all look like cons and guards. They wear the same-color uniforms. They even wear prison haircuts. My father's old playmate General Sprott is just about the finest-honed con I ever met in my life. He thought he took me all the way, but wait till I've dressed up that tape."

"So you're going to do that again?"

"Esther darling, in this particular moment of history the truth has got to be improved."

She smiled sadly and he wondered whether she was amused or had simply given up on him. In her present mood, Esther made him despair of ever being understood by anyone. But at least she seemed more tender than when he arrived.

He said quietly, soberly, "Apart from everything else I feel for you, I also happen to be very fond of you."

She sighed and looked away. "I know you are. Which is the problem."

This scene from so long ago has for me a wistful beauty it could never have had in reality. Almost certainly Esther and Timothy are no longer alive and I can only think of them as having always been young. Sometimes I wonder if years later, perhaps in the time of the Great Fear, they passed each other on a street without recognizing one another, both having changed so much. Among the many photographs that turned up in the iron box was one of Esther in color. Timothy had taken it on a beach and behind her the sea is intensely blue. Esther is wearing a bra and a kind of loincloth and there is no hint in her of *prima vera*. At twenty-seven and about one hundred and seventy centimeters she was a majestic woman with a broad forehead, Scythian nose and cheekbones, a wide mouth with full, molded lips, and large dark eyes that look out of the picture straight into yours. Her body is opulent and from her bearing she is proud of it, though I doubt if she appreciated Timothy's boast that it had been as well and truly laid (by him) as the cornerstone of the Sun Life Building.

Of course, it is true that there is no excellent beauty that hath not a strangeness in the proportions and Timothy recognized that this was the secret of Esther's power over his senses.

"Her eyes," he wrote, "were the kind that normally are matched by the sable hair of a beautiful woman from Spain or Portugal, but Esther's hair was a tawny gold. I asked her if this was a legacy of a female ancestor who had been raped on the North European plain by some Russian or German trooper and she gave me the look that can be the only reply of a sensitive Jew to a goy who asks that kind of wrong question. The idea that Esther's all-Jewish pedigree had been crossed by a rape was a mild aphrodisiac to me, though I hadn't the faintest understanding of why it was. In any case there was a wonderful mixture of genes in that girl. Her father, the little tailor and cantor, the gentle man who played chess and pondered the Talmud and Spinoza, had married a broad woman with big hands who loved him, and when Esther introduced me to her she did not smile but looked right through me. Between them, Mr. and Mrs. Stahr in a single generation had advanced their family in the New World as far as, or farther than, my own family had done in five generations. And now this wonderful daughter of theirs was sitting in judgment on me when the only thing I wanted to do was to screw her."

"Come over to the window," she said. "I want you to see something."

He joined her and pointed down over the cascade of roofs with the new highrises jutting up among them like tombstones. Farther down they could see the city's largest hotel nestling between the largest skyscraper and the old cathedral (the one with the twelve apostles standing in stone on the pediment), almost obliterated by the gigantic glass and ferroconcrete oblongs that had risen beside it.

"The top floors of that hotel have been turned into a fort," she said. "The whole cabinet and their families are there. The Prime Minister's mother is there. Dozens of corporation chiefs and bank presidents are there. The lobby is full of plainclothesmen."

"Good!" said Timothy.

"We've come to this and you call it good! Thousands of dynamite sticks have been stolen. After dark the streets are almost empty. Nobody knows how many cells are waiting to jump. I suppose you call that good, too?"

"For Christ's sake, do you believe all that crap? It reeks of a handout."

"My family came to this country to get rid of political maniacs and now it's beginning to look like the same story all over again and you think it's funny. Can't you see a fact even when you fall over it?"

Timothy laughed. "The thousands of dynamite sticks a fact? Who counted them?" He got up and returned to her. "Now you look at me, Esther. I've been around longer than you have and I know better than you do who the real bastards are. So you listen to me for a change."

"Listen to you! When do I do anything else but listen to you?"

"I know, I know, I talk too much. But this whole thing stinks. This crisis has been manufactured."

"Next thing you'll be telling me that what you call the Establishment has hired the kidnappers."

Timothy laughed again. "The Establishment! It would be a smart move if they did, but they haven't the brains. But the government is parlaying this affair into fifty times what it's worth."

She flared at him. "You make me sick to my brain. Crazy kids on the loose everywhere. Operators on the loose. Murderers on the loose. Do you blame *them*? No, you blame your own people. Another thing. Do you still have Che's picture on your wall? It's so long since I've been there I have to ask. If you do have it, take my advice and remove it, for the police might take it into their not entirely stupid heads to pay you a visit."

He screamed at her. "Two kidnappings, for Christ's sake, and everyone in this town goes crazy! I've just come from a place where they think in body counts of ninety millions. I could tell you – "

He was interrupted by a crescendo of howling police sirens and rushed back to the window. Ten stories below, cop cars were racing in from two opposite directions and the operation had the intensity of a commando raid.

"The cars slammed to a stop and the boys in blue burst out of them, some running into the apartment house, others around the sides. I jumped to Esther's phone, telephoned the network to ask Réjean to come over double-quick with his camera, and was told that Réjean had left half an hour ago. I watched for a long time and finally I saw the cops leaking out of the building, climbing into their cars, blasting off with their sirens, and driving off. 'Another *coitus interruptus*,' I said to Esther, and she told me she was going to make some tea."

While Esther was in the kitchen, Timothy watched the shadow of Mount Royal float down over the roofs and through the streets to the river. Lights had come on in the high buildings. Lights were shining from the upper windows of the hotel where the big-shots were sheltering and Timothy wondered if governments can really believe it when the wars they plan actually start. "To press the button that starts a war – my God, it must be the biggest thrill a man can know. But to press the button that starts a revolution" – Esther came in and his subconscious turned off. She poured him a cup of tea and he sipped it.

"This is good tea," he said. "How come you prefer English-style tea to European?"

"The minister they captured is going to be murdered," she said.

"Balls," he said.

"There's a terrifying personality in the cell that took him and when the police find him – I have a horrible feeling he'll turn out to be a man we've had on the show. If there's a single agitator or fanatic who's not been on our show, you name him. I remember this one and so do you. Him gabbling along about the moral necessity of kidnapping and political executions and you nodding your head as though that kind of talk was perfectly normal. I still can't understand how our show survived that performance. Or should I say, *your* show?"

"It's survived because they can't do without us. That's why it survived."

"If you and I are going to continue working together, we've got to agree on a few fundamentals."

"Such as?"

"Such as getting this program back to where it was before you turned it into an ego trip."

"There goes that damned gritty Jewish conscience again. All the way back from Washington all I could think about was how much I loved you. Why the hell aren't we in bed together instead of going on like this? What's come over you, Esther?"

"Reality, perhaps." Esther never gesticulated. She never shouted. "I'm guilty as much as you are. It was once so lovely I tried to pretend it would continue lovely."

He tried to laugh. "Let's cool this. Let's just a little cool this down. This so-called crisis – what does it amount to? The government will behave like they all do. Act stubborn and then surrender. They've made it clear they're looking for a deal. So what's going to happen? The cells will release the hostages. The government will fly the boys down to Cuba and after a few years everyone will forget about this and they'll return as patriots and heroes. But the moment they reach Havana – listen Esther – you and Réjean and I are going to fly down there and come back with a tape that'll go all around the world." He crossed the room, put his finger under her chin, and lifted it. "Know what I want to do above everything else? Not just spend a little time in bed with you but a whole night inside of you so we can keep waking up and start all over again."

She brushed his hand away. "Who gave you the idea that a woman likes to be used for a command performance? Now you listen to me for a change. If the government surrenders, this whole city will blow apart. There are people, Timmie, people you and I don't know, who'd find it very profitable if this whole country collapsed. What are you trying to do – dream yourself into insanity?"

He turned back to the window and stared in silence down at the city.

"I was as tight as a high-tension wire after she said that, for I knew she was right. To do my kind of work I had to be in extrasensory perception with what was around me. I didn't have to understand it. I just had to feel it, so maybe I *was* close to insanity. I saw the city's lights coming on and the beacon revolving on the top of the Cruciform and I felt invisible waves coming to me out of the city. I felt the hatreds compressed by three centuries of religion quivering down there like an agitated jelly, but this time the jelly wasn't edible, it was gelignite. The city where the System had so quickly turned half the population into non-persons. How many unknown, despised, exploited, frustrated, forgotten, and overlooked people down there must be singing hosannas in their souls now that the Establishment was scared pissless! *La Métropole – voilà la faiblesse!* So at last a handful of young men, nobody knew where they came from, they had found the path to the powder magazine of Métropole. Unseen and with precision – my God, and with such beautiful haughtiness – they had moved out of the Great Barrier Reef of unidentified humanity to plant the bomb, to seize the hostages, then had faded back unseen into the Barrier Reef from which they were hurling their ultimatums like conquerors. The non-persons of every Métropole in the world! The Dark People of Russia who rose when Lenin took another city nine wars ago! Esther was right. It *could* happen here. It *was* happening here. And I was here to record it."

He heard Esther's voice behind him. "Do you remember how long you've known me, darling?"

Her voice was so sad and gentle that it broke his mood.

"During all these four years have you ever seen me scared?" she said.

"Are you scared now?" His voice had become gentle.

"So scared I was sick to my stomach last night. Literally."

"Have I got anything to do with that?"

"If you'll sit down I'm going to try to tell you something I've never told to anyone. Not even to my own parents, though they found out about it. Give me a cigarette, will you?"

He gave her one and lit it for her. She seldom smoked and she never asked for a cigarette unless she needed it.

"Don't be hurt by what I'm going to say now. It won't do anyone any good if you're hurt by it." She paused. "Has it ever occurred to you that you have no mercy?"

He winced. "You mean I'm a sadist, or something?"

"Of course I don't mean that. I said you have no mercy. That's because you never found out what mercy is. I'm not criticizing you."

He rolled over on the sofa with his head on his forearms. "Go ahead."

"I know you've had an unhappy life. You're compulsively *sorry* for other people – lately for those who don't deserve it. Feeling sorry has nothing to do with mercy. Mercy isn't pity or feeling sorry for people. It's something nobody will ever understand unless he's had to beg for it. It's something that doesn't exist unless you're absolutely helpless in somebody else's power." Her hint of a smile was strange and distant to him. "Maybe Jews were born understanding what mercy is. Some of us are the most arrogant and proud people alive. Some of us are everything that goy Jew-haters claim we are. But I don't think there's a Jew alive, not even the worst, and that's saying more than you can possibly guess, who can't at least imagine what mercy is because there've been so many times we've found out that it wasn't worth while even begging for it. Last night I couldn't sleep."

He was still lying face down with his head on his forearms.

"That poor man they captured. He was twice on our show and you've not even given a thought to him. We had him only a month ago. Thank God you didn't try to cut him up. But he was French and you didn't. If he'd been English – . A middle-aged man with a wife and family. A proud man. A brave man who has known much about fear. Tied up, possibly gagged. Starved, maybe. Wherever that man is, he knows that his only hope is mercy and I don't think he's going to find it."

Timothy rolled over and sat up. "You're letting your imagination run away."

She made no reply, and looking at his watch, he saw they would soon have to leave for the studio. He also noticed that her eyes were closed. Was she as tired as that or was she simply intense? He remembered suddenly that she always had closed her eyes when she made love to him.

"Something cracked wide open inside of me and I remembered it and felt it again, the first time we made love, and it was not the fall of the year but the spring, one of those wonderful prematurely hot days we sometimes get in the middle of May. Never had I dreamed that so grave a girl could turn herself into what she became that night. It was a total union if only for a few seconds as the impossible happened and at last I was joined with a woman who loved me for myself and I understood what love is. This serious girl from the real world I had never known, this girl my family would have been lethally polite to, she was loving me for my own sake. The ancient history in her genes had judged me and found me adequate. The strength and acceptance of so many pilgrimages into so many destructions, into so many revivals, had emerged out of the centuries and I knew their power in her hard, imperious groin and the coiling of her muscles, and at the onset of a climax that must have shaken the room, suddenly she cried out: 'This is – *now*!' and just as her essence left her and entered me, and mine left me and entered her, in this most incandescent instant of my entire life what had to happen? My miserable mind bounced right back into the old jail and I thought, 'This is *now*? My God, the perfect title for my show!' "

In more moderate prose Timothy recorded that in literal truth it was a perfect title for his show and a few days later he told her how and when the idea had come to him and promptly felt guilty because he had offended her, Esther having hoped that this moment might also have been a different kind of climax in her own life. Under the title *This Is Now*, Timothy not only had far more material than he could even hope to use; he did not even have to understand it or interpret it. In those years most of the people who worked in the media were obsessed by what they called "happenings," and Timothy decided to base his show on nothing else but happenings. The one consistent line he trod was to use the happenings to make the Establishment look as bad as possible – something that in retrospect strikes me as redundant if not completely absurd. As Esther used prayerfully to ask him, what was the Establishment anyway? Anyone over forty? Anyone who had achieved something? Anyone who was not ashamed to use the word "duty"? Uncle Conrad, I remember, believed that the real danger in those years was that there was no real Establishment at all. Anyway, Timothy recorded that while he lay in Esther's arms he saw a cataract of program material flooding through his mind.

"I saw it all. My show could be a mirror of *Now* and there was no limit to the material *Now* could furnish me – drugged teenagers proving how moral they were to hate the politicians and their own parents; college presidents caught with their pants down; a victimized postman with seven children on inadequate welfare; a police captain almost certainly on the take; paroled convicts telling us what our jails are like; homosexuals and lesbians demanding proper respect; scientists, other journalists, generals, admirals, airmen, union leaders, pop musicians, whores who had written their autobiographies; politicians galore – all of them would jump at the chance of selling themselves to the public through me, and that would put them in my power. It's a matter of record that *Now* as I conceived and executed it proved inexhaustible. I even interviewed Bertrand Russell in England and he was so right, and so wrong, and so great, and so silly, and so wise, but above all he was kind to me and gave me the feeling that he was grateful because, though I reverenced him, I sensed the terrible contradictions he had had to live with for nearly a century. Without uttering a single overt remark, he made me know that he understood the chaos of my personal life and that we each felt pity for the other, and for the same reason.

"So on our first night together, silent in a white peace, I watching Esther intently as her eyes came slowly open and her strong face grew soft and radiant, I knowing that for the first time in my life I had brought someone into a state of ecstasy, her now-tranquil body gave a tiny *frisson*. Out of her hands as she caressed my skin I felt a vast and healing tenderness flow over me. Both of us were as silent as a country night.

"But soon afterwards my mind got busy again and I saw my program coming alive. I saw how I could use tricks with the lighting and shadows, how I could program the camera angles to make any kind of impression I desired without my victim even suspecting I was doing it. How I could edit with musical sounds, something like this – a politician speaks his punch-line and at a signal from me, a tuba player in the wings makes a noise like a farting horse. I saw also how I could fortify the satire and gain credibility with sincere, solid presentations of genuinely valuable people, how contrapuntally I would be able to display the multiple insanities of *Now*'s outrageousness to people, plants, animals, and all living creatures so that the public would have to stare at it, stare at it as I myself had stared at it helplessly for years, yes stare and stare at it so that I, Timothy Wellfleet, who had never before had a chance to do anything he wanted to do, with this Jewishly-wise woman beside me could become the Master of *Now*.

"So the dream was imprinted on my mind and I left it there for the time being. That night between sleeping and waking we made love till the robins woke us, and in the dawn and the pallor of sexual exhaustion, both of us naked, each with an arm about the other's waist, we knelt in the warm air before the open window and looked out over the roofs and through the gaps between the high buildings while the rising sun soared up like the song of a trumpet out of the eastern plain and poured itself across the river into the city.

"She whispered with her tawny-gold hair loose and her head turned away, she whispered, 'I have something I must tell you.'

" 'Yes, darling?'

" 'I love you.'

" 'I love you.'

" 'I'm *in* love with you.'

" 'I'm *in* love with you.'

"She paused and said very quietly, very sadly, 'But I can't marry you.'

"My arm tightened about her waist, my hand caressed the wonderful, opulent curve of her hip, and I, too, looked away, looked at that vast red sun lifting itself off from the horizon. She turned my face toward hers and surveyed me with a sweetness and gentleness I had never seen in a girl's face at any time since I was a child and Stephanie was there. But in Esther's eyes there was a look of fatality.

" 'It's not that I don't love you, darling. I'll always love you, I think. But I can never marry you.' Then she looked away and for an instant I thought she was crying. 'Why did it have to happen like this?'

" 'Because I'm a gentile?'

" 'It's cruel,' she whispered. 'More cruel on me than on you. Timmie, my beloved, why weren't you born a Jew?' Then she kissed me with open lips but very gently. 'So of course this gives you your freedom. I'll be here when you want me, but you're free.'

" 'I don't want that kind of freedom,' I said."

Now, three years later in her apartment, he wondered if things might have turned out otherwise if she had not spoken those words to him and meant them. He asked himself if it was really this strange rejection that had made him so reckless and driven him on without even looking where he was going, as though he had to fight tiger after tiger of his own invention in order to stay sane. She was sitting in an armchair with her eyes closed. He watched her open her eyes and the moment became trancelike.

"I've decided to tell you at last," she said. "I don't want to, but this much I owe you. If it wasn't for what's happening now I'd never have told you."

"Whatever it is, tell it."

Her voice came quietly, "When we first made love, you of course discovered that I was not a virgin."

Her mysteriousness was getting under his skin and making him irritable. "Did you think I'd expect any normal girl over seventeen to be a virgin?"

"Quite a few are. However, I'm trying to talk to you about mercy."

"I remember you saying I don't have any."

"I didn't say that. All I meant was that you don't understand what it is. Did you think—" her voice was shy, "that first lovely night we had together, did you think I might have begun when I was barely fourteen?"

"Great violinists begin when they're seven. That could explain why you're so terrific at it."

"Am I terrific at it?"

"Lots of men must have told you so."

He did not make her angry. Instead she smiled gently. "I know you pretty well, Timmie, and I know you didn't mean what you just said. Only one man ever told me what you told me and it was you. I remember thanking you and saying that if it was true, it was only because I loved you. Yes, I do have to tell the rest of it now." She looked away and her voice became almost impersonal. "Would you mind looking somewhere else than at me for the next few minutes?"

The trance in the room deepened. During an instant's silence he heard the distant wails of two different police sirens and estimated they were at least three miles apart. More than two and a half million people down there, increasing all the time, and a social scientist appearing on his show a month previous had offered, as his contribution to scientific knowledge, that in the city as a whole, an orgasm occurred on the average of every six and a half seconds.

Meanwhile Esther was talking in the detached voice of somebody reading aloud a newspaper column:

"It was a summer evening in the old street where we lived and a sickle moon was in the sky. I was one day over fourteen and I kept looking at the moon and thinking how nice it was that the moon was growing, too. I was thinking how much I loved my father for so many reasons, but also because he had called me Esther who was my favorite woman in the Bible. My father was so gentle, and he had never complained about having to live in a street like ours.

"Even our street looked beautiful that evening with the moon like a flower over the roofs. I remembered a pair of lines from a poem my Uncle Noah had told me in German—'Der Mond, die weisse Lilie,/ Blüht auf in Ihrer Hand.' I was only fourteen, so I said to myself, 'You're blooming out in God's hand tonight, Esther.' And then I saw them. I saw their faces and I froze.

"There were four young men, four of them on a corner with that look on their faces aimed straight at me. One of them looked like a rat. Another had a big chest and short, bowed legs. Another I can't remember at all but the leader was the one I would never forget. He had rusty red hair and he must have weighed more than two hundred pounds. He beckoned to me and said, 'Come here, you little Yid.' Then they came walking toward me spread out across the sidewalk like a net. I looked behind me and there were a few pedestrians about a block away. Across the street I saw two middle-aged men. When they saw what was going to happen they quickened their steps and looked the other way. It was like a human net moving at me and I ran down an alley where I knew there was a repair garage at the end of it. The garage door was open and I ran inside and screamed for help but there was nobody there. There was a back door and I tried to open it but it was jammed or locked and then they had me. They dragged me into the middle of the garage with that look on their faces and the leader said, 'All right, you know what it's all about so take them off.'

"I must have put both hands over my eyes. I must have tried to sink my chin into my body, for suddenly I saw stars and knew he'd hit me across my hands. I didn't know what to do. Went down on my knees, I guess, and begged them to have mercy and let me go but there was still that look on their faces – no, on all but one of their faces, and I knew the youngest one would not have been there if it hadn't been for the others. I think I said something about being only fourteen and that my parents were poor but the big one kept saying, 'Take them off.' He reached out to tear my dress off and I must have nodded. My father had made it himself and I couldn't stand the idea of it being torn. But when I tried to undo the buttons my fingers were shaking so they couldn't work. One of them held me from behind and the big one put out his hands and just tore the clothes off me and I was all naked there in the garage with my feet on the floor. It was solid earth and black with oil.

"Then the big one grabbed me and his hands were like rocks on my shoulders. The others took three seats out of some cars that were hoisted up on jacks and wedged them together on the floor. He put me down on the car seats and I rolled over onto my stomach. Then he picked me up like I was a cat or a dog and began rubbing me with his hand, and his hand was filthy. He put me on my back and one of them held me with his hands on my shoulders and suddenly it was like a huge red light splitting me apart – I can't go on telling this, I can't go on!" She stopped. "The man who'd been holding my shoulders got me by the throat and I fainted." She stopped again. "All of them were younger than twenty." After a moment she resumed. "It was dark for a long time. Then a light was shining in my eyes and I screamed because I thought they'd come back, but it was only the garage owner with one of those lights they hook up under car hoods when they're working on engines. He covered me with some kind of cloth. It was rough and smelled of oil and grease. I must have told him my name and address because soon I was in an ambulance on the way to a hospital. There were two policemen and one of them kept saying over and over in French, 'Tell us who they were, little girl.' Just like that, over and over. 'Tell us who they were and they'll wish they'd never been born.' "

Esther stopped talking and Timothy knew the story was over. Then she looked at him and added, "Now perhaps you'll understand why I'm not a fashionable cop-hater."

Her face had retreated far away from Timothy. He got up and went to the sideboard where she kept her liquor and poured out two stiff drinks. She refused hers and he poured it into his own glass. Normally he never drank anything before a show but now he thought he'd be unable to handle anything without one. He threw half of it down his throat and it seared his esophagus before it began to warm his brain.

"That guy with his hands on your throat," he said. "There was a Roman emperor who used to station a soldier by the head of slave girls when he raped them. At a signal the soldier'd squeeze the girl's throat. *Plus ça change*. Were those kids French or English?"

"Does it matter?"

"A great town. I hear a story like that and I ask whether they were French or English."

The atmosphere in the apartment was trancelike and the whiskey was reaching him. He turned on a light and his watch told him it was close to the time he had to leave for the studio. Esther also got to her feet and now she seemed quite normal, much less charged than she had been a while ago. He wondered if telling him this story was her way of telling him that all was over between them and she would never make love with him again. Christ, was it his fault if some punks gang-raped her when she was a kid? Then he wondered if that was why she had told him she could never marry a gentile.

She disappeared into the bathroom and he waited for five more minutes until she reappeared, tidy and collected and ready for the street with her bag on her arm.

"I'm all right now," she said.

When they reached the street there was a sharp bite of autumn in the air and the whiskey hit him with a crash.

"I've got to walk, Esther. That drink. I shouldn't have taken it. Maybe I'm just tired but it seems to be hitting me a little. You take a cab and I'll walk. I won't be long. It's just that I need some air."

"Yes, you'd better walk. If the guests arrive before you do, I'll look after them."

He saw a taxi coming and raised his arm. Its right flasher started to blink, it coasted in toward the curve and stopped, he opened the door for Esther, she got in, the cab drove off, and he was all by himself.

SIX

*I*F THERE WAS ONE QUALITY which Timothy professed to own in high degree it was a sense of place and he always insisted that the district he was now entering had more life in it than the rest of the city put together. I could agree with him, for when I was young it had also been my favorite district. Timothy's studio was located in a former factory not far from the shop where Esther grew up and her parents still lived. Its owner had retired and sold the premises to the network.

This was the quarter where most of the city's Jews had begun their lives in the New World. It had never been a true ghetto as some of their writers later said it was. There were many French families there too, even a few English, most of them working-class people. There was a discreet seasoning of quiet brothels only occasionally visited by the police, a few very large Catholic churches, one High Anglican church, and some neighborhood vaudeville and burlesque houses. However, it was true enough that if the city possessed what might be called a Jewish quarter this had once been it.

It was not that any more, not since so many of them had grown rich and moved out into stone houses and air-conditioned apartments in the west end, into the big deals, big cars, big golf clubs, and Miami

vacations where they talked with nostalgia of the dear old streets in
the years when a *zeyda* was still a patriarch and the bagels had tasted
so good, when the smoked meat was the best in North America and
nostrils were sensitive to the ancestral odors of the corner deli-
catessen. Now the quarter had been taken over by a new wave of
immigrants, mostly Greeks, Danubians, and people from the south
Mediterranean shore; even by some from the West Indian islands. In
the earlier days the district gave you a feeling of Riga and Bialystok,
but now you could smell the narrow streets of Middle Europe and the
little stone towns of the Inland Sea. And here, pronounced Timothy,
"The greed was as clean as a whistle. It was as sweet and innocent as
sexual desire before it is slaked."

There were many people in the street and it was still a genuine
neighborhood. These were the people, wrote Timothy, that he
wanted to reach above all others, though personally I would guess
they were the last people in the land he would have had a chance of
reaching. "I'm getting to them," he boasted, "before the System turns
them into Kraft cheese and Holiday Inns."

All officials detested Timothy and so did most of the other television journalists. The network bureaucrat in charge of his section had
smiled smugly when he shifted him out of the main broadcasting
house into this peripheral studio in the ex-garment factory. Timothy
threw a tantrum to make sure the man would keep him there, and
recorded that nothing is sweeter than to have an enemy do you a
favor when he thinks he's screwing you.

"Walking to the studio after leaving Esther I felt a surge of the old
confidence. The city trembled for me and it was a trembling
recorded on no seismograph. I saw a trio of young girls approaching,
probably Greek but possibly Lebanese, and each one of them looked
like an adventure. They were eyeing me and I knew I was recognized
and yes, I thought, yes – why not some time?

"Then I was sure I was going to be all right no matter how tired I
was, that I still had it, maybe more than ever I had it, and the city
trembled harder for me as I knew I would be able to seep into the
nervous systems of my armchair sitters, mate with their hidden fears
and truths, and make them identify with me as they would have to
identify with anyone who could project what I could project, which
was a saturating involvement in this instant of time when we had
obliterated the the past and made *Now* all there is, all the old

landmarks gone, all the old seamarks swallowed up in *Now*, world
with an end closer than you think. I saw more flashes of recognition
from passing strangers and what did I want with that sterile Broadcasting House on the Boulevard, that air-conditioned Versailles with
its identical neon-lit cubicles where sat and labored the shirt-sleeved
courtiers of King Common Man, most of them nice guys, some of
them such sincere and honest guys, some of them even competent.
But always there were the corridor schemers, the true courtiers of
King Common Man, whom they flattered, cajoled, terrified, entertained, stupefied, and conned, all the while knowing that no matter
how clever they were, no matter what they tried to make him believe,
he still would rule by Divine Right because he was the sole sanction
for their little mosquito dances under the kliegs and the big ideas
they made him pay for, their claws and stilettos honed for any rival
real or imagined, their chief fear – and it was a doppelgänger – their
absolutely accurate knowledge that if the Great King in one of his
unpredictable moments of sanity should ever get bored with them,
they would vanish as if they'd been vaporized.

"So what did I care what the real bastards, the bureaucrats who
called themselves Management, what they thought of me? Right now
they couldn't afford to get rid of me. So here in this district of
immigrants I savored with relish the smells of real work and ambition, sweat and human bodies, fresh vegetables and espresso coffee,
all those wonderful fruits and vegetables in The Four Brothers'
Market – what a title for a grocery store, poetry in that title! – and
those fish at Waldman's reeking of salt seas and themselves, the
shopmen in rubber boots and rubber aprons moving learnedly
among the boiled red lobsters, the olive-colored uncooked lobsters,
the sleek red snappers that shone like the Aga Khan's rubies among
the gray of haddock, cod, and halibut, all those fish in such profusion
it was hard to believe that soon there would be none left where they
had come from, everyone knew it but they kept on dragging them in,
sucking them up by vacuum into factory ships, another story in that
coming up soon. And after that still another, for an Ohio man who
had patented a process for making artificial beef and pork had
promised to appear on my show later in the year. To live on the
threshold of the possible extinction of all life above the insect and
virus level and to know it – at that instant the door of a disco opened
and a bearded youth with long shaggy hair staggered out glassy-eyed

wearing filthy jeans with a reasonably accurate design of a red phallus and black testicles woven into the crotch, and with him came the sour stench of whatever he and the rest of them had been smoking, and behind him followed the shriek of an electric guitar sounding like some kind of metal being tortured to death – *This is now!* – *Now is this!* – *All there is!* – *This is no-ow-ow!* And then I knew that I was with it in spite of what Esther had said, I was with it all the way.

"Then I stopped dead on a corner and spoke aloud:

" 'But where has she gone from me?'

" 'Where will I ever find her again?'

" 'Where will I ever find myself again?' "

When he reached the door of the studio building the last glimmer of twilight had faded out of the October sky and he realized that he had cut his time much too short.

SEVEN

AT HIS DESK IN THE OFFICE he became, at least outwardly, his cool professional self. Tonight's program had been set up two weeks ago and he had left it to Esther to invite the guests and give them a short briefing, also to prepare dossiers on them for him to scan before he went out to the cameras. He had asked her to get four people, but on reading the dossiers he discovered he would have only three.

The first was a woman of about thirty he had heard much about recently and had met at a cocktail party a month ago. She was said to be a rising poet and they had talked together for perhaps five minutes, during most of which she had placed her big hand on his forearm. A solemn face, a large full mouth, wide green eyes, and a body that could be fairly called sumptuous. He remembered that for a quick instant it had occurred to him that she might serve as a one-night stand. He remembered also that she had told him there was something she wished especially to say over the air, but now he had forgotten what this was. He scratched his head. Oh well, it would come to him later.

He picked up the next dossier, which was on Emile Chalifour, a separatist journalist-professor who had recently been fired from his university for fomenting student demonstrations and riots. Timothy had met him several times and knew him well enough to call him by his first name, but after reading Esther's notes, he knew him somewhat better. It emerged that Chalifour's father was not the exploited Gaspé fisherman he talked so much about; instead, he was in the construction business enjoying lucrative contracts with the provincial government. Timothy also learned that Chalifour had abandoned his wife and three children and was living with a nineteen-year-old Anglophone girl who was seven months pregnant, his wife refusing him a divorce because she was still a devout Catholic.

It was the second dossier that had really startled me when I first came upon it in the papers. Then I understood what André Gervais had meant when he told me in conversation I would have to revise my belief that Timothy had never had anything to do with our own lives. This second dossier was headed DR. CONRAD DEHMEL and on reading it I realized that Timothy had not known that he had married my mother. At the foot of the page, Esther had written a clear warning to Timothy:

"When you asked me to contact Dr. Dehmel, I don't think you knew much about him. The most important part of his life was lived in Europe in the terrible times. On no account should this be referred to on the program unless he brings it up himself. And some of it he will be sure to bring up."

Timothy had barely finished reading Esther's notes when he heard her footsteps approaching, and when she came into the office his mood was accusing.

"Where is the material on Dr. Jameson?"

"There isn't any."

"Why not?"

"I decided not to invite him."

"*You* decided! You're going too far."

"I'm trying to save *you* from going too far."

"That bastard Jameson's trying to screw up the Medicare Plan and I was intending to – "

"I know what you were intending to do. My brother is one of his internes and he's a fine man. He's not against Medicare, he's only against having the medical profession turned into a political football. Even if I had asked him, I'm sure he wouldn't have come."

"He'd have jumped at it. I know these doctors."

"You know nothing whatever about doctors. At a time like this, do you believe a man in Dr. Jameson's position would care to broadcast his appearance to the whole city? This place is so crazy that he's one of the men guarded in the top floors of the hotel."

"So you've left me with nothing but Chalifour and this professor?"

An impish smile appeared on Esther's lips. "Don't tell me you've forgotten your poet? She's out there waiting for you." Esther's smile widened. "Just how well do you know *her*, Timmie?"

"I can't even remember what she looks like."

Esther bent over and kissed his cheek. "Timmie, dear, it's just possible she took advantage of your good nature for the sake of mankind. She's a woman with a message. Anyway, you're tired out. You've been living on your nerves for a week and I'm at least partly to blame for that."

"Oh, for Christ's sake, what is it now?"

"That time I told you I'd never marry you because you're a gentile. I'm beginning to think you took it as a personal rejection."

"You told me it wasn't."

"You should forget all about me and find someone else and settle down."

" 'Someone else and settle down.' For God's sake let's get to work on this crummy program. After the Pentagon it's an awful comedown. Father's old playmate General Sprott, I wonder how long before it penetrates his crew-cut pointed head that the little brown men have licked to a frazzle the last, best hope of mankind? And you know, Esther? At bottom he's a nice man. That's what's so terrible about him."

"Timmie, we haven't much time left. That Madeleine Ball – have you read any of her poetry?"

"Have you?"

"Yes." Another feminine smile. "She's appearing with a cleavage of at least four inches, so maybe her poetry won't matter."

"So it's lousy! Oh well, she'll only be on a few minutes."

"She'll be on for the duration if you let her. She tells me she has something to say that will make you more famous than you are already. However, she doesn't worry me. It's the other two. I mean, having Chalifour on at the same time with Dr. Dehmel. They'll make an impossibly difficult combination. And why did you ask me to invite the professor in the first place? He doesn't fit into the kind of show this has become. I looked up the list of his publications in the university library and they run to three pages in four different languages. Why did you invite a man like him?"

"Because I've got my own sources and they didn't come from a library."

Esther smiled shyly. "Darling, you're tired right out, and no wonder. Why don't you let me take the program tonight?"

"Are you telling me I'm washed up? Well, let *me* tell *you* that I could bring anything alive tonight. And with those two dummies this show will need a rocket booster."

She bit her lip and turned away. Timothy noted later that if she had said nothing more he would have agreed to let her take over. But she did say something more.

"Lately older men – especially if they're dignified, distinguished men – they've been doing something to you that isn't good. You behave to them as though they're a bad smell in your nose. So please be careful tonight. That Chalifour is sure to be abrasive. Don't bait him into putting Professor Dehmel into danger."

Timothy came erect and looked straight at her. "This man Dehmel you think you know so much about – *I* happen to know he's an ex-Nazi and a racist."

Her face went white. "Where did you pick up *that* morsel?"

"I told you I had my sources."

"What source told you a thing like that?"

"Jason Ross – you remember Jason Ross, don't you?"

"That miserable little – "

"Come off it, Esther. Jason Ross is the most powerful student in the city, probably in the country."

"The most powerful student! Don't make me laugh."

"He's scared the administration pissless. And he's a good performer. You know yourself how good he is. We've had him here three times and he really socked it to them. He had his suspicions of Dehmel – he's got *really* good sources. He was born in Europe and he signed up for two of Dehmel's courses just to verify what he'd been told about him. He's an operator, Ross is. He gave me the real goods on this professor of yours."

In a voice frigid with contempt, she said, "Next time you're in the mood to get yourself conned by a phony like this Ross, you talk first with a real Jew. This Ross we can do without. A few more like him and there'll be people talking about pogroms. After I'd talked with Ross for five minutes I needed a bath."

She left him and he recorded later that her eyes had the same expression he had seen in the eyes of his wife when she had made up her mind to divorce him. He sank his head into his forearms and nearly sobbed, but he had a kind of desperate toughness that usually saved him from collapse and soon he straightened his shoulders and steadied his breathing. He opened a drawer in his filing cabinet and took out a piece of paper, glanced at it, then folded it and put it into the side pocket of his jacket. He recorded that he said aloud, "It seems that King Richard is himself again, and in more ways than one."

EIGHT

*B*EFORE I BEGAN WRITING this history I told André Gervais that the handling of time was going to be very difficult. This material has come to me from so many segments of time, some of which I never lived in myself. Even Timothy's material comes from different segments.

I have told you how it was for him when he was a child and quite a lot about him when he was at the height of his television career. André was informed by the Diagram that the crack-up occurred when I was in my late twenties. But did it? My own idea is that it began with Timothy's crowd, and Timothy was twenty years older than me. His age group was greatly disliked by ours, especially after they began copying the way we dressed and poached on our girls. We called them "the thirty-year-olders." I think now that we were as unfair to them as they were to the generation above them. We simply did not understand how much baloney had been jammed down their throats. As Timothy put it, "Instant marriage, instant family, instant coffee, instant jobs, and a trained consumer for the rest of your life." The programming of their ideas was changed as smoothly as the gears in the automatic transmissions of the automobiles of the time. No wonder poor old Timothy raved so frantically against the System. And with this clumsy introduction, I must ask you to bear with a short interlude while I take you back to what Timothy called "Those stone-dead years when I was doing my best to be like everyone else."

Before leaving school, in a craving to please his father and make him his friend, Timothy decided that he wanted to go to the Royal Military College instead of to a regular university. Nothing he ever did made his father so happy. Colonel Wellfleet had himself been an RMC man; so had his own father, one of his brothers, and two of his uncles in that older time when RMC was the prime stamping ground of the Anglophone establishment, its traditions and even its uniform straight out of nineteenth-century Sandhurst, most of its instructors burly, mustachioed ex-sergeants of famous English Guards regiments. Timothy spent two years there.

At times he could be fair even to people he disliked, and he admitted that the RMC he attended was not particularly exclusive, that the cadets really did come from what the Commandant called "every walk of life," and that the navy and the air force were there in addition to the army. But the very thought of anyone like Timothy in a military college ridicules itself.

When his third year lapsed around he told his father that all he had learned at RMC was to keep a tidy room and a straight back. Later on it mortified him to know that the sergeants had trained his reflexes so thoroughly that he could never get over the habit of sitting and standing like a soldier.

When he told his father he intended to drop out of RMC he expected an explosion, but Colonel Wellfleet merely seemed lonely and sad. What was the matter with RMC – had it fallen off? Timothy said there was nothing the matter with it if you liked the army.

"But you've known all along that RMC doesn't commit you to a military career. It's a training for almost anything."

"Oh sure, it's a training all right. Look at my shoulders."

His father rubbed his chin, glanced at his watch, and picked up the phone.

"I'm going to have a word with your Commandant. He and I did a spell in Staff College in the early days of the war."

Timothy sat still and erect during the conversation that followed over the telephone. Finally his father nodded and said, "Thanks, Cuffy, for being so frank with me. Next time you're in town give me a buzz and we'll have lunch and a splash together." He hung up, relit his pipe, puffed on it thoughtfully, and between puffs went into a soliloquy.

The Commandant had agreed that RMC was not the right place for the boy. Timothy had made no trouble, in fact he had put out a real effort, but he just wasn't the type. A long puff and a cloud of fragrant smoke from the imported Erinmore.

"I'd hoped it wouldn't come to this," the Colonel said finally, "but I'm afraid it has. You've become a problem."

A bank? No, that would never suit him. Another puff. What about investments? A long pause.

"From your expression I gather you're against investments, but you never know in advance about investments. I suggest that you take an aptitude test. Sometimes the most unlikely people turn out to be good at investments. I knew a man who wasted ten years of his life trying to be a painter. It took him all that long to find out he had no talent. Then he took an aptitude test and the test pointed to investments. Do you know what? That man astonished everyone, including himself. Inside five years he was a millionaire."

"Where is he now?"

"Dead, I'm sorry to say. As a matter of fact he committed suicide. Nobody ever understood why. He seemed to have a happy family. Nice wife and two splendid young sons. Queer things happen these days."

"Father," said Timothy, "I don't think I want to go into investments."

His father sighed. "Something tells me you're right."

The Colonel continued to think aloud. Insurance? He shook his head. Real estate? There was a strong gambling element there and it could be stimulating but – "No, you haven't the instinct. I've seen you play cards. Any ideas of your own?"

"I'd been thinking of becoming a teacher."

"The last refuge of the undecided," said the Colonel. Then once more he surprised Timothy. "But hold on a moment. There might be a great deal in that idea. One of the most successful men this city ever knew began as a schoolmaster and he taught tough subjects – Latin and Greek. He told my father something that made a great impression on me. Six years with schoolboys had taught him two priceless lessons, he said. First, he always knew when someone was lying. Secondly, he discovered that boys are just like grown men most of the time and that it was from boys that he learned what most people really want. So there you have two things – to recognize when people are lying and to know what they really want – especially if they're ashamed of what they want." The Colonel was warming to the idea. "And here's another consideration. These days teachers are being paid much more than they used to be paid. More than most of them are worth, in my opinion. But if that's what you want, give it a crack." A longer pause. "But of course you know yourself there's another problem here. You'll have to go to a university first. That will mean you've already wasted two years." He shrugged. "Oh well, what difference need that make? I lost more than five years in the war."

So the Colonel staked his son and Timothy enrolled for joint honors in Sociology and Political Science, which were prestige subjects in those days. He acquainted himself with a variety of girls, most of them of his own social class, and in his final year he fixed on a plump, rosy-cheeked blonde called Enid. Subsequently he found it "dismally funny the kind of ethics we used to have." Apparently the young people of his class were frank with each other verbally, if frank in few other ways. "I was too dumb then to know that Enid was even dumber. She had the hang-up, all right. She'd love to sleep with me – *sleep*, for God's sake! – but only if we first announced our engagement. So like a bloody fool I got publicly engaged for no better reason than that I was crazy for a regular lay."

But Timothy's father was delighted, because Enid's parents were old family friends. Marriage made it essential for Timothy to get a job even though his father was happy to stake the happy couple, but Greg Wellfleet was looking toward the future. Towards grandchildren and the future of his grandchildren. He therefore told Timothy that he must forget all about schoolteaching and that it was too bad he'd wasted all that time with Sociology and Political Science when he might have been studying Commerce. Once again he invited Timothy into his library and this time he didn't tell him he was a problem. He said he had the solution, but he took a long time to get around to saying what it was.

"Then it was that at last I found myself watching Father with a sad wonder. Then it was that I understood what had happened to him. I felt a great pity for Father. He no longer could recognize the world he was living in. He had become an exile in it. Instead of renewing his youth, he had become a well-heeled hangover from an age that had blown itself out. That young wife of his had only accelerated his aging. She was even blinder than he to the real world. I found myself thinking even then – long before I met Esther – what would he have been like if he had possessed the kind of courage to defy the stuffed shirts he had grown up with and marry some lusty immigrant girl who might have laid to rest that mighty animal in his loins and heart? You poor old bastard, I thought, while he was planning my future. The only time you were free to be yourself was in the war. You brave, sad, gallant man. Harnessed to a youthful replica of the poison that began to kill you when you were only twenty-two. Why did you *refuse* to understand me? Now your wealth is just another burden for your tired, frustrated shoulders to carry. I know a poet who lives with a long succession of girls and has no shame at all. He lets them support him. People swarm after him for his autograph. But you do have honor, and the only autograph anyone wants from you is your signature at the bottom of a check. You brave, sad man. So old before your time when your body and soul yearn to be young. Helping to liberate Holland didn't liberate you after all, for you came home to that bitch of a mother of mine and then you must have gone into a panic. Now there's no place for you in a world a-borning because it won't offer a man like you even a corner of itself to weep in. So here you are, a proved hero, searching the maps and travel agencies for some tropical island where you can escape the taxes and fence yourself in with others as rich and hopeless as yourself.

"As though I had been reading his thoughts, Father suddenly said, 'Your stepmother and I have been thinking of settling in Nassau.' So I said, 'Don't do it.' He said, 'Why not?' and looked at me hard. 'If you go there,' I said, 'the blacks will spit on your shadow when you pass.' And he said, 'I've nothing against the blacks. Why would they do that?' Then he turned away from me and said, 'I think I've found the solution for your problem.' "

The solution turned out to be an advertising agency which one of the Colonel's wartime friends, in fact his Adjutant, had inherited from his own father, who had also been a previous colonel of the regiment. So Timothy started to work in a business house which was respected, self-respecting, and dignified. Mr. Campbell was an obstinate man of high character who believed, and told Timothy at their first meeting, that while it was legitimate for an advertising man to dramatize the products he promoted, he must be as careful of the long-time truth as the editor of a first-class responsible newspaper.

"All the ads that's fit to print?" Timothy suggested.

Mr. Campbell gave him a stern glance to indicate that he did not appreciate flippant young men.

Looking back, Timothy marvelled that Mr. Campbell lasted as long as he did, for "His ethics were frozen in the prewar days when Canada was a dull and on the whole honest country with a dollar worth a hundred cents instead of twenty-five and when it was fatal to oversell anything from a detergent to a politician." When Mr. Campbell reached the end of his road, a bright young account executive smilingly described him as a time-adjustment casualty.

"So was the whole country a time-adjustment casualty, for what happened to it was as swift as a dream-sequence. For twenty years our dreaming capitalists had been selling out their companies to huge American combines which were wide-awake; or rather, the combines had been suavely and systematically engrossing them just as they had engrossed the smaller businesses in their own countries. One of them finally engrossed us. Mr. Campbell was retired with a generous block of the company stock, we became known as Campbell of Canada, Ltd., and just how limited we were we soon found out.

"Up from Madison Avenue came a thirty-five-year-old product of Phillips Andover and the Harvard Business School to modernize and reorganize us. His name was Melvin K. Goodwillie and it would have been hard to find a friendlier fellow. The moment he met me he said 'Hi!' and immediately called us all by our first names, including men twenty years older than himself. Soon he was sending us down in relays to New York to take what he called immersion programs in techniques which were more or less new to us, and there we met men as alert and friendly as Goodwillie himself, including the boss of the whole multinational whose name was Taylor W. Truscott. He also called us by our first names at first sight – silver hair with natural waves in it, a fast smile, a thin mouth, and pale blue eyes so alert to opportunity they could see around corners."

Mr. Truscott's message was that he welcomed this opportunity to expand into Canada because there the advertising industry still retained a a dignified image, "and we intend to keep it that way."

In order to dignify the image still further, Goodwillie was ordered to move the agency into the most prestigious (according to Timothy, one of Goodwillie's favorite words) tower in the city. In those days, as well I remember, you could hardly go anywhere without hearing some kind of music, and on the floors where the typists worked, piped-in music whispered softly from nine till five. On the floors where the account executives worked, the carpeting went from wall to wall and the windows from floor to ceiling "so that we could get the right perspective by looking down like Gullivers from thirty-eight floors onto the Lilliputian consumers swarming below." Silk screens depicting rural and mountain scenery in Canada adorned the walls and Goodwillie announced a poetry award of a thousand dollars for annual competition. Finally came the day when Goodwillie buzzed Timothy to come to the executive suite to witness the installation of what he called his *pièce de résistance*. He was just beginning a crash program in learning French.

Timothy arrived to see four husky French Canadians with the shoulders of ancient *voyageurs* manhandling into the suite the biggest Quebec armoire he had ever seen in his life.

Goodwillie beamed. "Genuine seventeenth century," he said.

The wood looked slightly dry-rotted, and when Timothy touched it and examined it closely he realized that it had been deliberately and carefully scorched and then stained.

"Mel," he said, "where did you find this eleven-dollar bill?"

Goodwillie laughed. "No hard feelings, man, but you guys don't even know your own town. You've lived here all your life and you never knew there's a business on Craig Street that manufactures antiques to order. This piece is perfect Louis Quatorze."

The next day Goodwillie summoned Timothy once more. "I just thought you'd like to see it operational. Just watch."

He pressed a button on the left side of the antique and out swung a tray bearing iced Coca-Cola, Seven-Up, two tins of tomato juice, six uniform glasses, and a bottle opener.

"*Pour l'heure du cocktail*. I had a small refrigerator installed inside of it. From now on, we hold our business luncheons in the executive suite." Goodwillie grinned. "Of course, this tray is for abstainers. You always have to watch out for them. More than one account's been lost by offering a drink to a dry." Pressing a button on the right side he said, "This is for real." Out swung a much larger tray bearing gin, vodka, Scotch, rye, and mixed martinis, also soda and tonic waters, eight glasses of varying shapes and sizes, and another bottle opener.

"*Les apéritifs*," said Goodwillie.

In those days Timothy wrote that Goodwillie wore Brooks Brothers pink on social occasions and nothing but charcoal black, thin ties, white shirts, and gold cufflinks when he was on the job. He also sported a crew cut. A few years later he was wearing unmatched jackets and pants, enormous ties, bushy sideburns, long hair carefully tailored, and a goatee "that looked Christawful on Goodwillie because he didn't have the right face for it."

But that Goodwillie was smart Timothy never doubted. Under his leadership Campbell of Canada boomed as it never had before. What most intrigued Timothy was that Goodwillie was sincere. When he described himself as "really dedicated to this country," he meant it. When he said, as he often did, that he had taken Thomas Jefferson for his model in life, he meant it. And when he said that Timothy's work for the agency was right on, he meant that, too.

"And what a thought *that* was to carry around. And what did it say about my character that Mr. Campbell had never trusted me while Goodwillie kept telling me I was by far the best idea-man in the whole outfit."

Glowing reports of Timothy's work went down to New York, Goodwillie explaining that in Timothy the company had acquired just what it most wanted, a smart native with a natural instinct for the industry who knew how to readjust the usual Madison Avenue presentations so that they had a genuine Canadian look.

"That's one thing we've learned," Goodwillie said, "that the British never learned. You must never give a guy the idea you're invading his territory. The British never thought about this and that explains why they lost their empire." Then, his face serious, his eyes excited, he said, "I've been talking with Mr. Truscott and Mr. Truscott has a big thing in mind for you. We're opening up in Iran. Mr. Truscott is in very big with the Shah. So how do you fancy this? He wants you to head up our branch there."

"For God's sake talk him out of it. That's the last place on earth I'd want to work in. Besides, I'd have to learn Persian."

So he stayed where he was and every year received a bigger bonus and more fringe benefits. He used to take Enid to the Costa Brava or the Côte d'Azur for quick holidays in the summer and to Val d'Isère for quick ski trips in the winter. He played squash regularly at the MAAA and once, when he and Enid were entertaining the Goodwillies to dinner, he even heard himself say that he'd never had it so good.

His work brought him into contact with the television people and that was how he met Esther Stahr. She was the first Jewish girl he ever knew and he was embarrassed to discover that she was much better educated than himself. He also learned that she felt sorry for him, as some people who have grown up poor feel for people who have grown up in a background like Timothy's. With Esther he could talk about books as he never could with Enid or his old friends. The agency work was beginning to desiccate him and he became an omnivorous reader. Every Saturday after squash he went to the book stores and came home with some new paperbacks. He read novels, poetry, biography, history, anthropology, and even some works in popular biology. He dreamed of becoming an author and after one of his business sessions with Esther he gave her the outline of a play he wanted to write.

He never got around to writing the dialogue, but I found among his papers a sketch of the play itself. He imagined a set with a gigantic television screen forming the back wall of the stage. Across this screen there marched or posed a steady procession of newsmakers, together with the worst of the news scenes they were responsible for. Politicians with their mouths opening and closing as they made their pronouncements; commercials cutting into them constantly; sudden jets of pop music; bombings, riots, hockey and football games; panel discussions between politely wrangling college professors – "Everything in the news which adds up to the vast war of shadows and images the world has become."

In front of this screen the actors on the stage itself were tiny. They were confined in a bare living room and were visible only in flashes when one of the roving spotlights caught them. They were ordinary men, women, and children trying to live with each other. He intended to give them no lines at all to speak. They were to mime their parts – making love only to quarrel, quarrelling only to give up and try making love again, much of the time just sitting with blank faces while the sound track boomed out from the screen telling them what to buy, where to go for their vacations, what to think, what to worship, what to do or not to do if they wanted to escape lung cancer, heart disease, bad breath, smelly armpits, or lack of love.

There were other characters in the play who would also be speechless. These were men and women dressed in the costumes of their times from Socrates and Jesus to just before the present. They moved in and out of the wings onto the stage. Longingly did the little mimes beg them to speak to them but they never did. Beg them to touch them but they never did. They came, they looked, and they disappeared.

This was Timothy's play and later on he wondered whether his inability or unwillingness to write it "was responsible for some of the things I did after I myself became one of those voices from the shadow world."

At first he and Esther had happy times just relaxing and talking together. She was the first person he had ever been able really to talk with. Enid did not even try. All she ever talked about, it seemed to him, was her children, her family, and prices.

After a while Esther decided that Timothy could become a television personality and in her quietly thorough way she spent more than a month preparing the boss of her section to let her set up a program examining the methods of modern advertising. She was a serious girl and she wanted to focus the program on a few serious questions. To what extent were American advertising methods responsible for the drastic change in the nation's character since the war? Why had a people once thrifty become spendthrift? Why had a people once calm become so erratic in their emotions and behavior? Why were so many of them in debt all the time? Her boss, who voted for a bland version of a socialist party, finally told her to go ahead. As Timothy put it a year later, "Dear old CBC, liberal to the second-last breath."

Esther was the *animateur* of this show and she had invited two other guests besides Timothy. One was the inevitable professor of Sociology, the second was a poet with strong opinions about what the ad-men were doing to what he called the language of Shakespeare and Yeats. They both assumed that Timothy was there to defend the industry and he gave them the surprise of their lives. He also gave himself the surprise of his own life. For when he realized that thousands of unseen people were watching and listening, "Suddenly my alienation and self-contempt turned into a salt tide and I said to myself, to hell with them, let the chips fall where they may."

Casually, as though he were telling the public what it knew anyway, he asserted that it was pure hypocrisy for liberal idealists to make the ad-man the goat for anything whatever. The ad-man had the same pedigree as any modern liberal you could name. Modern liberals were the outgrowth of nineteenth-century Wasp evangelicism, and what else was advertising but the logical conclusion of that? What were those old evangelical hymns like "Onward, Christian Soldiers" but singing commercials for the evangelical Protestant churches?

"We're in the direct tradition with our singing commercials. They weren't invented in the United States. They began in England. 'Hark the herald angels sing/Beecham's pills are just the thing.'

"Oh, so you want to know where we get our ideas? Some of them we dream up ourselves, but all of them have to fit into a general pattern programmed and computerized south of the border."

What did that mean, one of the guests asked. "Split runs," said Timothy. "We never heard of split runs." "Then let me explain."

"For instance," continued Timothy, "we take an original commercial from New York and we make it Canadian without changing a shade of the original message. We simply substitute the word 'Canadian' for the original word 'American.'"

Then he explained how they often imposed on the original Madison Avenue layout a quick camera shot of some well-known Canadian beauty spot like Peggy's Cove or Lake Louise, "so that your friendly filling-station man, who in real life is a bit-part actor residing in a New York suburb, seems to be filling *your* tank with that great-performance gasoline that sends *you*, a forty-five-year-old executive with grizzled hair but a trim waistline, purring along over the big Canadian land with that great performance and beside him the twenty-year-old blonde with blowing hair and the promise of a performance a helluva lot more interesting at the end of the trip."

"Actually," he went on, "the gas we use in our end of the Big Land is refined from just about the sourest crude you can get. Our own western crude is supposed to be the sweetest and maybe it is, but you can't get it here."

The poet, who had not known this, expressed wrath so extreme that Timothy guessed that the information had delighted his neurosis. The sociologist knew much more about what he called "the problem" than Timothy did, but he was so accustomed to being in opposition that he shifted his original ground and dilated to the poet on the dangers of economic nationalism. Are pollution and pornography any better, he demanded, if they're produced here and not imported? Then he turned to Timothy and asked him the same question that Timothy was to put to General Sprott a few years later.

"But if you really mean what you've been saying – I mean, if you really do have so much contempt for your work – how can you sleep in your bed?"

"Why shouldn't I? Without the kind of work I do the whole System would collapse and nobody, including yourself, would have any beds to sleep in at all. The System can no more run without us than an automobile can run without oil. That makes me the indispensable man."

"Do you like the present System?"

"Do you?"

"I asked *you* the question."

"Isn't it all we've got?"

"And you sleep in your bed?"

"I love my mattress and my mattress loves me. One of our most reliable clients makes it, by the way. It combines the maximum of support with the maximum of relaxation. It's been scientifically designed to be a mattress for all seasons and for all activities connected with mattresses."

This remark provided the poet with an opportunity to press him on the sexual aspects of advertising and once again Timothy took over.

"Let me ask you gentlemen a question for a change." He sighed and his voice was weary. "Do you really believe that old bromide that advertising is sexually based?"

"All you have to do is look at it," the poet said.

"Then evidently that's not what you've been doing. Oh, by the way, do you like sex yourself?"

"Well..."

"Why, man, it's the only lyric they've left us with. Next to motherhood it's the only human thing that's encouraged and our business is to make your sex life ten times more expensive than it has any need to be. Do you really believe we're so stupid as to think there's any money in honest-to-goodness sexual love? Take the most successful publication of our time. Take *Playboy* magazine. It's the most anti-sex magazine in the world. Not sex, but female meat. Do you seriously believe we're going to let anything like good, honest, passionate, lusty, free, non-phony, poetic, liberating sex compete with our products? Bastards we may well be, a bastard I admit I am myself, but stupid we are not."

The sociologist leaned forward and shook his head vigorously. He said that one of his graduate students had written a doctor's thesis containing a careful computation, percentage-wise, of the sexual imputations in TV commercials over a period of six months and that his figures, scientifically tabulated, indicated a conclusion very different from Timothy's.

"Definitely, Timothy, I have to tell you that your statement doesn't come near a correlation with these scientific findings. So what do you say to that?"

"I'd say it's one more proof, Professor, of why so many people are wax in our hands."

The poet wanted to know whether the advertising industry was the chief instrument in the American plan to take over the country and Timothy looked at him with one of those rueful expressions of his.

The Americans? What do you mean by American, anyway? The Americans aren't *planning* any take-over of this country. It's not that way at all. They don't even think about this country. It's our own people who want to sell it to them and not even that is planned. It's just one of those things that happens automatically. All kinds of nation-saving plans are floating around but what comes of them? Nothing. The beauty of the System is that it simply lets everything happen according to the engine that drives it."

"Which is what?" the poet asked sardonically.

"Greed," said Timothy.

The show lasted a full half-hour, during which Timothy revealed most of the trade secrets he knew, "which God knows should have been obvious to everybody," and all through the program his voice was casual, judicious, or bantering with a *fin de siècle* acceptance of the situation in which he found himself.

When the show was over the four of them went to a restaurant where they were served by a waitress dressed like a shepherdess in the court of Louis XVI. The poet recited some of his latest verses and one of his phrases was so piquant that Timothy asked him if he would be willing to offer it to Campbell's of Canada. The poet said he would indeed be interested if the agency would pay for it. When he suggested a fee of twenty-five dollars, Timothy laughed.

"With any kind of luck, I'll parlay that figure into at least five hundred. Give me your phone number and I'll call you in the next day or two."

This turned out to be another of his unkept promises, for the following morning the atmosphere in the office chilled the moment he entered it. During the next few days hardly anyone spoke to him and no new material came to his desk. Then Goodwillie called him in, inquired after his health, asked him if he had rested well the night before, and after a gentle cough got down to what he called the nitty-gritty by informing Timothy that this was one of the darndest things. He had done his best, but the head office had been on the line to him several times – "Well, I guess you know what I'm referring to." It was too bad that the head office tended at times to be remote. Personally he, Goodwillie, thought that Timothy's performance had been beautiful, he'd never seen anything more natural, really spontaneous, really sincere, but there were times when Mr. Truscott's funny bone wasn't in a mood to be activated. However, over and above and beyond this, he found it only just to say that he'd been thinking for some time that Timothy would be happier in another organization.

"Am I being fired, Mel?"

"Now Timmie, you know I'm not putting it that way and we're good enough friends for you to know I'd never think of putting it that way. It's just like I said, give or take nothing from it either way, I think it's in your own best interests to make a change. I'm perfectly sincere about that."

"And I'm perfectly sincere when I say I agree with you."

For he knew, as Goodwillie did not, that Esther's office had been swamped with phone calls and mail and that the letters were arriving in such profusion that she and her assistant would be busy on them for a week. Who was this fresh, courageous young man who at last was willing to tell it the way it was? Esther was delighted, and though Timothy was pleased because he saw a new door opening, he was otherwise unimpressed.

"What the hell," he wrote, "if you write or say anything really new you might just as well say it in Eskimo for all the attention anyone is going to pay to it. But if you say what millions of people have known for years without being told officially that they know it, they'll call you a genius. The funny thing is that nothing makes people sorer than if you con them personally and later tell them you did, but if you con the whole country it's entirely different. Expose something like that and it's better entertainment than anything you could possibly invent.

Of course, I didn't expect my little spit in the ocean of TV to make the slightest difference in the commercials or slay the sales of our processed foods and terrific cars. In the whole affair the only thing that interested me was the reaction of Taylor W. Truscott. He really disappointed me. He was as cynical an operator as I ever met and for God's sake I'd made him boiling mad. He must have thought that enormous pile of reeking crap he produced was a throne for his own ego."

A week later another ex-socialist who was a big bureaucrat in the network accepted Esther and Timothy as a team. He offered them a half-hour space one day a week for a public affairs and opinion program, in good time but not in prime time, and he gave them a guarantee of a six-weeks trial run.

I was unable to find out from the papers whether Timothy's wife had divorced him by this time or was still making up her mind to do it. At any rate, he and Esther had not yet become lovers.

Their show got off to a shaky start. Timothy was nervous and his first guests were non-political people whom he admired, and he had yet to discover that his inspiration nearly always came from hostility. If he was sympathetic to a guest, and he was often extremely sympathetic, it was always because the guest had been badly treated by his boss or by the authorities, or simply by the System. Their break came when the secretary of a federal cabinet minister, who had been making personal appearances all over the country, called Esther to ask for space on the program. Esther put her off for a few days until she had checked the man out in Ottawa. She returned with a dossier that scared Timothy. He asked her if she was sure the facts were absolutely correct – a precaution that never much worried him later on. Esther said they were undoubtedly correct; she had obtained them from a high civil servant in the minister's department.

"But dare we use stuff like this? It looks to me like a dynamite."

"It's our duty to use it," she said, and with youthful eagerness she added, "This man is a menace to the country."

When the minister arrived in the studio and they shook hands, Timothy was so nervous he could barely keep his voice steady. The politician saw his nervousness and immediately tried to increase it.

"He was a huge man, even bigger than he looked in his photographs, and he had narrow eyes in a bullet head. He had a hump on the back of his neck that made him look like a bison whose head was too small for it. He burned his eyes into mine like a pair of laser beams and when he turned on his smile that was the worst thing of all about him."

Timothy's military bearing, of which he himself was generally unconscious, must have made a slow impression on the minister; Timothy recorded later that after this initial opening the man became more cautious, though this did not prevent him from trying to take charge of the show and use it as a springboard for himself. There were no hooks in the first three questions Timothy asked and Timothy realized that the minister was taking him for granted.

"Suddenly I understood the essential vulgarity of power. In the presence of it, the average man can't help desiring its approval, as though some of that power might splash over onto himself. This thought drove my nervousness away and made me feel cold; Esther told me later that I sat up so straight and stiff that it was almost as though I were wearing a uniform. I decided the time had come to move in on him."

The instant the minister stopped talking, Timothy took a piece of paper from his pocket and laid it on the table before him. Looking up, his shoulders as erect as a guardsman's, he spoke politely as though he were genuinely puzzled and hoped that a matter obscure to him might be cleared up.

"Mr. Minister, I have here two sets of figures concerning that installation your department is building at Corway. The first one" – he stated the facts slowly and with a studious frown – "gives a cost figure of \$13,550,000. Now this second one" – another careful pause and a wrinkling of the forehead – "gives a figure of exactly \$20,000,000." Glancing up with no particular expression, he asked, "Would you care to comment on the discrepancy between these two figures?"

The politician reared back with his mouth open and his eyes on fire.

"Just what are you trying to insinuate by that question?"

Timothy smiled gently. "Sir, I appear to have been correct in believing that these figures would be familiar to you?"

The minister's voice mounted close to a shout. "Where did you get those figures? I demand that you tell me that."

Timothy smiled sadly and made one of the biggest gambles of his life.

"Isn't there something in the Bible about being sure your sin will find you out?"

The man's face almost disintegrated, then came together like granite. Timothy wrote that he could actually smell his fear. He wrote also that the man was such a natural authoritarian that when he was opposed by anyone he despised his anger made him stupid.

"Mr. Wellfleet, I didn't come here to have allegations – to be insulted – to – " he stopped, hunting for words, and Timothy knew that he had him.

"Mr. Minister," – the same calm voice – "is it true or false that the first figure was the lowest tender submitted to your department before the work began, but that it was the second tender that your department ultimately accepted? Is my belief also correct that the first tender was submitted by a proved company, while the second was – "

The minister's color changed, but not the bully in him. "Who do you think you are, the Auditor General?"

Timothy, though stiff with fear, managed to shrug laconically. "Well, naturally, if the Auditor General is in possession of both these figures – if he is in possession of them – due note will be taken in his next annual report."

The minister had a large vein in the left side of his forehead, just as I have one in mine. Timothy saw it quiver to the rise in this blood pressure, make a little jump, and turn puce.

"Are you aware of the implications in this line of questioning?" he said.

"Of course I am. I'm nobody, of course. I'm just an ordinary citizen. The real question is – are you aware of the implications here?"

"You – you little – " Timothy could almost see the man's tonsils, "you're the one who's going to be investigated, not me. You're on a government network. You won't be on it again if you think you can talk like this to a responsible public servant."

"If I have committed a criminal libel," Timothy said steadily, "you understand that the courts are at your disposal. But you know I've done nothing that concerns a court. I've merely asked you a straight question."

While the politician's mouth was still open, Timothy faced the cameras and said quietly, "And now we will pause for this message."

While they were off the screen for the commercial the minister glared at Timothy and growled. Timothy looked back at him with a mocking smile and that blew it. The minister leaped from his chair and grabbed Timothy by the shoulders. While he was still shaking him, the cameras came on again and caught the minister cold. Timothy rose to the opportunity of a lifetime.

"Mr. Minister, I must beg you to control yourself. You are being watched by hundreds of thousands of people. Thank you for joining us, but now we must continue with our next guest for the evening."

The minister stumbled when he walked out of the lights.

The following day Timothy's program made headlines all over the country. In the question period in Parliament the Opposition went after the government like a school of piranhas. The guilty minister had absented himself, may even have been ordered to stay away, and it was the Prime Minister himself who rose to receive the questions. The night before, Timothy had been scared white by his own audacity, but now he learned just what a partner he had in Esther. She had learned in the capital something known only to a few insiders, that the man Timothy had exposed had been intriguing for months to oust the Prime Minister and take his place. So it was with a serious expression but an inward satisfaction that the Prime Minister refused any comment beyond the routine one that the allegations would be fully investigated. He meant exactly what he said. They were indeed investigated and the man was driven out of public life. Timothy had also discovered something else that went to his head: that he had a rare talent for getting under the skins of powerful men and knocking them off balance. As he later reflected, "It takes one paranoic to catch another."

So it happened that Timothy Wellfleet, hitherto a young man who had considered himself a failure in everything he had attempted, found himself famous overnight. He was praised in the press as a courageous, intelligent, and honest journalist who had braved government arrogance in order to find out the truth. He even caught the attention of the cartoonists and one of them drew him in a metropolitan daily over the caption "Our Ralph Nader?" No praise could have meant more to Timothy than this and he later admitted that it went to his head.

"Then for the first time I tasted power and the taste was sweet. I said to Esther, 'Now we know the way we have to go. *De l'audace*, darling! *Et encore de l'audace, et toujours de l'audace!*' "

Esther reminded him that the author of this line left his head in the basket of the Paris guillotine, but she laughed when she said it. Explosive with relief they left the studio and began kissing in the back of the taxi taking them to Esther's apartment. This was the first night when Esther and Timothy became lovers, and he has recorded it previously.

NINE

NOW, TWO YEARS LATER, Timothy knew that if ever he again repeated Danton's famous line there would be no laughter in Esther's reply to it. Something total had happened. She would possibly love him; she would never allow him to be her lover again.

Reading his scattered notes and fragmented paragraphs two normal lifetimes later, certain that both Timothy and Esther have been dead for many years, I remember my mother's eyes when she said she had read somewhere that the saddest thing is that we must grow old and can never grow young. If only we could grow young instead of old, how many misunderstandings and miseries might be avoided? There were so many unnecessary destructions of happiness. This curious, marvellous woman, my mother. Emotionally she was a perfect harmony. Intellectually she was an explosion of contradictions. But what else are all intellectuals but bundles of explosive contradictions? And she was never an intellectual.

Anyway, Timothy knew now that the dream that began with Esther was over, but he would not admit – and perhaps he was right – that he was the one who had killed it. If she had rejected only his ideas it would not have mattered, but she had rejected his yearning for a brilliant mind with a body he could love with passion, as he had done. So now his old sense of the raw deal returned to him with a crash. He felt her physical rejection like a physical pain, and in a flood of anger and fatigue he muttered to himself, "All right, Esther, if that's how you want it, there are more fish in the sea than you."

He made his way to the make-up room but when he reclined in one of the studio's second-hand barber chairs in front of a powder-flecked mirror that had not been polished in weeks, he admitted to himself that Esther had at least been right about one thing.

"I was not merely tired. I was exhausted into a kind of ecstasy. When I closed my eyes to relax I had the feeling that the chair had taken off and I was flying in the dark. 'More sleep in God's forgotten name, more sleep you fool.'"

Then he was terrified that if he did learn to relax he would be destroyed. For as he saw it, he was not reporting the news as the others did. He was not hiding behind the usual rampart of facts and handouts. He was reporting what *made* the news, and if even under the rules as he played the game he never called a politician a liar to his face, he was compelling them to reveal themselves as the liars nearly all of them were, and if people wanted to call him irresponsible, all they had to do was turn the switch. As he put it himself: "The world was not my stage. I was the stage for the world.

"And this meant that I had to suck into myself all I could hold of what the world had become and hand it back so distilled and acid that in spite of themselves the armchair-sitters would have to see, hear, taste, and smell it. And how could anyone do that unless he opened his lungs and veins to the full, intoxicating brew of poisons, to all the dreads, lusts, ambitions, greeds, and inner terrors churning like microbes in the belly of the technological loneliness? How could anyone reflect *Now* unless he himself was manic-depressive, schizoid-paranoid, unsure, cocksure, uptight, downloose, dancing on banana skins balanced on tightropes, listening to a dozen different voices contradicting each other on the same subject in the same instant of time, knowing absolutely that except for the kooks, the cruels, and the godfathers legitimate and illegitimate, at the bottom of the universal fantasy there was only a single question that mattered – 'What is to become of me?' For I knew it – God damn you, God, I knew that unless *that* question was answered, and answered soon, this marvellous circus they told us had evolved out of You was going to blow up with a bang that would compete in its tiny way with that famous Big Bang the scientists (at least for the time being) were telling us marked Your first birthday."

The make-up room had been empty when he entered it and through his mind flashed the thought that the nicest people he knew were these kindly, matter-of-fact girls who powdered and primped the stars for the shows. Like a patient in a hospital bed suddenly aware that a nurse has entered the room, Timothy opened his eyes. This make-up girl was new and she was black. Evidently Esther had hired her while he was away to replace fat Gloria, who had bulged with Coca-Cola, French fries, and snacks before she became pregnant and grew so enormous he had asked her whether she intended to have her baby on the set.

To this new girl he said, "Use plenty of powder, please. I carry a heavy beard because I'm a hairy man, but at this hour in the day I rely on you to save my jaw from looking like Nixon's."

He closed his eyes and wondered if it would be a good idea to grow a real beard. Two years ago he and his cameraman had visited a university called Berkeley and found all the students wearing beards like bumper stickers—Lenin beards, Marx beards, Mao beards, Trotsky beards, even a few with Moses and Lincoln beards. He himself had settled for bushy sideburns and a solid mass of hair settling firmly on the top of his collar.

The girl's hands were working smoothly over his face and forehead and they felt delicious. He went into a partial doze in which Esther seemed to be talking with General Sprott. Old Eli down there in the maximum-security playing it cool. Old Eli waiting sharp and shrewd to press the button. Old Esther searching the corners of the earth with a lantern looking for a few dust pockets of righteousness.

He opened his eyes and this time he really saw the girl who was working on him. Small features, a full but disciplined mouth, impassive eyes, glossy black skin, and a neat little waist. How dull would the city be without these people bringing up all their vitality from the Caribbean. That racist professor, he was probably advising Immigration to keep them out. He asked the girl her name and she answered in a soft Jamaican accent.

"Miranda, Mistah Wellfleet."

"Call me Timmie, Miranda. We're all on first names here. Where did Esther discover you?"

"Through the Student Placement Bureau, sir."

"So you're a student? Don't call me sir, for God's sake. Didn't anyone ever tell you it's a disaster to be called 'sir' by a pretty girl?"

She did not answer and he closed his eyes.

"What kind of a time are you having in the university, Miranda?"

"It's all right."

"Do you encounter any prejudice there?"

"No."

"There must be some."

"I don't look for it."

"Some of your people ran into a lot more than prejudice a little while ago. They ran into half the city police force. Anyway, we're having a professor on the show tonight. I've just remembered his name. Dehmel. Do you know him?"

"I've audited some of his lectures."

"Like him?"

"I didn't audit his lectures because I liked him."

Timothy opened his eyes and said sharply, "Now that's a very interesting remark. Tell me more."

"I went there because my friend takes his course and he teaches people things they don't know."

He grunted and closed his eyes.

While Miranda was brushing and shaping his thick hair, his mind slumped into the state of a person half asleep and half awake "with the ideas charging through it like a pack of dogs chasing a bitch in heat." He should have let Esther take the show tonight. It was sure to be a dud and if Esther took it he'd lose nothing. That damned poetess, she'd conned him, but good. The separatist would sing his old song and the professor would probably utter the word "problem" in every third sentence. He was acutely aware of Miranda's presence close by, of her hands touching his skin, and it was an effort to keep his own hands off her. Why not? How could anyone be a part of *Now* unless he had made love to a black girl? He felt her strong little fingers kneading the nape of his neck and opened his eyes again.

"I suppose things have been pretty hard for you, Miranda?"

"No sir, not particularly."

"You're very brave."

She said nothing. Her face was an impassive mask and he closed his eyes again and was frustrated. "I simply had to have this girl with all that prehistoric history in those wonderful little loins of hers, all that body-lore they're supposed to have. I smelled from the cracks in this decaying building the fossilized sweat of those hundreds of thousands of woman-hours spent by the overworked and underpaid females who had labored here from 1924 until 1961 (smell of an abandoned barracoon?) until finally they had made the owner rich enough to sell his business, throw them all out of work, retire, and buy in Miami the house that he called a home."

When Miranda finished he stood up, scrutinized himself in the mirror, and did not like what he saw. He picked up his guitar, sat on a bench with the instrument on his knees, and began strumming it into a tune. He looked studiously at the strings, but glanced up occasionally to observe this girl who was making his imagination dance off into still another fantasy.

"Miranda," he said with a shy smile, "please be nice to us."

"What do you mean, Mr. Wellfleet?"

"Just be nice to us." He made a bravura flourish on the guitar, laid the instrument down, and stood up. "We're through, you see. Washed up. Kaput. Sexually sterile. We're going down, you're going up. Doom of the white race is in America. D. H. Lawrence wrote that forty years ago and corporative America hasn't caught up with him yet. Lawrence was a famous English writer. Doom of the white race is in America, he said."

She answered without expression, "I thought what Lawrence said was doom of our white *day* is in America."

"Good for you, Miranda. That's right, so he did. But it means the same thing. You know. We never understood. What I mean is that, well, I mean that we never understood women as women and our own women were – well, you know..."

Her face had become a black mask and it made him feel so ashamed of himself that he left her abruptly and went out to the small lounge where his guests were sitting with Esther. From a feeling in the atmosphere he sensed that there had been little conversation between them.

"Hullo, Madeleine," he said to the poetess and noted that Esther's estimation of her cleavage had been accurate.

She looked at him with determination. "You remember what I said, Timmie? You remember, don't you? I'm going to do it tonight. Somebody's got to say that word over the channels and this will be another first for you."

"Fine," he said and wondered what she was talking about. He still could not remember what she had told him.

He turned to Chalifour. "Allô, Emile. Comment vas-tu ce soir?"

Chalifour shrugged. "Comme ci, comme ça."

"Comme tout le monde."

He turned to Uncle Conrad. "Well, Professor, it's not often we have a man of your distinction on our little program. We're honored."

Timothy recorded that Uncle Conrad made a small, formal bow and spoke with a slight but attractive foreign accent.

"I have heard much about you, Mr. Timothy Wellfleet, and I have here – " he hesitated when he saw Timothy glancing at his watch and turning away. Then he took out of his pocket an envelope and touched Timothy's elbow. "I have here a message from somebody you know very well, somebody who is very fond of you. Perhaps you might read it?"

Suddenly Timothy wanted to urinate, but his watch had told him there was no time for it. He slipped the letter into a side pocket without even glancing at it.

"I'm sorry, Professor, but perhaps you might save it till after the show. I was in Washington this morning and I was late getting back. We've got to go onto the set immediately."

"I hope I will be satisfactory," Uncle Conrad said. "I have never before been on the television. I'm a little nervous."

"There's nothing to it, Professor. This isn't art or lecturing. This is just a few people talking together. Forget the audience. Just relax and say whatever comes off the top of your head. In this medium natural-ness is everything."

I could imagine the scene – Uncle Conrad taking some notes out of his pocket, looking at them through his bifocals, and saying there were things he had wished to say for a long time and he had made careful preparations. He was still trying to talk to Timothy, who was not listening, when the floor manager stuck his head into the door-way and said it was time. Timothy and the poet walked out together.

"You look great, Madeleine," Timothy said, which was the exact opposite of how he thought she looked.

Together they walked into the high-roofed, darkened studio where the cameramen and the floor crew were wired together with headphones clamped to their ears and the live audience was invisible behind the lights. Shining like an altar was the dais with its revolving plastic chairs and small tables holding the water glasses and ash trays. The dais was three feet higher than the floor, which made it easy to take those low-angled shots focussing on a speaker's lower jaw, a technique Timothy always demanded whenever he wished to make a guest look bad. Among his papers I found a notation that the control-ler of a television show had nineteen chances out of twenty to put anyone at his mercy so long as the control was his. Most inexperi-enced people's eyes narrowed in the glare of the kliegs and if a camera tilted up at a face from below, with the lights striking down from above, a man's eyes often looked opaque and dishonest, especially if he had prominent cheekbones. Another of Timothy's notes informed me that he had come close to ruining a cabinet minister by his use of the camera alone. The man had always been assumed to be handsome and wore a clipped military moustache. He was also an authentic war hero and an old friend of Timothy's father. "By taking nothing but undershots," noted Timothy, "we didn't make him look like a boob. We made him look like a rabbit chewing carrots."

Behind the dais and suspended from the roof was an illuminated globe of the world, slowly revolving. If Timothy wished to create an impression of alarm, the revolutions were speeded up and sometimes the show ended with the globe whizzing around and around in a blur of flashing crystals.

Timothy and Madeleine Ball took their seats on the dais and two cameras aimed at them with their ruby eyes shut. The floor manager's hand dropped. Timothy glanced sideways and saw the monitor screen come alive with the image of a girl looking like a pre-Raphaelite hippie twanging a guitar. The pitch of the music was high, anguished, strident with discords. Head thrown back, long hair hanging backwards almost to her hips, eyes half shut, body writhing, the girl looked so sexy that the studio received dozens of letters and phone calls every day asking for her real name, address, and telephone number, and this made Timothy laugh because "It never occurred to the boobs that any girl could look and sound like her and in reality be a homebody in love with one of the dumbest-cluck husbands I ever saw, and that she was putting on this act to pay the rent and also, as she put it, to finance a baby." She had proved herself a shrewd businesswoman, for when she signed the contract, instead of accepting a flat fee of two hundred dollars, she had asked for, and got, a royalty of seventy-five dollars for every time her little act was used as a signature. By this time she had hauled in several thousand.

Now her voice joined the music. With her face straining as if in a love-climax, her body writhing, she chanted four times over *This is now – Now is this – All there is – This is now ...*, the final *now* drawn out into a long quaver fading out into nothing.

The monitor cut off, the two cameras began to burn, and Timothy and Madeleine Ball were alive on the channel.

TEN

ABOUT THREE MONTHS after I asked André Gervais to search for a playback machine for videotapes, without much hope that he would find one, he called me to say that his organization had discovered an apparatus of a kind he had never seen and that he believed it might be what I wanted. I went in to Metro and by God, it was a real playback machine. What seemed a miracle of coincidence was where it had turned up. For years it had been gathering dust in the basement of a large old building in the country which now was part of a compound similar to my own. One of the aged inoperatives living there had recognized what it was and even knew how to operate it, but as he had no tapes it remained useless. When I asked some more questions, I suddenly realized that when I was a small boy I myself had lived in the building where it was found. It had been my old boarding school and I was there when Timothy produced this interview with Conrad Dehmel. I never saw this particular performance because the headmaster would not let us look at Timothy's show; he thought it disgraceful, subversive, and in bad taste. But though I did not see the show I certainly heard about its aftermath and even heard people asking why a man as intelligent as Conrad Dehmel had put himself at Timothy's mercy.

Uncle Conrad was a far shrewder man than I guessed during the little time I knew him. He must certainly have known what kind of a performer Timothy was, but if he had anything to say that he believed was important, he was never afraid to say it. Not only did Timothy have the largest audience in the country, he had exactly the audience Conrad wanted to wake up to their danger. The mood in our city at this time was making all our European immigrants nervous. They had seen in their own countries what kind of explosions can come out of paranoiac propaganda. They knew all about the techniques of the hidden operators who went down into *le milieu* and recruited violent and fanatical young men to do their dirty work for them. They could smell this kind of operation even when it was invisible.

There was also my mother. Even as a boy I knew there was a dangerous innocence in her, particularly in her feelings to those she thought of as "my children." If she had watched any of Timothy's shows, and I'm sure she had, she must have been distressed by many of them, just as she must have been pleased when he exposed a genuine evil, as he did very often. I can hear her telling Conrad that at heart Timothy was really a sweet person who had suffered from an unfortunate childhood. But though Mother was innocent she was always very careful. She had therefore taken the precaution of giving her husband a note to deliver to Timothy before the show began. She knew that if Timothy read it, Conrad would be safe from him and in this she was certainly right, for she was the only person he truly loved.

Another aspect of this affair that puzzles me somewhat is Timothy's ignorance that his older cousin Stephanie had married Conrad Dehmel. Mother had married Conrad some six years before this show occurred and her father – my grandfather – had died only a year before that. It would have been unusual of her not to have sent Timothy an announcement of the marriage. Possibly he received it and forgot all about it. Possibly he was abroad at the time and she did not know where he was. But even before she married Conrad, she had been living her own life and years might have passed without her seeing Timothy's father. I give up trying to explain it. All I know is that Timothy did not realize that Conrad was Stephanie's husband when he invited him to the program and in a later sequence I discovered that he did not find out until exactly a week too late. So the show took place.

Now the first camera was dollying in and Timothy at last remembered what his present guest had proposed at the cocktail party a fortnight earlier. "I'm going to use that word," she had said earlier. "You know – *that* word! It's in one of my poems."

A few years later "that word" became so commonplace that it sometimes appeared in the most conservative magazines and newspapers, but at the zenith of Timothy's career it was supposed to be a victory over the Establishment if anyone got away with it in the media.

Now Timothy was surveying Madeleine Ball with a critical eye and cursing himself for having invited her. The woman was big, she was lush, and she looked bold in a way that would make about ninety-nine percent of other women detest her. Had she been a professional whore – quite a number of whores appeared on the media in those years – she would have been a much safer prospect. "The male viewers would be titillated by her and the women viewers would secretly admire her because she was conning the men. But this God-damn female was not a whore, she was a poet, and that would mean that nobody would like her."

He opened blandly, "Well, Madeleine Ball, you've become one of the exciting new personalities in our city. Your poetry" – he held up a slim volume and looked at it in pretended admiration – "your poetry has been well received at least locally. But first will you tell me a little about yourself. Apart from poetry, what is your chief interest?"

She looked at him with her big eyes and said solemnly, "Making love."

"Just that?"

"Making love is a lot more than just that."

"Do you consider yourself a connoisseur of love, Madeleine?"

"I hate that word, connoisseur."

"Gourmet, perhaps?"

"Another of those false words. Applied to love it's disgusting."

Timothy smiled with suave hostility. "Just the same, Madeleine, your previous remarks indicate that you are, shall we say, at least interested in men. So what kind of man pleases you? Or should I say, turns you on?"

"That's a typical male question. Now you answer me this, Timothy Wellfleet. In love, what is the great difference between a man and a woman? I dare you to admit it."

"I think," Timothy drawled, "it might come better from you."

"You see? You don't dare admit it. Well, let me tell you the difference. A woman is capable of multiple orgasms and a man isn't. Now, what I claim is that every woman has the *right* to multiple orgasms. If she has to go through the hell of bearing children, to say nothing of sacrificing the best years of her life to rearing them, I claim it was established in the Great Chain of Being that at least she has this compensation. Nature agrees with me. Nature gave women a far bigger capacity for sexual greatness than she gave to men, and that's why men are jealous of women and won't admit it. If a woman doesn't get her multiple orgasms, it's always the man's fault. And since you ask me what kind of men interest me, you'd better believe it that the young ones don't."

"But you're young yourself," Timothy purred. "What have you got against your own peer group?"

"The average man under thirty goes after a woman like a lumber-jack after a steak. I've seen a lumberjack eat a one-pound steak in three minutes. I timed him."

"You talk of these multiple orgasms – I presume you're capable of them yourself?"

"That's none of your business."

Timothy was growing uneasy, even embarrassed, but before he could think of another question, Madeleine Ball was off again.

"Love-making should be a symphony. Even a fugue will do. There should be a minimum of four distinct movements in symphonic love. You begin with a largo. You move into an allegretto. Then into a scherzo – a period of playfulness and surprises. Then in the same key you let go into a prestissimo. That's symphonic love. Of course, it's not going to happen very often. But the fugue – yes, a fugal approach could be basic and it would be wrong to criticize it."

"And you're suggesting that you don't trust any man under forty even to be up to a fugue?"

"I don't trust many over forty, either."

"But you do know of a few?"

"Now here is something else a woman has to watch out for – the male connoisseur type who uses women as instruments to inflate his own ego. The kind that pretend they're doing something terrific for a woman when what they're really doing is making love to them-selves."

"And that's bad even if she gets – "

"It's another form of exploitation of women. It's the very worst kind."

"So your idea is a pair of artists – a man and a woman making a kind of Kreutzer Sonata out of it?"

"That was far from being Beethoven's best work. It's nervous and neurotic. But the Fifth Symphony – have you ever really listened to *that*?"

Timothy cleared his throat with elaborate timing and looked carefully at Madeleine Ball.

"However, Madeleine, I suppose you'd agree that the most impor-tant thing in your life is your poetry?"

"Of course I wouldn't agree with that. Living and loving are the most important things in my life. But yes, my poetry *is* important to me. You asked me to bring along two of my poems and I have them here. May I read them?"

Somewhat acidly, Timothy said, "That's what we've all been waiting for, Madeleine."

In a lugubrious voice she intoned her first poem, and when she had finished, Timothy asked her if she could explain what it meant. She looked at him in reproof and declared that nobody could explain a true poem because it existed in its own right and on its own terms. A poem was an act. It was an existential act. Then she went into her second and last poem.

> *Now do I feel again the stirring of the power*
> *the power implacable*
> *and will it be the god who comes?*
> *The god is there.*
> *I have not found him yet nor yet has he found me*
> *but he is there.*
> *And this I ask –*
> *When, upon this lovely dying star*
> *I lay again my body down –*
> *will it be the god who comes?*
> *The god Apollo – sure and strong?*
> *I would love to greet him.*
> *His would be all my secret parts and meanings*
> *if it is the god who comes.*

Here she paused, looked around, then resumed in a broken tempo, her voice sad and absolutely genuine:

> *Or will it be the usual jerk*
> *who'll spread himself out upon the sky of me*
> *and do what he calls the job on me*
> *and merely fuck?*

While she was intoning this, Timothy was off-camera grinding his teeth. When she had finished and they were on-camera together again, she spoke before he had time to open his mouth.

"Of course, this poem really needs a guitar accompaniment."

Timothy's hostility to women, which he seems never to have known that he had, flashed out like a knife.

"Why not an organ accompaniment?"

Her large, earnest face almost collapsed. Then, with the dignity of the totally humorless, and with complete sincerity, she drove one more nail into Timothy's ego.

"I should have known better. I should never have let you talk me into coming here. You – the famous freedom-fighter! Now I see that you're just another of the ones that use people. If people like you ever get power over us, you'll be three times worse than what we have now. I never claimed to be a great poet. I'm just a sincere woman. And I do think somebody out there *may* have been listening to me – really listening."

"Thank you, Madeleine Ball. I understand from the ratings there are several millions out there listening to you. And now we will pause for this message."

She left the set and Timothy sat cursing silently while the first commercial came on. "My antennae," he later recorded, "or whatever it is that does that kind of work for us, were picking up alarm signals all over the place." Then the cameras burned again and Uncle Conrad and Chalifour were on the dais with Timothy.

I studied this scene very carefully and played the tape over many times. André watched it with me the first time and became enormously excited. To him the whole thing seemed like a miracle. The commercials particularly excited him, and though the topics of discussion bewildered him because he knew nothing of their context, he was shocked by Timothy's performance. So was I. Parts of this section of the program were so raw and naked that I had no need of Timothy's subsequent notes to read his feelings. Anyway, Timothy himself later wrote an introduction to it:

"This had been one of those days that start beautifully and then turn sour. Esther, the police raid, the black girl, Madeleine Ball, and now Emile Chalifour. I looked at him and felt that at any moment the trapdoor was going to spring open. This man for an ally? My enemies must be laughing. Then I looked at the German professor and wondered how a man with an expression like his could even vaguely resemble the character described to me by Jason Ross. I remembered what Esther had told me about Ross and where did that leave me? With no choice but continuing my game plan or letting the whole program collapse."

Studying the tape, I saw Timothy's baffled expression as he gave a glance of furtive assessment at Uncle Conrad. Now, all these years later and living in a totally different age, the reappearance of Uncle Conrad was more than strange. It was a kind of revelation of my own lack of development when he was alive. A strong body, yet quick in its movements. A European face from west of the Elbe with high, wide cheekbones, a domed forehead, receding but vigorous gray hair swept back, eyes that looked straight at you, yet with a suggestion of irony I had not understood when I was a boy. Though the facial muscles were disciplined by experience and marked by a fading scar, I had the feeling that underneath the discipline a small boy had lingered, a youth of high endeavor was still there. I remembered Mother's pride in him and his own flashes of despair when people could not understand things that were so clear to him. "Conrad," I remember Mother saying once, "why do you have to keep on learning more than anyone's brain can hold?" This was a question he often had asked himself, for he is on record as believing that modern man knew so much that his knowledge was larger than the central nervous system of his brain could handle, with the result that many human brains had became like an overloaded telephone exchange where messages essential to survival failed to get through in time.

Clearly this was what was happening to the Timothy I was watching on the screen with Uncle Conrad. Knowing as I did what both of them felt about Mother, knowing that she was the only human being Timothy had ever loved and respected without reservation, I found myself a witness to one of those spectacles that wound and shock because they are so unspeakably clumsy, like street accidents.

Timothy's tense, baffled expression showed something close to panic as his gaze shrank away from Uncle Conrad and settled on Chalifour, a type which at that period might have emerged out of any city in the world between Los Angeles and Frankfurt. This is how Timothy described him:

"Chalifour was sprawling back in calculated, sullen insolence, his face three-quarters hidden by a shrubbery of unkempt hair with still more hair dripping over his shoulders and a semicircular moustache bushing out around a rosebud mouth. A medallion hung by a chain over a black shirt open at the neck, and a cigarette was in the corner of his mouth. He was skinny, with little muscular development, and the lower part of his body wore the uniform of his kind: a pair of not too clean, hip-hugging jeans carefully frayed at the cuffs and sold in the stores at five times more than a genuine workman would have paid for the real article. There he was, the perfect image of the fashionable bourgeois revolutionary against nothing more important than himself. But this was a judgment I dared not make aloud to anyone, because it might have applied equally well to me."

"Monsieur Chalifour," he began, "this morning I was in Washington interviewing an American general about the Viet Nam War and when I came back I found the whole city uptight about this so-called kidnapping crisis. In comparison to Viet Nam it looks pretty trivial to me. But what would you say?"

"It's not trivial."

"Do you approve of kidnapping for political purposes? It's not been done in the States, you know, though there are millions of protesters down there."

"The United States is a huge imperialist power. Quebec isn't. Quebec is an occupied territory. In an occupied territory, political kidnapping is not only legitimate, it's the only course left open to a people who are systematically treated like white niggers..." and so on and so on.

This surprised Timothy; he had expected Chalifour to play it much safer. He sat back and let Chalifour continue in an angry, sullen voice as though he were repeating a litany. More than twenty patriots were in prison, some of them for life. Their only crime had been to meet force with the self-respect of men who refuse to accept any longer a hundred years of injustice. It was the government that was treasonous, not the patriots. The government was nothing but a stooge of the imperialist corporations. The patriots had been too gentle for their own safety. Three times they had postponed the executions of the hostages and still the government would not move. Every postponement increased the danger that the police would track them down – and so on for another minute.

"Do you believe these execution threats are serious?"

"Don't you?"

Even in the hysterical mood of that time, this was strong stuff for anyone to deliver over the networks. Timothy looked scared for a moment and turned to Uncle Conrad.

"Professor Dehmel, you are a scholar of some reputation, I understand. Would you agree that the kidnapping – even the execution – of hostages is a legitimate weapon for revolutionaries who believe they are saviors of their people?"

"I would not agree. Neither, I think, would you."

"You don't have to put words into my mouth, Professor. However, you've said what I expected you'd say. One of your students told me you said in a lecture that the toleration of political kidnapping would reduce any society to the level of feuding Mafia families. You did say that, didn't you?"

A rueful smile from Uncle Conrad. "So a student remembered something I said! But if that's all he told you, he forgot other things I said. In the fourteenth century…"

"We're not discussing the fourteenth century, we're discussing the here and now. Many people – Monsieur Chalifour is one of them – believe the freedom fighters had no other choice."

"They have been told that, of course. Older people – men who are using them – they have certainly told them things like that. Perhaps even some of their professors used such language to them. There was a famous book we used to read when I was young – *La Trahison des Clercs* – 'The Treason of the Intellectuals.' What's happening here is not a new phenomenon, but if it continues long enough the results will be as they always are. Some intellectuals have much to answer for."

"Did these kidnappings surprise you?"

"I predicted them a year ago."

"And you stand by your statement that the Liberation Front is a Mafia?"

"I will not stand by a statement I never made. You know as well as I who are the Mafia. But these young men have been told that it is heroic, that it serves freedom, to kidnap and threaten to murder innocent people. I am an historian, and let me tell you that a crime is a crime, and crimes committed in the name of freedom are especially vile because they turn freedom upside down. That is to debauch a virgin."

Chalifour was twitching with fury and Uncle Conrad turned and said to him quietly, and with a smile, "Monsieur, I know *you* would never kill a man in cold blood. But please call things by their proper names. Don't make murder legitimate by calling it execution."

Chalifour's nostrils almost gesticulated. He smirked, spread his hands apart, puffed cigarette smoke out of his nostrils, smiled like a cat, and said, "Oh God, what next do I have to hear?"

Dehmel looked straight at him. "When I first came here this country was still innocent. Its people were kind and trusted each other. But look at it now! The same old sick propaganda. The same exploitation of paranoia by experts in paranoia. Even here, with the example of Europe before us, there is a desire among some people – and I wonder who they are? – to ruin our country and to use adolescents as their instruments to do so."

Again the twitch of the nostrils and the cat smile from Chalifour. "Did I hear you say *your* country?"

"I said that because I am a citizen of it."

Another cat smile. "And how long have you been a citizen, Monsieur le Professeur?"

"Ten years."

"Oh-la-la – my ancestors came here three hundred and thirty years ago and have suffered repression for two hundred and seven years."

Dehmel shook his head and smiled gently. He said, "I accept that you have longer territorial rights than I have, but let me remind you that all of us are citizens of the same world." He looked from Chalifour to Timothy. "Both of you are far too young to know what it was like in Germany before the Nazis came to power. Well, let me tell you that there are symptoms here, there is language here, that I have heard before. There's not a former European living in this city who wouldn't agree with me."

"An interesting comment, Professor," Timothy said suavely. "So now you come right out with it and compare people who belong to Monsieur Chalifour's movement to the Nazis."

"You are twisting me, Mr. Wellfleet."

"Am I?"

Now Uncle Conrad was looking at Timothy with a quick shock of recognition.

"Nazi is a very dirty word, and so it ought to be. Hitler made it so. He ruined an entire generation of Germans. He could not have succeeded had not the atmosphere been so charged with propaganda, and the governments too weak and timid to enforce their own laws." He turned back to Chalifour. "Monsieur, let me tell you something else. French is my second language, not English. I have many French-Canadian friends. I know their history and how difficult it has been. But I say this, and I think you know it, that only a handful of people in this province are happy about what is happening now. And I do not accept that a handful of frustrated intellectuals have the moral right to produce chaos because it's a quick way to increase their self-importance."

Chalifour broke out furiously, "What kind of chaos do you think our patriots are suffering in prison? Now you call them Nazis. If you'd ever been in prison yourself, and seen what it does to a human being…"

Uncle Conrad smiled grimly. "But I *have* been in prison. And bad though our prisons here may be, they are paradise compared to the one I was in."

The effect of this remark on Chalifour was extraordinary. Like many of the local intellectuals, he was very partial to Europeans and assumed they all shared his opinion of Anglophone North Americans.

"If you had said that in the first place, Monsieur le Professeur," he said with respect in his voice.

"There is seldom anything heroic about being in prison, unless you have accepted it as a moral choice. For me it was a terrible experience. There was no honor in it."

"But it gives you a certain right," Chalifour said, shifting his eyes to Timothy, "which other people have not earned."

Timothy realized that the program was being taken away from him. Not only was it getting nowhere, Uncle Conrad was dominating it. The suavity that made some viewers think of a coiled snake returned to his manner and he spoke with thoughtful deliberation.

"Professor, I suppose you know some separatists. Would you call them idealists?"

"The only ones I have met are students and yes – they are idealists."

"You were a young man in Germany when Hitler took over. Were the young Nazis also idealists?"

When Uncle Conrad was laboring to make a point he was blind to a trap.

"That is one of the things I particularly came here to speak about.

Yes, very many of the *young* Nazis were idealists, and of course nobody can be more easily manipulated than a young idealist. Well do I know it. I was young myself. The young are always the easiest targets for cynical politicians, especially for revolutionary politicians."

Timothy continued smoothly, "Professor, you are not in your classroom. Monsieur Chalifour and I are not your students – neither is the audience. We have heard all this before. The next thing you'll be telling us is that this is a Children's Crusade." His voice suddenly turned hard with contempt. "I've read some of the things you've written in the papers, and I think I'm right to believe that you think the separatists should be suppressed by force."

"I do not accept that statement as you make it."

"You're hedging."

Uncle Conrad gave Timothy one of those looks of his I well remember. "Let me ask *you* a question. Do you believe a democratic government has the right to make laws?"

"Naturally, but – "

"If it has the right to make laws, do you deny it the right to enforce them?"

"A very convenient way of dodging, Professor. Has our government ever had a law on its books that was not in the interests of the Establishment?"

"That's nonsense and you know it. To kill an innocent man is murder, and that's the law I was referring to."

Timothy shifted his attack. "I'll say this for you. You're certainly telling us where you stand. Recently you wrote an article comparing the separatists to Nazis and some time before you wrote a letter to the press supporting the authorities of one of our universities when they turned the police against black students."

Uncle Conrad took a handkerchief and wiped sweat off his forehead. He hesitated.

"Well?" said Timothy with a mocking smile.

"In the first place, Mr. Wellfleet, it is clear that you never read my article, because I most emphatically did not compare the separatists to Nazis. I compared some of the wild propaganda and emotions here to similar propaganda and emotions in Germany when I was young. So much for that. As for the affair of the black students, it had nothing to do with the separatist movement, but the causes of it were very similar. Immature instructors who dislike the Viet Nam War almost as much as I do – they inflamed those students because at the moment it is popular to make riots in universities. They made paranoiacs of some of them and in the end the university was nearly burned down. If it had been burned down, some of those students would have died."

"How very convenient to dismiss black students as paranoiac because they object to how they are treated here!"

Uncle Conrad lifted his hands and dropped them. "Is it really necessary for you to misunderstand me deliberately? They were students, period. Teachers, I think, should take what I call the Socratic Oath. It means this, that they betray their duty if they use their knowledge for any purpose but the students' good, and the test of what is good is simply respect for the truth."

"You have yet to answer my question about the Nazis."

Uncle Conrad sighed, then shrugged his shoulders. "By now I thought that everyone knew about the Nazis, but apparently you don't. What is important to understand is *why* they became Nazis – why Hitler's propaganda was so successful with the young. Everyone knows the political and economic explanations, but the deeper cause is often ignored." He took a deep breath and his face became very concentrated. "After the 1914 war, religion died out among millions of young Germans. This left a void in their lives and many turned to nationalism as a substitute for the religion they had lost. In the 1960s, religion also died out among the young all over the world and nationalisms of every kind are taking its place." He held up his hand as Timothy was about to interrupt. "Now understand this – because all Nazis were nationalists, it does not follow that all nationalists are Nazis."

Timothy looked at him with contempt, faced his audience, and said, "And now we will pause for this message."

The three panelists vanished from the screen and were replaced by a young man in a turtleneck sweater who displayed four sleek automobiles one after the other, caressing their hoods with the palm of his hand as though they were the bodies of naked women, and ending with a half-smile and half-snarl, "Why don't you fit your ego into one of *these* beauties?"

The cameras burned again and Timothy took over.

"Professor, you've been singing a pretty familiar song. Law and order – the American story in Viet Nam. Order and law. I think the time has come to get down to a rather important question" – a lethally quiet smile and a lilt in his voice – "were you ever a Nazi yourself?"

Uncle Conrad answered his smile and shook his head.

"You've told us that many young Nazis were idealists. Were you also an idealist when you were young?"

Again Uncle Conrad smiled. "Oh, I suppose so. I was certainly immature."

"And Nazi?" Timothy had snapped the words out, and now he was studying the older man with the expression of a judge who has found out a perjurer. "I have some reason to believe that you were a Nazi, Professor. And a very active one."

At last Timothy had succeeded in getting under the older man's skin. Uncle Conrad sat up very straight in his chair and there was indignation and contempt in his expression.

"Just what are you trying to imitate here, Mr. Wellfleet? Senator Joseph McCarthy? A police inquisition in a totalitarian state?"

Timothy later recorded that this did it. Up to that time he had not really intended to go the whole way, but when he heard himself compared to McCarthy and the police the adrenalin pumped solidly into his nervous system. He reached into his pocket and took out the slip of paper he had recovered from his files before the program began. It had been given to him by Jason Ross and he knew how Ross had obtained it. He had broken into Conrad's study in the university with a party of activist students and had ransacked the filing cabinets. The paper Timothy now unfolded had been taken, as I later discovered by inference, from one of Conrad's diaries. Timothy studied it, then looked up and surveyed Uncle Conrad coldly.

"Does the name Hanna Erlich mean anything to you?"

Whether Uncle Conrad flushed or turned pale I don't know, because at that moment Timothy had signalled his floor crew to alter the lighting and the camera angles. The effect was dramatic. Suddenly, Conrad Dehmel became another kind of person, and to an innocent viewer it would appear that this had happened because Timothy's question had unmasked him. He looked harsh, hard, cruel, and utterly ruthless. I saw him make a convulsive movement and grasp the arms of his chair.

His voice cracked. "Where did you get that paper?"

"It was given to me."

"By whom was it given to you?"

Timothy handed the paper over the table. "Do you recognize your own handwriting?"

Conrad put on his glasses, glanced at the paper, and looked up in dismay. "This paper was stolen. It was torn out of its context. It was – "

"I have asked you a question. Does the name Hanna Erlich mean anything to you?" He paused, searched Conrad's face, and added softly, "I think it does."

Conrad pulled himself together and the floor crew, sensing that something was wrong, made the lighting normal again.

Conrad said, "Men who had to live through the times I lived through should be allowed the decency of some personal privacy. This – this paper" – it was lying on the table and he pointed at it – "this has nothing to do with the purpose for which you invited me here."

Cold, contemptuous, pretending to make an effort to control his moral indignation, Timothy looked away and addressed the unseen audience.

"Hanna Erlich committed the crime of being a Jew and for this she was sent to the gas chambers by the Gestapo." Then he turned and pointed his finger at Conrad, "And if it had not been for you, this would not have happened. Because, Herr Professor Dehmel – if that is your real name – I have good reason to believe that you yourself were once a member of the Gestapo and that it was you who caused the death of this woman."

Conrad lurched forward in his chair. "Young man, you are doing a terrible thing here. Somebody has used you to do it. Such a thing, it should not be mentioned in public like this. You have no idea what you're saying. Who told you this terrible lie? To say that I was responsible for that woman's death – oh, what is the purpose of this? Hanna Erlich! Poor Hanna!"

He stopped with tears in his eyes. Then he rose and with a quiet and desperate dignity he made a short bow.

"I will leave you now. Perhaps I can bring myself to forgive you later, but for the present I call you a creature beneath contempt."

He walked off the set.

To leave a television set before the time was up was something that just did not happen. By doing so, Uncle Conrad ripped the mask off the program and left it naked and indecent. Timothy had almost ten more minutes and had nobody to work with except Chalifour, who now had come to detest him. However, Timothy virtually turned the show over to him and Chalifour talked in a vacuum about the separatist movement until the show ended with both of them sweating.

For what followed I have depended on Timothy's notes written some time later.

"The overhead lights went out and I said, 'Good man, Emile. You saved the show. At the end you were great. It was all yours.'

"But Chalifour was staring at me in rage, 'Shit la marde, but you're a bastard!'

"What are you talking about, Emile?"

"You're all the same. Even when you pretend to be on our side you're all the same. I could be arrested for tonight."

"Cool it. Nobody's going to arrest you."

"*Calvaire*, why didn't you tell me what kind of a man this professor is?"

"For Christ's sake, you've seen for yourself what kind of man he is."

"I've seen for myself what kind of a man you tried to make him look like. What were you trying to do to him?"

"I wasn't trying to do anything but get the truth out of him. He may have conned you, but he didn't con me. Pompous old bastard."

"You were using me. You damned English, you use everybody." He lit another Gitane. "That man's been in prison."

"How do you know he wasn't in prison for war crimes? Didn't you hear me say he was in the Gestapo?"

"How do *you* know he was?"

"I know, all right. I also know that twenty-four of your friends are in prison and this professor would like to keep them there."

Chalifour shrugged and Timothy also lit a cigarette.

"Oh, to hell with that professor. Tell me something, Emile – do you really think those hostages are going to be executed?"

Chalifour stared at him in cold suspicion. "How would I know that?"

"It was just a question."

"Then you can answer it yourself. Every *maudit* one of you is the same."

"What the hell do you mean talking to me like that? I give you space on one of the biggest programs in the country and you – "

"You sucked me in and used me. And now I'm going to be arrested."

Chalifour got up and left without saying good night. After spending a few minutes with the floor crew, who were reserved with him as they had never been before, Timothy joined Esther in the control booth. Her face was white.

"Well," he began, "now I suppose you're going to say that the show was lousy. At least we took on this big-deal crisis of yours."

She did not answer.

"Oh well, the Pentagon show will make up for it. That professor of yours was impossible. Is it my fault he was impossible?"

Without looking at him she said, "Go home and take a Seconal and go to sleep."

"Esther, what in *hell* is the matter with you today? Can't I do anything right?"

She looked at him as though for the last time. "Go home and swallow anything that will close your mouth and keep it closed for at least eight hours. Then come back here and play that tape over and have a good look at it. You've done plenty before, but tonight – there just are no words."

He left and went out into the street cursing her, for he was professional enough to understand that what he had just done might easily ruin his career forever. He felt like crying in despair. He began walking and suddenly felt a desperate need to urinate. He saw a narrow blind alley, entered it, and emptied his bladder against the closed door of a run-down and abandoned building at the end. After he had finished and was walking away, he realized that the building against which he had urinated had once been a garage.

PART THREE

Conrad Dehmel's Story
as told by
John Wellfleet

Aᴛ ᴛʜɪs ᴘᴏɪɴᴛ I am going to leave Timothy for a while, not because his story is ended, but because I have brought him to his first and only encounter with Conrad Dehmel, an almost accidental meeting that was to have terrible effects on us all.

Again it is early June. My seventy-sixth birthday is coming and this year we had a good spring, with the lilacs a week earlier than usual. It is true what the scientists predicted when I was young–that the climate would grow colder, but it has been much less cold than they said it would be and in these parts as erratic as ever. When we least expected it, lovely weather came in the middle of May and it is still here. It is so beautiful that I'm afraid it will turn cold again in August. And another thing has made me happy. André and his wife now have a little boy and they let me play with him.

From where I sit I can see the backs of those three old men and I wonder without interest what they're talking about. The last time it was about sex and they were telling each other that the young of today–they never meet any, of course–know nothing about it. The oldest of them is in his eighty-third year and he still smokes grass. He even cultivates a patch of the stuff near by. For a long time he has been in his second childhood and he lives entirely in the past – so far back that he's always talking about the great days when he was leading student demonstrations and parading around the streets carrying his placards. "Did I ever tell you about the time," I've heard him say a hundred times, "when we made the president of the university crawl under his desk and the President of the United States shit his pants?" He was born in the old United States and came up to this northern country to escape the military draft in that war that Timothy was so excited about. He insists he's going to live past ninety because both of his grandparents lived that long. What became of his father and mother he neither knows nor cares, but he still has enough energy to hate them and to blame them for what went wrong with his own life, which was just about everything, even before the real troubles hit us all.

I'm also watching a robin on the same patch of grass and wondering whether he is the same one I watched last spring or one of the little ones that were fed in the lilac bush. The chipmunk that used to come to my hand has disappeared and I don't know whether he was taken by a prowling cat or died in hibernation. I miss him. Though it was cruel cold in January and February, my health was better than it had been in years and my only complaint was an annoying arthritis in the left wrist that made typing painful when the weather was harsh. It's gone now, with the warmth.

It is just over a year since André turned these papers over to me and the people I have met in them are as real as any I have ever known. I was too young to have been involved in their time on the stage, but it was in the last years of their world that I became what is known legally as a man. I wonder if they sensed that they themselves were symptoms of what was going to happen to us all? It seems to have been automatic with people like Timothy to hate their elders and to put them down on every possible occasion, but I and my friends didn't feel that way. Now I can better appreciate the enormousness of the tragedy implicit in André's question about Conrad Dehmel last year – "If there were men like him with all that knowledge, why couldn't they stop what happened?"

Among Dehmel's notes I found this passage and it was written several years before he appeared on Timothy's program:

"In the relatively rare periods in the past that we call civilized, people understood that a civilization is like a garden cultivated in a jungle. As flowers and vegetables grow from cultivated seeds, so do civilizations grow from carefully studied, diligently examined ideas and perceptions. In nature, if there are no gardeners, the weeds that need no cultivation take over the garden and destroy it." Then followed a sentence that seemed to me quite terrible, even though I must ask myself whether it is true or not. "During my lifetime too many of the men who thought of themselves as civilization's gardeners, in nearly everything they did from the promotion of superhuman science to superhuman salesmanship, devoted the ambiguous genius of their programmed brains to the cultivation of the weeds.

They watered them with the jungle rains of the media. The klieg lights of the studios were their hothouses. They did what they did, and they still do it, with the best of intentions, because they cannot believe that the creative energy of the universe will never interfere with human ingenuity. If anyone said to them, 'Thou shalt have no other gods before me,' they would reply with a polite and pitying smile."

Is this overloaded? Had I read it fifty years ago I would have thought so.

But what of André Gervais and the small coterie of his friends? I cannot claim really to know them, merely to delight in them and in the way of an old man to love them. They feel sure that a time will come when human beings will be let alone to follow their own bents, to be joyful and adventurous, to entertain gracious thoughts and be responsible for their own actions and the work of their hands. They are discovering entirely on their own the excitement of moral philosophy. They are marvellously, beautifully ignorant of what men are capable of when they grow disappointed, sour, tired, or merely indifferent. Can they really succeed in ignoring the miserable remnants of the present Bureaucracy, which is the feeble descendant of the Second Bureaucracy, which in turn was the blindly barbarous successor of the Smiling Bureaucracy which controlled us when I was a boy? They are amateurs. They are sure that in time a bright new city will rise on the ruins of Metro. All I can say to them is God bless you, I hope you're right. All I can say to myself is that they have nothing to lose by trying; for we, without trying, lost everything.

Again, there is this notion of André's that there is a growing passion for books among the young people now. I suppose it's possible. But the poor boy cannot grasp the magnitude of what has been lost. He can't understand that the middle-aged of today, including his own parents, were worse casualties than I was, for they had no experience of anything before the Great Fear.

But to return to the books – and here I'm speaking only to myself. So many million tons of printed matter had been accumulated and stored away even before I was born that nothing short of the destruction of the entire planet could have obliterated all of it. So far as I know, most of the city libraries went up in flames. Even before that, the Second Bureaucracy had processed vast quantities of printed matter for fuel and animal foods. Certainly some books survived these holocausts. I was lucky enough to have saved many of my own books; luckier still to have found and collected several thousand others. I used to pick them up in odd places when I was still young enough to wander and when no authority was strong enough to care about me. One of the most precious of them all has been a magnificent encyclopedia in a single large, heavy volume. I know it almost by heart. But I still must ask myself how many of the young people will have André's enthusiasm and will want to read books.

André told me – I had not known it – that a few years ago circulating libraries began to appear and that there was one close to where I live. I visited the place and it was pathetic. I don't know what some of the others are like but this one reminded me of a library I had seen long ago in a small-town Sunday school where the shelves were crowded with a mishmash of books cast off by summer tourists or picked up from farmhouses after the old people had died. I saw a Gideon Bible, probably recovered from a rural hotel. *Gulliver's Travels* was there, and a battered collection of Shakespeare's plays, but the rest was junk. The young woman in charge was proud of the place, but when I asked her how she liked Shakespeare she told me she couldn't understand the language. I was trying to think of something tactful to say when she asked me if I had heard of a book called *The Idiot* by an author with a peculiar name she could not pronounce. The room nearly spun around. So Dostoyevsky had survived! The man who had foreseen so much of what was going to happen after his death was still with us!

"Where did you find *The Idiot*?" I asked her, and she told me that one of her friends had lent it to her. She did not know where her friend had found it and she had not liked the book well enough to read more than a few chapters. Her only comment was that it seemed a very queer book written about very peculiar people.

I was not suprised to learn that this was the only novel she had ever seen, for the Second Bureaucracy had been animated by a ferocious logic of the very kind Dostoyevsky had been the first to describe and understand. Unlike previous tyrants, they had not worried about ideas, knowing that there were so many ideas of all kinds floating around that they were bound to cancel each other out. But novels deal with individual lives, and they had hunted them down and destroyed them as though they were carriers of a plague.

To be fair to André, by no means all the surviving books were commonplace. The Destructions and their aftermaths were just as unselective as those ancient barbarians we read about in school who plundered the old Roman Empire. André and his friends were very lucky, for they possess some beautifully illustrated books and commentaries about the art and architecture of the old Italian Renaissance. God knows where they were found, but originally they belonged to a private library. When André showed them to me I even recognized the name of the owner written on the flyleaf. I think he was a friend of my grandfather. Possibly his children sold them when they had no money left.

André asked me if I would agree that he and his friends are beginning a second Renaissance, and what could I say to that? With all respect and affection for him, I can't see my young friend as a second Leonardo. Conrad Dehmel used to describe the original Renaissance as a mutation, and mutations are supposed to take centuries. Truly I can't estimate what is going on now or even guess what it will amount to. But I'm sure of one thing. Any rebuilding that will occur is not going to resemble the gigantic reconstruction programs of the cities of Germany and Japan after the world war that ended before I was born. The same technological system that destroyed them was able to rebuild them in record time. There is no system like that today. No power like that.

Often when I lie in bed unable to sleep, trying to understand what I am too old to understand, it comes to me that André and his friends now in their mid-twenties are younger in spirit than I was when I was eight years old. When I was a boy nothing seemed really new to me, none of the big events at all surprising. The famous moon landing, for example. Our whole school watched it on television but there was no element of surprise in that show. We all knew that if the Control had not been certain of success it would never have risked it. As for information, there was so much of it that we all seemed to be living in an international airport with nobody knowing anyone else and loudspeakers barking thousands of directions in several different languages twenty-four hours a day. Well, that's all past now, and André's hopes are yet to come. The time is overdue to return to Conrad Dehmel.

"For years I lived like a man in the jaws of a shark" – this sentence I found among Dehmel's notes and thought to myself, "So what is new?"

However, it was certainly a new idea to me to discover that when he was alive I knew hardly anything important about him except that he was my stepfather. I was much too young to know such a man, and my sister and I were away at schools in the country for most of the short time he and Mother lived together. I liked him well enough, though I thought he could be pretty ponderous at times. My sister Charlotte disliked him intensely, and ruined every attempt he made to be her friend.

For instance, the day she came home with a second-hand guitar and Uncle Conrad was so pleased.

"Why Charlotte," he said beaming, "you never told me you liked music. This is splendid. Let me get you a violin and arrange for you to take lessons."

As if a girl like Charlotte had any intention of spending hours a day learning a tough instrument like the violin! Looking back on that sister of mine she really comes out as the Bitch Original and how Mother produced anyone like her I never could understand. As we used to say, it must have been in the genes somewhere. But again I must return to Conrad Dehmel.

When he was murdered we thought it was because of the crazy politics in our city at that time, but even I doubted if this was the real explanation. Politics were crazy everywhere, because the world was going out of control. The same story day after day all over the world – kidnappings, hijackings, skyjackings, hit men, individual kooks blasting off with submachine guns on street corners, eminent people and unknown people dropping dead for no reason the doctors could explain, several new strikes every week, money losing its value year after year, arson incorporated as a recognized technique in the building industry, arson a pastime for sexually frustrated individuals, organized crime the second-biggest industry in the richest and most powerful nation in what we called – Christ, what a word for it! – the Free World. We took all this for granted and it was marvellously exciting. Through it all the Smiling Bureaucracy continued to smile whenever they appeared on the screens.

Charlotte and I were at school when Uncle Conrad was killed and his death made no sense whatever. Charlotte was an unfeeling girl and she said, "Oh hell, it was just one of those things. Maybe somebody mistook him for somebody else."

How appalling it is for me, a man older than Conrad Dehmel ever lived to be, to discover only now that Charlotte, without knowing the first thing about what she was talking about, was probably right.

For Mother, Conrad's death was an appalling thing and it almost broke her. Literally, she turned her face away from the world and this meant that she lost all control over Charlotte and me. Or is even this accurate? For we two were already going along with the wave. Charlotte had her first boy when she was barely fourteen, which was not unusual then, except that in her case the boy was a married man of forty-two who knew Mother, had tried to make her and got nowhere, then had turned to Charlotte as easier pickings. How unusual was that? André would be shocked at it, and now I am not so much shocked as horrified at it. This man, whoever he was, left Charlotte as soon as he got tired of her and she told me afterwards she was grateful to him because – the words are hers – "He was a first-class sexual technician, and he taught me so much that now the boys can't get enough of me." About six months after my twin was launched I had my first girl, and neither of us were sexual technicians. We were two scared, clumsy kids who thought we'd be out of it if we didn't start. Soon random sex became a habit with me like cigarettes. Charlotte and I knew we were hurting Mother and only now do I understand that she was far more sexual in nature, profoundly so because of her love of children, than either Charlotte or I could ever be. But she was too old-fashioned to talk to us much about sex. It had never occurred to her that we would go on the town in our teens.

I loved Mother. I truly did, but I was too young to understand how precious she was. Charlotte's behavior to her seemed to me at the time atrocious. I remember Mother looking at her in shocked despair – or was it the plain, honest contempt of a naturally great lady? – and saying: "So the serpent said to Eve as he coiled around the branch, 'Don't worry, little girl. I have the pill in my mouth and you can do anything you like. Look at *me*,' said the serpent smiling, 'in my mouth is the pill.'"

All Charlotte could do was to shrug and say, "For God's sake grow up, Mummy. I know what I'm doing. I'm safe as a boy."

Mother said sadly, "If only you did know what you're doing!"

She looked so wounded we both felt ashamed and guilty, but guilt was out of fashion for our generation so we became defiant and angry. We told each other it wasn't our fault if the world Mother had brought us into was not a world to her taste, or one that didn't give a damn what a woman like her thought about anything. There was a general feeling that our parents' generation had squandered the right to teach their children anything in the way of morals, and this explains why Timothy's program was so popular.

Yet I wonder now, indeed have wondered for years, just how much I myself squandered of the drive created by juvenile curiosity by satisfying while still a small boy what to a growing youth is the supreme curiosity. Without intending to, Charlotte and I made Mother feel that her entire life had been futile. When we were very young she had never lost her temper with us; she had been firm, but her love for us was always clear and wonderful. It was different now. She began to quarrel with us, and especially with Charlotte. One day she really took off against Charlotte for the kind of life she was living, but Charlotte came right back at her. "You had your fun, Mummy, and you were careless. I'm having mine now and I'm being careful. That's all the difference there is between us, so stop being self-righteous."

Mother's normally gentle face turned white and so stern I felt scared. But Charlotte glared right back at her.

"It wasn't fun I was having," Mother said, "I loved your father. When I knew I had conceived, even though it was only then that I was told there could be no marriage, I thanked God."

Charlotte may or may not have been feeling ashamed. I neither know nor care what she felt. But I remember what she said.

"That must have been a great day for God," she said over her shoulder and I felt like smacking her. But already she had stalked out of the room.

Now I am much older than Mother ever lived to be and it is an anguish to remember a scene like this. Poor Mother lacked the education to reason with us and this was her father's fault. He was a lovely gentleman but he tried to ignore the twentieth century. He did not believe that girls should go to college and compete with men, but he did believe they should be trained to be thoughtful of others, to have good manners, and to know how to keep a house and rear a family. He would have had no trouble if he had been born three-quarters of a century earlier. No matter what Timothy said against his own father, if it had not been for Mother's Uncle Greg, who bought Grandfather's house, Mother and her parents would have been destitute. It was a huge happiness for her when she married Uncle

Conrad and had a home of her own. Mother sat erectly and spoke and walked like a great lady who is also kind and she had no petty pride at all. More than once I noticed her looking at her hands. They were very small hands but they were marked by years of hard housework. "These two hands," I remember her saying, "have nothing to be ashamed of. They have earned their living."

Now she had neither husband nor home nor children who would let her care for them. After that developer destroyed her old home, she was reduced to a two-and-a-half-room apartment overcrowded with the antique family furniture she loved so much. And it was about this time that I did something pretty stupid, but I'm still proud that I did it.

I found out where that developer lived and one dark evening I rode out to the place on my bicycle. He lived in the most expensive area of the city, though hardly its best part, and he had one of those low-lying houses with huge windows they called ranch houses. This one was shielded from the street by a hedge that must have been at least two and a half meters high. The man had installed it fully grown and charged it off as a business expense.

There was nobody in sight, so I hid my bicycle in the hedge and crawled through to the other side and came out onto a wide lawn with a fountain in the middle of it and colored lights playing on the water. There was a blaze of light from those long, low windows and I walked up and looked in. A cocktail party was going on. About a hundred expensive-looking guests were standing around with glasses in their hands and servants in white jackets were shuffling through them refilling the glasses and passing trays loaded with canapés. I recognized the developer from his picture in the newspaper. He was standing near a big fireplace with artificial logs and pointing to a big oil painting that looked like an old master and may even have been genuine. I looked at his clumsy round face with round eyes and a mouth that also seemed round, and the worst thing about it was that it looked like a boy's face that had gone bad. His hair was sleek and very thick and black and I noticed that his hands were abnormally small and dainty.

Next door to this property was a new construction site. He and his kind had been thumbing their noses for years at the zoning laws by the usual expedient of bribing officials, and if this didn't work, they let loose batteries of lawyers against any citizens' groups that tried to keep them out, and if that didn't work, sometimes they hired arsonists to burn the place down. I went to the site and came back with two large stones. From a distance of only eight meters I threw them one after another through the window and the crash of the breaking glass was beautiful. It was nothing like so beautiful as the behavior of the developer and his guests. He and at least half of them dropped their glasses and fell flat on the floor and I saw some of them crawling like caterpillars to get behind the furniture. They must have thought a machine gun was going to open up on them. Then I remembered that this man was sure to have bodyguards and I didn't wait any longer. I skipped back through the hedge, pulled out my bicycle, and pedalled down the nearest side street to the first lateral avenue below. Nobody chased me and when I searched the newspapers the next day there was no mention of the incident. Men like that son of a bitch didn't want to give other people any ideas.

I never told Mother about this because it would have upset her. If anyone had tried to enter her own house and there was a child in it, Mother would not have stopped at killing the man to save the child. But what I had done was an act of vengeance, and in her nature there was never any vengeance. But I'm still glad I did it. If a System won't punish people who ruin others – well, as a lot of us put it then, to hell with the System.

Uncle Conrad had not worked long enough at the university to build up an adequate pension and living costs were rising at the rate of twelve percent a year. He had published many learned articles, but there had been no real income from these. Fortunately one of his books on the history of the Roman Empire remained in print. Later it even went into a paperback and shortly after his death enough people wanted to read it that they supplied Mother with a small income which at least kept her off welfare. She also got a job in a settlement house for orphans and the children adored her, but Charlotte and I had to be withdrawn from those two country schools. The feeling between Charlotte and Mother was now too bad to be mended and they seldom saw each other. Charlotte moved from one petty job to another and lived with a succession of boyfriends and this routine went on for nearly ten years until she shacked up with a pyschotic who strangled her. For myself, after throwing those rocks through the developer's window, I finally began to behave better.

It was no grief for me to have to leave that boarding school. I had always detested it, and I now moved in with Mother and finished my last two years in a city high school and worked over the weekends to help out with the bills. I still made love to a few girls without really loving any of them and at home Mother's sadness was like a weight on my chest.

There was one night I have never forgotten, for it accentuated her withdrawal from the world. I had come home late after spending the evening with a girlfriend and I found Mother in a chair, not reading or listening to music but just sitting there. Her face was young and radiant and when I came in she looked at me in that surprised way of hers.

"I've been daydreaming," she said, and I asked her what about.

"It was that Christmas morning in your grandfather's big house when all was well with us all. We children got up early for the tree, but your grandmother said, 'No, you children must eat your breakfast first.' And that's what we did. After breakfast the whole floor of the living room was covered with the wrappings we took off our prezzies and everyone was so happy. But the best came after that. Your Aunts Rosalie, June, and Louise and I put on our warm clothes and sat down on a big toboggan with me in the front because I was the youngest and the smallest. Then we coasted down the hill with our arms full of presents for Granny. Granny lived lower down on the mountain. It was so lovely! The snow was pure white and the sun made the whole world glisten for the birthday of our Lord. It was the purest heaven." Then her face clouded over and she looked older again. "Poor John, if only you could have been young in the years when I was young. If only you could have known how sweet life can be."

I thought to myself, though I didn't say it aloud, "Oh God, Mummy, please don't think like that. There are so many exciting things if only you'd give yourself a chance."

So there were Mother and I, two hopeless misfits in the international airport our world had become. I had always known that Uncle Conrad's death had been a catastrophe for her, but it was only after reading his papers that I learned that quite possibly it was an even worse disaster for myself. I was naturally an eager student, though lazy and unsystematic because I found no stimulus in the teaching system. By the time I was twenty I'm sure I could have appreciated Uncle Conrad more than I did when I was a child. He might have given me some mental armor for what lay ahead, perhaps even some moral armor. Not many of us had either. In my last conversation with André Gervais I told him that there may never have been a time in the past five centuries when young people were as defenceless as in those very years when we were told that the young had never been so free. Perhaps we were, but nobody told us something that Uncle Conrad understood – that freedom has to be paid for and is the most expensive thing in the world.

Shortly before he died, Mother persuaded Uncle Conrad to write the story of his life and this I did not know because she never told me. That's what she meant, of course, the time she cried out, "All our lives were in those boxes."

At first Uncle Conrad refused to write his story because he did not think it would interest anyone and he was afraid that his training as a professional scholar would make it impossible for him to write in an intimate style. But Mother was a determined woman and she finally got her way. So here am I, more than half a century later, left with what he began and was not allowed to finish.

Conrad Dehmel has given me a much more difficult problem than I had with Timothy because some of the most important part of his story is written in German. I could speak German when I was young but had forgotten much of it. Fortunately I have a dictionary and a grammar and finally was able to translate it into English. In his methodical German way he had accumulated an arsenal of information in the form of notes, diaries, and personal letters. He had the scholar's tendency to play down dramatic incidents, but at times the drama could not help getting the better of him. From the way he begins I think he intended this record solely for Mother's eyes, but I can't be sure even of that. At any rate, his opening is characteristic of the man I remember and no more professorial than he usually was in a relaxed mood. Now for a time I can sit back and let him speak for himself.

PART FOUR

Conrad Dehmel's Story
as told by himself

*D*EAR STEPHANIE, you are probably the sanest person I ever met in my life, but forgive me if I mention that your kind of sanity reminds me of a French farm woman I was told about many years ago. In the early days of the First World War, this woman's farm became a battleground. German trenches were on the east side of it, French trenches on the west, and her house was in the middle. She paid no attention to the war because this was her property. Every morning, regular as a clock, she opened the farmhouse door and waddled out to milk the two cows she had tethered in her field. German soldiers on one side of her and her cows, French on the other. The moment she appeared the soldiers on both sides rose from the trenches and cheered her. They knew she was saner than they were and a genius of sanity compared to the politicians and generals who had sent them there. But as soon as she returned to the house with her milk pails they jumped back into the trenches and began shooting at each other.

Every time I remember that woman I feel like a fool. I have always had to ask the question "Why?" and now after all these years I ask myself what good that question does for anyone in a time like ours. And when I tell you this, I know you are too sure of yourself to pay any attention to it.

When I first arrived in America, I came to the United States from a ruined and disgraced Germany, came at a time when most people believed that merely to have been born a German was to have been born into a state of original sin. I had expected to find a new world. Instead I found one that was doing its best to grow old without taking the trouble to grow up. Well, I've already told you why I had to leave the States.

When I arrived in this country I knew hardly anything about it and after a few months it began to bewilder me. It was like a palimpsest

written over by authors who all contradicted each other and generally seemed uninterested.

Innocence, dear Stephanie, is a lovely quality, but to retain it too
long is to live beyond your moral income. You may not believe this,
but the Germany I grew up in used to be innocent. "The famous
German honesty" was very real and that is why Hitler was able to
make himself our master. The French, the English, and the Italians
have never been innocent in this way. Right up to the end of the war,
when all was lost and everyone knew it, young German soldiers
obeyed orders without question and fought, battle-drugged, to the
last cartridge. For what? To buy time for the war criminals to escape
with their lives and their loot.

If I speak of innocence with bitterness it is because, oddly enough,
it can make a man too arrogant for his own safety. It did that to me
when I was young, and I had much less excuse than you people have
here. This century has been relentless to everything an innocent
person values. The strange creatures who have bred in the rottenest
parts of our woodwork are quite possibly our real controllers today.
The true international underworld is not composed of gangsters but
of brilliant men, few of them with police records, none of them
attractive in themselves. But I tell you, some of them have the I.Q.s of
genius. As the great man after whom I was named once wrote, they
have kicked themselves loose from the earth and now they are
kicking the earth itself to pieces.

Remember Switzerland, Stephanie? Orderly, Zwingli-Calvinist
Switzerland? Remember her with her beautiful lakes in her beautiful
mountains resting rich and calm on a solid foundation of organized
crime? And some of the characters who have gone to earth there – do
you remember them with their lizard faces chauffeured around in
der Schweiz in their Mercedes and Rolls-Royces, and in their hooded
eyes did not you yourself read the question they will never be able to
answer? How long? How long before I'll have to find another refuge
for my money? How long before some investigation in another
country finds my record and names me? How long before the cancer
arrives? How long before the kidnappers come for my children and
grandchildren? How long before they come for me?

But I must stop this or you will lay down the papers and agree with
my original intention not to write at all. So now I will go back, as I
sometimes have done when we talked together in the evenings with

our apéritifs beside us. I will return to the time of childhood and begin with my name.

TWO

MY FATHER CHRISTENED ME CONRAD because at a very special moment for him, when his single-track mind was sure that his young wife had conceived the night before, he happened to be reading a novel by Joseph Conrad and came upon the description of a certain woman that "she was simply a person to whom life spoke imperatively in terms of love." This my mother told me twelve years after I was born.

He was sitting alone on the sand of a Baltic beach and he was on his honeymoon. On this July morning the air shone as though it were polished, the sky was without a cloud, and the limp sails of becalmed yachts broke the blue of a glassy sea. My father reread the sentence from Conrad, looked up while he pondered it, and saw a dense cloud of black coal smoke rising up beyond the horizon. He laid down his book and concentrated on the smoke.

Only one kind of ship could make that much smoke and he watched while the masts, the funnels, and finally the hull of the latest battleship in the Imperial German Navy came over the horizon. A high bow wave showed that she was steaming at full speed and when she shifted her course my father nodded, knowing what it meant. I have seen a picture of that ship and I can tell you she was harsh, ugly, angry-looking, but formidable. My father's interest in her was purely professional. He picked up the Zeiss binoculars he was carrying and watched her guns point up to a forty-five-degree angle and waggle as they steadied in for the range. Then he saw eight globes of orange fire burst out on the far side of the ship, the four midship globes outlining the stark lines of the hull and the upper works. Ragged balloons of black smoke were spewed out and hung in the air long after the ship had steamed beyond them. A minute and a half passed before the booming shock of the salvo struck the shore.

My father knew all about this warship and only a fortnight earlier he had dined with her officers in their wardroom. He also knew she was going through her first trials and was firing at a series of towed targets that he could not see because they were beyond the horizon.

He watched her fire three more salvos at three-minute intervals and nodded with professional approval. Her guns were new and her officers were not straining them by too rapid fire. The ship altered course once more and headed north and he watched until her hull went over the horizon and disappeared. Then he returned to his book and reread the sentence about the woman to whom life had spoken imperatively in terms of love.

This new battleship was a proud and very expensive instrument of the first great fantasy that seized the people of my native land in the early days of the century. In his own and much less expensive way, my father was another.

He was a naval officer born in the old Hanseatic town of Rostock in a family connected with the sea for centuries. His hair was golden blond and cropped short, his eyes were bright blue, his face was lean and high-colored, his body tall and hard from exercise. He was an educated man, far from insensitive, who loved art and music. His discipline was awesome and it was bolted to the only things he had been trained to value – his service, his country, and whoever might become his wife. I have always been a worrier, but when my father was in his prime he never worried about anything more complicated than the gunnery system of the ship in which he was the chief officer. He had studied mathematics and optics at Göttingen and mechanical and electrical engineering in Hamburg and he had advanced so rapidly in his profession that he had been promoted over the heads of officers many years older than himself.

Father's morality was so meticulously compartmented that he never suffered from any interior moral conflicts until after the 1914 war. If ever there had to be a choice between his duty to his ship and his duty to his wife and family, it was understood that the ship came before the wife, just as the nation came before the ship. If the ship were ordered to commit suicide for what a superior officer considered the greater good of the Fatherland, he and his brother officers would obey without even thinking. As it turned out, just such an order was given to his ship during the First War.

My mother, as I have told you, came from a Catholic family in the city of Freiburg in the southwest corner of Germany where most of the people look different from the blond, fair-skinned Nordics of the Baltic region. My father met her in the Prado in Madrid where she was looking at the pictures with her parents. The moment he saw her he fell in love with her but he was very correct about it. Hearing them speaking German together, guessing that her bearded father was a professor, he approached them, clicked his heels though he was not wearing uniform, bowed, and begged permission to introduce himself. Two days later he asked her to marry him. Two years later she did marry him.

My father was a good man in those years and so were most of the young men of the old fighting races of Europe who so diligently and high-mindedly slaughtered each other when I was a child. To my students of today he would seem preposterous and probably horrible; to him they would have seemed worthless and contemptible. He was a product of what somebody has called "the age of the hero" and my students are the products of what somebody else has called "the age of the anti-hero." And I, who witnessed his tragedy, and pray God I may not also have to witness the tragedy of these his opposites, I whose life was spent in a limbo between him and them, I mourn for him in an impersonal way beyond grief, for it is a mourning for a species that with absolute courage did what they thought was their duty and thereby became the most destructive generation the world has ever known.

Now this man was on his honeymoon. This man whose disciplined face would still look lean, taut, and ruddy at sixty (and in a frightening way would also look innocent and bewildered) was releasing into a young girl all the pent-up tenderness and suppressed poetry of an over-organized but essentially adolescent character. I'm sure it never crossed his mind to wonder what his wife would look like when she was middle-aged, or how either of them would feel when they knew in advance what the other would say about everything. I'm sure that it never occurred to him that it might be possible that they would ever disappoint one another. If in fact they did – and indeed they did – he would never admit it even to himself.

It so happened that my mother did conceive a child the night before my father read the Conrad novel and watched the new battleship firing her 280-millimeter guns. When he knew for sure that a child was on its way his happiness was the greatest he had ever experienced because his own family had never been prolific of boys and he was sure that his wife had conceived a son. Nor was his happiness diminished by his certainty that in a few years his country would be at war and that his own chances of survival were likely to be small, for everyone knew that the young German navy was smaller than the British. But this knowledge he locked away in a separate compartment of his brain, and so it was possible for him, in the mood of the moment, to believe that this sentence of Joseph Conrad was a divine revelation.

I like the name Conrad well enough and I love the books of the great man after whom I was called, but about that particular sentence I can see nothing remarkable. If there were not millions of women to whom life speaks imperatively in terms of love the human race would have finished itself off long ago. The dedicated efficiency of those millions of boy-men like my father in serving the dreams of messiahs, megalomaniacs, and ordinary cheap politicians would have guaranteed it. Incidentally, the country he admired most was the very one he was training himself to destroy, England. He was also a strict Lutheran and continued to be one after he married Mother in a private chapel in the Freiburg Catholic cathedral.

When I was working in that American university, I knew a young psychologist who was researching a mass of evidence to fortify one of those brainstorms psychologists often have. He was a great one for the Oedipus complex and he had a theory that the social and political results of our two big wars could best be understood by a computation of how many children had spent the first years of their lives living with their mothers and knowing their fathers only as pictures on a wall. He had worked out a rough estimate of how many millions of men, now of student age, fell into this category and from this he deduced a growing hostility to male authority leading into the present permissive society. He asked me what I thought of his idea and what else could I say but that I myself was one of his specimens, along with millions of other Germans who were children in the First War. I had to tell him that so far as the Germany I knew was concerned, the exact opposite had happened to what he had taken for his conclusion, for most of my generation had worshipped Hitler and died for him. But his example of the picture on the wall remained with me. For when my memory began, this was all my father was to me.

He stared gravely out of the frame with a gloved hand clasping a telescope, and if it weren't for the telescope and the naval cap he could have been mistaken for a high-class undertaker in the dark, long-coated naval uniform of the day. Like most German naval officers of the time he wore a small moustache and a short, spiked beard beginning at the bottom of his lower lip and terminating just under the point of his chin. Beside him was a larger photograph of his ship surging through the sea with a mighty bow wave and a vast pollution of coal smoke belching out of her two squat funnels. Her name would mean nothing to anyone now, but after the Battle of the Skagerrak (the English call it Jutland) she was the most famous ship in Germany. In the early stages of the battle her guns destroyed two huge British ships. Later, when the battle turned against the Germans, she and the other ships in her squadron, all terribly battered and one of them unable to fire a single gun, were ordered to charge and even ram the entire British fleet – four wounded battle cruisers against twenty-four untouched battleships. The four ships were to do this to give the main German fleet time to escape from the trap the British had caught them in. With their usual love of the macabre, our newspapers called this "The Death Ride of the Battle Cruisers." Which it wasn't, for somehow those four burning, half-destroyed ships wallowed home in the night to their harbor.

In Germany this battle was celebrated as a great victory, though actually it was a great defeat. Everyone was talking about it and strange men visited our apartment to congratulate my mother. There was one old man I have never forgotten, I loathed him so much. He was tall and thick. Out of a bull's hump neck there upthrust a narrow, pear-shaped head shaved completely bald. He wore a handlebar moustache like the Kaiser's, his face was seamed with duelling scars, and for years he had been boring everyone he knew by telling them about the great day in 1871 when he rode into Paris at the head of his regiment of Uhlans. He kept jabbing a stubby, cigar-stained finger at the photograph of my father's ship. "Such casualties!" he kept saying as though the idea was beautiful. "Such casualties! Two hundred and fifty-seven dead on her decks and so many more wounded and she fought the whole British fleet and came home." Stiff as a poker he bowed and kissed my mother's hand. But Mother was white, drawn, and still, and I watched the fingers of her left hand tapping the arm of her chair. For all the time this horrible old man was boasting about the casualties, she still did not know whether her husband was one of them and neither did I.

Several days later the news came that my father was alive but had been severely wounded and had been decorated by the Kaiser himself with the Knight's Cross of the Iron Cross. It was not until several years later that I learned that his guns had been responsible for the blowing up of two famous British ships and (to use the delightful word of today) the vaporizing of nearly three thousand human beings.

In those days we lived in an apartment in the old city of Freiburg-im-Breisgau on the verge of the Black Forest – my mother, my grandfather, and myself. During the first two years of the war I only once saw my father because he was on the other side of Germany with the navy. Occasionally we all went out to the railway station to see my mother off on a short visit to the north to spend a few days with my father, and when she came back from the third visit I overheard her telling my grandfather that my father was depressed and irritable because the authorities would not let the navy go out to fight. I, of course, was a tremendous patriot and filled my drawing books with crude pictures of German soldiers bayoneting French soldiers and German ships sinking English ships, but after the famous sea fight I lost my taste for this sort of nonsense.

When my father was released from hospital he came home and stayed with us for a month – not long enough for him to become completely real to me but certainly long enough to become unforgettable. His back had been gouged by a shell fragment and it was to remain painful for the rest of his life; some spinal disks were injured and in those days nobody understood how to treat them. I'm sure he wished to be kind, but to me he seemed remote, brooding, and ominous. He never learned to be wise, but within the limits of his profession he was exceedingly intelligent and he must have known that after the failure of his ships to drive the English off the seas it was impossible for Germany to win the war. He never spoke a word to us about the great sea fight. When his leave was up and his ship had been repaired – it took nearly four months before she was fit to fight again – he left us and went north, his eyes having seen what few men see.

It was around this time that Grandfather took me in hand. He was my mother's father and he told me many things, including something of my own origins.

Like many people in my region of Germany I had Frankish genes along with a variety of others inherited from the huge anonymity of time and the ebb and flow of various peoples and the tramplings of forgotten armies throughout the ages. In Mother's family there was a legend that a male ancestor in the eighteenth century had been a

Jewish chamberlain to one of the old archdukes. There were many stories about these Jewish chamberlains, for even before Hitler there was a tendency among Germans to believe that Jews have some kind of occult power. Years later one of my gymnasium teachers informed me that there was Jewish blood in the royal family of England and that it came from the chamberlain of some half-witted archduke or elector who had hired the Jew to run his province for him. That particular teacher became a Nazi long after I had left him, and when Hitler came to power, he elaborated on the story by explaining to his pupils that King George V was actually the grandson of Benjamin Disraeli, which meant that King George VI was at least one-quarter Jewish and that it was no wonder that he and President Roosevelt got on so well because everyone knew that Roosevelt was a Jew born.

There was much music in Mother's family. Her great-grandfather had been a child prodigy who had once been presented to Beethoven, but when he grew up the best he could do was to become Kapellmeister in a provincial city. Mother herself was a fine pianist, almost but not quite good enough for the concert stage. She had the same glossy black hair that you have, Stephanie, but her body was frailer, small in the bones, which is unusual with German women. This must have been an inheritance from her great-grandmother, the wife of the Kapellmeister, who had come from a line of Italian musicians. (I suppose that was why the story got around that we had Jewish blood.) She had the soft, deep eyes of many Italian women, which may explain why images of dark, still water so often come to me when I am tired or troubled, for the first time I saw her eyes they were smiling in wonder at her first baby, who was me.

She was very different from the general run of German women in those days. Most of them had been trained to think of themselves as Roman matrons and the war made some of them much fiercer than the men to whom they were supposed to be subservient. The lady living on the floor above us was a majestic hater, but Mother was not like that. She loathed war and her love for my father must have been remarkable if it made her marry a professional officer. But she also loved the moving waters of rivers and seas and perhaps she thought the navy different from the army. As in fact it was.

But my grandfather—he was the man about the house in my childhood and a wonderful old man he was to me. He used to talk with me as though I were an adult and he was very outspoken about the war, though he was probably more reticent outside the house than in it. He understood very well what it would lead to. He used to remind me that he was just as much a Frenchman as a German because he had been born in Strassburg and had lived there for twenty years before the Prussians took the city from France and made it a part of Germany. He had been a professor of Philology in our university for more than thirty years, but he was retired the year the war broke out and he had to live with us because his pension had shrunk to less than a quarter of its value in purchasing power. He was a proud man who looked older than his actual age, for it was the fashion when he was young for men in their twenties to try to look like men in their forties. He became a widower five years before I was born. He had always been thrifty and he told me that the Latin phrase for "debt" was "another man's money." He used to earn a few extra marks by playing the organ in our cathedral and in the last winters of the war, which were exceptionally cold, he would let me walk out with him in the early morning when he went to the Minster. I used to sit on the edge of the organ bench while he played.

Sometimes as a special treat Grandfather took me with him at night when he went to the cathedral to practise. The only illumination came from the flickering votive candles and the light on the organ console. When it became known in the city that Grandfather played there almost every night, numbers of people came to listen. They were troubled people who never spoke, they were just there, and I used to *see* the music. I mean I saw it literally, especially if it were the music of Bach or Händel, saw it mounting like the risen dead in and out of the Gothic shadows. The most visible music of all was an organ version of Bach's Eightieth Cantata, the one you like so much, which was based on the old Lutheran war-hymn "Ein Feste Burg Ist Unser Gott." When Grandfather played it he pulled out all the stops and the whole cathedral shook with it and first I thought the music was a picture of Germany surrounded and fighting for her life, then I saw the music grow into the boughs and mountains of the Black Forest, then into the cathedral arches, then up and out toward the hands of the Supreme Ally of all living creatures who have the will and courage to go on living no matter what their lives are doing to them. "Nicht Bach," said my grandfather, "sondern das Meer." And I marvelled that the composer whose music is the most oceanic of them all should have a name which means "brook."

The early mornings were the most exciting times. On winter days Grandfather and I would get up in the dark and dress and go out and see the gables and the red roofs of the city coming up sharp against the first light. Our breath was visible as it puffed out in little clouds, the morning giving us its energy as we walked through the narrow, winding streets of the Old City. Usually we took the narrow little Herrnstrasse which led directly to the back of the Minster, but I liked it when Grandfather chose the curving Salzstrasse with clean mountain water gushing through deep stone gutters between the sidewalks and the cobbles of the street itself. It was a little longer but it was more beautiful. We heard the angelus from the slim spire of our cathedral of red sandstone, the scars of old cannonballs on its walls, and I remember Grandfather remarking that people had been listening to those bells for nearly seven hundred years. When we left the apartment we always had to cross the bridge over the little Dreisam River which comes down from the Black Forest beside the Schillerstrasse where we lived. Most mornings there were mist patches over the water and the current flowing over the terraced bottom was just fast enough to keep it from freezing, though there were pockets of shell ice along the shores. The city was cold, clean, silent, and orderly, the war was barely a hundred kilometers away, and I was a child.

Just across the river was the massively angular medieval Schwabentor, which had been a city gate in the old days. It made me think of armored knights riding out to the wars of my storybooks, but on several dark mornings we saw modern soldiers marching through it with the solid, rumbling tramp of infantry under full pack, tired men in worn, patched field gray and flat forage caps, their Mausers slung by straps over their shoulders with the barrels sticking up like a hedge of broomsticks, their heavy coal-scuttle steel helmets secured to their packs. In the stillness of early morning we heard the tramp, tramp, tramp of two thousand boots hitting the cobbles in the plodding, businesslike march of the German army, and we knew why they were here and where they were going. The southern front near our city was the quietest in the West and any troops sent there had been collected from the tag ends of divisions which had been chewed to pieces on the big fronts farther north. They marched with the blank eyes of men who had learned long ago to live without hope and each soldier stared at the jogging pack of the man just ahead of him.

"So we've come to this," my grandfather said the first time we saw the soldiers. "Things are so bad they're moving them at night so the people won't see what they look like."

It was only then that I began to be afraid, and the fear grew rapidly. It was only then that I knew in the way a child does that most of the things they had been telling us in school were lies, that the French were not cowards and the English were not bad soldiers and that perhaps we were as much responsible for the war as they were. When we entered the cathedral in the last winter of the war it was often so cold my grandfather had to warm his hands over the votive candles before going up to the organ loft to play. The people who came to early Mass seemed different from the ones who came at night. It was not the music they craved but the Mass itself and I saw them huddled like bundles in their shabby clothes praying for the souls of the dead and the lives of the living.

The war, *Der Krieg* – I used to think it was everywhere. It was in the desperate hardness of everyone's work and in the eyes of the people who knew we were losing yet hoped for a miracle, for now the government was telling us that if we lost the war we could expect no mercy. The war was in the flat of our neighbor, Studienrat Zimmermann, the night his only son Alphonz, home on a five-days leave, invited us over so that he could play piano-violin duets with my mother. His three younger sisters looked at him adoringly and after he had finished playing he pushed back his forelock, looked at his rough hands, and smiled in a strange way and said, "This I will remember when..." and did not finish the sentence. Sure enough a month later, just after we had been told by the newspapers that our men had broken the British Army in the north and were advancing on Paris and that we would win the war by the summer, the word came that Alphonz had fallen at last.

THREE

*T*HIS IS WHAT TROUBLES ME now I am no longer young, now I am living in another country on the western side of the ocean and I see that this new country has suddenly become nervous with discontent and does not know why. It troubles me that fear is different from discontent and that there is something in discontented people that makes them crave fear just as it makes people crave sex or the bottle. Fear – a distant fear and not the terror of bombardment or torture – a distant fear is very exciting. In those days in the war it heightened my sense of everything. It made the city and the cathedral, the music and the spring flowers when finally spring came, seem more poignantly lovely than they have ever seemed since. We were always saying how much we longed for peace, but the suffering and the hunger had to go beyond bearing before people began to talk of giving up. And when that happened the whole country turned hideous.

I remember the horrid look on the face of another schoolboy when he told me my father was sure to die and that it would serve him right for the coward that he was. We got into a fight immediately and the boy was stronger than me and made my nose and mouth bleed pretty badly. All these boys whose fathers and big brothers were in the army were now cursing the navy because their parents told them the sailors skulked in harbor while the soldiers fought and died. What this boy meant was something I had been dreading anyway, that when the war was hopelessly lost the navy would be ordered to save its honor by sailing out to certain death against overwhelming odds, for the English who had been too strong for them from the beginning of the war were now reinforced by the Americans. By this time the politicians and the newspapers were talking about fighting to the last drop of blood. By this time also I was old enough to have a pretty clear idea of what happens to a warship when the shells explode inside it. I became insomniac with visions of my father lying wounded on a steel deck frying to death when the deck turned white-hot from the fires. But that last drop of blood – I used to wonder how they measured it out, how they were sure there was any left in the body, did they squeeze it out like the last gob in a toothpaste tube or what did they do?

"*Quatsch!*" said my grandfather when I asked him to explain. "*Quatsch* – like everything else they tell you."

Mother was seldom home after breakfast, if you could call the tiny roll and the cup of *ersatz* coffee a breakfast. She went to the hospital where she nursed wounded soldiers and often it was midnight before she returned. She looked terribly tired and thin like everyone else, and being slim anyway, she had too little flesh to hide the crow's-feet about her eyes and the constant fear for her husband gave her chronic headaches. There was so little to eat that this was called the winter of turnips, and as our bellies shrank, the British blockade was blamed for it. Actually, as I later discovered, the real cause was not the blockade at all, but our generals' insatiable appetite for human lives. They were so hungry for men that they conscripted the majority of our farm workers. Of course, when the war was over, the continuance of the blockade was very effective in creating the mood for the next war. Anyway, towards the war's end, as has happened in so many other wars, we were hungry all the time. Often I could not sleep because of hunger and when I did sleep I sometimes dreamed of wolves in the snow. But in the last winter of the war, again because of hunger, occurred one of the happiest and proudest days of my life.

Lying awake one night I suddenly thought, "Why am I lying here when there are hares in the forest?" I dressed quietly, collected a few necessaries, and slipped out of the apartment and down the stairs into the silent city. The only sound was the whisper of the Dreisam under the bridge. I had read in a boys' magazine how to set snares and was sure I was going to be successful. The ground was frozen, there was a film of snow on it, and I knew the hares would be gray. It was a short, steep walk out of our part of town into the Black Forest and when I reached higher ground I followed the footpath into the trees. When I came out from the trees I looked down on the city lying below open to the sky and a last quarter-moon. The slim spire of the Minster rose out of its heart steadfast and beloved.

I went back into the trees again and after a short walk came to a small clearing where there was an abandoned cottage built of thick logs morticed with plaster and held together by S-shaped iron clamps. I had seen it before and knew it had belonged to a solitary forester who had gone to the war. I tried the door but saw it was double-locked with a huge padlock and a heavy lock with a bolt. Then I went back among the trees and set two snares about a hundred meters inside the tree growth. I waited near by and listened for nearly an hour. The frost was searching for my bones when I heard a squeak, almost a scream like a tiny infant's cry. I shivered and waited until I heard another scream. "I've caught the hare and the hare's wife," I thought, and came out from my hiding place and killed them with blows of a stick on the backs of their heads. When I removed them from the snares I saw a film of blood at their throats and now it was dawn. The moon was pallid and low in the sky and the air had the pallor and promise of a windless dawn. I walked home proudly with the furry animals. They were heavy and hung limply and I was tired and achingly hungry when in full daylight I reached home and climbed the flight of stairs to our apartment on the second floor.

By this time Grandfather had returned from the Minster and he growled at me, "Where have *you* been, Bubi? Your poor Mother is frantic. She went to the hospital but she is frantic. What have you been doing?"

Then he saw my two hares and I swear that the lips of that disciplined old man actually slavered. If old people are healthy, hunger can be even worse for them than for the young.

"Ach, Conrad! Zwei Hasen! Zwei Hasen! Du liebe Zeit, was hast du getan?"

After I had swallowed a cup of *ersatz* coffee and a crust of bread, he told me to run to the hospital and tell my mother I was safe.

It was a Saturday and Mother would not have to get up early next morning. When I came home from the hospital, I found that Grandfather had already skinned and cleaned the hares and laid them out ready for Mother to season and cook them. He held up the skins.

"These will make two pairs of good mittens. One for your mother and one for you. I'll make them myself."

When Mother came home she seasoned the hares and put them into the oven to bake. She boiled a whole swede turnip and I tell you that never afterwards did I feel so proud as when Grandfather chuckled and said, "Conrad has given us a feast. But a feast he has given us." After dinner, which we ate slowly, relishingly, Grandfather turning to me from time to time and saying, "Ach, Conrad, was für ein Knabe bist du!" Mother smiled with tears in her eyes and said, "How proud your father will be when I write to him about this." For many minutes we sat feeling the good food working inside us and then Grandfather went to the cupboard and carefully measured out into two thimble cups the last of his old cognac. Smiling broadly he said, "Nunc est bibendum." He and Mother sat close to the amber-colored porcelain stove – I had spent the afternoon walking the railway line with a sack and had picked up enough coal to partially heat our living room for two days – they sat there turning their glasses and warming them with their fingers and palms, sniffing the cognac and touching it with the tips of their tongues.

Grandfather must have become drunk with the food for he broke into a Latin student drinking song. Mother went to the piano, caught up the tune, and joined him, and because I knew the words I joined in, too. Then Grandfather took a beer mug from the mantelpiece, one of those German porcelain *Krüge* decorated with grotesque medieval figures, and he waved the empty mug in time to the music. When the music stopped he gave us one of his rare, wonderful smiles and announced that he felt ten years younger. Indeed, he could even say that he felt fifteen years younger. Then his smile became almost crafty, his beard spreading because of it, and he looked at Mother and said, "Trudi, when I was a young man I did not comport myself like a Herr Professor. I can tell you that when I was a young man in Strassburg I knew some girls, but never once did I see a girl like you." Mother smiled back at him and said, "I hope that isn't true." He pretended to be shocked and said, "Do you say that I ever tell a lie?" And she said, "What will I play for you now – Mozart?" Grandfather, no longer drunk with food, said decisively, "No, the Titan!"

Mother sat down at the piano and her face became composed and contemplative as she selected what to play. Then she began Beethoven's last sonata, brooding, all its creator's violence absorbed into his final gentleness, holding within its sounds so much of our condition that words can never express. We sat still, bathed in the music, and when she finished, Grandfather rose and kissed her cheek. Then he said something that to me was meaningless, though many years later, remembering it, I understood what he meant.

"Beethoven may have been born in Bonn, but his family was Flamand."

Those were the last and only hares I caught. When a country is starving, it doesn't take long for the edible wild animals to disappear even in a forest as large as the Schwarzwald.

Grandfather was the first of the many men I have known, myself included, who saw the disintegration of their world. He had grown up in a time in which most university lectures in Europe east of the Rhine were given in Latin and when scholars thought of themselves as an international brotherhood. He was nauseated by the Germany that grew up after the Franco-Prussian War. "Germany!" he used to say in anger. "When I was young it wasn't this. It was the home of the German people. It was the land of poets and musicians and thinkers."

He made me think of an indignant old bear when he went down on his knees to pry open the briquets of pressed coal dust we used in our porcelain stove. There was never enough of them to take the chill out of our rooms in January and February and soon there were none at all. Even the briquets had been harnessed to propaganda. When we pried them open we saw pressed into their insides the words GOTT STRAFE ENGLAND. Of all the things that disgusted Grandfather, this made him the most disgusted of all.

In the war's last year I acquired from Grandfather a sense of time unusual for a boy, a sense young people today have not at all, so far as I can see. I myself lost it entirely when I became a university student, and this also was natural and perhaps healthy. The young can do nothing if they have to carry the past on their shoulders. Now that I am old it has returned to me. It's simply a feeling that the present moment is unreal because it is a product of the past and a transition into the future. It was not that Grandfather lived in the past, though naturally he did a little. Rather it was that he saw the present with such experienced eyes that he often seemed to be living in the future, which would become real only after he was dead. At the time this frightened me. Now it only makes me feel lonely for him.

"They will tell you about the Laws of History when you go to the university. Don't believe them. This war wasn't caused by laws, it was caused by fools and spoiled brats."

Grandfather was no romantic as my father was, even as I myself have been, and this was natural in a classical scholar. One night while we were waiting for Mother to return from the hospital, the windows blacked out in case of an air raid from the French, the old man in his worn black suit shabby about the knees and elbows hanging loose on a body that once had been robust, he spoke to me as though he were speaking to himself.

"Queen Victoria," I heard him say. "Old Queen Victoria, she should have lived forever."

I had no idea what he meant and for a long time he did not explain. He picked up an empty meerschaum, stuck it between his teeth, and hunched forward breathing air fiercely through the stem. It had been months since he had had any tobacco to fill it.

"Twice I heard Victor Hugo speak," he said finally. "Twice also I heard Humboldt. He worked in Paris for twenty-one years before Germany became a religion, then he lectured at Göttingen and I was there to hear him. Brahms and Wagner I have heard conduct their own music. Saint-Saëns also. And now what do we have? Strauss!"

He made an abrupt turn of his whole body and looked at me with the expression of a scholar studying a new manuscript. What he saw there I don't know. After a while he looked away and seemed lost in his own thoughts and it must have been ten minutes before he spoke again.

"Money won't be worth the paper they'll print it on. The fools know it already. When the old emperors began putting lead into the *denarius* and the *drachma* they sealed the fate of the Empire. Foreigners are going to come in here from all over Europe and buy property for a song. Our people have believed everything they were told and it's no wonder we have fools for our rulers. It's going to be years. Years it's going to be before anyone will even dare to understand what all this means. How many states are going to disappear? States have their seasons like the leaves of a forest. They come and they wither but the people remain. When you're as old as I am, living in a world so different I can't even imagine what it will be like, let me tell you that men are not going to be different from what they are now. Queen Victoria should have stayed alive another twenty years at least. With that woman alive, he'd never have dared do it."

I looked at him with my knees pressed together and my chin on my hands and my elbows on my knees. There was a hole in one of my long black stockings and the skin showed very white through it. Then I heard the old man talking again.

"I saw her once. I saw her in Bonn. It was the day they unveiled the statue of Beethoven. I think it was the last time she came to Germany but I may be wrong. I saw her as clear as anything. A stout old lady, very short she was. Oh, she was a brown dumpling with her yellowish face and the big pouches under her eyes. People said she got the pouches because she took to drink after her husband's death. People will say anything and believe more. All those Hanoverian princes had pouches under their eyes. You know she was his grandmother, I suppose?"

"Do you mean" – I was almost afraid to say it – "do you mean the Kaiser?"

He nodded, his head steadied, then he nodded again. "They said she was the only person who could do anything with him. He was much younger then, of course. Everyone said how handsome he was. A face carved out of marble, one fool newspaper said. People will call a prince handsome even if he looks like an adenoid. When I was

young they called Franz-Joseph handsome. So is a block of wood with
hair growing out of it. The Kaiser is a spoiled brat. What I remember
is his fool's mouth with that imbecile moustache sticking up on either
side of it like the horns of a cow. How many nations have been ruined
by spoiled brats! But at least this one was afraid of his grandmother.
Our wonderful All-Highest was afraid of that dumpy old woman in
black." He chuckled. "Would you like to know what I saw happen that
day in Bonn?"

"Of course, Grandfather."

He chuckled again. "Well, you see, when they pulled the cord and
let the drapery fall off the statue, Beethoven's back was to the balcony
where the royal party was and of course the Kaiser thought himself
insulted and began shouting. What a nation of shouters Germany has
become lately, to be sure. The Kaiser was in a tantrum. But you'd
never guess what happened next. The old Queen always carried a
small ivory fan and now she took the fan and slapped the Kaiser's
wrist with it. 'Be quiet, you bad-mannered boy,' she said. 'What else
would Beethoven do but turn his back on a bad-mannered boy?' He
stepped back and blushed like a tomato and never another shout
came out of him that afternoon. He was bowing and scraping to her.
Oh, that old woman should have lived forever."

I have often wondered whether Grandfather really did witness this
scene or even whether it actually happened. He would never have
said anything he did not believe to be true, but he had reached the
age when men are apt to believe that things they were told when they
were young were things they themselves had seen.

Grandfather had never asked more of life than what he assumed
was his due as an honest Christian and a competent scholar. He had
grown up in a time when most people in our part of the world knew
exactly where they stood at any period of their existence. They
understood what was to be admired and what was to be despised and
if they were in a profession like his, they knew how much they would
be earning twenty or thirty years later if they worked hard. They knew
how much to spend and how much to save, and when their working
days were over they knew their pensions would be paid in money
worth what it had always been.

All this was gone now and Grandfather knew it. His sadness was
not for himself but for his loved ones who would have to live in the
chaos left by the war. He had married in early middle age and his wife

had been eighteen years younger than he. She had died bizarrely a few years before the war. She had accompanied him on an archaeological holiday in Asia Minor and while they were poking about in the ruins of Ephesus she walked on a viper and the snake had struck her and she died of it. His two sons had been killed in the army, the younger one fighting the Canadians in Flanders, the older by the French in the Champagne. His other daughter, my Aunt Toni, had married a Frenchman who had been one of Grandfather's favorite students. This man had obtained a post in the University of Poitiers, but when the war came there were no more letters from France. Early in 1915 one of Grandfather's friends who held a chair in the University of Basel wrote to say that he had received a letter from Toni saying that her husband had been killed on the Aisne and that she herself had been interned as an enemy alien.

Grandfather taught me Latin by word of mouth and this reminds me of the night when there was an air raid and in the far distance we heard the thudding of bombs. At that very moment a storm broke out with a great roar of wind and the sound of the explosions was lost in the thunder and wind. Later they told us that a French plane had crashed in the Black Forest and that the pilot had been taken to a hospital. He was very young and had been horribly burned and he screamed all the way through the streets. Now with the wind shaking the house and the thunder crashing, Grandfather began talking to himself in Latin. I heard him say something I did not understand, but it had a sombre resonance like the tolling of a bell. When he realized I did not understand he translated it into German, "And in a rush of wind the gods left the city." He was silent for a time and so was I, for I was listening for more bombs and was afraid. Then he spoke again: "I wonder where the gods are going? To America? I think not, because America is only an extension of ourselves. Perhaps they will go to China. It will be interesting to see what they do there."

He was silent again. An old man, a small boy, and the war.

Grandfather was not famous and never had any ambition to be so. He was just a retired professor of Philology proud to have studied under Mommsen and to have read a few kind words written about one of his monographs by Wilamowitz-Moellendorf. Probably he was a dull lecturer on principle, because he believed it wrong to let emotion interfere with anything scientific. Yet for all his heavy beard and his mane of gray hair – when younger and heavier he had looked a little like Brahms—when I knew him he was closer in spirit to a small, enquiring boy than to anyone his own age. He used to talk sometimes of rebirth and I thought he meant the resurrection of the body but after a while I knew he was talking of something larger than that.

Grandfather lived long enough to see the soldiers marching home in good order after their defeat and I was standing beside him on the sidewalk with the silent people watching. Now you must understand that Freiburg was always a quiet city, a gracious city close to France and Switzerland, with no heavy industry or conflicts between capital and labor. It was the only place I knew and for me it was the center of the world. The soldiers marched in their worn, patched, and muddy uniforms and broken boots and the crowd had pity for them. But suddenly a man in the rear began to shout, "Nein! Nein! Nein!— Feige!" I felt a shiver pass through the crowd and this was ugly, for many of these watching people had lost sons and husbands and lovers and these returning, beaten soldiers at least were still alive, but to call them cowards was shameful. The man in the rear continued his shouting and I looked at him and his face was crazed. He was shaking his fist at the soldiers and a few in the crowd were with him. I heard a woman say, "He had four sons and they were all killed." But when I looked at Grandfather, and heard the murmur increasing in the crowd, his face frightened me. It was not merely that his face was emaciated with hunger but that the last dregs of hope had been drained out of it.

"These people will obey orders again," I heard him mutter. "When the orders are given, yes, they will obey them again. They have learned nothing and they will forget nothing."

For the next three days Grandfather was so withdrawn that he seldom answered when we spoke to him and barely tasted the few morsels of food that were his portion. I had the feeling that he had gone away from us into what was left of himself and that his immediate surroundings meant nothing to him any more. On the third night there was a beautiful sunset and I pointed out the window to the spire of the Minster. He opened his eyes and looked at the spire and I heard him murmur, "Yes." A little later he stirred out of his immobility and went to bed and Mother and I had nothing to say to each other. Mother rose and went into his room and came back and said, "He's asleep."

He was still asleep the next morning when Mother left for the hospital. I had nothing to do because in the state of everything at the time the schools were closed. About ten in the morning I tiptoed into Grandfather's room and saw him motionless on his back, his beard spread out over the coverlet. I touched his forehead and it was cold and I knew he had died in his sleep.

My desolation was something I cannot describe, but later when I saw him in his coffin, all the lines of struggle and disappointment wiped away in a white calm, I felt a serenity and knew that in the end each one of us is alone with something that may be infinity. His life had been lived as best he could live it. It had been all his own at the beginning; it had been shared with many others for many years, it had been all his own at the end. This was the first time I ever saw a dead man and it came to me that this kind of death has nobility and that all of us should be allowed to look like this when we die and not to be mangled or shredded to death as happens in war, or recorded as a statistic as tends to happen now. "The Lord has given, the Lord has taken away, blessed be the name of the Lord." What this line means, dear Stephanie, has been taken away from nearly all the people alive today and I think that all the material things that the machines have given to people have not made up for the loss of it.

Mother was white and silent but not distraught. She tried to reach my father by telephone but the system had broken down. The whole country had broken down though it did not carry a single visible scar from the war. We heard that the Emperor had fled to Holland. We heard there was no government at all. We heard many things I forget. There was a quiet funeral service for Grandfather in a corner of the Minster attended by Mother and me and a few old people who had known him. Then he became a memory and I used to wonder what God said to him when He received him. And so, for me, the first great fantasy of our century came to an end.

FOUR

NOW WE HAD TO LEARN what total defeat in war can mean.

Hunger turned into starvation, for the victors kept up the blockade until a few frightened, outraged men in stiff collars and frock coats signed a peace treaty which most people today believe guaranteed the even greater fantasy that obsessed the world twenty years later. Actually I don't think it provided anything more than the excuse for it.

We had known, of course, that the naval crews in the great port cities of the north had mutinied just before the Armistice was signed and that they had shot and killed some of their officers and arrested some others. We learned that returning soldiers had shot at the sailors and that in the northern cities the hunger was terrible.

Every day I searched through the railway yards with my sack collecting coal; so did dozens of other boys. I went into the woods hunting for beechnuts or anything edible I could find. In the winter the influenza came and many hundreds died of it in our city alone. My mother also came down with it and for a few days her situation was serious, but she had great resolution and her longing to keep alive for her husband may have been what pulled her through. There was no chance of his coming home for a long time because his ship had sailed out with the rest of the fleet to surrender to the British and was anchored in the bleak waters off northern Scotland where winter nights are so long that in December and January there are only a few hours of daylight.

"Anyway," I remember Mother saying, "your father will not be hungry because the English have plenty of food."

"But will they give him any?" I asked her. "They don't give us any."

Mother managed a smile. "That is because we aren't living with them, dear, and they can't see how hungry we are. But your father and the other sailors are living with them. The English are not barbarians. They will give them food."

It was many months after the end of the killing before Father came home and I saw Mother sobbing in his arms. To me the scene was awful. His embrace of my mother was not even human, it was more like the reflex of an officer returning a salute. Almost immediately he broke from her and his eyes swept the little living room of our apartment. I suppose he saw me there but he gave no sign of recognition, and when I saw his face I froze with fear, for if this man was my father, then my father had the expression of someone who had stared into the face of a madman. I have told you, Stephanie, how disciplined he was and I have told you also how romantic he was. As a boy who knew what the word "discipline" means, but had yet to learn what the word "romantic" means, I understood with that quick insight of a teen-ager that this man could now become dangerous to others. Worse, I knew he had become dangerous to himself.

He stood in the center of our living room and I made myself small and watched from a corner. I saw his eyes fix themselves on the photograph of his ship rushing through the water with that great bow wave and her two squat funnels belching the black smoke and her huge guns elevated. For nearly a minute he stared at the picture while in my mind I saw the ship lurched over on the cold sea bottom with fish swimming through its insides and even through the barrels of those terrible guns.

Erect, his lean face taut, my father turned swiftly around. It was a movement which must have caused anguish to his wounded back, for he turned with his shoulders high and stiff as though he were at attention. I saw some gray hairs in his short, spiked naval beard. When he spoke his voice was like a cry of pain.

"Trudi!" he said in a high-pitched voice. "Trudi!"

"Lieber Gottfried, ich bin hier."

"Our own men, Trudi! Our own sailors! The communists got to them. A miserable, crafty peasant from Silesia, a stoker in the *Helgoland* – he raised the Red Flag on his ship. I never liked that *Helgoland* class of battleships; the design was stupid, it wasted firepower. Twelve big guns but a broadside of only eight. I wrote a memo to the Kriegsmarine but they..."

"Du lieber Gott!" I thought. "Du lieber Christ!"

"The sailors put that damned stoker in command over my admiral. It started in the battle fleet, of course. The battle fleet only fought for a few hours in the whole war. It didn't start in our scouting force because we fought often, but in the end it spread there too. That damned stoker! When I refused to surrender my personal weapon a sailor hit me in the face with an iron bar."

I looked and saw the scar. It would be with him for the rest of his life.

"They put us in irons. German sailors did that to their own officers. In the end the soldiers had to come in and put them down. The soldiers didn't betray because they'd been allowed to fight. When those damned politicians surrendered, where were our soldiers? On French soil, on Belgian soil, on Russian soil. The army was never defeated and the navy –"

My mother was pale and as she looked at him I knew she was feeling desperate.

But my father was obsessed and his voice became so high-pitched it frightened me.

"They never gave us a fair chance. If they'd let the navy out in the beginning we could have won the war in an afternoon. *Our* squadron went out often and we proved we were better than the English, but they kept the main battle fleet in harbor for nearly two years before they gave it a chance. If they'd let it out in the first week we'd have won the war. We proved it. We had better ships and superior firing efficiency. We had better shells and optical equipment and our ships could be hit again and again and still keep fighting. Every time we hit an English ship, it blew up. But by that time the English had many more ships. We nearly destroyed their battle-cruiser fleet at odds of five against nine. The fact speaks. When the English officer in Scotland examined my breech-locks he couldn't believe what he saw. 'We never had anything as good as this,' he said."

"Du lieber Gott!" I thought again.

Then he told us how they had scuttled the fleet at Scapa Flow.

"Exactly one week before those damned politicians signed that peace treaty. The shortest night of the year and in that sub-arctic place it was still bright enough to read a newspaper at midnight. Von Reuter had us over to the flagship in the anchorage that night and the English didn't notice a thing. He gave us the orders, we went back to our ships, and we gave the orders to the men and this time they obeyed us."

He had been speaking as though Mother and I were not in the room, as though he had to prove something to God, perhaps.

"At exactly noon on the next day, the day of the summer solstice, with English warships all around us, the imperial ensigns rose to the mastheads of seventy-four German ships, and every one of those ships was sinking. There was nothing the English could do to stop us now. Our ships went down with their flags flying because our men remembered at last that they were Germans. The navy lost its honor in Wilhelmshaven because the men had been kept rotting for years and the communists got to them. That damned stoker, he's still at large. But that day in Scotland our men saved the honor of Germany."

No, Stephanie, mutinies never succeed in Germany unless the orders come from the top and then it's not revolution, it's a *putsch*.

I saw Father hunch down on the couch, thinner than I had ever seen him, his hands limp on his knees, and I knew that his balance had been shattered. The compartments that had divided his life and at the same time held him intact had cracked open like the steel compartment doors of his sunken ship. He would still believe that he loved his wife and might even believe that he loved me, but his true home had never been any house or apartment where Mother and I might live. It had been his profession and now his profession was gone. Now he was an officer with no men to command, a sailor with no navy to serve. As though we were not there, as though he were entirely alone and thinking of his sunken ship, I heard him hum a tune and I knew the words of it: "Auf einem Seemannsgrab/ Da blühen keine Rosen." As you don't know the German language, Stephanie, that means "On a sailor's grave no roses bloom." I can't imagine a sailor in the British or American navy singing a song like that. I'm German enough to be moved by it, especially as it was sung in the last war in circumstances far more heartrending.

Now more than ever it became a question of how we could live, for the country was bankrupt and there must have been five hundred thousand officers without money or jobs. We were lucky to be in Freiburg in those times, for it was a small, orderly city as I told you, and before my father came home there were no food riots as there were in the large cities of the north. Occasionally during that year morsels were obtained from the countryside – a few eggs, once a whole chicken, sometimes fresh milk, and after the peace was signed the allied food relief began to reach us. I was back in school again and was making good progress in the gymnasium, for Grandfather had trained me well. If we were desparately poor in the first two years after the war, we were at least no worse off than nearly everyone else.

Gradually the old human ability to accept whatever happens took charge. The war was over, it had been lost, the Kaiser had gone, nobody understood the new democratic government, least of all those who were in charge of it, but somehow the people were surviving. Now they were saying that the war had been lost by everyone except the Americans, that we had won the moral victory, and that the Treaty of Versailles was such a farce that not even the Allies could believe in it.

Two years after the end of the war our personal fortunes changed. Germany had been allowed to retain a tiny fleet – a few obsolete battleships and cruisers that could be a threat to nobody except the equally obsolete Russian Navy, whose sailors had shot nearly all their officers during their Revolution. One of Father's brother officers, a man senior to himself, was back in the service and he arranged for Father to get a job as a marine engineer. Young though I was, I sensed that this job was only a stepping-stone back into the service and that many mysterious plans were being made in secret. This new job meant that we had to leave Freiburg and go north to live in Bremen. It also meant packing all our belongings, crating the piano and the tables and chairs, and obtaining wooden boxes to hold the china and books.

On our last evening at home when everything had been packed except a single couch, the piano, and a few chairs, I watched Father go down on his knees with a hammer and nails intending to nail down the cover on a box of books. He paused to look at one of the books on the top. As I have told you, he had a deep appreciation of art and I had often studied his collection of those large, heavy books of reprints of paintings by the great masters of Europe. One of his favorites was Goya and now he picked up the Goya volume and stood for a while glancing through it, with the late afternoon sunlight entering the window making the scar on his cheekbone look red. Still holding the book, he sat down on the couch and beckoned me to sit beside him.

The book was *Les Désastres de la Guerra* and my eyes followed page after page of it as he slowly leafed his way through to the final page containing the scroll with the single word "Nada" inscribed on it. He stared at this in silence and I thought I understood what he was trying to show me – that the war had been Nada, the heroism, the suffering, the great victories and the final defeats, the millions of dead and mutilated, the total surrender, the bankruptcy of the country and the starvation – "Für Deutschland, alles Nada." I said it aloud.

When my Father heard it he stiffened. He sat erect despite the pain in his back and his eyes grew opaque and strange. His whisper was far more terrifying than a shout.

"Nein! Aber n-ei-n!"

Across the room my mother watched him without expression and I knew she was growing remote from him.

Then I saw a grimace, you could not call it a smile, distort my father's face.

"Mistakes," he said softly, almost cunningly. "Just a few stupid mistakes. But now, you see, we understand just what those stupid mistakes were."

As his blue eyes fixed themselves on me I knew, though at the time I lacked the words to express it, that my father had completely surrendered to his own pride and will. I knew also that the war had not ended after all, that wars as terrible and stupid as this one can never end. And immediately my father confirmed it.

He snapped the book shut, replaced it in the packing case, and stood up.

"The next time there will be no mistakes," he said as though the matter had been decided forever. "But until then there is much work to do and when we are ready there will be swine to take care of."

I left the couch and went to the window and saw the Minster spire serene against the aftermath of a November sunset. Father nailed down the cover on the box and sat down again and I continued to look out across the red roofs to the spire. So never again would I walk out in the dawn with Grandfather or sit with him in the organ loft while he filled the cathedral with music. As I thought this, an invisible presence seemed to touch my shoulder and a voice whispered, "He does not understand what he's saying. Even though he is your father he understands nothing. He never will."

Music had begun in the room and it was Mother playing the Goldberg Variations. It was one of Father's favorites and that was why Mother had chosen to play it, but after a few minutes he rose and went quietly out the door. He had gone out for a walk because now he was less lonely with himself than he was with us. I followed the music through its intricate journey until at last it came home to the same largo, child-simple lyric with which it had begun. When the music ended, Mother remained seated in the silence, her hands folded in her lap, her head bowed.

All these things I have written I saw first as a child and understood as a child and the last things I saw as an adolescent. In Germany a child was believed sentimentally to have the perfect wisdom, but this did not deter some of our teachers from treating us like morons. Not long after this evening I began my higher education, the over-powering discipline of the German gymnasia and universities. Just as I had been "a good boy" while living with Mother and Grandfather, now I was being trained into something very different – a good student on his way to becoming an ambitious professional, a young man dazzled by the maze of professional knowledge. I was on my way to becoming a learned fool.

PART FIVE

Conrad Dehmel's Story
as told by
John Wellfleet

I HAVE NOW REACHED a long gap in the records and will have to rely on Conrad Dehmel's diaries and notebooks, on some of his professional publications, on letters, photographs, and the occasional patch of narrative by himself.

Contrary to what his grandfather had believed, that First Great War did not destroy Europe. It was followed by such an explosion of intellectual and artistic energy you could almost believe that the slaughter of all those millions of young men had served as a fertilizer to some of the survivors. So much happened in those years. So much passion was spent. Everywhere new oceans of knowledge were discovered and eager men dove into them.

The year the Dehmel family moved to Bremen, Conrad's parents had another son they called Siegfried. His mother was now forty years old, the birth was as difficult as it was unexpected, and it left the mother weak for several years afterwards. Siegfried was physically robust, his hair even blonder than his father's, his temperament was cheerful and boisterous, and by the time he was five he was playing with toy warships in the family bathtub and was determined to join the navy as soon as he was old enough. To his father, Siegfried was a greater joy than Conrad ever was.

Eight years after Siegfried's birth, Conrad matriculated from the gymnasium and went to the first of his three universities. It was at Göttingen that he made his doctorate. His field was History and for him History seems to have included nearly everything connected with the human race. As his working tools he used "four and a half languages," the half-language at that time being English.

The work-load of those German students would have emptied the classrooms of any university I ever knew. The best ones did hardly anything but work and some of the scientists spent whole weeks in their laboratories, dozing a few hours at a time on camp cots when they had experiments cooking. Conrad prepared himself for his career like an athlete training for the Olympic Games. He got up at 06:00 hours every morning and spent twenty minutes in vigorous calisthenics. Sunday was his walking day and no matter what the weather he usually covered about thirty-five kilometers. Often he took an early train in order to walk in the Harz Mountains.

On weekdays he did nothing but study, and the routine was much the same with his friends. Their sole recreations were the occasional concert or a night with a girl, but they were seldom companions of their girls as we were with ours. One of Conrad's friends, a philosophy student, went to a brothel every Saturday night: "Sleeping with a girl you like is a waste of spiritual energy. Going to bed with a *poule* is a release of it."

Usually these students quit work around 22:00 hours and went to the beer halls, but not even there did they relax. They talked shop together and the mathematicians and physicists worked out equations on the backs of their beer mats and discussed them while they sipped their beer and nibbled their pretzels. After they went home, the waiters collected the beer mats on the chance that the equations were valuable and they could sell them.

A weird place a German university in those far-off days. As Conrad later admitted, "We lost our heads completely. We were sure that we were going to change the world. It was such a marvellous time for Science that it seemed certain that humanity at last might make a quantum-leap forward. The politicians, the generals, the old hierarchical orders who had made and lost the war were finished – *kaput*. A wonderful new world was dawning and we would be its creators and high priests."

The historians also called themselves scientists and they no more trusted the literary historians who reported the past than they trusted the newspapers that reported the present. What they wanted was hard evidence – documents, inscriptions, artefacts, the leavings in ancient tombs, chemical analyses of old coinages, papyri, lost alphabets. It was a great time for archaeology and Conrad twice joined digging expeditions in the old Middle East. The historians of this time were more interested in what had destroyed civilizations than in what had created them, apparently believing that if men could discover the mistakes of the past they could prevent politicians from repeating them in the future. When he was older, Conrad would admit that in his university years he became totally blind to the present.

This was a bad present for most of Europe and for Germany it was a terrible one. Not many students were like Conrad and his friends. They were young, they were frustrated, they were angry, and they wanted fast action. Some of them joined political and duelling clubs. Some of them drilled at night in the secret armies and many of them hated the new freedom. "Wir scheissen auf die Freiheit" (we shit on freedom)—this was one of their slogans. But Conrad and his scientific friends not only despised people like these, they ignored them.

When the time came for his doctoral thesis, he decided to base it on the papyri collections his grandfather had described to him. They had been found in the Sahara Desert west of the river Nile a few years before the First Great War. Though Conrad was to go far beyond this early work, he must have retained an affection for it because I myself heard him speak of it more than once. The only thing that interested me about those papyri was the story of how they were found. I liked the story so much that now I'm suspicious of it, but for what it's worth, here it is.

One day an English archaeologist was exploring the desert on a camel looking for signs of buried monuments when the camel stumbled on a protruding rock and he fell off the animal's back. When he got to his feet he noticed that the rock was marble, so he took his spade and dug around it and the top of an arch emerged from the sand. This could mean one of two things. Either it was the top of a solitary temple or under the sand were the ruins of a lost city.

A few years later a digging expedition came out from England and a city it turned out to be, a sizable one in ruins, and the rock on which the camel had stumbled was the pinnacle of the civic theater. The rest of the remains were what might have been expected: a stadium, public baths, some official buildings in partial ruin, the lines and even the names of a maze of streets. The only valuable discovery was made in the city dump. Here were dug out thousands of papyri accumulated over several centuries. They were covered with Greek writing in violet ink, many were torn or mutilated, but the dry sands of the desert had preserved the writing and most of them were legible enough to be read or restored by the same kind of ingenuity required by code-breakers in wartime. There were enough papyri to keep several platoons of scholars busy for more than seventy years.

When I was young this kind of material would have bored me to death, but now Conrad's description of it gives me an eerie feeling. Suppose André and his friends succeed in building a new city, how new will it really be? I won't live long enough to begin to answer that question, but certainly the resemblances between this vanished city and some cities I knew in my youth are embarrassingly close. It was a collection of ghettos. One district was a ghetto in the original meaning of the word, for it was known officially as "The Jewish Quarter." And sure enough, evidence turned up in the papyri that when things went sour the majority blamed the Jews for it and beat them up.

Studying Conrad's notes and trying to decipher the German of his thesis, I found myself reading about a community of perhaps a hundred thousand people living out their life-spans in their own little corner of a huge power structure which pretended to rule the known world. The papyri showed life as ordinary people have lived it in all ages – thousands of mortgages, bills of sale and purchase, inventories of small and big merchants, of stewards and managers, notices of sheriffs and auction sales, bills of lading for the flat-bottomed boats that took on cargo at the city docks and sailed down the canal to the Nile and then down the river to the great city at its mouth. Even beyond, sometimes; even as far as Naples. There were many personal letters, quick glimpses into obscure private lives, some poignant, some ridiculous. There were many edicts from the Central Bureaucracy in language even more pompous than we got from ours. And as time passed, there was a deluge of appeals for relief against tax collectors and the labor organizers of the Bureaucracy.

By the time I had worked my way through Conrad's monograph I had acquired a fellow feeling for these vanished folk. This was their little plot of earth and it had been good earth. What for more than fourteen subsequent centuries was an unmapped waste of drifting sand, in their time had been a prosperous farm country with thousands of hectares under cultivation, watered by inundations from the Nile fed into it by a complex system of irrigation canals. In its earlier years the city was prosperous. It had its own town council, its banks dealt in a reliable currency. It even had a social and athletic club and I was amused to discover that its membership was rigidly restricted. No Jew or lower-class person had a chance of getting into it.

If left to itself, this city might have prospered indefinitely, but of course it was not left to itself. About two centuries after the record began, the control of the Central Bureaucracy was up for grabs and between them the politicians and the military ruined the whole district. Just before the final collapse, the city's population reached its highest point and the people were proud of how big it was. The crowds swarming into the stadium broke all previous attendance records. Where did all this urban population come from? It could only have come from abandoned farms. Finally the currency collapsed and was worth nothing and soon afterwards the record ceased for an entire century.

When it resumed it revealed a new kind of world uncannily still. The town council had vanished and so had the middle class. The city's principal buildings were now filled with nuns and monks – some thirty thousand of them altogether. As for the farmland, all of it was now the personal property of a single family headed by a man who spent most of his time in the imperial capital and came home only to supervise his stewards, oversee his rent collectors, and exercise his race horses in the stadium. Conrad records this letter written by one of the boss-man's tenants:

"To Apion, my kind lord, lover of Christ and the poor, all-esteemed and most magnificent patrician and duke of the Thebaid, from Anoup your miserable slave on your estate called Phraka, I, your miserable slave, desire by this petition for mercy to bring to your lordship's attention that I serve my kind lord as my fathers and forefathers did and pay the taxes every year."

In a footnote to this document, Conrad wrote: "Man is a thinking animal, a talking animal, a tool-making animal, a building animal, a political animal, a fantasizing animal. But in the twilight of a civilization he is chiefly a taxpaying animal." When Conrad made a point, he always underlined it.

A few years after Anoup wrote this letter the record ceases entirely. The Arabs came in and destroyed the last remnant of the old Bureaucracy. Did they massacre the inhabitants? There is no proof that they did. Did the people simply give up the place and move somewhere else? Nobody knows that, either. All that is known for sure is that for nearly fourteen centuries the sands of the desert blew in steadily and buried the place. If the Englishman's camel had not stumbled on the pinnacle of the civic theatre nobody would have heard of its existence; not a word about the magnificent duke who was such a lover of

Christ and the poor, to say nothing of Anoup. What will André make of this little story, I wonder?

But for Conrad Dehmel his study of this lost city was the overture to the entire course of his future life. His monograph was given a first-class rating by his professors and after it was published it came to the notice of a famous historian who wrote him a letter of congratulation. This man was a Russian of vast learning who had emigrated to America to avoid being liquidated by the new bureaucracy that had taken over his own country. When Conrad wrote to thank him for his letter, he asked if he himself might go to America to study under him. The Russian offered a better prospect.

At that time the largest collection of papyri in the world was housed in London in a famous place called the British Museum and the man who had found the papyri was now the Professor of Papyrology in Oxford. The Russian arranged with this professor that Conrad should be granted a fellowship to study in London. He promised Conrad that if his work in England was successful, he would recommend him to a post in the Grosser Kurfürst Institut in Berlin. Anyone with a good post there was supposed to be set for the rest of his life.

In a time when the whole world was nearly broke and jobs were as scarce as snowballs in August, this would have been heady stuff for any ambitious young man and Conrad had become exceedingly ambitious. He noted in his diary that his entire life's work leaped before him in a kind of map. After the papyri and routine studies in Politics and Economics, he would concentrate for several years on the history of art. Then he would set out to complete what he called "My Grand Design." He would harmonize traditional History with the new findings in Psychology, Biology, and Anthropology and out of the mixture he would develop a new Moral Philosophy based on a combination of all these elements. Quoting an earlier German professor, he wrote in his diary: "I know where I stand now, but it may take the rest of my life to build the roads to take me there."

None of this will make any sense to André Gervais or anyone else of his age. It makes no sense to me, either. The Germans of that time were famous for their addiction to grandiose projects and the time would come when even Conrad would ask himself what real difference there is between the ambition of a man who sets out to conquer all the people in the world and that of the one who sets out to conquer all the knowledge in it.

The trouble with Conrad was that he had put so much of himself into his academic work that he knew hardly anything else. At twenty-five he was still a virgin. Now with a fine job and what looked like a sure future he could afford to marry and the time for marriage had come.

TWO

*E*VA SCHMIDT was the only daughter of a minor provincial industrialist. All I know of him is that he spoiled his daughter, suffered from chronic constipation, and went annually to the sulfur baths at Wiesbaden. Conrad had met Eva through one of her three brothers whom he knew in the university. There are no photographs of her, but Conrad later described her as a picture-postcard Germanic beauty with flaxen hair, a light skin, and the kind of figure they called *vollschlank*, which meant simultaneously buxom and slim. I knew a few German girls and one of them was great to know and another was very good, but they were of a much later generation. In Conrad's youth a German bourgeois girl was supposed to have no future outside marriage. Eva was twenty-four, her father reeked with money, and if Conrad had not been so engrossed with his books and documents it might have occurred to him that if nobody had wanted to marry Eva before, there must have been a good reason.

After a wedding much too expensive for his taste, they spent a two-weeks honeymoon in Paris before setting out for London. Conrad was reticent about his personal life and he has left me with only a few facts about his time with Eva. I assume that the honeymoon was a sexual disaster and that what followed in London was worse.

His working routine would have been pretty awful for any young wife even if she loved him, was intelligent, and had some inner resources of her own. Eva was invincibly stupid and sexually frustrated. In London Conrad worked eight hours a day in the Museum on those ancient papyri documents and in the evenings he read learned books connected with his work. He had assumed that Eva would keep herself busy seeing the London sights and learning English, but she had no interest in London and detested all the English people she met. She learned no more of their language than was necessary to do some elementary shopping.

This provincial heiress had grown up in a large house with servants and she thought it degraded her to have to live in a small flat in Bloomsbury. As she had never learned to cook, they ate most of their meals in cheap restaurants in Soho. It was even worse when it came to entertainments. Eva knew too little English to follow a play or a movie. Conrad loved classical music and she liked Viennese waltzes and second-rate jazz. After three orgasmless months, Eva discovered herself pregnant and the marriage collapsed. By this time she loathed Conrad and decided to escape from him. Without telling him she was pregnant, she left for home, spent a few days with her parents, and then went to Berlin for an abortion.

During the next two months Conrad wrote her a letter three times a week and she answered none of them. Finally he returned to Germany and found her just where he expected, at home with her family. There must have been some ugly scenes before he finally concluded that the only solution was divorce.

It was at this point that he discovered just what he had got himself into. Eva screamed at him that if he wanted a divorce he would have to pay for it. The price she named was more than he could afford, and she knew it. He had ruined her entire life, she said. No man would want her after what she had been through on account of him, and so on and so on.

I don't know what the German divorce laws were at this time and Conrad did not mention them in any of the material he left. Though he was a baptized Catholic he no longer belonged to any formal religion. Eva was probably a lapsed Lutheran, so religion was no impediment to divorce providing they both wished it. I would have guessed that he could have divorced her for desertion, but as the decision seems to have depended on her, I can only suppose that she had some legality on her side. Anyway, he went back to London.

I wish I could say that Eva Schmidt merely entered Conrad's life and left it, as a person may enter a hotel by the front door and go out by the back. Certainly he believed that this was what she had done and though he felt mortified and ill-used, he must have been relieved not to have her around any more. He never expected to see her again, but it did not turn out that way. Some years later they met each other in Germany, and in circumstances where she had all the advantages and he had none.

Conrad's experience with Eva, and much more his love for the next woman in his life, saved him while still young from turning into the intellectual dinosaur he was well on his way to becoming. I can say this for him, he was willing to learn from experience even though he never got over his compulsion to make big generalizations. Here is one of them:

"If History is the study of men in society, I can thank Eva Schmidt for teaching me something most historians ignore, namely that fifty percent of the human race is composed of females."

On the same page in the diary follows another notation that raised my eyebrows a little:

"It is reasonably certain that Henry VIII contracted syphilis when he was a young man and this could explain much that otherwise is mysterious. When young, Henry was amiable. Could not the megalomania and cruelty of his later years be explained by the fact that the disease in its third degree damaged his brain and made him paranoic? The beheading of his wives made him famous, but it was of minor historical importance compared to the megalomania that refused to accept the authority of the Pope. This led, of course, to the policy of aloofness from Europe and the establishment of the Church of England. Hence it follows that this unknown woman who shared her disease with Henry was an extremely important historical agent. What would the Archbishop of Canterbury say if it were proved that the Church of England would never have existed had it not been for a wandering spirochete?"

As this singular *pensée* followed his previous reference to Eva Schmidt, I toyed with the notion that Conrad himself might have picked up a dose from a London prostitute after she left him. But I don't really believe it. It was just another of the ways in which his over-complicated brain tended to work.

Now, before I continue, I must deal with an exasperating problem that has nagged me ever since I began this record. It concerns the dating.

As anyone old enough to remember will recall, the old dating system in which I grew up was abolished twenty-five years ago and replaced by the new one which took off from that particular year, which became our Year One. This was part of the Bureaucracy's plan to obliterate the past. It was tied in with their Diagram. They calculated that after enough time had elapsed, the Past would be reduced to such a jumble of legends, propaganda, and inaccurate memories that none of the younger people would be able to think about it even if they wished to, or blame the Bureaucracy for having cheated them. For a while this colossal fraud seemed to be working; it worked well enough to make me wonder whether I myself had really lived through what I had seen. Until I met André Gervais I thought they had got away with it. Now it seems they haven't.

Anyway, in our present system I am writing in the year 25. But as almost everything I write about happened during the old system, I will use the old system in my story and hope that any younger people who read it will at least be intrigued by the novelty.

I now resume in the year that used to be known officially as the nineteen-hundred-and-thirty-fourth year of Our Lord. André knows who Our Lord was because I lent him my Bible and he was fascinated by the Four Gospels. That Jesus Christ had lived more than two thousand years ago was something he could not grasp because he had never had the chance to understand time and its passage. The name of Christ he had always known. Everyone knows it and uses it, for it has survived as a swear word. If any of my readers are curious, all they have to do is to change the date 1934 to what in derision I call 80 BTB; that is, eighty years before this Third Bureaucracy abolished the old system.

THREE

ONE DANK AUTUMN NIGHT after Eva left him, Conrad Dehmel went to a concert in a famous London auditorium which a few years later was destroyed by bombs dropped from German aircraft. During the first movement of Beethoven's Seventh Symphony he sat immersed in the music, his eyes closed, his chin resting on the heel of his hand. When the first movement ended and he opened his eyes, they came to rest on a young woman in the cello section. All through the allegretto which followed his eyes never left her.

By this time Conrad had made a variety of friends in London. Some of them were English, but his closest friends were Germans and Austrians who had come to London to escape the bureaucracies in their own countries. A few of these were musicians. Three weeks after the concert he met this young cellist at a Sunday supper party given in honor of an exiled Austrian pianist who had been playing in London. Eva Schmidt had made Conrad cautious of women, but by nature he seems to have been a romantic and I certainly know that when his emotions were aroused he was the least cautious of men. He fell in love with Hanna Erlich and it was the real thing.

I can envy him. For though I have made love to more women than I can remember, and to some whose faces and bodies I remember but whose names I have forgotten, though I was very fond of Valerie and truly loved Joanne, I never *fell* in love in my entire life. No salmon ever sang in the streets for me because of any girl I knew; no sky ever blazed with Perseids. A psychiatrist once congratulated me for this, calling me a realist free of illusions. He was a fool. Even before I was thirty I understood that this was the price I had paid for becoming promiscuous at fourteen with girls as promiscuous as myself.

Like most Germans and Japanese, Conrad was a camera buff and I have more than forty small photos of Hanna Erlich. In most of these pictures she has a happy expression, in some a piquant and enquiring smile, in a few others a deep reflectiveness suggesting the sadness of a civilized person at the end of her civilization but still refusing to believe it. Her brows slant up delicately into a wide forehead. Her nose is too slim and aristocratic to have been a thoroughly satisfactory organ, for it pinched her antrums and she often suffered from sinus headaches. Conrad said she seemed tall because she carried herself well, but when I examined a picture of the two of them standing together I noted that the crown of her head was no higher than the lobe of his ear and he was not an especially tall man. In her teens she had studied ballet and she moved with a grace and litheness that were a revelation to him after the clumsy stiffness of Eva Schmidt. He said that her voice was a rich contralto with a throb in it. Though she was only twenty-five years old, her hair was a rich silver shot through with darker tracings like the pure old silver that does not reflect the light but absorbs it. If I had ever met a woman like her when I was young I would have been wild for her, but by now you probably know me well enough to understand that I'd never have had a chance with her.

Hanna's family was a part of the mosaic of old Europe that even in my youth was still a legend. The Erlichs were entwined with a long European experience going back into the past for centuries. My continent, the democratic continent, never had known anything comparable.

Hanna's paternal grandfather had been born a Conservative Jew, but he became agnostic and all but two of his grandchildren married gentiles. The old man took ironic pleasure in reminding his Jewish brethren that he was much more a typical Jew than they were: "If every one of Father Abraham's descendants had married only Jews, there'd be more of us in the world today than Chinese." Yet all the Erlichs were proud of their Jewish genes and traced their lineage back to the aristocratic family that had emigrated from Spain centuries earlier to escape being burned alive by the Christians.

The first of Hanna's purely Jewish ancestors to become German was the descendant of one of these refugees from Spain. He was a Polish citizen and held the chair of Chemistry in a famous Polish university. A Prussian king invited him to settle and teach Chemistry in Berlin, and from this time onward the Erlichs were integrated into the Teutonic core of old Europe. All of them prospered and some of them became distinguished.

Hanna's father was a doctor who had served as a surgeon in the First Great War and this changed the course of the rest of his life. The physical mutilations had been horrifying enough, but what seemed far worse to Dr. Erlich was the state of mind which had brought on the war in the first place. Even before 1914 he had been interested in the teachings of Sigmund Freud and had audited some of his lectures in Vienna. Now he returned to Vienna and became Freud's pupil for several years. The name of Freud can mean nothing to André Gervais, as I found out when I tried to describe him to André as a "mind doctor." Dr. Erlich finally left Freud because he could not accept Freud's insistence that the main cause of aggression is sexual. He went to Berlin and practised psychiatry on his own.

The Erlichs were a far more stimulating family than any I ever knew. They loved to argue and discuss with each other and they had much to argue and talk about because they were involved in most of the important areas of Central European life in the last years of its glory. Hanna's Uncle Karl had married into an old Swiss family, had become a Swiss citizen, and was the director of a large bank in Zurich. A great-uncle had for a time been Minister of Finance in Austria, an older cousin was a physician and professor of Medicine in Cologne, and her father's oldest brother, a senior partner in one of the great German shipping companies, made his home in Hamburg. His youngest brother, Hanna's Uncle Helmuth, was a professional soldier. During the war he had reached the rank of full colonel, had won several decorations for valor, and now was a major-general in the small but exceedingly efficient army of the young German Republic.

Every Christmas the families reunited, entertaining and being entertained in rotation in each other's homes. Much music was played and after the women had gone to bed the men relaxed with their cigars and *kirsch* and argued about everything that interested them. Each was a proved professional in his field, but all assumed that the ultimately important things were art, science, music, and literature, and they agreed that with the exception of science, none of these should be confined to national borders even in wartime. They had intimate friends in five different countries and all of them were fluent in at least three languages. The major-general spoke five, including Russian.

As I think I have indicated, Conrad was a pretty conventional young man at this stage of his life, but coming from a family like the Erlichs, Hanna had been living on a different plane from his. She was the first truly modern woman Conrad had ever met, and in a time and country where most women were systematically kept down, she was an astonishment to him. She was even more disciplined than he was, but she had no sexual hang-ups whatever. She was never promiscuous and would have felt contempt for the way my sister and I lived when we were young. Just when she and Conrad became lovers I don't know, but it was probably a month or so after they first met. Soon he was asking her to marry him. His work was going so well that his post at the Institut in Berlin seemed reasonably certain and then he would have enough money to buy off Eva Schmidt. But Hanna would not consider marriage and refused for a reason that Conrad, incredibly, refused to take seriously.

For Hanna knew, as Conrad's ambition and concentration on his work had blocked him from knowing, that huge events and appalling personalities were poised to intervene in the personal lives of every living soul in Europe. Love as Conrad understood it meant permanence. Love as Hanna understood it in that particular time meant love in impermanence.

It is bizarre for me to have to think of Hitler again. So many books were written about him that some of them must still be around. Even André has heard his name, though it means no more to him than Attila or Torquemada meant to me when I was André's age. My parents' generation never tired of talking about him and his war and they bored most of us to death. But when political troubles began in my own country when I was still a boy, I knew that Uncle Conrad was much more worried than most of our own people were. I remember hearing him say to Mother, "The tragedy was that hardly any of us took Hitler seriously until it was too late. I should know, for I was just as blind as the others."

But there was one person in this story who took Hitler seriously even before he gained power and this was Hanna's father. When she was spending Christmas with her family, and all the relations were there as usual, Dr. Erlich asked her one evening after dinner to come into the library with him.

He asked her what people in England thought of Hitler and she said they didn't take him seriously. He asked what she herself thought of him and she said she had thought very little about him. Hanna and her father were exceptionally close, so close that her mother may have resented it. When she absorbed the expression on his face she felt frightened.

"What I'm seeing, Hanna, is something only one other person I know is seeing. What I'm seeing is something unthinkably terrible. This man is soon going to become this country's dictator."

She looked at him incredulously. He nodded and went on. "There's a limit to what the human mind can stand. Too many calamities have happened too fast. The war was lost. The Treaty was terrible. The middle classes lost all their savings in the inflation. Still the people held together, and two years ago most of them were working. Then pouf – inside a few months everything fell apart and now there are at least seven million Germans out of work."

"But it's the same everywhere else. Look at England. Even America."

"That doesn't make it the same. England is an old nation, but Germany has never been sure of herself as a nation. She's falling back onto what she always was – a collection of tribes. America? If an American is out of work he may feel guilty. He certainly will feel angry. But a German out of work feels sick in his mind."

A silence fell between them and finally the doctor said, "If I were to tell you that the neurotic symptoms of a large number of my patients are becoming alarmingly similar to Hitler's, would that seem important to you?"

She looked at the sadness in his face and nodded, "Yes, it would. If you said it."

"You see, this republic of ours never grew out of the people. It was imposed on them by victors who have totally discredited themselves. Now it's falling apart." He paused, looked away, and said very quietly, "Germany is on the verge of a mass psychosis and Hitler is going to be its catalyst."

She still could not really believe him. She said what most people were saying, "But this little man, he's been nobody all his life."

"That's just it, Hanna. Most people in Germany have been made to feel like nobodies. The young believe that nobody wants them. But Hitler wants them and he will find them. He's probably found enough of them already."

How can I describe this man Hitler to André and his friends? A squat figure, an unsavory face, a ridiculous moustache, short legs, a backside shaped like a basket, a raucous, uncouth voice—I read somewhere that he had only a single testicle.

Hanna asked what her soldier-uncle thought of Hitler and her father smiled wearily.

"Your Uncle Helmuth is a civilized man. Unfortunately, civilized men will be the last to recognize what I've been seeing. He tells me the Officers' Corps is now the best since Gneisenau and I'd take his professional opinion that it is. No wonder I've not been sleeping well. There's only one man I know among the officers who sees what I'm seeing. You've met him. He's often been at our house. You've played chamber music with him."

"Admiral Canaris? Does *he* agree with what you're telling me?"

"But Wilhelm is alone." He pointed his pipe at her. "I ask you never to mention—not to anyone—never mention anything I may ever tell you in private about Wilhelm Canaris. Yes, indeed he's alone. The rest of our officers are the most professionally professional men in the whole of Europe. They have no idea how isolated and arrogant they are. All but a few of them despise Hitler, but he sees through them like plate glass. When he gets power—and I say *when*, not *if*—the first thing he will demand is a huge army. Can you imagine any professional soldier objecting to that? It would not be unpleasant to your Uncle Helmuth if he were promoted to lieutenant-general and commanded a corps. They'll all be promoted. All the sergeants will become lieutenants, all the lieutenants will become majors, and so on."

She sat silent for nearly a minute; they both sat silent.

Then Hanna said, "I suppose Uncle Helmuth thinks the army will be able to use him and then control him."

"He hasn't told me that."

"But he thinks it?"

"Probably. But I tell you, the army won't have a chance with him. Those generals follow the rule-book, but Hitler talks directly to the volcano underneath the rules. Nothing in their experience has prepared them for a man like this. When has anyone in this country known how to strike straight through the rules to what lies underneath them? It's as clear as daylight to me what has happened to this man. When he gets power he will make it happen to the whole country."

"But what *has* happened to him? To me he's just a crazy little man who talks nonsense. What *has* happened to him?"

"I wonder if even you will believe me. A total inversion of his original character – that's what has happened to him. I've seen it in a few patients – generally they were criminals. None of them had abilities but this man has incredible abilities. Let me put it to you like this.

"Using our ghastly professional jargon, let's start with the preposterous German authoritarian superego that demands more of people than any individual can fulfill. You know it yourself. The soldier who is supposed to be incapable of fear because he's a German. The philosopher who is never satisfied to understand a few things perfectly but must set out to understand everything in creation. The planner who is expected – and who expects himself – to foresee every possible difficulty before it occurs. One could go on and on." He paused. "In Hitler, this impossibly tyrannic superego has combined with a particularly ferocious and cruel id to crush out his original ego as though it had been caught between a hammer and an anvil. Adolf Hitler the little corporal? Adolf Hitler the dreamer and failed artist? This man has literally ceased to exist and an entirely different man has been born."

Hanna listened in silence and when her father stopped talking neither of them spoke for nearly a minute.

Finally she said, "So he's insane – is that what you're telling me?"

"Psychotic certainly, but so far his psychosis is under control. It's working for him. It's what gives him his incredible self-confidence. He has a perfect eye for everyone's weakness – especially for the weaknesses of the powerful."

The doctor went on to say that he took another war for granted and that it would not be pleasant to have to pray that his country would lose it.

"For when he comes to power he will be absolute, and he will act with such speed that nobody will believe it. But Hanna, there's something else and it's why I beg you to return to England and stay there."

Then he began talking about Hitler's obsession with the Jews and he asked her to remember that in Hitler's eyes the long service of their family would mean nothing whatever.

"I'm one-half Jewish and you're one-quarter Jewish, but in Hitler's country we will all be Jews whether we've practised the religion or not."

He talked to her for nearly an hour more. Finally she asked him if he himself intended to emigrate and practise in another country.

"Your mother wants me to leave, but not even she believes what I believe. As she has no Jewish blood – as Hitler would put it – she'd be safe enough. At least for a while. At my age I feel it would be professionally dishonorable for a psychiatrist to walk away at the moment when a psychotic is about to become his country's ruler. But you're too young, Hanna. You could do nothing here. Your whole life is before you and you have a duty to that."

When Hanna returned to England her father's warning seemed unreal. The English had far too many troubles of their own to worry about Adolf Hitler. Only five weeks after Hanna had left her father, Hitler not only gained power, but gained it legally. There must have been some people in England who were concerned, but Hanna never met any. Just as her father had predicted, he acted with lightning speed. He drove the communists underground and soon he would destroy them. He began to get the unemployed off the streets and back to work. Knowing that no other nation would agree, he even proposed universal disarmament. As for his attitude to Jews, most foreigners and even many Germans refused to take it seriously.

Now I come to Conrad. He had certainly known about Hitler and the Nazis but had thought of them as a bunch of ignorant crackpots. Like nearly everyone else, he refused to believe they were serious about the Jews. When Hanna tried to warn him, he reminded her that Jews were in control of many of the key positions in universities, hospitals, and the law. This had caused inevitable resentment, he said. It had caused resentment in Austria for years. But – as my generation would have put it – what was new in that?

Hanna gave up arguing with him and suggested that he write to his father. He did so, asking him specifically if Hitler really meant what he was saying against the Jews. He got an instant reply warning him never to ask such questions again, never to utter any kind of criticism against a leader who was Germany's savior.

A letter like this would have told the mature Conrad all he needed to know, but Conrad was not mature then. As Dr. Erlich had said to Hanna, trained men of reason are the last to recognize the bared teeth of the human ape when it appears before them. Half a century later, when I was young, it was the same story all over again.

Matters came to a head between Conrad and Hanna in the summer of that same year. He had finally published the results of his long researches and within his narrow speciality they had been well received. The famous Russian scholar wrote him a letter of praise. He also wrote to the Director of the Grosser Kurfürst Institut in Berlin, and in August of that year Conrad received a letter informing him that a post on its staff was his for the asking.

Now for the first time in his life Conrad could look forward to financial security and even to a modest fame. Having finished his work with the papyri, he was ready to enter the world of Renaissance art. Full of joy and deeply in love, seeing his Grand Design developing just as he had planned it, he asked Hanna to dine with him in celebration. This time it would not be Soho and a carafon of Chianti, it would be the Savoy and champagne.

It was not until dinner was over that the roof fell in on his head. He was sitting relaxed sipping Turkish coffee, looking at Hanna and feeling like a sailor who had finally come to harbor after a long and dangerous voyage. Then he realized that Hanna had been silent during the whole evening and that her eyes across the table were remote and on her face was an expression of withdrawal he had never seen before. His euphoria began to evaporate. He reached across the table and closed his hand over hers, but there was no responding pressure.

"Hanna darling, what's the matter?"

She looked back at him and said, "I'm so proud of you. I'm so happy for you."

Then she looked away and he felt a chill.

"There seems to be something I don't understand," he said.

"Yes," she said in a small voice. He saw her make a compulsive movement, take a handkerchief out of her bag, and wipe her eyes.

"Is it something I've done? Is it something I've said?"

She shook her head violently, "No!"

"Then what is it? Has something happened at home? Are your parents all right?"

She turned to him in a surge of grief. "I should have insisted on making you understand long ago. I tried in so many ways but you never heard me. Don't think I blame you. Don't think that, please don't. I was so happy and happiness is going to become so rare. I've had such happiness with you I'll remember it for what's left of my life."

He stared at her in total incomprehension. "For what's left of your life! What is it you're trying to tell me?"

"What I've been trying to tell you for so long and you couldn't listen. I didn't say *wouldn't*. I said *couldn't*. Oh my God, but I understand you. Yes, I do. Nearly everyone in Europe is like you, but to accept what I accept – they can't."

He was hurt, bewildered. "I seem to have lost you."

"It's me who has lost you." She was panting with emotion. "Haven't I told you, dear – haven't I told you I can never go back to Germany the way things are now? Haven't I asked you to try to find a post in America?" She bowed her head, put her face in her hands, and said, "No, all that I said isn't true. I only wished you to do it for your own sake. I wouldn't have gone to America with you, either."

"Hanna!" He was shocked. He thought something had happened to her mind and he had always assumed that she was more mature than himself. "Hanna, you've either told me too much or you've told me too little."

"Can't you for once let me be a woman? Can't you?"

Later in his diary Conrad wrote that his intuitions knew exactly what she was trying to tell him but that he could not accept it. For if he did accept it, what would become of the ambitions of more than ten years, ambitions much deeper than a mere post in a famous institute? He was barely able to realize that the true reason for his relentless work had been a drive to release himself from his father without making his father despise him.

Hanna said, "You'd set your heart on it. It was to be your liberation. Now you've got it."

He exploded into the usual rationalizations of nearly everyone at the time, including the most hard-boiled statesmen in the world. He stopped talking when he saw the expression on her face.

"What does your Uncle Helmuth think?" he said.

"I don't know what he thinks now. A year ago he thought exactly as you told me your father thinks."

"Aren't both of them in a better position to know than you or I?"

She smiled desperately. "Of all the heroines of antiquity, the one I've most pitied was Cassandra. I'm not calling myself a Cassandra. I'm calling my father one. Uncle Helmuth? I'd take his opinion on music and rose-growing and even on soldiering if he ever mentioned that – which he never has to me."

He sat silently and she watched his face.

Quietly she said, "What about the Jews, Conrad?"

He winced. There was nothing to answer to that question now. She pushed back her chair and rose.

"Let's go outside into the air while it's still light," she said.

Holding hands they strolled down to the Thames Embankment in the twilight of a summer evening, sensing the majesty of the grand old city that most people still thought of as the capital of the world.

"I'll be sorry to leave London," he said.

"I'll be even sorrier to see you go. I'll be very sad to see you go."

His nerves tightened again. "I'm shaken. I thought I understood you."

She pressed his hand. "And so you have! Understood me as I never dared hope I'd be understood by any man. Body and soul when we've loved you've understood me."

They leaned in silence against the parapet, their arms about each other's waists, he feeling her hip's curve through the light dress she was wearing, she knowing that the beauty he had discovered in her own body had become sacred to this man. They watched the lights on the moving water and their gaze followed a late excursion boat passing downriver toward Greenwich.

"The tide is going out," she said.

"Do you mean that symbolically?"

"I was just looking at it. It's drawing out fast."

He remembered his grandfather's words about the gods leaving Troy and again was aware of the pressure of her hand on his own.

"Please don't be offended, Conrad. You're a scholar and I'm only a musician, but when I was in the university I used to hear professors and students talking about history just as I've heard you talk about it. For me, it's made by men, and I'm afraid professors seldom meet the kind of men who make it. I've met a few. My father and my uncles have met many. But none of them has met a man like the one who's making history in Germany now. I suppose you know his police have you in their files?"

"Why should they bother about me?"

"Oh, Conrad, where have you been living?"

He stared bleakly at the river and the lights coming on in the city. Recalling the evening a few months later, he was to write that he knew that what she was telling him was the truth, but he knew it only in the way that a man knows that one day he is going to die.

Hanna was talking again. She was telling him some of what her father had told her, that Hitler's psychosis was still under control and that it would remain so just as long as he was successful, as long as he received the echo from the people that he was the genius he felt himself to be.

Conrad almost exploded. "Him a genius! You tell me your father believes that?"

She gave up. She knew how it had been with him and so many others for a long time, that the word "genius" was sacred and applied only to men like Goethe and Beethoven.

They found an empty bench and watched the lights grow brighter as the last glimmer of twilight vanished into a moonless night. They sat there and listened to London, to the sonorous rumble of London as I myself would listen to it nearly two generations later with Valerie and in that very place. With Valerie who now was dead, along with much of London itself. What a marvellous name for a city was London! Rolling, deep-toned, fuller in sound than Roma and almost as heavy with experience.

Conrad began talking. "Do you remember that man from Munich we met last year, the one who'd been in New York? How he said that he resented New York because it made him feel like nothing, but that when London gave him the same feeling he couldn't resent it?"

He drew her closer, turned her head to his own, kissed her, and felt the warmth of her breast.

"No darling, in spite of what your father says and with all respect to him, Hitler won't be able to get away with it. I know our generals are political children and our admirals aren't even that, but even if they can't control him, there are others who can and will. The French have been stupid and malicious about Germany, but they'll certainly know how to look after themselves. And finally there's England. There's London. It's still the capital of the world."

"Have you ever lived in France?" she asked quietly.

"Only for a fortnight with Eva."

"I've spent a year and a half in Paris and I tell you the French will do nothing but quarrel among themselves. As for England, she seems tired to me, but perhaps she's only confused. My Uncle Helmuth, by the way, has the greatest respect for England. As he puts it, she still has one more good war in her. He also thinks – or thought – that for this reason Hitler won't provoke her."

He touched her cheek and found it moist with tears. "Hanna dear – why do you cry?"

"I'm sorry, Conrad. I'm terribly sorry but I can't –" she choked back a sob and said, "It's going to be an awful time we'll have to live in. It's a terrible time to have fallen in love, and I have! I have! The millions of people who are falling in love all over Europe and don't know what I know! I envy them because they don't know." She straightened, her voice steadied, and she looked out over the river. "Who signed this letter you got from the Institut?"

"The chairman of the board."

"Had you ever heard of his name before?"

Startled, he asked why she had asked such a question. She repeated it.

"No, I never heard of him, but board chairmen come and go. He's somebody appointed by the government. The Grosser Kurfürst has always been a state institution."

"So Professor Rosenthal didn't sign the letter?"

"Why should he have signed it? It wasn't in his province."

"Do you really believe your Professor Rosenthal will keep his directorship much longer?"

With this she reached him hard, for Erwin Rosenthal was the man under whom Conrad had intended to work in Berlin. He was the world's greatest living art historian. He was also a Jew. Conrad protested to her.

"The very fact that Rosenthal is still there proves that the situation isn't so bad as you think."

She rose to her feet. "Then go, Conrad, for you'll never believe me till you see for yourself. You have decided to go home. Your life is yours, as I've often told you. So go home and see for yourself."

He was so disappointed that his mind felt bruised by her words. Later he would record that when he heard her say this it was as though she had planted a time-bomb in the foundations of his life.

"Hanna, is this your way of telling me you'll never go home?"

"For my father and brother and sister I will go home if they need me. I've begged all of them but my father to leave. I understand why he's decided to stay. He tells me that Mother would be in no immediate danger because in Mother there's no Jewish blood – as these crazy barbarians would put it."

Again he was astonished. "But none of you have been Jewish for a century!"

"We've never denied our Jewish ancestors. Why should we? Incidentally, it would do us no good if we did."

"Hanna – this anti-Jewish talk of his, it's only propaganda. It's been going on in Europe for centuries. Propaganda, that's all."

"Indeed it is," she said softly, "and horribly successful propaganda. How many Christians like Jews as Jews? Individual Jews – often. But Jews as Jews? How many Jews like gentiles as gentiles? Individual gentiles, often." She paused and said, "Look at me, Conrad!"

He looked at her.

"Just why did you – you yourself – think it important to mention that my family had not been Jewish for a century?"

He could not answer this because he could not deny what her question meant. She put her hand on his wrist and continued.

"It's far more than that, of course. Far worse. Not even the Jews in Germany can bring themselves to believe what's going to happen to them. It's too incredible to believe it. My father is certain that Hitler's obsession with the Jews is the key to his psychosis. He thinks it's the one thing about which he's entirely sincere."

"So you're telling me he's mad?"

"What is 'mad'? A word."

"Well, if he's insane, how has he been able to do what he's done? Seventy million Germans aren't insane."

"Neither are the frock-coated Victorian gentlemen who run the French and British governments. They're saying just what you're saying. He can't be insane because look what he's doing. He can't be insane because he's pulled a great nation out of despair and he's getting the people back to work. And of course they don't want to discourage him because he's cleaning the communists out, and with the communists destroyed, their investments will be safe."

There was a long silence between them. London rumbled reassuringly around them. He felt tears in his eyes.

"But what of us, Hanna? What of us?"

"I will marry you if you can get rid of Eva. But I won't live in Germany with you and I won't even think of marrying you until you've gone home and seen for yourself. If I talked you into abandoning your ambition you'd resent me for the rest of your life."

"I'd never do that."

"You're human, Conrad. Indeed you'd resent me if that's what you thought had happened. So go home, Conrad. Go home and make up your own mind after you've seen it there."

That summer the weather was hot over most of Europe and before Conrad left England they spent a week together on the Channel shore of the Isle of Wight in a small cottage lent them by one of Eva's friends. The south coast of England swarmed with holiday-makers but they had a small private beach to themselves. The transatlantic liners of the time passed close to the shore on their way in and out of Southampton and one night a huge one hove into view. High on her masthead shone the lights of an enormous swastika and they both knew what that ship was. She was the swiftest vessel on the oceans and she was calling at Southampton on her return voyage from New York.

In Conrad's diary of that week, the last peaceful one he was ever to spend with Hanna, occurred this single line: "We made love every day and all the goodness of life was in it."

The week ended, they returned to London, he packed his bags, packed his books into massive wooden boxes and nailed down the covers on their tops. Hanna went down to the station to see him off on the boat train. When the train started he leaned out the window of his compartment waving to her. The sun streamed through the open cleft in the station roof making a partial rainbow in the smoke and steam. It fell on her silver hair and as the train gathered speed he watched her grow tiny, but he still could see the little flicker of white from the handkerchief she was waving to him.

FOUR

*T*HE SHIP THAT TOOK CONRAD HOME was another German liner making Southampton its port of call *en route* from New York. He had not been aboard more than an hour before he felt the tension.

There were passengers returning after many years in the Americas to serve the new Germany. He saw a group of arrogant, loud young men, some of them with Latin features, who had been born in Argentina and were coming to Germany to enlist in the Nazi army. They all wore swastikas in their buttonholes. At dinner that night Conrad's waiter informed him that he was hoping to rejoin the navy, that he had served in the last war and had been in one of the battle cruisers at the Skaggerak. Noting Conrad's name on his placecard, he said, "Herr Doktor, our chief gunnery officer had the same name as yours." He named the ship.

"He was my father," Conrad said.

"Korvettenkapitän Dehmel ist Ihr Vater! Wie geht es ihm? He was the best gunnery officer in the fleet. Nobody who was not there could know how good he was."

The waiter stood very erect when he took the order, and the others at the table looked at Conrad with respect.

Afterwards, strolling through the ship, Conrad noticed an elderly Jewish couple huddled in a corner and wondered why they were going to Germany. Their faces were expressionless but they seemed afraid. He crossed to where they were sitting, bowed, and invited them to a cognac. The old man seemed grateful.

"You are very kind. For myself, I will take only soda water, but for my wife a small *kirsch* would be good. Indeed you are kind and I would like you to let me pay. The waiter refused to serve me."

Conrad looked over his shoulder, beckoned to the waiter, who came over grudgingly.

"A *kirsch* for the lady, a soda water for the gentleman, and a cognac for me."

The waiter hesitated. Conrad stared at him and said, "I have given you my order."

He turned back to the old couple.

"I am a professor of History," he said. "Or should I say, I am about to become one. Do I intrude?"

"You are very kind, Herr Doktor."

An uneasy silence followed and finally Conrad broke it. "Have you been long in America?"

"Two years," the old lady said. "We have a son there."

"I have not been in Germany for quite a long time, but I read the newspapers. I am curious why you should be returning?"

The old man shrugged. "It is necessary for business reasons. Also, two of our sons and our daughter and our grandchildren are there."

The waiter came with the drinks, set them down with a truculent air, and Conrad paid him.

"If I need you again," he said to the waiter, "I will call you."

Turning to the elderly couple he said, "I am not a Nazi and you may talk freely. I am engaged to a German-Jewish girl who is now in England."

"It is better that you should not become conspicuous by talking with us," the woman said.

He realized that she meant it; realized also that his sitting there made *them* conspicuous, so after downing his cognac he rose, said good night, and went out on deck.

The ship was now steaming in the twilight through the Straits, England hazy to the north, France a little clearer to the south, and as they passed the lights of Calais, Conrad saw a passenger spit in the direction of France.

He paced the deck until darkness fell, saw the lights flickering from many other ships, and smiled ruefully as he remembered that this very expanse of water had not so long ago been known in England as "the German ocean." As they steered deeper into the North Sea a wind rose and the ship began to heave violently in the shallow waters. He went down to his cabin and heard somebody vomiting in the stateroom next to his own and though he was not seasick himself it was long past midnight before he finally fell asleep.

The next day they were in the Bight and the sea was calm again and the only white water he saw was the foam of quick swells breaking against the rock of Heligoland. Soon afterwards his short voyage ended at Cuxhaven with the band playing "Deutschland, Deutschland über Alles" and several hundred passengers standing at attention while they roared out the chorus of the Teutonic hymn. Then they jostled each other against the railing, waving down at a sea of relatives who were waving back from the dock.

It took him more than two hours to clear customs and immigration. There must have been a hundred expressionless men in black uniforms and helmets and he wondered what would be the fate of the Jewish couple he had spoken to the day before. Probably nothing more than rudeness and harassing delays. When his own turn came the immigration official greeted him cordially.

"Congratulations, Herr Doktor, on coming home. Germany needs men like you."

Customs took longer and his trunks and boxes of books were searched carefully. Then the tops of the packing cases containing the books were smartly nailed back into place and he was through. But still more time had to be spent putting the trunks and packing cases into storage until he could find an address in Berlin to which they could be sent.

By the time the boat train reached Hamburg it was late in the afternoon and when he came out of the station carrying his two suitcases he saw the streets filled with burly men in brown shirts and breeches. There had been a big Nazi rally that day and it had just broken up. Banners were stretched across the streets from lamppost to lamppost bearing political slogans in huge gothic letters. Pictures of Hitler stared like ikons out of the shop windows. Sitting in a taxi on his way to a hotel he thought there must be great fear in the city because only a few years ago Hamburg had been the chief communist stronghold in Germany. He registered in the hotel and after dinner he walked for an hour without seeing anything important.

The next afternoon the train that took him to Berlin had three cars packed with soldiers, strong young men in the old field-gray. They were having a happy time, their faces were flushed, and their singing was like thunder. He reached Berlin just before sunset, registered in a small hotel in a side street, and after dinner again went out to walk the streets. He did not wish to go to his parents' until he had sensed the atmosphere by himself.

The last time he had been in Berlin the city was a mirror of despair. There were many beggars and in Germany begging was the ultimate disgrace. But it was not these he had noticed, it was the prostitutes. Swarms of them along the sidewalks of the Friedrichstrasse, females on one side of the street and young males on the other with painted lips and mascaraed eyes. On that evening he had been walking with a student friend who was an economist and his friend had remarked that the surest test of a nation's economic condition was the price of a whore. He spoke to one of the girls and asked her price.

"Four marks," she had replied.

Now there was not a whore in sight and he wondered where they were. He passed a cabaret that seemed vaguely familiar and on an impulse he turned back and went up the stairs to see what it was like now. There wasn't much to see: a few middle-aged men sipping drinks and talking little, three entertainers idle in front of their instruments on a tiny stage in a corner, some semi-private booths called *séparés* where men could take girls for two marks and they could rub one another. Tonight the booths were empty but there were three hard-faced blondes at the bar who seemed to be waiting for customers.

He sat down at a table and ordered a beer. The girls at the bar turned around on their stools and one of them beckoned him to join them. He paid no attention and after a few minutes the biggest blonde came over, planted herself on a chair at his table, and asked if he was alone.

"Do you see anyone else with me?" he said.

"It's still early. The show hasn't begun yet. If you stay till eleven o'clock you can see us all naked. *Lebende Bilder*. In public we're not allowed to move our hips. We stand like statues. But you should see how we can move in private. Will you stay till midnight?"

"No."

She shrugged. "I can get off for a little while so long as I'm back here before eleven o'clock. I have a place near here. Why don't you come? I can give you a good time."

She named her price and said she was very good because he could see for himself she was a big girl and a lot of woman. She said she was unusual because she could adjust herself to all sizes. Not many girls could do that, but she had always been able to do it. It came naturally to her because she liked it so much. She would do anything he wanted but for some of the things the price would naturally be higher.

A waiter had come over and was standing by the table and he asked him to bring the girl a beer. The man came back with an opened bottle of bad champagne, filled two glasses, and put the bottle in an ice bucket on the table between them.

"I ordered a beer," Conrad said.

The waiter smiled. "But this is a lady. She drinks only champagne."

"So that's how it is. All right, how much?"

He named the price; Conrad paid him and noted that the markup was only a hundred percent. In a place like this he had expected it to be more. Business must be bad, and looking about at the nearly empty cabaret, he guessed that it was very bad. He asked the girl where she came from and she said from Breslau.

"You're English, aren't you?" she said next.

"Why do you think that?"

"I can always tell an Englishman. An Englishman's clothes are always so chic. We like Englishmen here. How do you speak such good German? If it wasn't for your clothes I'd have thought you were a born German."

"I made my studies at a German university."

A small-time political informer, of course. What revolution no matter how noble had ever neglected to enlist the whores? He left her with the champagne and walked for another half-hour. Berlin was hard and naked under a full moon and there were few people on the streets near his hotel. Suddenly he heard loud voices and just ahead of him some big men in brown shirts and breeches were erupting onto the sidewalk from an underground rathskeller. They were all in early middle age, thick through the chest and hips, and the bellies of three of them bulged out over their belts. He smelled stale beer and they stared at him with stupid and automatic hostility as he passed. The original wave of the movement, he thought, the first of the bully boys, the beefsteaks brown outside and red inside. Suddenly he was seeing history instead of reading about it. Smelling it, too. Unseen behind these goons would be the young ones coming up, lean, hard, cold, and trained.

The hotel lobby was empty except for the night porter. Conrad said good night and asked for his key. Only then did he notice behind the desk a colored photograph of the Leader and under it was printed a jingle:

> *Trittst du als Deutscher hier hinein*
> *Soll stets dein Gruss Heil Hitler sein.*

The porter was bigger than any one of the Brown Shirts he had passed on his way here: a brutal body, an ex-bouncer for sure, in the last war probably a corporal and now a *Blockwart*. He must have weighed at least 110 kilograms and Conrad took in the beetling eyebrows, the thick-fleshed face creased into a permanent scowl, the square moustache, the shaven head the color of cement with a few veins showing living between the skin and the bone. A single spike of pepper-and-salt hair jutted up from his scalp just over the center of the forehead. With the key in his hand he stared at Conrad.

"Heil Hitler!" he barked.

"Danke, gute Nacht."

The porter's mouth opened so wide that Conrad saw its red roof. His thick thumb jerked backwards over his shoulder in the direction of the Leader's picture and he bellowed, "Heil Hitler!"

Conrad looked back at him levelly, but he felt the fear of the civilized man in the presence of the barbarian. Before Hitler had taken charge, it would have been inconceivable that a man like this porter could have talked like this to a gentleman. But Conrad was also his father's son. I, who had no father I ever knew, could I ever have responded to a man like this as he did?

"You will speak to me properly," Conrad said.

The porter stared at him.

"You are insolent," Conrad said. "I have just returned from London. I have not been in Germany for a long time. What's the matter with you?"

The porter looked at him and laughed sneeringly. "Your passport!"

"I presented my passport when I registered. I left it in my room."

The porter bent over the register and Conrad watched his thumb travel backward over the list of guests and finally stop. Then he looked up with a smile and the smile was not pleasant.

"Sie sind Herr Dehmel?"

"Herr Doktor Dehmel."

"A German name and a German passport. Heil Hitler!"

They looked at each other and Conrad shrugged. "If you insist."

"Then say it."

"Adolf Hitler is the Chancellor of Germany. Didn't you know that? Now, give me the key."

The porter looked at him dumbly and handed the key over. Conrad went to the elevator cage, pulled open the folding metal door, went inside, closed it, and creaked slowly up to the third floor. He was unnerved because he had felt such a useless fury against the man, and when he rose and turned on the light he took his diary out of his suitcase and sat down at the little table. This is what he wrote:

"Hanna was right and I was blind. I have come home to the unthinkable. You can smell the fear and the rottenness. It reeks like the smell of stale boiled cabbage in a slum. It is unthinkable to know that it is dangerous to be writing these words. Hanna was right again. I knew more than I know now about the reality of history when I was a child and Father came home after the great battle. Now history has stepped out of the books and documents and is looking me over. I can smell her breath but I can't read what's in her eyes. I'm afraid of her. I'm afraid of myself. I'm afraid she will make me know I'm a coward."

He tried to write more but nothing came, so he stowed the diary away in his suitcase under some dirty clothes, locked the suitcase, and put the key in his pocket. He turned out the light, went to the open window, and leaned out. Opposite was the wall of another building, a small, cheap hotel similar to his own. A light flashed on and he saw a man and a woman enter a room. The man was stout and heavy and so was the woman. Without even looking at each other they took off their clothes, the woman lay down on the bed and spread her thick legs, and the man followed her. With the light still burning they fornicated. It was quickly over. The man rose, washed himself at a small basin, and put on his clothes without speaking. Then he nodded to the woman lying on the bed and went out the door. When he was gone she sat up, brushed her teeth, yawned, put on a nightdress, and yawned again. Conrad saw her hand move to the switch, the light vanished, and again he was confronted by a dark, blank wall.

FIVE

*T*HE NEXT MORNING he phoned his mother. Three weeks earlier she had written to tell him that she had a spare room where he could sleep until he found an apartment of his own.

"Are you well, Mother?"

"Nothing to complain of, certainly, at my age."

"Your voice sounds tired, Mother."

"I must make it sound better for you. Dear Conrad, it's so good to hear you again. Are *you* well?"

"Never better," he lied.

He asked about his father and she said he was working twelve hours a day and had been in Kiel for the past ten days. He would be home soon but she did not know when. He asked about his young brother Siegfried, whom he hardly knew as a person, and she said she would tell him about Siegfried when he arrived at the apartment.

He went down carrying his suitcase and asked the day porter to call him a taxi. The day porter was a thin, gray-haired, stoop-shouldered man with a racking cough. Conrad asked him if he was well and after another shuddering cough the man said, "It is nothing new. The mustard gas."

"I have been in England for several years and have met some men there who experienced the mustard gas."

"Natürlich."

When Conrad said "Guten Tag" the porter said "Grüss Gott."

"Are you from Bavaria?" Conrad said.

"My mother was. I was born in Baden."

"Freiburg?"

"No, Offenburg."

"That's where they have the big statue of the Englishman Sir Francis Drake, isn't it?"

"The first man who brought the potato to Europe. Yes."

Conrad knew that Drake was not the first man to bring the potato to

Europe but for once he restrained himself from talking like a teacher and saying that the Spaniards had brought it from Peru.

"Eine schöne Stadt, Offenburg. I am from Freiburg."

"Eine schöne Stadt."

Conrad felt better when he went outside into the sunlight and hailed a taxi. On the way to his mother he looked intently out the window and Berlin in the sunshine was a different city from Berlin in the night. It was brisk, full of purpose, and not too many uniforms were on the sidewalks. The streets were cleaner than the streets of London, but there was nothing remarkable about that. They had always been clean. The first time he was in Berlin he had seen a street-cleaning machine spraying the pavement in the middle of a blinding rainstorm. He paid off the taxi and entered the four-story building where his parents lived, and when he examined the small register of the tenants he saw that they lived on the top floor.

His mother looked older than she had three years ago, more withdrawn, her expression resigned and sad, but her kiss was as warm as ever when they embraced.

"Well, Conrad, are you glad to be home?"

He understood that the question was not routine. He sat down, filled his pipe, and puffed it alight.

"I don't know yet. But tell me about yourself. Are you playing as well as ever?"

She lifted her right hand. "The arthritis has come to me finally. So far it's only in the wrist but it will be sure to spread to the fingers. Then of course I won't be able to play at all. However, this is to be expected. Meanwhile the important news with us is that your father is going to be promoted to rear-admiral. It should be official any time now."

He put another match to his pipe, shook it out, and set it down in an ash tray.

"Are you happy about it?"

Her slim shoulders moved in a half-shrug. "For him, yes. He feels vindicated. You were such a little boy when the news came about the great battle. Do you remember it?"

"I'll never forget it. I remember everything each one of the neighbors said about it. And I remember even better how Father looked when he came home on leave two months later."

"He has not been forgotten by his old comrades. One of them is now the Grand Admiral. The Grand Admiral stood on the bridge beside Admiral Hipper on that day."

"Is Father happy?"

"As I said, he feels vindicated. He's never been so busy in his life." She smiled again, this time in wry amusement. "I was never studious myself, but here I am with a studious husband and a studious son. But they both study such different things."

"When will Father be home?"

"I can never be sure of his movements and neither can he, but he should be home soon. As I told you, he's in Kiel at present. They are making great plans for the navy and some of your father's ideas have been adopted."

Conrad puffed his pipe slowly, then held it in his palm and looked out the window.

"Mother," he said, still looking out the window, "I know I must have seemed unkind. I mean, seeing so little of you these last half-dozen years. I can't talk about it, Mother. I only hope you understood."

"Yes, I understood. I was sad, yes, but I know you pretty well, Conrad."

He drew on his pipe several times more, then swung his head back and faced her.

"I'd like to talk to Father now. Do you think he'll talk to me – really talk to me?"

"You're his oldest son. Of course you should talk to him."

"I want to ask him if they're going to make the same mistakes they made the last time."

"If you ask him that, he'll tell you they have studied all the old mistakes and won't repeat them."

"I heard him say something like that when I was a child. He said it the night you played the Goldberg Variations. I've never forgotten the expression on his face when he said it."

She did not reply and there was a silence of almost a minute before Conrad broke it.

"Mother, no country in Europe wants war except Germany."

"The people don't want it. I don't want it."

"Not even the young?"

She sighed. "They have no idea of what war is like."

"All this talk about not repeating the old mistakes – don't they realize that the only mistake that mattered the last time was that the war happened at all? Don't the soldiers and sailors understand that?"

"If you asked your father that question, I suppose you know what his answer would be?"

"That he is a sailor and that politics is the business of the government?"

She nodded.

"Does he trust Hitler?"

"I truly can't say yes or no to that. He never makes it necessary to ask him. What he does say is, look at Germany now and remember what it was like before Hitler became the Chancellor. Many people say that. In Germany everyone is working again. So your father says, the facts speak."

"Soon there will be new facts and they'll speak, too."

"Conrad, please! There's nothing I can do. There's nothing I can say except that he is my husband."

She asked if he was ready for coffee and while she was making it he stood up and looked out the window appraisingly. Certainly this was the best apartment his parents had ever lived in and this was the best district, though for him it had none of the loveliness of Freiburg by the little Dreisam. When she returned with the coffee he asked about his young brother Siegfried, whom he hardly knew.

"I have not seen him all summer. He's still in camp with the Hitler Jugend."

"So Siegfried swallows all this?"

"All the youth believe in it. Poor children, they have no choice. But Siegfried is enthusiastic. He's very proud to belong to the Hitler Jugend. He has always been strong and he loves the training."

Frau Dehmel sipped her coffee and sat with folded hands.

"So," Conrad said. "If war comes, Siegfried will be just the right age for the first battles."

"He is already assigned to the navy."

"I'm glad it's not the army. The navy won't be strong enough to fight for years."

With no change of expression, she said, "Siegfried intends to serve in submarines. He's fascinated by them. He dreams of torpedoing ships. He loves to study technical things about submarines. One torpedo, one ship. Twelve ships sunk on every voyage. That's the way he talks about it."

"Oh, my God! So it's going to be just the same as the last time."

Conrad relit his pipe and walked to the window feeling unnatural. Looking out the window with his back to her he asked if she would play something for him.

"I play so badly now."

"Does it hurt your wrist to play?"

"Not too much."

She rose from the chair, went to the piano, and sat for a moment with her head bowed, thinking. He would always remember her in this posture. Then she lifted her hands and began playing one of the last Beethoven sonatas, the one in A-major that begins with a quiet, rippling contemplation, and he remembered that this was what she had played for his grandfather that night in his childhood after he had brought home the rabbits. She finished and he said it was lovely. She said it was lovely only in her mind and returned to her chair.

"When I knew you were coming home," she said, "I visited the Institut. The public doors are closed for the rest of the month because they're making renovations inside. You will have to enter by the door leading into the basement. You will find somebody there who will take you to Professor Rosenthal."

"Have you met Professor Rosenthal?"

"I didn't ask to meet him."

"Why not?"

"I thought it best not to."

She left him again to get their lunch. She had everything ready and only ten minutes elapsed before she came in with a soufflé, delicious after the restaurant meals he had been eating in London. He thought of Hanna and wanted to tell his mother about her, but instead he asked if she had heard anything of Eva Schmidt. Her expression hardened.

"She came here three weeks ago and asked a number of questions about you. I have the impression that you would have little difficulty in getting a divorce from her now."

"So she wants to marry somebody else?"

"She didn't say that, but it was obvious to me that she does, so I made some discreet enquiries. He's an officer in the Gestapo. I suppose you know what that means?"

"Are they as bad as they're supposed to be?"

"Much worse. Your father is worried about them because

Himmler is using the secret police as a cloak to build a private army of his own. The regular army officers despise them, of course. Your father's not afraid of the Gestapo on his own account, but he's afraid they'll disgrace the country. He didn't believe me when I told him that it won't be long before the officers in all the services will be afraid of them." She looked at him and she had never seemed more serious. "For your own protection you must tell me this truly – does Eva hate you very much?"

"I think she despises me."

"Don't be surprised if I say that I hope that's true, but I don't really believe it. Soon after she came home from London she became a Hitler Girl, but she's beyond that now. She's the mistress of this Gestapo officer. He's very important and he has an evil reputation. He's a married man with children and Eva is stupid enough to believe that he'll leave his wife to marry her. You mentioned a girl you met in London but you told me nothing about her. Is she English?"

"No, German."

I can imagine the shy smile with which Conrad continued. He was always shy about his personal feelings.

"How the man who was obtuse enough to marry Eva Schmidt should have been lucky enough to discover Hanna Erlich I can't understand. She's been wonderful, Mother."

Her face tightened. "Erlich, did you say? That's frequently a Jewish name."

"None of them have been practising Jews for nearly a century. Her mother isn't Jewish at all."

"That might not make much difference. By the way, your father knows a Major-General Erlich. Is there a connection?"

"He's Hanna's uncle. She's connected with some very interesting people."

His mother seemed relieved, but not entirely so. "If a Wehrmacht general is her uncle, that could make her safe – for a while, at least. I can't help hearing a lot of professional service gossip. The high command still believes it can control the government. I hope they're right, but I'm only a woman. Anyway, General Erlich has a very good reputation in the service."

"Hanna's father is Dr. Erlich, the psychiatrist. I've never met him, but he sounds like a fascinating man. Some things Hanna tells me about his ideas seem strange, though. He believes that the thing

Hitler is most of all sincere about is this craziness about the Jews. Do you think he's right?"

She compressed her lips and laid her hand on Conrad's knee. "It's safe for you to talk like that here, but in public you must never speak of him as 'Hitler.' Only as the Führer."

"Hanna says she will never return to Germany while he's in power except on one condition – if her family needs her. Do you think she's exaggerating?"

"Do I think? Most of us have decided that the best thing is not to think at all. As you know, your father has nothing against the Jews, but he becomes very uncomfortable if I ever ask him about that aspect of Hitler's government."

A long silence fell between them and finally his mother broke it.

"I've never interfered with your life, Conrad. I don't want to worry you or make you change your habits, but I have to tell you this. You have always been outspoken and I've loved you for that. But you've also had a tendency to think aloud. Now please listen to me, carefully. You've been away so long that you simply don't understand how things are here. Don't mention certain words in public. Don't mention the word 'Russia' in a bus or a streetcar. It is best not to talk about politics at all. But if you do – and I suppose you will do it – make sure you know who you're talking with. And make sure it's in a public park or a room with the doors locked."

His expression froze as their eyes locked.

"Has it really come to this?"

"It came to this very quickly. Suddenly it was here. You know that slogan of theirs – 'Today we have Germany, tomorrow the whole world'? We didn't take it seriously. It seemed too insane. But the young believe it now. For them it's a certainty. If you say something often enough and loud enough – " she lifted her hands in the old gesture and let them drop in her lap, "for the young the program is all settled. They believe that every detail has been worked out. The Leader is infallible and the young follow him – like Siegfried, deliriously happy."

He sat in silence and remembered Hanna saying that Hitler was a genius. He looked at his watch and rose to leave for the Institut. Then he looked down at his mother and felt sad and helpless, knowing she loved his father and therefore had to accept what her husband wanted against all her better judgement. He wondered if there are many things more destructive that one person can do to another than what his father's one-track mind was doing to his mother. He looked at her steadily and full of pity.

"Mother?" he said quietly.

"Yes, Conrad?"

"I have been very stupid these past years. Trying to escape, I suppose. Escape into the safety of History and now into – well, as you said, I've been living in England. What's happening here seems unreal in England. If I've been living there, a German, and couldn't really believe it, why should anyone be surprised that the English believe it even less? But when they finally do believe it – "

She said nothing. He bent, caressed her cheeks with his fingertips, and kissed her forehead. He felt a profound and helpless love for her.

"Mother?"

"Yes."

"Tell me something. Do they think here – I mean the Nazis – do they think the English are stupid because they're so casual?"

"How do I know what they think?"

"At the moment the English leaders are old and blind. But there are other English – I've met some of them – and they're terrifyingly intelligent. They're never more dangerous, these men, than when they seem casual. Does Father understand that?"

The son and the mother looked at each other and later Conrad recorded this in his diary:

"At last I was growing out of the intellectual cocoon I'd been living in ever since I went to the university. This was the first time it had ever occurred to me that it might be interesting to understand my mother and her thoughts. Like most sons who have had a loving mother, I had taken her for granted. Now for the first time I was watching her tragedy.

"She had understanding, deep and experienced, but she had no authority. She had two sons she loved and who loved her, but they were diametrically opposed. She had a husband she loved and who loved her, but their interests were so different they might have been living on different planets. She had loved her country and now her country had become Hitler's. She had an understanding so total that she had resigned herself to the fact that her understanding made no difference.

"Tears filled my eyes and I embraced her and she welcomed it. Then she stood apart from me and said quietly, 'I love your father. I love Siegfried and I love you. To you I am closest, but this is a luxury I cannot afford to show.' We had been such a disciplined family that such intimacy was rare with us. You, dear Stephanie, also belonged to a disciplined family, but in your family it was the mother who was dominant. It was easier for your mother than for mine.

"Then Mother said, 'I don't know if this matters, but your father has always agreed with what you said about the English. He thinks the best of them are the most intelligent people in the world. So he tells me that just because they're intelligent, England will be either neutral or Germany's ally.'

"I said, 'Oh my God!'

"Then I kissed her on the forehead and said that I had to leave."

When he reached the Grosser Kurfürst Institut he entered by the back door as his mother had told him, descended to the basement, and after wandering through many corridors found the porter in a glassed-in cubicle equipped with a small telephone switchboard. The man looked almost as big and brutal as the night porter of his hotel and he was reading a Nazi tabloid called *Der Stürmer*. Behind him was the same picture he had seen in the hotel and the same slogan:

Trittst du als Deutscher hier hinein
Soll stets dein Gruss Heil Hitler sein.

He dispensed with any kind of greeting and asked the porter how he could find the chambers of Professor Rosenthal. The man laid down his paper and stared at him truculently.

"What do you want with Rosenthal?"

"I am Dr. Dehmel. I have come here from London to work with Professor Rosenthal."

The porter's heavy face broke open into an insolent smile. "Well, Herr Doktor, if you want to see Rosenthal, you'd better see him now. Follow me."

Behind the broad and muscular rump of the porter, his pants an acid green exuding a faint smell of masculine sweat, he plodded up one flight of metal stairs and two flights of marble stairs and followed down a long corridor to a large door, which the porter jerked open without knocking.

"Rosenthal!" he bellowed. "Are you still there, Rosenthal? Come here."

A small, delicately formed man emerged from an inner room. Professor Rosenthal looked about fifty years old, had graying hair and large, humorous eyes, and was immaculately dressed in a light-gray suit. He spoke to Conrad as though the porter were not there.

"And you, I believe, are Dr. Conrad Dehmel? I'm so happy to meet you at last."

"He says he's Dehmel," the porter barked.

"And so he is," said the professor.

Conrad turned to the porter and said quietly, "You are very rude and very insolent. In future when you speak in my presence you will be polite."

The big man was taken aback; his mouth opened and stayed open while he thought of something to say.

Conrad looked straight at him and said, "It might interest you to know, porter, that I am well acquainted with some people you should respect. My father is a close associate of the Grand Admiral of the Reich. I have told you to be courteous. Now, have you understood?"

The stupid face solidified, clarified, and the hulking body crashed to attention.

"Bestimmt, Herr Doktor!"

"That's better. Now I request you to leave us."

"Hitler!" the man barked, went about face, and marched away like a soldier. Professor Rosenthal closed the door, locked it, and turned to Conrad with a smile.

"That was nicely done, Dehmel. I had forgotten that your father is a naval officer."

"I believe he will soon be a rear-admiral."

"Even if he wasn't, that blockhead would have believed you. You spoke your lines very well indeed. Suddenly I feel much better. Shall we sit down and talk quietly?"

The professor seated himself erect and small behind an inlaid seventeenth-century desk, his fingertips pressed together. Conrad sat in a comfortable chair opposite him.

"So, my dear Dehmel, you have been living in England while most of this was going on here. How long is it since you returned?"

"I reached Berlin only last night."

"And already you see how it is here?"

"I can't believe it."

"As a Roman historian you should have little difficulty believing it. If you give a barbarian a centimeter, he immediately demands a meter. Give him a meter and he demands a kilometer." The expressive hands dropped to the desk. "You have seen already how it is with me. But I wonder if you know how it is with yourself?"

"With myself?"

Though the professor smiled again, he was looking at Conrad very carefully. He waited for Conrad to speak.

"Herr Professor," Conrad said, "how is it possible that a man like that porter could dare speak to you like that?"

"You know, I suppose, that I am a Jew."

"But a man like you, sir!"

"Fortunately I have some influential friends and at the moment the authorities do not think it worth their while to make me a minor *cause célèbre*. In other words, I don't expect to be arrested within the next few days. But let me tell you, Dehmel, if I were to continue to stay here much longer I would soon find myself in a camp. As it is, they have merely dismissed me. I had been expecting it for some time, but the dismissal arrived only two days ago. I immediately wrote to tell you this, but you must have left London before my letter arrived."

Conrad stared at the great scholar he had honored so long and there was nothing he could think of saying.

"I wonder how long it will be," the professor remarked, "before Europe understands that these people intend to do exactly what they say? It is quite fantastic. At least ninety percent of this nation have entirely ceased to think." He rose from his desk. "Perhaps it would be better if we went into the inner room. That oaf may return and put his ear to the keyhole."

Conrad followed him and saw many closed packing cases lying on the floor and one still open, half filled with books.

"As you see," the professor said, "I have almost finished packing. I intensely dislike doing things in a hurry, but these last two days I have been in a very great hurry. Somebody may change his mind about my exit visa. If nobody does, I will be in Brussels within forty-eight hours.

Thank God – or thank my wife's foresight – she and my three children have been there since last May."

Conrad glanced at the packing cases. "At any rate they allow you to take out your property."

"Not entirely. They will let me take out five hundred marks. The rest of my savings, except for a small sum I deposited in a Brussels bank two years ago, they will confiscate under the cover of what one of their officials told me is an emigration tax. It is difficult to accommodate one's self to the mentality of these people. They allow me to take out my books, though they could sell them abroad. But then, as you must have heard, they burn books these days and some of the books they have burned were extremely valuable. Remember Danton? 'In the face of the kings of Europe we throw the head of a king.' For them it would be, 'In the face of civilization we blow the smoke of burning books.' And speaking of smoke, would you care to smoke yourself? I don't smoke any more, but by all means do so if you feel like it."

Conrad took out his pipe, stuffed it, lit it, and felt terrible.

"Sir," he said slowly, "what I have just seen and heard sickens me. For years I've looked forward to working under you. Possibly even *with* you. Apart from your learning" – he hoped the professor would not think him unctuous – "it's also your style. There's delight and wonder in the style of your scholarship, Herr Professor. It was the proudest moment of my life when you accepted me."

"Thank you, Dehmel. Ever since my friend Rostovtzev wrote to me about you, I had been looking forward to working with you. You're an excellent scholar for your age." He shrugged. "Basic scholarship is absolutely essential, but of course it's only a tool to help us understand larger things. You may go far with experience. I'd have liked to go a few steps of the way with you, but it seems impossible."

Feeling every moment more miserable, Conrad said, "You do me too much honor."

"That remains to be seen," said Professor Rosenthal quietly. "Many things remain to be seen."

There was something in Rosenthal's expression that made Conrad feel even more uncomfortable.

"Sir," he said, "I can't imagine anyone being able to fill your position here. But I suppose I must ask you who has been nominated to it."

The professor, his face grave, was silent while he studied Conrad. Then he nodded as though he were nodding to himself.

"It is, of course, possible that they merely wished to surprise you. They enjoy surprising people. Surprising people has been the secret of their success so far."

"I don't follow you, sir."

"Are you sure you don't?"

Conrad was completely confused. Then, with an expression the like of which Conrad had never seen, Rosenthal confronted him.

"Since you say you don't know who my successor is, I will tell you. It's you."

"What!"

The professor's face was stern. "You heard me, Dehmel."

"But sir, this is incredible. This is absolutely impossible. I knew nothing of it. Do you believe I would have come here if I'd known *that*?"

The older man's face, which for an instant has been as implacable as the face of a judge of Israel, softened and became urbane again.

"Forgive me, Dehmel."

"For what, sir?"

"For being careful. I didn't really believe that you knew. But these days – " he shrugged slightly, "these days to be sure even of a certainty seems a dangerous luxury. Forgive me, anyway. Of course you didn't know."

"Sir, believe me, if I had known – I don't know what to say."

The professor laughed quietly, then uproariously.

"I see nothing to laugh at, sir," said Conrad.

"If you were my age, you would. Perhaps after a few more years you will understand why I laugh. For one thing, you are going to receive a salary much higher than you anticipated. They told me the figure, and it's thirty percent more than I ever received in my life. As the Devil is supposed to have said to Faust, the world is yours."

Conrad flushed and said, "Professor Rosenthal, if a Jew can't help being what he was born, neither can a German. That's not fair."

The professor ceased smiling. "*Touché, mon cher Dehmel*."

"But why me? That's what I can't understand. Why do they appoint *me*?"

"I didn't understand it either, but since you told me that your father is about to become an admiral, perhaps that explains it."

Conrad sat erect and looked straight into the professor's eyes. "My father has been a naval officer for all of his adult life, but he's never been a Nazi and he isn't one now."

"Hardly any of our naval officers are Nazis, but they are certainly officers."

The wise Jewish face looked into the earnest, wounded eyes of the young German and Conrad did not speak.

"You are an officer's son," the professor said reflectively. "Officers here obey orders. Therefore it might be assumed that you would do the same. That's the logical explanation." He shook his head. "Which is why I don't believe it's the right one. Nothing here is normal, Dehmel. What we have here is the logic of *Alice in Wonderland* – a book I'm sure none of them have read. Logical conclusions proceeding from absurd hypotheses. Logic can never explain the Nazis. Why, for instance, do they take such elaborate steps to demonstrate that their monstrous crimes are legal? Frankly, I have no idea why they appointed you. What I do know is that you'll find yourself in a very strange situation."

"An impossible one."

Still holding his distance a little, the professor went on: "However, for a young man wishing to become an historian, this could be a unique opportunity."

Conrad continued silent and the professor surveyed him.

"Providing, of course, that you survive. Providing, again, that any world survives that may be interested in history and truth. There is only a single historian alive today who has had the experience to understand these people. That's Rostovtzev, of course. He saw Lenin in action. He even met him personally. The rest of us have studied historical texts that never dealt with people like the Nazis."

Rosenthal put his fingertips together and contemplated them. Had he imbued himself so deeply with the art of the Renaissance that he had absorbed the gestures of a bishop? Conrad wondered. Rosenthal continued.

"All the European foreign offices are floundering because they're dealing with something they've never had to deal with before. They can't bring themselves to accept that a maniac from the flophouses of Vienna has become the total will of a modern civilized nation. *Das*

Land der Dichter und Denker! They think he's only playing politics. And by God, so he is! And what politics! *Kleiner Mann*, *was nun*? The little people love him."

Conrad remained silent, remembering bitterly what Hanna had told him in London.

The professor continued to think aloud. "At least these Nazis have made some of our high-flown survivals of nineteenth-century academica wonder what they were talking about when they became portentous about what they call 'the dignity of history.' The only dignity I ever found in political history was the incredible capacity of ordinary people to survive what governments have done to them. Most of our German scholars lost little time in losing *their* dignity lately. But who am I to blame them? We were all trained to be rationalists, *n'est-ce pas*? Not the stuff out of which martyrs are made, Dehmel. The Nazis knew that not many of that sort would risk torture for the sake of an idea."

"Bruno did."

"Bruno was in holy orders. But Galileo didn't, and who has blamed him for not giving the priests the pleasure of burning him alive? One can die for the love of a dear one. For a very dear one, I can imagine a man betraying his soul. But to die for an abstract principle that will probably be proved wrong after we're dead? It would have done science no good if Galileo had gone to the stake." He paused. "I have been very lucky. Because I'm a Jew, the Nazis absolved me from the necessity of making a moral choice. But for an *echt* German like Heisenberg the dilemma may become a terrible one."

Suddenly, Conrad shouted, "No!"

"No to what, Dehmel?"

"I refuse to accept this position. Me, coming here to be a student under a great man and then to be asked to take his place! I refuse, I tell you. I refuse. I also would like to have a little dignity."

Again the professor placed his thin elbows on the table with the fingertips touching. Watching those subtle, experienced eyes observing his own, Conrad suddenly realized that Rosenthal was beginning to like him.

Rosenthal smiled. "You know, Dehmel, I'm beginning to think that our pompous friend Spengler should be taken seriously. His reasons for his theory about the decline of the West are typically romantic, and explain nothing. But his conclusions? If Hitler loses this war he's going to make – and in gloomier moménts I'm not sure that he will – what is the world going to be like thirty or forty years from now? Will there be anyone left who will even understand what ethics are? Or will they only consider expediencies?"

Conrad had nothing to say. He was too miserable, too shocked, and above all too ashamed of himself for having been so confident in his own intelligence. Two days of Hitler's Germany!

Years later in Canada he wrote it down:

"They humbled me for the rest of my life. My old dream of earning the right to belong to civilization as its interpreter vanished. What was needed now was not to belong to the old civilization, but to survive this nihilism in order to preserve the seeds of a new civilization. My response to the challenge was not intellectual. It was purely physical. It was animalistic. As they would say today in English, so I thought then. Fuck you bastards! I'm going to survive you."

But the professor was speaking. "We must be practical. Please try to listen to me. I know why you're disturbed, but in conscience I must advise you to make no issue about the position they're giving you. You must accept it." He held up his hand as Conrad was about to protest. "A moment, please. I don't think you have any choice. The administration will be no problem for you because the Institut has been taken over by the party and functionaries will manage it. As for the history of art, there are only two arts they're interested in. One is the art of controlling the masses and the other is the art of war. A month ago one of them was here and told me the Führer has a great interest in art so long as it's Aryan art. I had to listen to it with a straight face."

"Does Hitler really care about art?"

The professor smiled. "You seem to have forgotten that he once was an artist himself."

Conrad made a gesture of contempt and the professor smiled again. "Have you seen any of his pictures?"

"No."

"I have. Some of his watercolors are very delicately done."

"Do you really mean this?"

"So delicately done that they scared me. The contrast between those sentimental, *petit bourgeois* pictures and what the rest of the man is – my God, Dehmel, the split in his personality must be appalling."

Conrad looked out the window to a pigeon bobbing its head as it strutted along the window ledge. The bird suddenly took off and flew out of sight and Conrad looked back again to Professor Rosenthal.

"In other words, you're telling me he's insane."

"If he loses his war he'll certainly be called insane. But if he wins it?" He shrugged. "As for his henchmen, hardly one of them would get a job with any responsible business company in the land. By themselves they're scum. But they're gamblers and he gives them the confidence to believe they can't lose. Are you familiar with the work of Professor Oster in Princeton?"

"Isn't he the comparative philologist?"

"That's the man. He and I have had a correspondence for quite a few years and thanks to him I expect to be going to America soon. I have been offered a post in the Flexner Institute in Princeton. But to return to Oster.

"He understands some fifty languages, but what sets him apart is that he has used them to study the common denominators in cultures. It seems important to Oster that in every culture – even in subcultures – gambling has always been a favorite pastime."

Conrad had no idea where this was leading and said so. The professor continued.

"Like most of us, I had assumed that gambling is simply a stupid habit leading to a waste of time and money. But as Oster sees it, gambling for pleasure is a sport and like all sports it's a sublimation of a profound instinct. Without it we'd still be in the trees. The biggest gamble in our evolution must have happened when our forebears came out of the trees and took their chances on the ground with the snakes and the lions. If these pedants who talk about the 'laws of history' understood the role of the gambling instinct, maybe they'd understand what makes history. Hitler and his gang, every man-jack of them, they're not only gamblers but gamblers on an enormous scale and so far they've been lucky. And against them what do we see? Not one among the present leaders of France and England. Not one among our German communists." He gave a contemptuous shrug. "Lenin was a prime gambler, but Thaelmann and the rest of our communists were doctrinaire bureaucrats. That's why they're dead or in concentration camps."

Conrad was confused and said nothing. Neither did the professor, and Conrad interpreted his silence as a signal that the interview was over. He looked at his watch, got to his feet, and apologized for having overstayed his time. But the professor had been thinking of something else.

"Not at all, Dehmel. My packing is almost finished and I was hoping you'd have lunch with me."

"I'd be honored, sir, but surely—"

Rosenthal waved the protest aside. "My last lunch in Berlin—I would not like to take it alone. But as it would be difficult to talk of serious business while we're walking to the restaurant, and inadvisable to talk seriously about anything when we get there, I think there are a few matters I should tell you before we leave."

Conrad sat down again and said, "When I told you I intended to refuse this position, I meant it."

"And when I advised you not to refuse, I also meant it."

"But why?"

"Take my word for it."

Thinking of Hanna again, realizing even more what a blunder he had made in coming home, he said, "Why can't I go to America myself?"

"Because you didn't think of it before you came home and accepted a job here." The professor twinkled. "However, when in the course of human events—as the Americans would say—you should wish to come to America at a time when it would be safe for you to escape from here, don't hesitate to let me know. My friend Einstein has also been invited to Princeton. I'll be seeing him in Brussels in a few days."

"Will even Einstein have to leave Europe?"

"Yes, and for stronger reasons than any of the rest of us. You know, Dehmel, Einstein is the least worldly man I have ever met. He's not at all like me. Now I suppose I'll have to spend the rest of my life in an ivory tower working on the history of art, and I assure you that the ivory tower is not a habitat that suits my temperament. For Einstein, of course, it would be perfect. He could continue to dream in higher mathematics and play his violin badly and listen to Mozart played well and take his rambles in the countryside and forget where he was after he had lost himself in contemplation of a wildflower or a snowflake. Such a life would be perfect for Einstein and this I find sad. Because for him of all people the ivory tower will be impossible."

"I don't understand."

"You were in Göttingen, were you not? Surely you know what the physicists are up to these days? I was told that you know Heisenberg personally."

"I met him several times, but I can't claim to know him."

"As I mentioned before, I pity Heisenberg. Such an aristocratic mind must despise the Nazis, but the Nazis will crave his knowledge. At any rate, those marvellously innocent, intricate equations of Einstein's finally resolved themselves into a single conclusion so small that it could be printed in large letters on a postage stamp. Yet out of that equation there may come – I'm told by experts that it's sure to come – the means of producing a small sample of the primal force which exploded the original matter of the universe. I don't have to tell you that at no period in the history of the world could it have come at a worse time than now."

Conrad sat still, his mind churning. The professor then remarked that there were some details about the Institut that he should tell him and for the next half-hour he gave a factual description of the organization as it had been during his own time there. He then discussed some of the men who would be Conrad's colleagues and finally Conrad interrupted him.

"But these men are all senior to me by years. It would be intolerable for them to have a young man like me as their Director."

"Under normal circumstances it certainly would be intolerable, but the present circumstances aren't normal. All but two of them are frightened men. The two who aren't have a great admiration for the military, and for Hitler. But there are three men who I think will be reasonable."

Conrad shook his head. "No, I can't."

"I'm not saying it will be pleasant for you. But if you are tactful and very careful, there are at least three colleagues who would understand and even respect your personal position. Before I leave, I intend to speak to them about you."

"Sir, this grows worse and worse."

"You will discover ways. I suppose you know that the department which now controls this institution is the Ministry of Public Enlightenment?"

"Goebbels?"

"Of course."

Conrad felt sick. He also felt more frightened than he had ever been in his life.

"Is there no way I can get out of this? I'm determined to refuse it. I'd be in an impossible situation."

The professor, who had managed most of the time to look cheerful, now looked grim.

"Dehmel, I've decided that I like you. I've warned you twice not to refuse. Believe me, I know what I'm talking about. These people are insecure. If you refuse they will take it very personally."

Conrad looked at the floor, his pipe cold in his hand. "When am I supposed to begin working here?"

"On the first day of next week."

Conrad looked up, feeling sudden relief. "In that case I'll return to England tomorrow."

"Poor man! Do you seriously believe you would be allowed to leave?"

"Would they know?"

"They would know, all right. You are a German citizen and that makes you a property of the state. You accepted a position here while you were still abroad. You may be sure they have made many enquiries about you before you came home. Now, by coming home, you have signalled to them that you have accepted them and approve of them." Suddenly Rosenthal laughed. "By God, that could be the reason why they appointed you Director!"

Conrad was aghast and felt weak at the back of the knees.

"Perhaps I was wrong in thinking that your father's rank had anything to do with their decision. Men like Goebbels have a fanatical hatred and jealousy of the old military and naval castes. Anyway, it doesn't really matter what their motives were. You're here, and they won't let you go."

Conrad was breathing heavily. "But what can I do? What can I *do* now?"

"Learn to dissimulate, like millions of others. You know the old tag – *qui non vult dissimulare, non potest regnare*. In your case it will not be a matter of dissimulating in order to rule, but in order to survive. It won't come easily to you, which is one reason why I like you. But I'm afraid you have no other choice."

A long silence fell between them and Conrad sensed the older man's sadness. This man whose work he had reverenced, on whom he had pinned so many of his own hopes – it was shattering to see him treated like this and talking like this. He thought of Hanna and wondered whether he would ever see her again. She had known the truth, had told him the truth, had even warned him that Rosenthal would be dismissed, but because he had been so set in the tradition of the old German scholarship he had refused to believe her. He could almost hear the clang of the gate as it shut on him.

Professor Rosenthal had risen to his feet and was smiling again.

"*Alors, mon cher Dehmel, allons au déjeuner.*"

SIX

*T*WO DAYS LATER Conrad rented a small furnished apartment not far from his parents. All he had to do to settle in was to order his book boxes from the station, unpack them, and hang up and put into drawers his clothes. If he had to get out in a hurry his books would have to be sacrificed.

The next evening his mother telephoned to say that his father had returned from Kiel and wished to see him, but that he was very tired and would have to be at his desk at 0730 hours the next morning. Conrad was to meet him in the Admiralty at 1145 hours and he wondered what this might mean. His father was so methodical that he must have a reason for such a particular time.

It was another bright morning with a cool breeze flooding the streets as Conrad walked through central Berlin toward the Admiralty. There was a tang of autumn in the air and this clear wind had blown down across the Baltic from Scandinavia. Tension had been growing in him steadily since he had said good-bye to Professor Rosenthal and he hoped that a brisk walk would ease some of it. Under his present circumstances a meeting with his father might easily be traumatic.

When he reached the Admiralty the warrant officer on duty at the doors was expecting him. He was a rugged, cheerful, brown-faced sailor in his middle forties and when Conrad told him he had an appointment with Captain Dehmel, he smiled broadly.

"Rear-Admiral Dehmel, Herr Doktor. Your father's promotion

became official this morning and we're very happy about it here. I had the honor to serve in the same ship with your Herr Vater in the war. I served in 'Bertha turret' – she was the second one forward and the only one that was not destroyed. Your Herr Vater was the finest gunnery officer in the fleet."

"That says much."

"With respect, Herr Doktor, it says more than anyone who was not there could ever know."

"A sailor I met on the *Albert Ballin* on the way home told me the same thing."

"And now he's Rear-Admiral."

Conrad was passed on to another sailor who led him to his father's room. A male secretary was inside, a lieutenant in uniform, who asked him to take a seat and said that the Rear-Admiral would be back very soon. Five minutes later he was. Conrad rose, father and son shook hands, and whatever emotion the father felt on seeing his son after these years was compressed into a single sentence:

"I'm glad you decided to come home."

Conrad congratulated his father on his new rank, Gottfried Dehmel nodded, and they both sat down, the father behind his desk. He turned to the lieutenant and said, "Dismissed for two hours, Richter." The lieutenant left the room and the father surveyed the son and the son the father.

Gottfried Dehmel had reached the time in a lean man's life when at last his age was beginning to show. The scar on his cheekbone where the sailor had struck him now seemed a natural part of his face. His forehead was at least an inch higher than it had been three years ago, his hair was grizzled, and he had shaved off his moustache and small, spiked beard. He had never been a heavy man, but now his body was so wiry it made Conrad think of "a network of finely integrated nerves held in place by the armor of lean, hard muscles." He asked his father if his back still troubled him.

"Much less. I have found a Swedish physiotherapist who has done wonders. The sciatic pain has gone and he has taught me exercises to control the muscles which support the spinal column. Much more is known about backs these days. How did you find your mother?"

"As always."

"Yes," Gottfried Dehmel said quietly, "as always." He looked down at his desk and toyed with a pencil. "I have been told that you have been appointed Director of the Institut." He raised his officer's eyes and looked at Conrad severely. "Is this correct?"

"It seems that it's true, but it's not correct."

"It certainly isn't. You must refuse it."

"I told Professor Rosenthal that I wished to refuse it."

"Then you have not refused it officially?"

"He told me I'm in no position to do so. He said that Dr. Goebbels would take a refusal as a deliberate insubordination and insult."

The Rear-Admiral's face gave an involuntary twitch of disgust. He looked down at his desk and again the fingers of his right hand toyed with a pencil.

"There are some things these days that I don't –" he decided not to finish the sentence and changed it to another. "However, you can avoid this embarrassment if you volunteer for the services."

"I have not been trained for the services, Father."

"I wasn't thinking of the routine services. I was thinking of the Intelligence. A scholar's training is just what's required there. Thank God the Abwehr has been retained by the navy. Its Chief is a most remarkable man. In the last war he served in the *Dresden* and later in submarines and Intelligence. I suppose you know the record of the *Dresden*?"

"I'm afraid I've forgotten."

Gottfried Dehmel frowned. "People forget too quickly. She was the only light cruiser to escape when the English finished off poor von Spee in the South Atlantic. She dodged the English for nearly four months until they trapped her at Juan Fernandez Island. Her entire crew was interned by the Chilean authorities and put in a camp on the island. This officer escaped to the mainland and walked through the Andes *in winter*. He reached Buenos Aires and got passage back to Europe on a neutral ship. After that he began his intelligence work in Spain. A man very rare, Conrad, very remarkable." He glanced at his watch. "I will introduce you to him at 1230 hours. We may even have lunch together, the three of us. We hold the same rank, but he is senior to me and much more influential."

"But I have no intention –"

"We can discuss that later. Meanwhile, I believe you have little confidence in our navy. Well, let me assure you that if you serve as I suggest, you will become a part of something far more valuable to your country than you realize. I'm permitted to show you certain things on the understanding that you don't talk to anyone else about them. Will you give me your word?"

"That will depend on what you tell me."

"It will be nothing dishonorable or political."

"Then I give you my word."

"Intelligence, to begin with. Ours was generally bad in the last war and the English made fools of it. Let me promise you it won't be bad the next time."

Gottfried Dehmel went on to describe the kind of navy he and his brother officers were planning. He never raised his voice but his eyes shone with pride as he spoke. There would be five, possibly eight, of the most powerful battleships ever built, ships so strong they boggled the mind. They would be constructed of specially hardened steel and would be divided into so many watertight compartments that a torpedo on their flanks would be no more dangerous than a bee sting.

(Conrad's note: "I had a vision of hundreds of men frying like pork in those labyrinths of specially hardened steel when great shells pierced their armor and exploded inside. In the case of two of them, this is precisely what happened a few years later.")

His father was going on: Two super-battleships faster and stronger than anything the English had would be ready in eighteen months. The three ships the English called pocket battleships were ready even now. Splendid new heavy cruisers, more than two hundred submarines, even aircraft carriers much more modern than the antiquated ones the English had. As the English would have to disperse their ships to guard their trade routes, a fast German squadron could pick its own moment to break out. It could concentrate at sea and be refuelled and revictualled by supply ships. It would be fast enough to avoid any stronger concentration and strong enough to destroy any force weaker. In this way England could be starved into making peace. But above all there would be a signalling system unlike anything ever known. It would be lightning fast, it would be infallible, and its codes would be unbreakable. This was the ultimate secret weapon the Leader had spoken about. Its details, of course, he could not reveal to anyone.

Conrad listened to this, watched the pride in his father's face, and felt despair.

"How long will it take to produce this navy?" he asked finally.

"Six or seven years."

"The way Hitler's going, do you seriously believe you're going to have those six or seven years?"

"Get into the habit of calling him the Führer and don't judge him by some of his favorites like Goering and Goebbels. He made that promise to the Grand Admiral. No matter what the provocation, the Führer will keep out of a major war until the fleet is ready."

"Did the Grand Admiral believe him?"

"Why do you persist in asking questions like that?"

"I have been trained to ask questions, Father. Now I'll ask you another. Do you think the English will do nothing while all this is going on?"

Gottfried Dehmel made a gesture of impatience. "How many times do people have to be told that the last thing we want is a war with England? And the last thing England wants is a war with us."

"Then why in God's name all this preparation?"

His father surveyed him with the quiet smile of an unsubtle man who thinks he is being farsighted.

"For centuries the English have been the most aggressive nation on earth. But what is England now? A tired, divided country. Their socialists hate us, naturally. But their aristocrats hate their socialists worse than they hate anyone else. I don't mean the English like us. They have never liked any foreign country. But they're shrewd enough to know that Germany is their only shield against Bolshevism. They don't want to see us stronger than themselves, but they have no choice in the matter. Therefore" – Gottfried Dehmel smiled triumphantly – "if we have a strong navy and profess friendship, the English ruling classes will insist on remaining neutral. Indeed, I wouldn't be surprised if they became our ally against the East."

Conrad said nothing and thought, Oh my God what a people we are! Will we ever understand what we do to ourselves?

His father rose to his feet. "Come," he said, "I have permission to show you something."

He opened a door in the rear of his study and switched on a light, and Conrad followed him into a small room where he saw what looked like a miniature navy.

"Models of the ships we intend to build," Gottfried Dehmel said. "Some of them are built already."

Each miniature ship-model was mounted on a wooden stand with its name engraved beneath it. Looking at the names, Conrad remarked that at least six ships bearing the same names had been sunk in the last war. Then he noticed that most of the cruisers and battleships had identical outlines and asked his father why this was so.

"So you noticed that!" His father was pleased but shy about it. "It was my own idea that their outlines should be identical. Any gunnery officer would see the point of it. In wartime conditions at sea, it is almost impossible to estimate the size of a ship merely by looking at it. At ten thousand meters a heavy cruiser can easily be mistaken for a capital ship and *vice versa* if their outlines are similar. I'll give you an example. At the Skaggerak my ship destroyed the British *Invincible*. Her guns were as heavy as ours but we knew she had no protective armor. If we hit her, we knew our shells would penetrate and explode inside her. We also knew she was attached to their main battle fleet. Now if this ship had carried two funnels instead of three, we would have known she was a stronger ship than ours and have sheered off. But we recognized her immediately, we engaged at close range, and we blew her up with a single salvo. So you see the value of this idea. When I proposed it some years ago to our present Grand Admiral he saw it, too. But staff officers are always conservative and we had a long struggle before the idea was accepted."

This was a long speech for Gottfried Dehmel and Conrad listened to it unhappily. His father passed his hand lovingly over the outline of one of the giant ships.

"The keels of two ships of this class have already been laid. Isn't she beautiful? Fully loaded she'll be forty-eight thousand tons. She'll have a complement of about twenty-five hundred officers and men. Ships even larger are on the drawing boards."

The very image of compact, massive, brutal power, Conrad thought as he looked at this model. Yet she was graceful because of her flared bows and perfect symmetry. He turned away, his father snapped off the light and closed the door, and they returned to his office and sat down again.

"Are you planning to serve at sea again, Father?"

"If the war comes soon enough – yes, I'm sure they'll give me a command."

"So the plan is to fight England again?"

Sitting behind his desk, Gottfried Dehmel rubbed his chin thoughtfully. "You've just returned from England, so tell me. Do they want another war with us?"

Conrad wondered what was the use of saying anything, but he tried.

"Of course the English want no war. But if anything's calculated to make them fight, it's this great navy you're planning. Nobody wants war but Germany."

His father replied irritably: "Don't you even read the newspapers? We have a naval treaty with England."

"Which Hitler will break the moment it suits him."

"The Führer." His father became more irritable. "We build this navy as a guarantee of peace with England, which means peace with western Europe. You're a scholar. You know what the Romans said. If you want peace, prepare war."

"The English have also studied Roman history, Father."

"Conrad," Gottfried Dehmel said earnestly, "I wish us to agree with one another. Germany wants no war with Europe. Russia is the ultimate enemy of Europe. It has always been our destiny to defend Europe against those barbarians. It's so long since we've talked together I don't understand you. You seem to forget that my family came from North Germany. For centuries we Prussians kept the barbarians out. All Germany demands is that our position should be accepted. All Europe understands this. Even the French understand it. Hasn't the Führer obtained everything he demanded without firing a shot? What he has demanded, and will demand, is nothing more than Germany has earned and what Europe needs. Did you meet any Englishmen except professors?"

"Some, but their professors aren't like our professors."

Gottfried Dehmel frowned. "Yes, I suppose you're right. But still, they're only professors." His chin jerked up. "I ask you – who is there who can frustrate Germany's destiny now?"

"God, perhaps."

"I have already told you that in the navy we are religious men and I can't understand what you mean by that statement."

"It was hopeless," Conrad wrote that night in his diary. "My father was beyond recall. I had known it ever since our last night in Freiburg, just as I had known that he was totally honorable. Being myself a German I understood him in his emotions. But being his son, I was devastated."

Conrad said quietly, "This is all very logical, Father. Before I came home I might have argued logically as you have been doing. It didn't take me long to know that logic is helpless in this country now." He looked his father in the eyes. "How do you reconcile your honor with what this man is doing to the Jews?"

As though an electrode had been touched to a different part of his brain, Gottfried Dehmel's expression changed. He sat down and again toyed with his pencil.

"The role of anyone who has been trained to serve his country as a soldier or a sailor is very difficult. The Jews? Yes, the Führer's opinion of them is not a secret."

Conrad said nothing.

"But within our service we can be responsible only to the service and the nation. There are some excellent Jewish officers in the navy and the Grand Admiral has no intention of dismissing them."

"In that case will not Hitler dismiss the Grand Admiral?"

"The Führer." Gottfried Dehmel frowned and shook his head. "He is a genius and Germany is his life. Because he is a genius, we accept that he has certain peculiarities. Also, because he is a genius, we know that he needs the navy. The Nazis are not religious. I don't deny that. But as I told you, we in the navy are religious men and divine service is held in all our ships. We have our own traditions, which to some extent are shared with the army, but still they are different, and between the two of us, I wish the Grand Admiral was in charge of the nation's strategy." He paused. "Now let me tell you this. When the Führer inspected our newest ship, we received him with the traditional naval salute, not with the Nazi salute, and he accepted it. So! Does that answer your question?"

"No."

"I don't understand your attitude at all."

"It grieves me, Father, that you don't. But I'm afraid you never will."

Gottfried Dehmel looked at his wristwatch and rose. "Now, Conrad, it is time for us to meet the Admiral."

Conrad also rose and in a quick explosion of lonely affection, the father put his arm about his son's shoulder.

"I wish you to understand that I'm proud of you, Conrad. It's a scholar's duty to ask difficult questions. The admiral we're going to meet is familiar with your work and that has made me proud. It was he, not I, who requested this meeting. How splendid it will be, Conrad, if you and I can work together, you in your *métier*, I in mine!"

The austere man's voice broke and tears filled his eyes.

"My son, I loved you before you were born."

In his diary Conrad was to write later, "One of the most horrible of all human tragedies is surely this, that an honorable man's devotion to his profession can lay his life and honor wide open to a scoundrel. At last I understood how right Hanna had been when she said that a terrible time was coming. It was already here. My father in opposition to Hitler? The Grand Admiral in opposition? The gods were laughing at them as they swallowed the bait whole.

"But immediately after this thought came to me, I met a man who had swallowed no bait."

SEVEN

*T*HE REAR-ADMIRAL who was the chief of the Intelligence Service of the nation was a year younger than Gottfried Dehmel, but in comparison to him his father seemed to Conrad like a schoolboy. The Admiral was short and bowed in the shoulders, yet seemed sturdy and enduring, even though Conrad sensed that when younger he had suffered from ill health. His thin silver hair was brushed flat across the top of a high forehead and the sensitive lobes of his long ears fitted closely to his skull. The eyes made a mystery of his face. Most of the time they were veiled, but at moments they could flash open unnervingly bright blue. When he bade his guests welcome he spoke with a slight lisp.

While he and Gottfried Dehmel exchanged commonplaces, Conrad was silent and observed his host. He felt drawn to him instantly and did not understand why. The Admiral's study, for that was what he called it, was more like the room of an absent-minded professor than like that of a man of power and mystery. Its shelves were littered with papers, there was a camp cot in a corner, and on his desk was a model of an obsolete light cruiser. Conrad supposed it was the Admiral's old ship, the famous *Dresden*.

Suddenly Conrad was aware that the Admiral's eyes had opened wide and were concentrated on himself. For an instant he had the sensation that his entire personality was being filtered through those eyes into an exceedingly subtle and calculating brain behind them. Then the Admiral smiled and his eyes became a turtle's.

"I have much looked forward to meeting you, Herr Doktor," he said.

Conrad felt instantly at ease with him. "Thank you, sir. I'm as flattered as I'm surprised."

The Admiral rose and turned to Conrad's father. "I suggest we go to lunch now, Dehmel. As I told you, I'm interested in your son's scholarly work and I understand he's just returned from England. One is interested in intelligent people who have just returned from England."

They left the room, went downstairs, and passed through a gauntlet of salutes to a staff car waiting at the door with two small naval flags mounted on its front fenders. A warrant officer with his hand at the salute opened and closed the door for them and they drove off. When they reached their restaurant the maître d'hôtel greeted them obsequiously and showed them to a table in the rear far corner. The tables near them were empty.

The Admiral said drily, "Lately some of our friends have been planting deaf-mutes in places like this to read people's lips." They took their seats and he changed the subject. "I hope you care for asparagus. I confess to a lifelong weakness for it."

So they started with golden asparagus *au gratin*, passed on through Vichyssoise to Heligoland lobster and then to fruit. During the luncheon the Admiral encouraged both Conrad and his father to talk, but spoke so little himself that Conrad wondered whether he was listening to a word they said. It was not until the fruit that he emerged.

"Herr Doktor," he said as he peeled an apple, looking at the apple while he spoke, "did you like the English?"

"Most of the ones I worked with I liked."

"You were fortunate. I have liked few English I have met, but this may have been because of my profession. I have always wished to like them because I admire them. Their philosophers are not up in the clouds as so many of ours are. They are instinctively Aristotelian. They understand that the highest morality is to consult one's own interests and this leads them to examine with shrewdness what their interests really are. The best of them know that this way of living requires intelligence and immense mental discipline." He paused, smiled faintly, and went on, "I am always disappointed when an Englishman behaves like a scoundrel. I have known some who have done that. But generally speaking, one must respect them. They eat lightly at lunch. We and the French eat far too much in the middle of the day."

Clearly the Admiral never ate too much at any time of the day. He had ordered a bottle of exceptional Moselle, but took only a single glass of it. The Dehmels followed his example and when lunch was over and they rose from the table, the bottle was more than half full. They were driven back to the Tirpitzufer and when they arrived the Admiral turned to Conrad's father.

"Could you spare me your son for a short time? I'd like to talk with him."

"Certainly, my dear Canaris." Gottfried Dehmel smiled happily and to Conrad he said, "I forgot to tell you that the Herr Admiral is also an exceptional scholar."

"A very weak scholar. An amateur merely. A student – yes, I would admit that."

Alone in the untidy office with this strange character who seemd so un-German and un-military, Conrad wondered what all this was about. He was offered a cigar and said he preferred a pipe. The Admiral lit a most fragrant cigar and contemplated Conrad through a thin veil of smoke.

"You know, Dehmel, I have always thought of myself as a European. Have you?"

Conrad smiled and felt at home. "Yes, sir, I also."

"Three centuries ago my family was not German, but of course there was no Germany then. Apart from the English and the Scandinavians, we were all Europeans then."

"My grandfather used to tell me the same thing, sir, when I was a child. He was born in Strassburg when it was under the French, but he did his professional work in Freiburg-im-Breisgau."

"So I understand."

The Admiral contemplated his cigar and said that he had read some of Conrad's publications and had found them interesting. He asked how much further his work had gone in England and Conrad spoke of it for several minutes. He even ended by saying a few words about his Grand Design.

Canaris looked at him almost affectionately. He smiled and said, "Yes, of course. It is excellent to aim for the sky when one is young. Then perhaps one may acquire the energy to do a few small things of value." He smiled again. "You know, Dehmel, I find epigraphy and papyrology very satisfying just in themselves. That's where you find the human raw stuff that never changes and saves the world from its geniuses. Those inscriptions that old megalomaniac Mommsen collected! They're windows on centuries of domestic scenes. You know them all, I'm sure. That one on the tombstone of the Roman soldier: 'Here I lie, Marcus Manlius of the 22nd Legion. I ate a lot, I drank a lot, I loved a lot of women. Nobody can take this away from me.' Those Roman tombstone formulas to dead wives from widowers: 'With whom I lived for so many years without a single quarrel – *sine ulla querella.*' A record of the real world, Dehmel. A record of the undefeatable human being who has had to live under governments." In what seemed to be an afterthought, but wasn't, he added, "What was done to Professor Rosenthal was a scandal."

Conrad hesitated, then blurted out, "Sir, can you help me? You seem to know all about this situation at the Institut. What should I do now?"

"About accepting the directorship?"

"That was the last thing I ever dreamed of, but I was told I may have no choice."

"Did Professor Rosenthal tell you that?"

"Yes, sir."

"He told you correctly. The minister in charge is a very venomous man."

"Did you know Professor Rosenthal personally, sir?"

"Intimately, and for many years. It was through him that I learned about your work."

Conrad had not realized that Rosenthal had thought so highly of him and flushed slightly.

"I suppose," the Admiral said, "you are wondering why I could not save Rosenthal. There was no chance of that. He prevented Goebbels from looting a priceless manuscript that belonged to the Vatican and nobody could preserve his position after that. The best I could do was to make it possible for him to leave the country with his life."

There was another silence and Conrad restrained himself from breaking it until the Admiral spoke again.

"I sympathize with you, Dehmel. This is a sad time for scholarship here. It's a sad time for everything we value. However, your training may play a protective role until better times come. I can't be confident that they'll come, but one must hope."

"I don't think I understand."

"They know that scholars with your kind of training could be useful to them. There is a British epigraphist I have met." He mentioned the man's name. "He was born in Scotland but on his mother's side he is a direct descendant of Marcus Niebuhr. Did you meet him in England?"

"I was introduced to him once in Oxford, but we had no conversation."

"He's still doing meticulous work in deciphering and reconstructing fragments of old Greek inscriptions. He has an incredible memory and an uncanny knack of finding missing links in the evidence. He is a very gentle person. Outside of his profession he appears as naive as a child." The Admiral smiled ruefully. "Those English! In the last war this childlike man did us a great deal of damage. Well do I know it! For a time I was his opponent. He broke a vital Turkish code and this played its part in some of our disasters in the Middle Eastern theater. The French gave him a Legion of Honor. The English gave him nothing." The Admiral looked at Conrad with a faint smile. "Well?"

Conrad thought carefully before saying anything. He remembered his father's suggestion that he join the Intelligence Service and he did not like the idea at all. As though reading his thoughts, the Admiral spoke again.

"A place could certainly be found for you in my service, but not in the code department. Mathematicians are needed for most of the codes now in use. All great mathematicians tend to be eccentric. As one might expect, the English are by far the most eccentric of them all. For the Leader this could be very bad. However, our service employs all kinds of people and a place could be found for you in it. I don't think you'd enjoy it. Our generals are excellent tacticians, but any kind of understanding of long-range strategy is beyond all of them except one. The Grand Admiral understands strategy well, but the navy here is minor compared to the army and the air force and if war comes he'll be up against a navy four times larger." The blue eyes fixed themselves on Conrad. "Does my candor disturb you?"

It not only disturbed Conrad, it frightened him.

"I was about to say, sir" – Conrad hesitated, then plunged – "you mentioned Intelligence. I don't think I'd care to serve the military plans of this government. Even less its cultural policies."

The Admiral made no comment.

"Is it true, sir, what I have been told, that all military preparations have been perfectly calculated? That a master plan exists and that everything is ready?"

The little admiral hunched forward as though the weight of his head had increased.

"In what major war has everything been successfully calculated in advance? Our Leader has some remarkable intuitions, but more than once he has said that he advances into the future with the sure step of a sleepwalker." He shrugged. "There can be no question that he is a genius of a kind. However, though geniuses have won many campaigns, I can think of only three who have made and won great wars."

The next silence lasted until Conrad broke it.

"My father has told me there are great plans for the navy."

"Prodigious plans," said the Admiral drily. "Now let's talk of more congenial things."

For the next half-hour they discussed various scholars of ancient and modern history and Conrad felt like a student undergoing an oral examination. Then the Admiral changed the subject again.

"I am acquainted with Major-General Helmuth Erlich," he said.

Conrad started slightly and the Admiral permitted himself a faint smile.

"An able man, but not so interesting as his brother, the psychiatrist."

This was said so suddenly, yet so naturally, that for a moment Conrad suspected a trap. Again his instinct told him not to dissemble.

"Sir, is there anything you don't know?"

"I know too little and too much. I also find myself in an uncomfortable position, but I am used to it. Occupying uncomfortable positions has been what our Leader would call my destiny." He looked sideways out the window. "Have you ever thought, Dehmel – this is a serious moral question – have you ever thought how it is with men who believe that the only way they can defend honor is by being dishonest?"

Conrad had often thought of it; he was thinking of it now. He did not say anything.

"However, in such a situation I suppose one's duty to one's country's welfare is the thread that most men cling to. It's not enough, of course." He changed the subject again. "I understand that you are engaged to Dr. Erlich's daughter?"

"If I had my way I'd be married to her now."

The Admiral nodded.

"Is her family safe here, sir?"

"For the time being, yes."

"But in the future?"

"Who knows? Or perhaps I should ask you how much of the future you have in mind? As I foresee it – and I don't foresee it clearly – the time will come when nobody will be safe in it."

"If her family is in danger," Conrad said, "Hanna told me she intends to return to Germany."

The brilliant blue eyes looked directly into Conrad's. "And so she will. I know your fiancée. Yes, she would do it."

"What would you advise me to do now, sir?"

"For the time being – that's what many of us say these days, for the time being – I'd advise you to accept the directorship. As Professor Rosenthal told you, you have little choice in the matter anyway. Later on, circumstances are sure to change. When they do, please feel free to come to me if you think it would be helpful."

The Admiral rose, nodded gently; Conrad bowed as he shook hands and left the Tirpitzufer in a daze.

EIGHT

*T*HE NEXT WEEK Conrad took up his post as Director of the Grosser Kurfürst Institut. Three days after he had settled into his office and had had barely enough time to learn the names of the senior members of his staff, he was ordered to report to a department of the military bureaucracy. There he found waiting for him a straight-backed major-general in full uniform with a pale, coarse-featured face that looked as if it had been frozen stiff years ago. The general looked him over and said curtly that he had received assurances that he, Conrad Dehmel, was reliable.

"I have been told that you have a professor in your Institut who is an expert in the art and history of the Mongol peoples? Is this true?"

"That would be Professor Heidkamp."

"Are you acquainted with his work?"

"Only with the general nature of it."

"I am informed that this professor has made a detailed study of the political and military methods of Genghis Khan. You are to tell him that we require him to make a brief summary of Genghis's military methods, especially his use of cavalry. Has your father ever discussed military matters with you?"

"Naval matters a little. He doesn't profess to know much about the army."

"But at least you understand that though strategic and tactical realities never change, weapons do. You understand that the last war was unsuccessful because machine guns and barbed wire neutralized the cavalry and made victory impossible. In the next war the role of the cavalry will be taken by tanks which can ignore machine guns and barbed wire. As Genghis was the greatest cavalry commander who ever lived, we require a precise analysis of his methods. I wish to have this analysis within a week."

The general then dismissed Conrad as though he were a subordinate officer and Conrad returned to the Institut longing for somebody with whom he could safely laugh hysterically. He called Professor Heidkamp to his study, apologized for disturbing him, and told him what the general wanted.

Heidkamp was a stringy, stoop-shouldered, bald-headed man, nearsighted, with a shuffling walk and a breath that Conrad could smell halfway across the room. When he heard what the general wanted, he burst into a cackle of ecstasy.

"So! So-o-o! It's what I've always dreamed of. At last the importance of my work is recognized! And by the General Staff! What do I care now about *dummkopf* professors? The General Staff!" He thrust forward two thin hands and grasped Conrad's. "Herr Direktor, Heil Hitler! Gott sei Dank, a German is my Director! Herr Direktor, thank you very much!"

Two days later, Heidkamp's summary was on Conrad's desk and he read it with disgust. He knew little about the Mongols except that their name had been a horror word for centuries among the peoples of eastern Europe. Now it appeared that their example was going to be used by Hitler's Germany. He read and reread the summary with a feeling of increasing contempt for its author. This miserable little man was not only marinated in his subject, he was intoxicated by it.

Here it was, though, the old horror story. Brash treachery followed by raw terror. First spies, posing as ambassadors, appeared to look over the lay of the land. Then came merchants to open up trade and spread stories about the invincible ferocity of the Mongols. Then followed the armies. When they invested a city, many citizens were so paralyzed with terror that they killed their wives and daughters and committed suicide. If a walled city offered resistance, every single inhabitant was butchered. After a few such examples it was assumed that no cities would resist, but some of those that surrendered without a fight fared little better.

This part of the professor's report Conrad read with scant interest, but soon he came to the specific tactics of the Mongol armies. Their cavalry probed the lines of the defenders until they found the weak point (the professor's word for it was *Schwerpunkt* – the hard point – and for the victims this was exactly what it was). Massed archers saturated the hard point with a bombardment of arrows, then the cavalry charged through it in column like a battering ram, killing everyone in its narrow path. Once through, the cavalry columns fanned outwards and back again, swirled around and around until the enemy was encircled. The enemy was then destroyed by archers on horseback and dismounted riders who went in to finish them off with spears and swords. There were seldom any survivors.

The professor's report ended with a slavering appeal: "I am only a poor scholar, but this has been my subject for years. For me, Herrn Generalen, your request for my help has justified a long life of lonely study. I have always yearned to serve my country, the greatest in the world. In profound humility and in the greatest hope, I can swear before God that against tactics like these no army has ever survived. If today, with tanks and total ruthlessness, these same tactics are followed, they will be as invincible as they were when the great Genghis invented them. Heil Hitler!"

So this miserable little man thinks he will become immortal as the architect of victory in the next war, Conrad thought. The entire episode worried him so much that he asked the Admiral for a few minutes of his time. Canaris glanced through Heidkamp's summary and handed the papers back to Conrad with a mischievous smile.

"It occurred to me that something like this might be useful to you," he said.

"To *me*?"

"You cooperated instantly, so this may relax their suspicions a little."

"But if they suspected me, why did they insist that I be the Director?"

"You are not dealing with normal people, Dehmel. Among other elements in his make-up, the minister is a failed scholar even though he did make his doctorate at Heidelberg."

"I still don't understand."

"The motive behind your appointment is obvious enough. Professor Rosenthal nominated you for a fellowship in the Institut and I have explained to you why Goebbels hates him. What could have wounded Rosenthal more than to have you – a beginner – immediately put into his place?" The Admiral held up his hand. "Rosenthal is far too big a man to hold this against you. As for this staff-general who ordered you to get that report written, he is a general only because he was one of the original party members. In the last war he was a sergeant. One stripe above our Leader, one might say. He wants to make himself important. It so happens that Genghis Khan's tactics as described by your professor correspond pretty closely to those our generals intend to use anyway. This general knows this. He also knows that in the war plan Genghis's name is not mentioned. Obviously he hopes to get the credit for having discovered it."

This is one of the two incidents Conrad recorded of his activities as Director of the Institut. The other occurred in the summer before the war broke out, in the third year after he had left London. He was ordered to go to Paris to represent the Institut in some kind of international conference on culture and the arts. It was not a mission that he relished. In Paris he was treated with contempt by most of the French scholars he met because he was a German who obviously collaborated with the Nazis. One Frenchman, a communist, called him to his face a running dog of fascism.

But there was another scholar who was very friendly and seemed much superior to the rest. He was a tall, young-looking professor from Oxford whose name was familiar to Conrad. He twice invited Conrad to drinks and they discussed Conrad's work in England. This man's subject was Modern History, but he knew personally all the men with whom Conrad had worked in the British Museum. He also had a high opinion of Professor Rosenthal. Finally he told Conrad he would very much like to visit the Grosser Kurfürst Institut.

By this time Conrad's antennae had become sensitive, and on his return to Berlin he reported his meeting with the Englishman to the Admiral.

"Invite him at once," the Admiral said, "and let me know when he's coming."

A few weeks later the Englishman arrived and it turned out that he also had friends in the Berlin Rot-Weiss Tennis Club, for he was a doubles player with an international reputation. After a few days of talking with Conrad and his colleagues, he said good-bye and left the premises in a private car driven by a chauffeur. Conrad guessed that his next port of call would be the Admiral's apartment. It was not until long after the war that Conrad discovered that this professor was one of the most efficient of all the operators in the British Secret Service.

The visit to Paris could have been Conrad's opportunity to defect and go to Hanna in England, but if he did so, he knew there would be reprisals against his parents. He telephoned her from Paris and was told by the landlord of her old apartment that she had moved and had left no forwarding address. Then he called the office of the orchestra and asked if she was still attached to it. She was, but at the moment was on holiday somewhere in Scotland.

His frustration was total. He had written her several letters and he supposed she had received them because they were not returned. They had been very cautious letters. In nearly three years he had received no word at all from her and he was hurt and bewildered. He thought she might at least have arranged with her Uncle Karl in Switzerland to get a letter to him. The sudden thought occurred to him that Hanna might believe he had gone over to the Nazis, for this was a time when few people knew what to believe of anyone.

A few weeks after his return from Paris, he received a formal notice from a government department that his marriage with Eva Schmidt had been dissolved. Simply that. Again he was puzzled until he remembered his mother telling him that Eva had become the mistress of an important officer in the Gestapo.

Shortly after this, the war broke out and the trap closed on him. He had known all along that war was inevitable, yet when it came he admitted – like millions of others – that he had not been able to believe it in his emotions. He wondered if he would be called up for military service, but no call came.

The German armies won their first campaign in a few weeks and seemed invincible, but after the victory, Conrad's father was glum and ill at ease. "Things are happening in Poland I did not believe possible," he said, and refused to elaborate. He had no need to. Conrad also knew that the Nazi police had begun a systematic massacre of the leading men of that country.

"Only then did I realize that they were sincere in their insane racial ideas," he wrote in one of his diaries. "How hard it is to accept that an insane evil can be real."

Gottfried Dehmel was finding it even harder to accept it. For more than twenty years it had been an article of faith with him that his navy was an honorable service which had been smirched by revolutionists and betrayed into surrender by the peace treaty. After a long and difficult career he was now a rear-admiral. He had become a consummate professional and in the first winter of the war he was given an independent command for the first time in his life. It was a small, fast, powerful squadron and his orders were to break out into the Atlantic and attack British convoys. He was also forbidden to engage if he encountered a convoy escorted by a British heavy ship. His task was to raid, not to fight, for if his ship were damaged in a fight it would be slowed down and unable to escape the concentrations the British would certainly send out to get it.

He led his squadron north through rain, heavy fogs, and finally through snowstorms until he was far north of the Arctic Circle. Then he steered west and finally south and began quartering the ocean for prey.

Two weeks passed during which he saw nothing but the cold gray waves of the North Atlantic. He refuelled from a pair of cruising supply ships and continued his search. The Atlantic remained wide and empty but he was sure he would find something and the next week he did. He shot up and sank on three successive days three lone merchant ships, in each case making sure the crews were taken off in boats and given enough blankets, food, and water for a chance of life. Then, just as he was turning for home, came a morning when a cloud of smoke five kilometers wide grew up into the sky over the western horizon, soon to be followed by the masts and hulls of more than forty ships.

This was the moment Gottfried Dehmel had been waiting for. He fanned out his squadron and was closing the convoy at full speed when he saw in the middle of it a massive battleship. He recognized her type instantly; he had seen her sister ship twenty-four years earlier when his squadron charged the British line at the Skaggerak. He knew her guns were heavier than his, but she was old and slow and her guns were probably old, too. He was sure he could sink her and was maneuvering to fire a broadside when his flag captain reminded him of the orders not to engage a ship of that power. He cursed. While one of his cruisers exchanged fire with an English destroyer, he signalled the squadron to break off and used his superior speed to run over the horizon for home. On his arrival at Wilhelmshaven he was met on the dock by the Grand Admiral, who pinned another decoration on his chest on the orders of the Leader. He was mortified.

"I could have come home with a much better victory than von Spee's," he told the Grand Admiral. "In God's will, why didn't you let me fight?"

He was ashamed to have to accept the medal and when he read about the affair in an English newspaper which had entered the country from Sweden he was so enraged he could hardly speak:

"An enemy squadron centered on their newest and most powerful battle cruiser, supported by two of their most modern cruisers, met one of our convoys in the Atlantic. The convoy was escorted by a single battleship and a few destroyers. The moment the German admiral saw a puff of smoke from our battleship's funnel, he turned tail and ran for home, just as the Germans always did in the last war."

This was the last time Gottfried Dehmel was allowed to go to sea. He was so angry that the Grand Admiral was afraid that if he let him out again he would disobey orders and fight against any combination of ships he encountered. Meanwhile, Conrad's younger brother Siegfried had been at sea almost continuously as first officer in a submarine that destroyed more than forty thousand tons of shipping in a period of six months. Though he was still very young, he was soon given his own boat and during the next year and a half he became a national hero. His single boat did the British more harm than the whole of his father's surface fleet put together.

The war went on. Victory after victory for Hitler until Germany became master of the whole continent. Conrad felt he was living in a vacuum of total unreality, that the Institut had become a prison where the work he did was as meaningless as the work of convicts in jails.

One morning when he was clearing his desk of the usual traffic in bumf the buzzer sounded and it was the porter calling from downstairs. Conrad had fired the *Blockwart* who had been there when he met Professor Rosenthal. This man was quiet, elderly, and courteous.

"A lady is here who wishes to see you, Herr Doktor. She calls herself Fräulein Lindenau and she says she knows you."

Conrad knew nobody of that name, but he asked the porter to send the lady up. When he heard the knock and opened his door he turned pale. Hanna Erlich was standing there.

She came in, he closed the door, and they searched each other's eyes. Six years had passed since they had parted and now the world was worse than even Hanna had anticipated. They joined hands, kissed each other lightly, drew back, closed again in a fierce embrace. But there was no intimacy in it. An invisible line had been drawn between them. She sat down in an armchair and he behind his desk. He thought she looked at least ten years older since last he had seen her. Hanna wondered if she would ever know him again. He wondered the same of her.

She said almost formally, "I hope you understand that it was for your own safety that I didn't answer your letters."

He had a sick feeling as he realized he was resenting her. "Surely you could have written me something. You didn't have to sign your name. I would have recognized your handwriting. Even after the war began, you could have got some message to me through your Uncle Karl in Zurich." She said nothing and a new idea occurred to him. "Or was it for your *own* safety?"

She said coldly, "If I was thinking of that, why am I here?"

"You were right, of course – what you told me in London. I hadn't been home two days before I understood how right you were. I thought I let you know that in the first letter I sent you."

"I understood. You wouldn't have had to spell it out. You were never stupid, Conrad. Merely at times unobservant."

In an unnatural silence they continued to watch one another. Then he understood why she had come home.

"Has it happened to your family?"

"My father was arrested six weeks ago."

"How did you learn this?"

"My Uncle Karl in Zurich. Uncle Helmuth kept in touch with Father, so he knew when the arrest was made. There was an agreement that if it happened he would telephone Uncle Karl and speak a sentence which would be a signal. Then Uncle Karl would let me know."

"What of your brother and sister?"

"They went to America before the war began."

"So now there's only your father and mother and uncle here? Where is your father?"

"In Dachau."

"Oh, my God!"

(This was one of the concentration camps I told André about, one of the worst.)

"Did they send him to Dachau simply because his grandfather was a Jew?"

"The actual charge was grand treason."

Conrad's hands were shaking as he tried to light his pipe. "Was it real, or did they invent it?"

"One of his patients turned out to be a police spy. He pretended to have a nervous breakdown because of what's happening here. He was not the only patient who came to Father for that reason."

Conrad's pipe was now drawing but the hand that held it still shook.

"The police seized all of Father's files. What this has led to in the case of other patients I don't know. But I'm sure he would never have kept files on patients who were critical of the régime."

"Was there nothing your military uncle could do?"

She was unnaturally calm; frozen calm as people can be when they have heard a death sentence.

"Uncle Helmuth has not been arrested yet. But when Father was arrested my uncle was demoted to the rank of lieutenant-colonel in a line regiment."

"An invitation to take the old German choice and get himself killed on the battlefield?"

"I suppose so."

There was a silence. Then she said, "I see you have learned, Conrad. But *what* have you learned?"

He still did not understand the cause of her reticence. "Have you spoken with your Uncle Helmuth since you came home?"

"Not yet. I must be very careful. I suppose I can see him somehow. Uncle Karl is my only real hope now. He has a strong position in Switzerland. Quite a few of your government people have secret accounts in his bank."

"*My* government people! Did I actually hear you say that?"

She ignored his shock and continued in an expressionless voice. She told him that on her Uncle Karl's advice she had obtained a Swiss citizenship a few months before the war broke out. Otherwise the English would have interned her as an enemy alien. Quite a few of her old friends – and of Conrad's also – had been shipped out to Canada.

"I don't blame the English," she said. "Their backs were against the wall and they had no time to sort out the good from the bad. There were probably no bad ones. So the first of all the anti-Naxis were arrested by the only country that's fighting Hitler."

He was silent for nearly a minute. Then he said, "Why did you change your name, Hanna?"

"I didn't change it when I first took out Swiss citizenship. But now with my real name I might not have been admitted to Germany and would certainly have been suspect if I did. Uncle Karl made the arrangements. In matters like these the Swiss are very good, especially if they're bankers, as Uncle Karl is."

"How did you go from England to Switzerland?"

"The way many do these days. I took a ship to Lisbon. Then by train to Switzerland."

She told him she had a new life story and a new profession. She was attached to the Swiss Red Cross.

Conrad shook his head. "They'd never let anyone in the Red Cross visit one of their camps."

"Naturally, but it's a cover."

A thin one, he thought, if the police began to sniff. He rose and looked out the window at the bare branches of the lindens. A thin drizzle of cold rain was falling and the sidewalks and pavements glistened. He came back to his chair.

"Have you any hope of seeing your father?"

"At least I know he's alive."

"You know this through your Uncle Helmuth?"

"Uncle Helmuth can tell me nothing now. I know it through a man much more important."

Conrad, who had been slumped in his chair, jerked upright. "Is this man Admiral Canaris?"

It was her turn to start. "What made you mention that name?"

"I happen to have met him. My father introduced me. The Admiral told me he knows you and that he's a friend of your father's. He admires you very much, Hanna."

When he said this her entire manner changed and in a flash he understood why. He became bitterly hard-angry.

"So all along you've been wondering where I stand – is that it? You know, because I told you in a letter, that Professor Rosenthal had been dismissed just as you assured me he would be. Didn't you understand that in a letter that would be opened and read, I could say no more than that I had been made Director in his place? Didn't you realize I had no choice?"

Her face had softened and there were tears in her eyes. "It's been horrible. I've been horrible."

He said nothing and waited.

"You say you had no choice," she said. "Isn't that what they've all said? Yes, indeed I asked myself how you could have taken Rosenthal's place. I'd never met anyone who'd so set his heart on a position as you'd set yours on this Institut. In London you met many of our friends who were refugees. After you left it was dreadful for me. Apparently two people can love each other as beautifully as we did and still remain strangers. I didn't know what to think. So I wondered if you'd been hypnotized by him just as your father was. For that matter as a lot of Englishmen and Frenchmen were."

He felt that a great weight had been lifted off him. He spoke very quietly.

"It was Germany that hypnotized my father, Hanna. Germany and the defeat in the last war. I wasn't hypnotized at all. I was merely blinded because I'd buried myself in books. In two days – in less time than that—I knew I'd made a terrible mistake in coming home. But it was too late. I did everything I could to avoid the directorship. Professor Rosenthal told me I had no choice. Admiral Canaris said the same. It's no more my fault that I was born pure German than it's your merit that your grandfather was a Jew. I never forgot you for a single day all these years. You may think of me what you like."

She lowered her eyes but she did not weep. She was too strong and too sad and determined for that.

She said very simply, "Let's try to forgive each other. We've never been married, but that's what married people have to do with each other again and again—so I'm told."

He became businesslike. He asked where she was staying and she gave him the name of a small hotel he knew.

"It would have been safer if you'd registered in the Adlon. A *Blockwart* in one of those little hotels is more dangerous than a dozen policemen in a large one."

"I've seen him. He's a stupid brute."

"All the more dangerous to someone like you."

He rose, went around the corner of his desk, put both hands into hers and drew her to her feet.

"Eva divorced me a year ago," he said. "Will you marry me, Hanna?"

Her large eyes opened and so did her full lips. She put her arms about his neck and he felt her breasts against his chest. Then she drew away and sat down again.

"I didn't come home to get married, Conrad."

He returned to his desk. His pipe had gone out and he lit a match and puffed it alight and became businesslike again.

"Have you any plans about your father?"

"Not yet."

"I suppose you realize that by yourself you can do nothing? If you make enquiries about him you'll either blow your cover and be arrested as a spy or be told to mind your own business and take the next train back to Switzerland. There's only one thing I can think of. I must tell Admiral Canaris you've come home and see what he can do."

"He knows that already."

Her face, he was thinking, now looks more Jewish than it ever did before. Why not? She was relearning what dozens of generations of

Jews had learned for centuries from the savagery of Christians.

"It's strange, unnatural, and terrible here," she said. "The people go about the streets and look normal. Everything that's real is hidden and is never mentioned. Do they know it's there – all those people on the streets, do they know it?"

"How are you taking me, Hanna? I have the right to ask that. How are you taking me?"

She said nothing.

"All right, then, you won't answer. So listen. I've learned more about what goes on in this country than you could possibly have learned in England. For one thing, there's a silent civil war between the regular armed forces and the Nazi party's army." He made a violent gesture as though he were throwing away something slimy and loathsome. "My father won't discuss it, but in his job he must be going through hell. As for my title as Director here, it means nothing. I hate it. I guessed that sooner or later you'd come home. That may be why I've stayed here."

She looked at him with clear eyes. "Conrad dear, I said let's forgive each other. But I think I should never have come to see you."

"Thank God you did."

"When I decided to return I swore I'd never put you into danger. But I longed to see you and here I am."

"Thank God you are."

They both rose and embraced and his hand traced the curve of her hip. He led her to the window and they looked out at the lindens in the rain.

"It looks so normal, doesn't it?" he said. "So normal those people think it will always be like this. But the time will come, and sooner than you may think, when those buildings and those trees will be blasted and burned to cinders."

He went back to his chair and she to hers.

"Listen carefully, Hanna dear. A few days after I returned, my father introduced me to Admiral Canaris. It was at Canaris's request because he was an old friend of Professor Rosenthal. I was vain enough to believe what he told me – that it was because he was interested in my work. Tell me, how well did he know your father? How well did he know you?"

"They were close friends for many years. There was a great affection between them. They both knew so many secrets and it made them lonely with ordinary people. He was always charming and delightful with me. I often played chamber music with him."

"Do you know anything of Canaris's politics now? Anything definite?"

She put the tip of her index finger to her lips. "My Uncle Karl told me – no, I can't say to anyone what he told me. Not even to you can I say it."

He looked back at her steadily. "You don't have to. He has told me nothing definite, but I can guess. The stakes he is playing for are terrifyingly high and he can't jeopardize them even for his dearest friends. So let's let it go at that."

Conrad smiled with some bitterness. Now he knew definitely that it had been solely on Hanna's account that the Admiral had protected him. This also explained the charade about Genghis Khan and that *Scheissfresser*, Professor Heidkamp.

He said quietly to Hanna, "However, quite apart from Canaris, there's also my family. As you know, my father is a rear-admiral. My young brother Siegfried, whom I hardly know at all, is fanatically *Führertreu* and has become a national hero. So I can assume that at the moment I'm not suspected. At least I can try to do something for your people, Hanna. And first, I beg you to leave that hotel at once. If the *Blockwart* sees you there a few times more he'll be certain to ferret around. He's probably searched your drawers and luggage already. Do your clothes all have Swiss labels?"

"Most of them."

"I suppose no English labels?"

"Of course not."

"Then please go back, pay your bill, collect your baggage, and take a taxi to my apartment. Do you need money?"

"No, thanks. I've just come from Uncle Karl."

"I'll give you my address."

He wrote it down on a card, phoned the porter to order a taxi for her, and waited until she left. Then he went into one of his bi-weekly meetings with his staff that never accomplished anything important but had to be held. Three-quarters of his colleagues now detested him because Professor Heidkamp approved of him.

That night after they had eaten, the invisible wall between Hanna and himself seemed to have disappeared, but they soon found that something more subtle than a wall had taken its place. When they went to bed to make love, Conrad was devastated to find himself impotent. She was gentle with him and told him not to let it trouble him.

After a time he said, "I'm trying to understand this. It's been such a long time and I've dreamed of this every night before I fell asleep. Every nuance of your face and eyes and body I know better now than when we were together in England. The memory crystallizes everything. Now all I can see is how you are more beautiful than I'd even been able to guess before. God damn it, you've got into my mind and I seem to have lost you in my senses. I can't understand it, Hanna. I don't know what's happened to me."

Naturally I wonder if there had been other women in his life during those years of separation. To me it would seem abnormal if there were none. And if Hanna had been like the women I knew in my own young days – but I don't suppose she was.

Hanna said, "It will come back. I know how it is with you. It's with me, too. I gave you no help at all."

Toward midnight he had relaxed enough to recover and they made love with a fierce desperation, but there was no gentle peace in the aftermath. It would have been astonishing if there had been. When things are terrible and uncertain, what's the use of sex except as an escape? In such a time, what is a deep love but a commitment that can numb the senses? Hanna must have understood this before he did, for Conrad records that she actually said it.

"It would be easier for both of us if we just liked one another as acquaintances." She also said, "Please God you won't hate me before all this is over."

"I love you more than I ever did," he said.

It was not a sentimental phrase. For me it has the ring of literal truth because I experienced something similar myself just before the Great Fear. That love can defeat the joy of love is one of the diabolical ambiguities many of us have to live with.

PART SIX

John Wellfleet's Story

ANDRÉ GERVAIS SAID TO ME, "I want to know where the truth is." I wonder how much truth I can find for myself, much less for him.

The next part of Conrad's story becomes so murky that I can barely follow it. I'm sure he told my mother only episodes of what he was involved in during those days. He kept very irregular diaries in that time when it was dangerous to tell the truth even to yourself. Much of what he wrote that has come down to me was written long after the events. It is certainly enough to have brought me to new dimensions in my belated discovery of the stepfather I called Uncle Conrad. It also brings him very close to me.

When I was young I knew little about the Germany of Conrad's youth and early maturity. I knew that most of its famous cities had been blasted into moonscapes and charnel houses, the decomposing ruins of hundreds of thousands of human beings stinking in the ruins for nearly a year. Yes, I knew this had happened, but I knew it only as a fact. When I went to Germany thirty-five years after that war it was hard to believe what had happened there. The cities had been completely rebuilt and many of the finest buildings were exact duplicates of the historic ones that had been destroyed. I have now discovered that Conrad himself played a small part in making this possible.

Now I am forced to link up my own experience of total destruction with his, and Germany is the touchstone.

When I first went to Germany it was the most prosperous and efficient country in the whole of Europe and this gives me some real hope for the aims of André and his generation. Any recovery they may make is sure to be much slower than Germany's because they will have to develop a technology, yet I am sure that long after I am dead there will be real civilization on this planet, better than the one in which I was born. I had several German friends when I was young, including a big blonde girl from Hanover with a majestic figure who once spent a skiing holiday with me. She made love with such gusto that I thought I had slipped a disk in my back, for it went into total spasm and for a week I was almost helpless. She was a physio-therapist by profession and our holiday ended with her giving me treatments mornings and evenings and spending the rest of her time on the slopes by herself. She was a grand girl. I was genuinely fond of her as she was of me, though the fondness never grew into love.

What seems important to me now is that all my German friends had been born after an appalling catastrophe and that none of them even mentioned the Hitler years. Nor did I ask about them. They would have had little to say if I had, for their parents had drawn a veil over their horrors just as André's had drawn a veil over ours. For years I have taken it for granted that nothing that ever happened in this world was as terrible as what happened to us. Now I believe that on a purely personal level it was even worse for people like Hanna and Conrad.

I lived through the erosion and the final self-destruct of the vastest human complex that could ever have existed in the entire Galaxy. None of us dazed survivors knew, or ever can know, whether this *had* to happen. People had been making doomsday prophecies for years, but they didn't really believe it would end as it did. How could they?

Some time ago I tried to write about the Great Fear, but I don't think I was successful in describing it. What I wrote was true so far as it went, but what were the actual facts?

Right up to the beginning of the Fear, the Bureaucracy continued to smile at us. Their computers computed us, their pollsters polled us, their con men conned us. They even conned themselves. Behind them moved in the shadows those faceless men who juggled what they called the world's economy. Slowly, we came to realize that the true power was seldom in the hands of our governments, but there was always plenty of beer and sex, the stadiums were crowded, and the action spilled out into the living rooms of everyone with a television set, which in my country meant about ninety percent of the population. The Deer Park of the old French king had become democratized and it was at least more salubrious than the original one, for most of us washed and didn't have to use civet to drown our body odors. Decadent? We were constantly called so. Yet I'm reasonably sure that it wasn't decadence that brought on the Great Fear.

About ten years after Uncle Conrad's death, whole peoples in what the journalists called the Third World began to erupt. We saw them on our screens, mobs as large as a million or more, packed body to body like swarming insects, some of them blasting off with the guns our businessmen had sold to their former chiefs. We knew nothing about these people, but anyone could see they were screaming support for the usual Savior who was promising them a new life. All this would not have mattered to us if they weren't sitting on top of an ocean of oil. Without oil our System could no longer continue as a System. So naturally their Saviors thought they had us by the balls.

They pretty well did. Soon our money went out of control. People who had labored for years when money was worth something now found themselves desperate. A murmur circled the world multiplied by hundreds of millions of murmurs – "What is going to happen to me? What can I do?" All we could think of doing was to blame the politicians we ourselves had elected. Now that it was clear to us that our leaders were as helpless as ourselves, we felt we were living in a vacuum and it was in the vacuum that the Great Fear was spawned.

Nature, I was told in school, abhors a vacuum. Soon a handful of unknown individuals silently moved into it. They had taken a hard look at our bureaucracies and had decided they would be gutless because for years we had insisted that they be gutless. These operators began a new kind of terrorism that made our old-fashioned kidnappers, skyjackers, and bombers look like bush-leaguers. It was obvious that they were highly educated, because no ignorant person could have done what they did.

The first cell built and planted a bomb in a great city and demanded an enormous ransom in gold and diamonds. They gave the Bureaucracy a time limit of only twenty-four hours to pay up. If the Bureaucracy refused, they said the bomb would be exploded by remote control, the city destroyed, and perhaps a million people would be killed. The communiqué issued by this cell was so precise in its scientific details that the experts knew they weren't the usual run of kooks. Later, when the bomb was found and disarmed, it turned out to be exactly as the communiqué had described it.

A half-hour before the ultimatum expired, the Bureaucracy surrendered. Its front man came onto the screens and informed the world that the crisis was over, but this time he was too scared and shaken to smile at us. I happened to be in Paris at the time, sitting with a girlfriend in a brasserie and looking at the screen. The French people were tense and silent, some of them were white-faced, and the atmosphere in the little brasserie was acid with fear. The front man's speech was translated into French, but what interested me most was his face. He looked like an ordinary, well-intentioned man who had just discovered that the ground on which he thought he had stood all his life had vanished from under his feet. All I can remember of his speech is something like this: "While it is intolerable, and in the future must not be tolerated, for a great civilization to be blackmailed in this fashion, the facts speak for themselves. We were given no time to track these people down. We were presented with a brutal choice between gold and diamonds and the lives of a million people. What else should we have done?"

Most of us agreed that there was nothing else they should have done.

During the next year there were bomb blackmails in five more metros and only in the fifth did a bureaucracy refuse to surrender. The bomb exploded and killed half a million people. The bureaucracy that had defied the terrorists was execrated and forced to resign. Then we were all on the roller coaster. Money did not merely decline, it collapsed, and what we called the Western world went into hysteria. This was the climax of the Great Fear.

God knows my friends and I had despised the Smiling Bureaucracy. To jeer at our so-called rulers was part of what we called our Life Style, but never would we elect a bureaucracy that would compel us to change our ways. As I said to André soon after I met him, who will stop the music when everyone is having a ball?

But there were others who thought differently; there were millions of others who thought very differently. Suddenly people like us discovered that we had become targets. Those unknown millions we had dismissed as red-necks felt against us a rage deeper than anything they had felt against the bombers. Furious voices spewed out hatred and loathing against my whole generation. We were the spoiled brats who had been responsible for all their woes. We were the ones who had destroyed their authority over their children and foisted our own laziness and sensuality onto everyone else. We were the ones who had insisted on abolishing capital punishment, had sneered at the police, had sympathized with the murderer and not with his victim, had pretended that crime is the fault of society as a whole and not of the criminal.

They turned with especial fury against our women and some of them bellowed from street corners that they were all whores. Their hatred was soul-shrivelling. These people who roared for law and order – and they craved order far more than they craved law – now took to bombs and guns themselves. Their first target was the Smiling Bureaucracy, which had ceased smiling for some time now. Even in my own small nation two cabinet ministers were assassinated. They also went berserk against others – against the men who had made millions by saturating us with sex magazines; against the millionaire kings of the rock music; against actresses who had become sex symbols. Some of them were beaten up. A girl who had been advertised as "The most luscious sexboat in the world" was found in her New York apartment with her throat cut. I met a man who claimed to have known her and he told me the whole thing was crazy. She was just an ordinary girl of humble parentage who had been conned into the act by some agents who had pocketed about ninety percent of the profits.

Though at the time I did not understand it, I know now that this was no ordinary political revolution. It was an upboiling of subterranean wrath that had been seething for years. Against this fury the Smiling Bureaucracy was helpless and was swept into the discard, to be replaced by what I have called the Second Bureaucracy. This was a coalition of several so-called governments and after a summit meeting of its front men it was given international powers. It cracked down everywhere. Millions of private homes were searched, hundreds of thousands were thrown into jails without trial, and the masses applauded. When two of the blackmailing cells were caught, the authorities announced that they were composed entirely of intellectuals. They were publicly executed. These executions did not happen in my country, but we saw them on our screens.

I could not believe that what was happening was real, neither could my friends. One day Joanne and I were walking hand in hand in the city and she was wearing slacks. She was so graceful in them, they outlined her exquisite little figure so precisely, that it was a joy merely to look at her. Suddenly a police siren screamed, a car slammed to a stop beside us, two cops jumped out and grabbed

Joanne. When she struggled, one of them slapped her face so hard he broke her glasses and without them she was half blind. When I tried to help her, the other cop back-elbowed me, cracked my septum, and knocked me rolling. By the time I got to my feet with my nose gouting blood, they were driving off with Joanne in their car.

I knew where their station was and fifteen minutes later I arrived on foot with my nose still bleeding. I was confronted by the same pair of cops who had arrested Joanne, both of them with sneering grins on their square faces. Without a word they frog-marched me into a back room, pushed me down onto a wooden chair, and shaved off my beard with cold water and ordinary kitchen soap. Then they cut my hair so short it was only a fuzz on my skull. They made me look at myself in the glass and for the first time they laughed. Then they jostled me out the doorway and sent me stumbling into the outer room where I saw Joanne very pale and dressed in a long, drab skirt and a smock of some coarse brown material.

"How does your little friend look now?" one of my two cops said and guffawed. As his fist was clenched I knew he was hoping I would answer him back. However, to keep the record straight, I must admit this much: Our local cops had become mean and rough with their fists and sometimes their boots, but they never went in for the systematic, refined tortures that were commonplace in some other countries.

They released us with jeers. Holding my arm, Joanne walked with me to her apartment where she kept another pair of glasses. Her hands were cold and she could not stop shivering. She was like a woman frozen and I was like a man frozen.

The kind of life we had always known now closed down like a summer bungalow when the winter comes. International travel was banned except for some of the Bureaucracy and the huge tourist industry ceased. Strict morality laws were passed. Sexual promiscuity was forbidden, though this was a law they were not too successful in enforcing. To be found with drugs of any kind meant a prison sentence. To be caught selling hard drugs was death. But this was not the end. Indeed, the Great Fear abated now that the mass of the people believed they were under an authority strong enough to rule them.

When the end finally came I was incredibly fortunate, if to survive was really a good fortune. I had a cottage in the hills outside Metro and in it were all my books, most of which I still have. I was planting vegetables when the earth where I was kneeling hit me with a shock that struck up through my knees to the top of my skull. I got to my feet and staggered about as the earth continued to pulsate against my soles. I thought it was an earthquake. Then far off in the area of Metro I saw towers of flame and smoke rising into the high sky. Soon came a surging sound roaring in a profound bass as though the firmament had become a colossal, sonorous drum. I don't know how many minutes passed before the shock waves of air arrived. They knocked me off my feet. I saw the trees bending, screeching as though in a terrible agony as the wind tore them and broke them. Distant flames continued to billow up into the sky and with them a vast smoke that covered thousands of square kilometers. The darkness for a time was so intense that the sun was entirely eclipsed and so it remained for several hours. Toward evening the sun reappeared as a lusterless disk in the sky.

For many years, indeed from before I was born, people had dreaded what we called the nuclear bombs, which would have produced results like this but would also have contaminated the entire earth for as long as a century, so that all living creatures in the hemisphere, even those who had survived the blasts, would die of disease, and life would come to an end on our little planet. Something profound and mysterious, something blessed and almighty in the genes of humanity, had created a taboo against these bombs. Trillions of dollars were spent on them, but no bureaucracy used them. André Gervais will never understand the genius of our scientists. They were sincere men, pure-minded men, devoted to their countries and even to mankind. They bypassed the taboo. They invented what were called "clean bombs," which had a destructive power less than that of the nuclears but nevertheless tremendous. These were the bombs that did the trick.

This was the end as I experienced it and I can't even remember the date on the old calendar. It was so quick, so colossal, and pretty well so universal that my best guess is that the huge computer networks of the rival bureaucracies had become so overloaded with conflicting data, some of it fed into them by panic-stricken or merely incompetent technicians, that they suffered the equivalent of a collective nervous breakdown. I can think of no other explanation. The rival bureaucracies had been playing chicken with each other for a half-century, but none of them wanted it to come to this. Anyway, the underground and undersea hardware began flying to and fro across the globe and this, as we used to say, was *it*. And if what I believe happened actually did happen, it was so impersonal that there was no more malice in it than in a combined earthquake and volcanic explosion on a global scale.

That is why I'm sure it was worse on a personal level for people like Conrad and Hanna than it was for us. To have your world annihilated by a computer balls-up is not the same as to be strapped naked to a table in a police basement and have your backbone and rib cage stripped by steel whips, your fingernails and genitals torn out with red-hot pincers, or your brain blown by electric shocks so powerful that an ignorant policeman can reduce the world's greatest genius to a screech of agony, all these things being done by men as human as yourself. This man Hitler made everything personal. Whether he was the worst man who ever lived I do not know – there has been plenty of competition for that title – but it was Admiral Canaris's opinion that he was not so much a human being as a universal catastrophe.

As I try to follow this mild-mannered, silver-haired sailor flickering through Conrad's story I can hardly believe him real. Conrad wrote that he was the most morally brave man he had ever met, and in another context that only Germany could have produced him. He had been a successful spy long before anyone had heard of Hitler, so I suppose he enjoyed that kind of work. There can be no question about his courage. He was a realist who knew that his ultimate chances of escaping death by torture were bound to be precarious. According to Conrad, he had deliberately chosen to live in a maze of contradictions – on the one hand, to do what he could to prevent Hitler from winning the war, on the other to save Germany from the mindless vengeance of enemies who had come to hate her worse than any nation had ever been hated in human history. Double games, triple games, multiple games. I can see now that the work of all those intelligence agencies, plotting deceptions more complex than the chart of the world's weather systems, had a great deal to do with the *fin de siècle* into which I myself was born. The techniques developed during that war became endemic after it. They lingered and bred in the bloodstreams of the nations and no moral antibiotic was discovered to neutralize them. The deliberate murder of truth led to the murder of people. In our case it led to the self-murder of a civilization.

PART SEVEN

Conrad Dehmel's Story
as told by
John Wellfleet

*I*N THE TELEVISION INTERVIEW between Conrad Dehmel and my cousin
Timothy Wellfleet, all of twenty-five years after the end of the Hitler
War, Timothy virtually stated that Conrad had been a member of
Hitler's murder police and had been responsible for the death of
Hanna Erlich "because she was a Jewess." It was the most odious of
all his performances, yet it was not so much malicious as it was
irresponsible. You may remember that he had nothing to go on but
the word of an ego-tripping, revolutionary student who had broken
into Conrad's office, searched his files, found what looked like
incriminating information, then carefully replaced the papers so that
Conrad did not know they had been tampered with. I also told you
that though Mother was a very trusting person, especially of those she
loved, she was also very careful. If she had known how vulnerable
Conrad turned out to be, she would have implored him to avoid
television interviews like the plague. So now it is clear to me that
Conrad did not tell her everything about his time in Germany under
Hitler.

To my astonishment, I have discovered from Conrad's own narrative that for a time he *had* been enrolled in the Gestapo, though his
motives were far different from what Timothy made them out to be.
In the end, his position became as horrible as the Admiral's. It was a
long and twisting journey he took before he came to the end of his
road.

It began a few days after Hanna's return to Germany when he went
to the Admiral for help and advice. He found Canaris more depressed
than usual, and before Conrad opened his mouth, he told him that at
the moment there was nothing he could do for Hanna's father.

"You think I have influence? Yes, I do have some. But only so long
as I can deal with these people. That influence I must protect at all

costs to myself and even to my friends." He sighed. "The arrest of Dr. Erlich was sure to happen sooner or later. These people who control our country are never so vindictive as when somebody touches their neuroses. That's why they're going to ban the psychiatric profession. That spy of theirs who posed as Dr. Erlich's patient was sent – he was sent to do just what he did."

"Do you know who sent him?"

"Goebbels, of course. He's the only one of the lot with enough education to be disturbed by the insights of a man like Dr. Erlich."

Conrad asked if the doctor's position was hopeless.

"Nothing is hopeless until it becomes so. This at least I must continue to believe." His blue eyes concentrated on Conrad. "Dehmel, I'm going to ask you a direct question. In comparison with your own life, how important are the lives of Hanna and her father?"

Conrad hesitated. "Of course, I have never met Dr. Erlich."

"Quite so," said the Admiral and waited for him.

Conrad had the German obsession of trying to balance every side of a question. As he assessed his position, he knew that if he travelled alone he might have a chance of surviving the phantasmagoria and doing the work he felt he had been born to do. But having thought this far, he stopped thinking altogether. "The image of Hanna's silver hair, of her dignity, of her whole mind and body in the power of the police, blotted everything else from my mind and I blushed for shame."

Before he spoke the Admiral said, "It's my duty to tell you something else. The odds are heavy that anything you may try to do for Hanna will be useless."

"I can't leave her. I can't do such a thing."

Watching him carefully, Canaris said, "Are you being romantic?"

"I don't think I understand your question, sir."

"I think you do. If you don't, you should. To all of us our personal lives are more important than the lives of others unless they've been intertwined for a long time. You and Hanna have had very little time together. Without her, you might survive this insanity and have a long and useful life before you. So think carefully."

Again Conrad shook his head.

"Are you aware," Canaris said, still looking at him, "that Hanna at the moment places her father entirely before yourself? That family of hers is a very old family. It's not like yours or even like mine. They argue and disagree about nearly everything, but in a crisis they draw together to protect each other. It's their categorical imperative. At the moment, Dehmel, you stand on the outside. I think you should understand what this could mean. I think you must realize that you'd be inhuman if at times you won't resent her bitterly for what you have involved yourself with in order to help her family." He paused. "Be frank, Dehmel. Is what I'm telling you a shock?"

Conrad drew a deep breath. "Less of a shock than it would have been a week ago."

"Then think very carefully about the question I've asked you."

The remark hung in the air for several seconds during which the older man's eyes never left Conrad's.

"Will it depend upon my courage?" Conrad said.

"Ultimately, yes."

"How can I know that I have the courage?"

The Admiral hunched forward. "Who can ever know that until he's been tested? However, people can accustom themselves to almost anything. If a soldier isn't trained, he's sure to panic the first time he's in battle. But step by step one gets used to things." The Admiral's voice became decisive. "If you really want to protect Hanna, the time has come for you to prepare yourself. I think you should begin by joining my service."

"Would there be any difficulty about leaving the Institut?"

"At the beginning there might have been, but not now."

"Would questions be asked about my loyalty?"

"Naturally. We have had a revolution in which the scum of the gutters has come to the top. They all distrust and dislike each other. Without Hitler they'd soon be at each other's throats. I have no fear of saying this to you. If you took it into your head to report me, it would become my duty to have you disappear."

Conrad flushed, flared for an instant, then smiled tightly and said "*Compris.*"

The Admiral also smiled tightly. "French is such a convenient language when one is embarrassed. I've often wondered why. Yes, I see you have learned a few things."

"My question was, sir, would I be under suspicion? Your service is something different from the Institut."

"Not seriously at the moment. I'm not thinking of the reputation for loyalty earned by your father and especially by your young brother. That would weigh very lightly with them. I mean that your record since you returned from England has made them believe that you would never have the courage to be other than subservient."

Conrad flushed. "But you yourself . . . "

The Admiral brushed his pride aside. "Certainly I myself. Listen carefully, Dehmel. All intelligence services are snake pits and mine isn't the only one in this country. Do you know anything about intelligence work?"

"Not really."

"Much of it is routine, of course. Do you know anything about the English service?"

"Only that I've been told it's the best."

"That's very true. It is." He smiled enigmatically. "The English intelligence service has been directed by aristocrats or near-aristocrats for several centuries. These are the only kind of people who can keep their characters intact in the work they do. Intelligence attracts some of the bravest men alive. It also attracts a swarm of unstable, mercenary, and unreliable scoundrels. At the moment I have two double agents and one triple agent working for me. I retain them because I think I may be able to use them to my own advantage." He rubbed his long, straight nose and said with his faint lisp, "In this, of course, I may be very wrong. I presume I have been infiltrated by several British. Possibly by a few Russians. But what worries me are Nazis who are trying to undermine me in the interests of their own party service. With these, of course, I remain on the most cordial terms. Do you understand this kind of language?"

"I'm beginning to."

Canaris went on in a factual tone, "It's a poisoned cup we drink, but we do have our own perverted ethics. In this profession the most relentless enemies know they are spiritual brothers so long as they remain sane – which some of them don't. Because of the unspeakable crudity of the rival agency I think I have lost the respect of my opposite number in England." Another pause and another scrutiny of Conrad's expression. "Do you still follow me?"

"I'm trying to."

"You see, though this Englishman and I have never met personally, we're old acquaintances. In the last war he tried to kill me." The Admiral smiled wistfully. "Understand – there was nothing personal. It was his duty, just as it was my duty to kill him if I could. On that occasion I outwitted him. I have little hope of outwitting him again. Nor do I wish to except in small, unimportant matters. I believe I have almost, but not quite, lost hope of making him understand me. In this I may also be wrong. It's possible that he understands my position perfectly. So now I must ask myself what *I* would do if I were seated where he is, and when I ask myself *that* question, I have little to hope for." Canaris smiled wanly. "The Nazis will never understand these English. Sometimes I wish the English had taken the trouble to understand themselves. Their brains have already doomed Hitler, but they left it too late. They'll keep Hitler from winning the war. They've almost done it already. But they will lose the war just as we will. The winners will be the Russians and the Americans."

"But they aren't even in the war!"

"They soon will be. Plans have been completed to attack Russia. I implored them not to do this, but I was told I'm only a naval officer and know nothing of soldiering." Another pause. "In the end the Americans are sure to come in."

"But why, sir? Why?"

"Hitler is making this a world war. In a world war, how can the most powerful country of all remain neutral?"

Conrad sat in silence. Then he said, "Sir, are you telling me Hitler is mad?"

"Why bother with labels, whether he is mad or not? He's a peasant with enormous power."

Years later Conrad wrote that it was at this instant that he realized for the first time that he was in the presence of a profound tragedy; that it was not a personal thing, but that Canaris was caught in a chain of mathematical equations from which there was no escape.

"You have been like a father to me," he said formally, "and I thank you."

Canaris bowed his head slightly but said nothing. His expression was so lonely that it made Conrad think of a mind trapped in the collapsing vaults of history. Finally the Admiral straightened and became practical.

"To begin with, your scholarly training qualifies you for a variety of posts in my service. It's full of weaknesses, but it's still an excellent professional service. Therefore, if you work for me, I will expect you to be professionally competent, and above all, professionally accurate."

"Naturally, sir."

"I'm thinking ahead. One year ahead. Two years. Perhaps even as long as three or four years, to the moment when the Leader will understand that he has lost this war he has made. He will never admit that he has lost it. Not even to himself will he admit it. But he will know it. That is how he is. He will know it, but he will not admit it. And when that happens, the time will come for Hanna's father and therefore for her. Yes, it will surely come."

Conrad shivered but he asked no questions.

"Nothing can prevent it from coming because of her devotion to her father. It is essential that you understand and accept this *now*. Otherwise you will be unmanned by surprise when the moment comes."

Conrad nodded.

"Very well, you will be inducted immediately." The Admiral permitted himself a wry smile. "My friend your honored father will be delighted, I'm sure. Now everyone in the family will be in the navy except your mother."

The next day Conrad was inducted with the rank of lieutenant and took the oath of allegiance to the Führer. In Germany he always wore the dark-blue uniform but the only time he was aboard a ship was the occasion when he and his parents were invited to visit his brother's submarine when Siegfried was awarded the highest decoration for valor in the land. His father was proud and smiling. Siegfried, very young and blond but with tight, ruthless lines about his mouth, was proud and grave. His mother kissed Siegfried and even managed to smile, but when she pressed Conrad's hand afterwards he knew how she felt. Both of them understood that Siegfried's luck was sure to run out sooner or later.

Conrad found his work in Intelligence a relief after the nothingness of the Institut and at times he may even have found it exciting. Like the Admiral himself, he had to do accurate work while longing for the day when Hitler would die and the war would finally end. Because he understood several languages and had established contacts with some foreign scholars, he served at first as a courier. He appeared at various times in civilian clothes in Spain, Portugal, and France and four times in the Vatican. Often he was not told the nature of these missions. Usually he delivered disguised packages containing microfilms to men he had never met before and would never meet again. Sometimes the rendezvous was in a railway station, sometimes in a public park or an obscure restaurant. In the Vatican the techniques were probably more polished, but there is nothing in the record describing his visits to Rome. Out of the blur of this part of his life there emerged, like a knife-thrust in a dark alley, this single note: "If I'd been caught by the Gestapo en route to Lisbon with *that*, I'd have been tortured into confession and finally shot."

But Conrad was surviving and so were Hanna and her father.

A full year before this mission to Lisbon, Dr. Erlich was released from Dachau with the marks of the torturer on his body. They had begun by breaking his nose, as our own police liked to do to prisoners in the time of the Second Bureaucracy. After this overture they put him through the routine of more complicated though not fatal tortures. Physically he was almost a broken man when he was released. Hanna met him at the prison gate. His hair was thin and snow-white, he was emaciated by starvation, and he walked with a limp. In her role as a member of the Swiss Red Cross she was professionally cheerful. The tears came later. And it was Hanna, not the Admiral, who told Conrad how her father's release had been worked.

One of the highest officers in the Gestapo had deposited in a secret account in a Swiss bank a large sum of money extorted from Jews and converted into American dollars. If an ordinary person were caught transferring money outside the country he would have been sent to a concentration camp, but many higher officials did so and took it for granted that others were doing the same. What put this man into Canaris's power was something that could only have happened in Hitler's Germany.

He was a violently sensual man and there was a young Jewish woman he was mad for sexually. In spite of his high rank he did not dare be seen with her in Germany: his many enemies would have used it to ruin him. He therefore arranged for her to emigrate to Switzerland. Her family, including her husband, were still in Germany, so he was sure he had her under control. This officer was in the Intelligence branch of the Gestapo, the one that was making so much trouble for Canaris, and his business often took him to Switzerland, where all the belligerents had spies and listening posts. In Switzerland he could safely visit his woman. Sumptuous surroundings were an aphrodisiac to him and he insisted that she live in luxury. He opened in a Zurich bank a checking account in her name. She must have been a remarkable actress, for she made love to him with such expertise and variety that he believed she was as mad for him as he was for her.

Over a period of more than ten months, this woman had been using his money to bribe minor Nazi officials to furnish the rest of her family with emigration visas. When they were all safe in Switzerland, she had a private meeting with the Director of her bank and told him the whole story. The Director was Hanna's Uncle Karl. One of the lady's own uncles had been a friend of the Erlich family for years. Within forty-eight hours Admiral Canaris had on his desk all the evidence he needed.

A brief meeting with the Gestapo officer was all that was required to have Dr. Erlich released from Dachau. Then Canaris put the screws on harder. He demanded for the doctor an exit visa to Switzerland and at this point the Gestapo man became terrified. He said it was impossible because Goebbels had a personal hatred for Dr. Erlich and would surely know if he had escaped to Switzerland. If that happened, then he – the Gestapo man – would have to implicate Canaris and both of them would be ruined.

The two operators came to a compromise. Dr. Erlich would be allowed to live with his wife in a small Alpine village near Munich, where he would be required to report weekly to the local police. He would also be given new identification papers under a different name.

During all this time, Hanna preserved her cover. Her duties were routine, mostly arranging for letters and food parcels to be delivered to prisoners of war. She always informed the police when she made one of her rare visits to her parents and the police assumed it was part of her work. Nor did she and Conrad live under the same roof, though they met from time to time until their separate apartments were destroyed by British air attacks. I can't imagine that their love for each other was any release to them. It must have been somewhat as it was for Joanne and me in the time of the Second Bureaucracy. And, of course, they both knew that such time as they had was running out.

For just as Canaris had predicted, Hitler finally brought most of the world against Germany. The air attacks became steadily more terrible, and as the range of the bombers increased, Berlin was battered again and again. Life in the city became so dangerous that Gottfried Dehmel sent his wife out of the city to live in Freiburg.

It was during this time that Canaris discovered a new role for Conrad. They both knew there was no hope of peace while Hitler was alive; they knew also that another year of this kind of bombing would smash the German cities into heaps of broken stones. Conrad now became one of a variety of men (some of them architects and art historians) who catalogued the country's most famous buildings and assembled the plans and designs of the ancient cities. These were stored in safe places in the hope that Germany could be rebuilt after the war. How large a role Conrad himself played in this operation I don't know, but certainly after the war the old Germany rose like a phoenix from its ashes.

Conrad dated the turning point for Hitler with the death of his brother Siegfried. For two years the submarines had been so successful that the sailors believed they could starve the British into surrender. Then suddenly, within a single month, the British destroyed seventy U-boats. The German Admiralty knew they were using a new kind of weapon but they did not know what it was. This meant that the German navy was virtually finished. Among the boats that failed to return was Siegfried's.

It had been a long time since Conrad had seen his father, but when this news arrived he visited him. He found a man whose face proclaimed more than grief for his son. At last Gottfried Dehmel understood that once more his beloved country had lost a great war.

Conrad said to him, "I've been thinking that it's only the losers who can have ultimate dignity."

If his father heard this remark he gave no sign of it. His eyes flashed open and he began to shout.

"The idiot! The maniac!"

Conrad remembered his last night in Freiburg when he and his father had looked at Goya's war pictures. He said nothing. His father went on:

"He lied to us. He broke his promise to us. If he had waited till the navy was ready, nothing could have prevented us from winning this war. Now millions of American troops and millions of tons of food and matériel are pouring across the Atlantic as though it were a lake. Those fool generals and politicians! This is the second time they've refused to understand what sea power means. This war must end while there's still something left."

"Does Hitler know it's lost?"

Gottfried Dehmel stared out the window and made no comment.

Now, just as Admiral Canaris had predicted – and Dr. Erlich had predicted even before the war – Hitler's personality went out of control. He was far from the only one who had preached that Jews were the curse of mankind, but now in the profundity of his psychosis he believed that they were responsible for all the shames and miseries he himself had suffered since the day of his birth. Some time before this he had given orders for what he called the Final Solution of the Jewish Problem, but now this became his chief aim. Though he never admitted that he had lost the war, he knew that he had lost it, just as the Admiral had said he would know it. Now he was determined to exterminate all the Jews of Europe before he was exterminated himself.

A week after visiting his father, Conrad was in Freiburg staying with his mother in a small flat near the Minster. Her hair was now very white. The arthritis had closed in on her fingers and she could no longer play her piano, but her eyes were as gentle and understanding as they had always been. She thanked him for having gone to his father after the death of Siegfried.

Conrad said, "Mother, you always knew it would come to this, didn't you?"

"So did you, but we both hoped it wouldn't."

He stayed in Freiburg for several weeks. He knew and loved every corner of that city and now that he was seeing Germany in terms of doom, he haunted the Minster and the Minster Platz of the ancient section of the town. He met with the Burgomaster and with several of the aldermen and learned that they also were making plans for the reconstruction of the city if it was destroyed.

I will now turn the narrative back to Conrad as he himself wrote it. This section of the papers I left to the last because they were written in German, and my own German, which never had been too good, had become extremely rusty. I finally managed to translate it, and it is my own translation I am offering now. Though it is addressed to my mother, Conrad himself says there are many things about this period of his life that he had never told her before, and as she could not read German, it seems probable to me that she died without ever understanding why he was killed. Nor, for that matter, did anyone else.

PART EIGHT

Conrad Dehmel's Story
as told by himself

*Y*OU KNOW , Stephanie, because I made no secret of it, that at the war's end I was in the Belsen concentration camp and would have died there if the British Army had not arrived and liberated the survivors. I have never tried to describe the experience because nobody could describe its reality. Everyone, of course, has seen pictures of the walking skeletons. But nobody who was not there has smelled them or has had to sleep beside the corpses.

You have seen the faded scars on my body and sometimes you have heard me scream in the night. You must often have wondered if you were married to two different men – the calm scholar and, perhaps, the hidden horror. I have loved you and I still do, but for years it has been impossible for me to love myself and now I feel compelled to tell you why.

Belsen? The thousands of corpses stacked there like cordwood? The guards, Germans like myself, and what they did and what they were? I never told you of one incident that has seared itself into my memory cells. A few weeks before the British came, a starved prisoner collapsed and fell on the ground a few meters away from me. I was weak and starving too, but when I bent down automatically to help him, a guard cuffed me aside, turned the man over on his back, and carefully smashed four gold teeth out of his mouth with a hammer. The man was still alive. He had enough strength left to moan and sob. The guard put the teeth into his pocket and I stood there watching him.

Nor did I tell you how it happened that I was sent to Belsen. After the war was over, anyone who had been in a concentration camp was regarded as a martyr or a hero. A sentence to a camp exonerated even a German from any kind of collective guilt. Naturally, some people believed I was in the German underground.

But there was no underground among the German people during that war. The police were everywhere and made any kind of popular revolt impossible. All the young men were mobilized into the armies, and the fighting was desperate. Night after night the allied planes bombarded the cities. The only resistance to Hitler came from a tiny group of high officers and it completely failed.

During the early days of the war I played an ignoble part; my sole purpose was to survive. But this changed when Hanna Erlich came home because her father had been arrested. I have confessed to you my impulsive, idiotic marriage to Eva Schmidt when I was blown up with delusions of intellectual grandeur and I have told you how deeply and happily I was in love with Hanna when we were both in England. But I never told you the whole truth about this. Hanna in England was one thing; Hanna in Hitler's Germany was another, for in Germany her sole purpose was to protect her parents. I have also told you a little about Admiral Canaris, who was my protector in those days.

I was in Freiburg visiting my mother when a call came from Canaris ordering me to return to Berlin immediately. I arrived several hours behind time because the city had been struck by a ferocious air raid the night before and half a kilometer of railway track had to be cleared before trains could enter the city. I emerged from the ruins of the station into a wilderness of shattered buildings with fires burning everywhere and the smoke so thick that the central city was in twilight though the sun was shining brightly above it. People with smoke-blackened faces and desperate, enduring eyes were coming out of mass shelters and basements and plodding to work. Corpses were scattering here and there, fire engines were squirting water, fire hoses wriggled like pythons across bomb-holed streets. My lungs were dry and aching from the smoke, my nostrils were desiccated. There were blizzards of scorched paper, geysers of water spouted up from shattered mains. When finally I reached the Admiral his face was dusky and his eyes were red.

Canaris did not rise when I entered his room. He remained as he was, his small body hunched forward and his chin on the heels of his hands.

"How many more nights like this can our people stand?" he said as if to himself.

"Was it much worse than usual?"

"Yes, and less than what will come later." He took a deep breath as though to clear the smoke from his lungs. "However, I didn't summon you from Freiburg to tell you that. The time has come at last. At any moment Dr. Erlich may be picked up. As Hanna is with him now, she will be picked up, too."

I said nothing and waited. His next question was not long in coming.

"Those trains – those freight trains with Jews packed into them like sardines – have you seen any of them?"

"So it's true?"

"Most people know nothing of them." The Admiral nodded toward the window through which we could see the drifting smoke. "With all they are suffering and will have to suffer, who should blame them if they don't think about what he's doing to the Jews? Yes, it's true. It's so unbelievably true that not even I believed it would come to this."

The Admiral's eyes closed, his head sank into his hands so that only the white cap of his hair was visible. It was the first time I had seen his mask crack open.

"Oh, Dehmel, so many of us have longed for this country to be honorable. Now on account of this man we are hated and despised as no people has ever been. There will be no mercy. The vengeance will be terrible. They have decided to destroy us." He drew another ponderous breath and coughed. Then his voice firmed. "I will continue in the way I have chosen, but I can't hope to last much longer."

We sat there and coughed. I watched Canaris pick up a pen and doodle aimlessly on a scrap of paper.

"Can you do nothing for the Erlichs, sir?"

"My position is so slippery I may be arrested myself. My service is a travesty of what it once was. The party has virtually taken it over. I've had to be devious, Dehmel. Very devious and for such a long time that my brain feels like a weary muscle. So many balls in the air at once. Sooner or later one of them is bound to drop. They have always known that Dr. Erlich is my friend. For me to intervene on his behalf would not only be useless, it would be fatal to us both." He paused and looked me in the eyes. "However, it is not known that you wish to marry his daughter."

"Has Hanna blown her cover?"

"No, but she's with her father. She feels he can't be left alone. Three weeks ago her mother went to Switzerland to visit the doctor's brother there. You can guess why she went. She was stopped at the border when she tried to return a few days later. She is still in Switzerland. Somehow Goebbels has found out where the doctor is. The change of name – somebody must have talked. Sooner or later they will come for him and if Hanna is there..." He lifted his hands and let them drop.

I waited for more. It soon came.

"If you still mean what you once said to me, you may be able to save them if you're lucky. Don't be shocked by what I'm going to propose to you. Your only chance is to join the Gestapo."

I murmured, "Oh, my God!"

"In a Gestapo uniform you might pretend to arrest them and get them away from that village before the exterminators arrive. No local functionary will question a man in the black uniform."

"And then?"

"You must hide them somewhere. In some place where they can stay until the war is over. That could be sooner than you think."

"But would the Gestapo accept a man like me?"

The Admiral's expression was resigned.

"I've told you many times that these people are not normal. Himmler hates all professional officers like your father. He knows what they say and think about him. He also knows he can't do without them."

"I don't follow you, sir."

"I'm still on terms with Himmler. I still have a certain power over him. What that power is I have mentioned to nobody but himself. Anyway, I took the liberty of telling him that you had asked me to recommend you to the SS. The idea of your father's son wanting to join his gangsters is not unattractive to this chicken farmer."

"Would he want me to spy on my father?"

"Probably."

"My father never has spoken about him in my presence."

"He's an outspoken man. Never?"

"He was always careful until my brother was lost."

"Your father and I have had several conversations these past few months. He's a man I respect very much, but he's not fitted for the situation we're in now. However, say nothing to Himmler about him that you do not know to be true. He knows much about your father."

I was silent.

Canaris said, "I may be wrong. I often am. But I believe Himmler will accept you."

I rose and went to the window and looked out at the smoke drifting through the street. Even when Germany was everywhere triumphant, my intuition had told me it would finally come to this, but only in recent months had I truly believed it. Berlin was half destroyed already. Soon it would be totally destroyed. Many people had already dug caves out of the shattered masonry and were living in them with the corpses underneath. Soon all the German cities would be smashed. But the land would remain. The wonderful, varied land of forests and rivers and plains and mountains would still be there after the Devil had gone back to hell.

Bombs from an earlier raid had fallen near by and destroyed half a block. The ruins were outlined by the blackened stumps of torn linden trees. I turned away and sat down again.

"Is there any discharge from the SS?"

"Don't waste your time thinking about that."

"But doesn't the training take months?"

"In your case I don't think so. You would be employed as a functionary."

"Would I be ordered to take part in this – this thing against the Jews?"

"That is precisely why I make this proposal to you."

I began to tremble. "No, sir! Not even for Hanna. She'd kill herself if she knew this was the price of her life. She'd kill me, too."

"I did not say you would *have* to do it. I said you'd be *ordered* to do it. I'm not pretending your position won't be horrible to someone with your temperament. Even a few weeks of training with them will be a nasty experience. And if you help them escape and desert afterwards, as I propose that you do" – he shrugged – "you know what they will do to you if they catch you. But this is how I see it. If Himmler accepts you, they will give you a very short course of instruction. This operation against the Jews is now so enormous it has created a bureaucracy. They're very short-handed and they don't require the military types for much of this kind of work. They're now in such a hurry I doubt if your training period will last more than three weeks at the most. At the end of that time – perhaps even during it – tell them your mother is in Freiburg and has taken seriously ill. Ask for a few days' leave to visit her before they post you somewhere else. Whoever is your commander will probably grant this because you've been sent to him by Himmler. But don't try to hide the Erlichs in Freiburg."

I asked if it would be possible to get them into Switzerland. Perhaps the Gestapo officer he had squeezed a few years ago could be used again?

"Not unless he rises from the dead. He was killed by Russian partisans six months ago. No, I see no way of getting them into Switzerland now. The Swiss themselves are very nervous and with good reason. We're pressing them one way, the Allies are pressing them another."

"Why do you tell me not to hide them in Freiburg? Nobody knows them there."

"Do you know anyone in the city apart from your mother who would take them in?"

"No."

"There's a Gestapo headquarters there and any newcomers would be investigated. There's also another reason. At any moment the Allies will land in Europe. The invasion is sure to come through France, though the Leader thinks it may come in several other places. These past two years the English Intelligence has been uncannily clever. But they and the Americans will invade and they are sure to succeed. When they break through and close in on Germany, Freiburg will almost certainly be bombed to death."

"But it has no military significance whatever."

Canaris's expression did not change. "The air power of the Allies is now overwhelming, as you can see for yourself. Their air marshals are also functionaries. Blowing up cities has become their business, and with each passing month there are fewer cities left intact. One has the power. One uses it." He paused. "You are fond of walking. Do you know the Black Forest well?"

"Most of it."

I sensed then what was in the Admiral's mind and asked him to give me a few minutes to think.

In recent weeks I had often thought of the Black Forest as a refuge for Hanna and her father. I had even formed a tentative plan. The last time I visited Mother, I had gone for a walk to the place where I caught the hares during the hunger in the First War. The forester's cottage was still there and an old widower was living in it alone. He was the same man who had been the forester many years ago when I was a boy. His cottage was empty at the time I caught the hares near it, because he had been drafted into the army at the end of the war. He had been gassed and wounded in Flanders, but after the war he had been given back his old job. When Hitler's war began, a great deal of timber was cut in the forest, but for some reason very little was cut in this area. Though the man's meager pay had come through regularly, he told me that it was more than a year since he had received any instructions. At first he was unwilling to talk, but when I told him about the hares in my boyhood the old man smiled.

"There are many hares now. I also have a small garden." Then he said in a resigned voice, "They have forgotten all about me."

The forester's mind seemed vague, but when he and I sat in the sun and smoked our pipes – I had given him the first tobacco he had seen in more than a year – he began to talk. He spoke slowly, in fits and starts. He said his first wife had died so long ago he could hardly remember her. His second wife was also dead. By her he had had three sons and they had all been killed in Russia.

"One of them intended to take my place, but he can't because he's dead. They've forgotten all about me."

Birds chirped in the forest, I saw a hare come out and squat in the sun, and we smoked in silence.

As though he were talking to himself, the forester said, "The Austrians got us into the first war and we lost it. Now another Austrian has got us into a worse one and we'll soon lose it. That's how it happens. Three sons. I'm all alone here. No work. They don't tell me what to do."

The old path I had followed as a child had been widened into a corduroy road which passed the cottage at a distance of about a hundred meters. The cottage was invisible from the road, which was overgrown with a short covering of grass. I asked him if it was still used and he shook his head.

"There's another one about three kilometers away they use very much."

On my way back to the city I had examined the surface of the road and calculated that if I could acquire some kind of vehicle I could convey Hanna and her father to this place along with rations and bedding. There was even a well behind the cottage near where the garden was. There were cooking utensils and an old stove inside. The forester might accept us and of course he could be paid, if only with tobacco. But I did not believe he would be influenced by a bribe. He was of the old stock of the old Breisgau; he was a tribesman.

I looked Canaris in the eyes and said, "All right, I'll try." And with those four syllables I committed myself.

A week later, wearing my naval uniform, I appeared before Himmler. I had seen many pictures of this man, but only when he was performing in some public affair in an imposing setting. The reality of Himmler alone in his office was very different. He was a dumpy, slope-shouldered little man almost chinless, hollow-chested and wide-hipped, pot-bellied and myopic behind rimless pince-nez that glittered in such a way that they seemed to mask the chilly eyes behind them. He made me think of a pettifogging clerk with nasty personal habits and a disagreeable body odor.

Himmler surveyed me as though I were a lifeless object, picked up a note from his desk, appeared to study it, then laid it down.

"I understand that you are the son of Rear-Admiral Dehmel?" he said.

"Yes, Herr Reichsführer."

Himmler made some coldly poisonous remarks about the navy and its admirals and I was chilled and terrified. I had never met a man before who held such monstrous power and it was not reassuring to realize that in himself he was a total nothing. By his mere appearance this little creature seemed to define the preposterous character of the entire regime. Somehow I managed to articulate that the sailors had done their duty as they saw it.

"Then why have they done so badly?"

"Herr Reichsführer, do you believe my brother Siegfried did badly?"

"When I said the navy did badly, I was not referring to young submarine officers. Naturally, the *Jugend* are heroes. They grew up under the Führer. But their commanders?" He did not even shrug. He left it in the air.

"Herr Reichsführer," I said, "if you are thinking about my father, he is a brave and loyal man. Unfortunately he is also an old-fashioned man who cannot understand the kind of world we're living in now."

"What do you mean by that?"

"The treachery, Herr Reichsführer. The last time I spoke with my father he was very worried. I told him that if our naval Intelligence had been half as good as England's, my brother would still be alive and serving the Führer."

With no expression, Himmler said, "You are a protégé of Admiral Canaris. Are you criticizing your protector? If so, tell me why."

"What can Admiral Canaris do when there are so many traitors?"

His chilly eyes became chillier. "That is very interesting, what you say. What do *you* know of these traitors you speak of?"

"Nothing of them, Herr Reichsführer. If I knew their names, I would have informed Admiral Canaris. I simply know they exist."

"How do you know this?"

"What other explanation can there be except traitors in high places?"

"Explanation for what?"

"For the victories the British and Americans have been winning. Without treason they could never have done it. Africa – Sicily – Italy. Always they win by surprise. So there must be traitors, and in high places."

A flicker of light appeared in Himmler's little eyes and he said, "Yes, what other explanation is possible?"

Then the flat face turned cold again and he asked me what I thought of the Jews. Did I know that the service I wished to join was now committed to the Final Solution of the Jewish Problem? Did I know what the final solution was?

I had expected this question, had been told to expect it, and I had rehearsed my answer. I was trembling when I made it, for I had never had experience with these high fanatics and I still could not believe that anyone would take seriously what I had been told to say. I looked at him earnestly.

"I don't deny, Herr Reichsführer, that when I was young there were some individual Jews I thought I liked. It took me far too long to realize that the supreme proof of the Führer's genius lies in this – that he understood the Jews as nobody has ever understood them. The Romans loathed them. 'This disgusting people' – that is how their historian Tacitus described them. But he did not understand them. Neither did the Christians. We had to wait until the Führer made us realize that though they are human in the anatomical sense, they have always been a disease within every civilization they have infected, and that no civilization can hope to survive unless they are exterminated."

I had been told that Himmler's little eyes could smile at his wife and child with adolescent sentimentality but for me they remained cold as a snake's.

"Am I supposed to be impressed by that statement? You repeat only what the Führer was saying when you were still in school. Just when did *you* come to share his opinion, Professor?"

This question I had also expected and was ready with an answer.

"I remember the day precisely, Herr Reichsführer. It was the day after the Führer became Chancellor and I knew that at last Germany had found her savior."

His eyes remained a snake's. "In that case – quite a long time after the date you mentioned – why did you return from England to work under the Jew Rosenthal?"

"I returned to serve Germany, Herr Reichsführer. I knew that Rosenthal was sure to be dismissed."

The snake's coil tightened. "I am very well informed, Dehmel."

"One knows that, Herr Reichsführer. One is thankful for that."

"I have filing cabinets containing many more than a million names and incidents. I review them constantly."

I bowed and said nothing.

"Answer me this – why, the day you arrived from England at the Grosser Kurfürst Institut – why did you defend this Jew against a loyal German you later dismissed?"

This question I had been sure would be asked and as I still remembered with bitterness my first day at the Institut, I was able to answer with real indignation.

"I did *not* defend Rosenthal, Herr Reichsführer, though that stupid oaf of a *Blockwart* probably thought I did. I am not accustomed to insolence from a *Kerl* like him. The man was a fool. Loyal, certainly, but a hopeless fool. I wished to talk privately with Rosenthal before he left the country. I wished to learn some of his connections abroad. All I learned was that he knew Einstein – or pretended that he did. He was very clever and very slippery. I still wonder why he was allowed to leave with his life."

Himmler nodded. "He did know Einstein. They're both in the same place in America."

For nearly a minute Himmler was silent and expressionless. Then he murmured as though he were talking to himself.

"These Jews are so difficult. I have never been hostile to them. I even tried to like them. But they remain Jews and they can never be anything else. They have given me a terrible problem. They have made me do things that may injure my reputation."

Again he fell silent and for the next few minutes he seemed unaware that I was in the room. There were many papers on his desk. He picked up one after the other, glanced at them, and initialled them. A filing clerk of death and murder, I thought, and stood before him wondering whether another paper would be initialled that would send me to my end.

Suddenly he looked up. "You will report to Gruppenführer Krafft in Munich. One of the secretaries will give you the address and the date."

"Thank you, Herr Reichsführer."

Himmler extended across the desk a limp, clammy hand. "Hals und Beinbruch," he said.

I left him, spoke with the secretary, and was given a date and an address in Munich. I saluted, pocketed the information, and asked where the men's room was. I locked myself into a toilet cabinet and vomited with such violence I felt as though I were vomiting up some of the tissues of my stomach. Weak, wet, sweating, and pale I got to my feet, wiped my face clean with a handkerchief, and opened the door of the cabinet to confront a Gestapo sergeant.

"I had too much to drink last night," I said to him.

The sergeant's face was a block of expressionless bone and muscle.

"But it wasn't really that," I said. "To meet the Reichsführer – to be accepted by him when I hardly dared hope I'd be accepted – it was too much for me."

"What can I do for you, Herr Leutnant?"

"A car to my lodgings, if that's possible."

"Bestimmt, Herr Leutnant."

The man crashed into a salute. I replied with a casual naval one.

The next day in Munich I was inducted into the Gestapo. My fingerprints were taken and checked against those on the dossier which Krafft had ready on his desk. He asked me a series of routine questions about my past career and turned me over to a doctor for a medical examination. The doctor stabbed a thick finger up my rectum with such violence I nearly screamed from pain and shock. He grinned at me.

"So you're not a homosexual. What a pity! However" – he was still grinning – "it was a necessary medical examination."

Later that day I was fitted for the black uniform and the next morning my training began. It occupied me entirely and I discovered it would take a good deal longer than Canaris had expected. For more than six weeks I studied manuals, listened to lectures, spent four hours a day in rugged and exhausting physical exercises, underwent weapons training, and was instructed in various methods of making arrests. I had been in the Gestapo for more than two weeks before the western Allies landed in France. The first communiqués were vague and made light of the situation and I was afraid it was another failure like Dieppe.

The pace of the training became faster and harsher. One morning a senior officer barked at me to stand at attention. I did so, and without warning he slapped me hard across the face with the back of his hand. It was a test, of course, and as I had heard about it I did not flinch. Later I was put into a section of twenty young men with blank faces and powerful bodies and taught some routine methods of quick killing. Finally I received a summons to appear before Krafft once more.

"You have done quite well," he said. "At least adequately well. I will now tell you what lies ahead."

Here Canaris had been accurate. My work with the Gestapo would be purely bureaucratic. I would be assigned to a small district in Hungary where I was to order a compilation of the names and addresses of all the Jews living there. Those still at liberty I was to have arrested and finally I was to make arrangements with the railway officials for the trains that would take them to the gas chambers and the ovens in Poland. When I asked when I was to leave for Hungary, Krafft became irritable.

"The damned bombing is causing delays everywhere. In France alone we've lost thousands of freight cars and hundreds of locomotives. Anyway, your training is not complete. You must still pass your final stage."

He did not tell me what the final stage was and for another week I was put through even more exhausting physical drills and weapons training. It was now midsummer and the weather was hot and humid. I worried constantly about Hanna and her father because time was passing and I was afraid they had already been arrested. If there was any reliable news about the battle in France we were not told of it. The first real information came to me by chance at the mess table when a senior officer joined Krafft and I overheard the conversation. This officer looked tired, strained, and very worried. He had just returned from Normandy.

"It's not good," I heard him say. "We knew the English and the Canadians would be tough but we thought the Americans would be soft. We were wrong about that. Of course, none of them are in our class, but that fool Goering has left us without an air force. Their planes are over us like an umbrella from dawn till dark. The bombing is unbelievable. The fighting is worse than anything I ever saw in Russia."

I kept my eyes fixed on my plate. So the invasion was successful. So Hanna and her father might have a chance if they were still free. I myself might have a chance. And surely the British and the Americans would know there were men like Canaris in Germany who could do away with Hitler and make peace with the West before the Russians came in and tore what was left of the country to pieces.

When the visiting officer departed I finally made my gamble. I told Krafft that I had just learned that my mother, who was in Freiburg, had been diagnosed for cancer. I wanted to speak with her physician to learn the exact nature of her case. As she might have little time left, I begged for a few days' leave to visit her before going to Hungary. Krafft looked at me with suspicion.

"Your final sessions begin tomorrow. You will have three of them on successive days."

I asked him what they would consist of and he said casually, "Interrogations."

Stephanie, those next three days were the second most horrible I ever spent in my life. The sessions I attended lasted from four to six hours and I had to watch what they did to the victims strapped to a bloodstained table and I had to hear their screams. I had to look on with a frozen face, for Krafft kept watching me. If I had protested, fainted, or vomited I would have been disgraced in Krafft's eyes, and any chance of rescuing Hanna would have vanished.

After the final session Krafft became very friendly. He clapped me on the back and called me *ein ganzer Kerl* (a fine boy) and told me he now trusted me completely. He also said I might have four days' leave to visit my mother in Freiburg.

"Give your respected mother my greetings," he said. Then he added reflectively, "Those interrogations weren't much. Those men broke very quickly."

"Two of them screamed in French and one of them screamed in Czech."

"Did they? The difficult ones were the Germans in the early days. Communists. Swine of course, but they were at least Germans. Most of them died before they talked. What a waste!" He smiled at me. "You'll enjoy your work in Hungary. I think you'll enjoy it very much."

I hoped to get some more information about the battle in France but he was indifferent.

"The Führer will soon take personal charge of the situation and settle it. So now, on your way to Freiburg! Report to our barracks when you arrive and if you need anything, they'll provide it." He then gave me requisitions for a Volkswagen and gasoline and shook my hand. "Heil Hitler," he said. "Heil Hitler," I said.

TWO

I TOLD YOU, Stephanie, that I have found it impossible to love myself. It was this experience that started it. The next day, driving in the Volkswagen to the mountain village where I hoped to find Hanna and her father, I was no longer the same kind of man I had been before. Even now as I write this I can hear the screams of those tortured men, but that morning they deafened me. I felt worse than a murderer. I wondered if the shame and horror had passed into my face and I soon discovered that it had.

Hanna and I had not seen each other for more than five months and when I appeared at the door in my SS uniform her face went pale and she flinched away with loathing in her eyes. Let nobody blame her for that. This was a time so unnatural that almost anything could happen and I realized that her first thought was that I had joined the Gestapo in order to save my own life and that part of the deal was to arrest her father and possibly herself. I was in partial shock anyway and her attitude paralyzed me. But her father understood instantly and closed the door behind me.

"So you are Conrad!" he said and smiled and shook my hand.

Hanna was still staring at me. "How long have you been wearing *that*?" she said and pointed at my uniform.

Then something like fury exploded inside me and my voice shook. "I've planned everything. You must leave here at once."

"For where? Dachau?"

Dr. Erlich intervened. "Hanna – please! You're not yourself. Listen to what Conrad is trying to tell us."

"I've found a place where I can hide you both," I said. "It's in the Black Forest near Freiburg. I have a car to take you there. Believe me, it's your only chance."

"I asked you how long you've been wearing that uniform," she said.

"Longer than the Admiral told me would be necessary. It was his plan. He told me this was the only way to save you."

"Hanna hadn't heard from you for months," the doctor said gently. "She was very worried about you and this – well, it's a surprise."

Hanna's disgust was leaving her, but I was still hurt and angry.

"You mean Admiral Canaris did –" and she pointed at my uniform.

"He told me my only chance of saving you and your father was to join the Gestapo. He arranged it with Himmler. Do you think I enjoyed it?"

"It's done something to your face."

"I'm afraid it has, Hanna."

"We won't go with you. No matter what you have in mind, we won't go with you."

My temper broke and I shouted at her. "Has the hell I've been through these past two months been useless? Do you think I intend to go back to Gestapo headquarters? I have two civilian suits in the car and when the time comes I'm going to burn or bury this horrible uniform."

At last she believed me. Her pallor turned into a flush, but she remained stubborn.

"The day I first saw you – when I came back to Germany – I told you I'd never endanger you, Conrad." Quietly she added, "I still mean it. No, Conrad, we won't go with you."

My nerves were screaming at me and I think I screamed at her, "For God's sake why do you have to be so stubborn? Endanger me? I've endangered myself and there's no turning back. There's no possible alternative for any of us. More than two months have passed since Admiral Canaris warned me that you and your father could be picked up at any moment. Do what I say, for God's sake, and stop arguing."

Dr. Erlich put his hand on his daughter's arm. "Hanna dear, we both understand how you feel, but please be reasonable." He turned to me and said, "I learn nothing here and Hanna can only guess what's been happening. She's thought and worried about you every day, Conrad."

The doctor had a way with him and my voice became normal again.

"What's happening is what both you and the Admiral predicted. The liquidation of the Jews has become almost as important to Hitler as the war. He knows he's lost the war, but he thinks he still has time to destroy the Jews. We have no time to waste, Doctor. We can talk all we like on the way to Freiburg."

I looked out the window and saw some villagers standing outside watching. Dr. Erlich also looked out the window.

"These village people rather like us," he said. "They think you've come to arrest us."

"That's just what I want them to think." I gave the doctor an appraising glance. He seemed frail, but probably in adequate health for the journey. To Hanna I said, "How soon will you be ready to leave?"

She was herself again, her very efficient self. She was already packing a carton with all the food they had. While doing so she told me they had two suitcases already packed and ready.

I threw open the door with a theatrical crash and stalked out, not a man but a uniform, and barked at the villagers to clear out and ask no questions. They knew what my uniform meant and they vanished. I drove the Volkswagen to the back of the house where we could pack it without being seen. I asked if any arrests had been made in the village and Dr. Erlich said there had been none.

"That's good," I said, "because this isn't the normal way we arrest Jews in the Gestapo."

It was a cruel thing to say and Hanna winced.

"So you were taught to do that, too?" she said.

This day was the only one on which I felt totally bitter against her. "I was taught, but I haven't done it. Will that satisfy you, or do you wish to continue humiliating me?"

Dr. Erlich, of course, understood us better than we understood ourselves. "How long will it take us to reach Freiburg?" he asked gently.

Looking at my watch I saw it was now eleven o'clock. "It's about two hundred kilometers to Freiburg. If the roads are clear, we should be there by early evening."

"There have been many planes overhead recently," he said.

"German or allied?"

"Both, but mostly allied."

"Are the Allies shooting up traffic on the roads?"

"Possibly, but here there's nothing to shoot at."

We drove off, and as we passed through the village main street I noticed a few movements of curtains and knew we were being watched. I took the road for Munich and I'm not proud of what I said then, but Hanna had wounded me and I said it.

"If this was a real arrest, we're going in the right direction. Just beyond Munich is Dachau."

Dr. Erlich said quietly, "Of course, Conrad. But Hanna has also been under great tension."

After Munich I turned west and there was little traffic on the road. We rolled on. It was quite incredible, but gradually I relaxed. The doctor was in the front seat of the little car, Hanna in the rear with the carton of food, the suitcases in the trunk ahead. I was thinking, "If it hadn't been for Hanna I would not have horrified myself and now she despises me for what I did for her sake." I was thinking, "But those men would have been tortured anyway, so why should I feel degraded?" I thought again, "But I *was* degraded. Hanna knows it and she's biting me for it." And again, "But how can she possibly know it?" And still again, I recalled that in her work with the Red Cross she must have discovered pretty accurately the training methods of the Gestapo, and it was with bitterness that I thought that I had never loved anyone as I had loved her and now she seemed to have contempt for me.

After a time I felt her fingers touch the back of my neck and gently stroke it and at last I began to feel better. Some day I would tell her about witnessing the tortures, but I could not tell her now. Perhaps I never would tell her. Perhaps I would never tell anyone.

Until now, all these years later, I never have.

A half-hour after leaving Munich we overtook a column of tanks moving slowly ahead of us. I guessed they had come from Russia and were going west to reinforce the new front in France. I exchanged salutes with an officer standing in the turret of the leading tank and we passed on ahead of the column. When we reached Augsburg the center of the city was in ruins from a recent raid and it took some time to get through. Beyond Augsburg we saw a formation of heavy American planes flying west, which meant that they had discharged their bombs. Where, I could not even guess. I muttered to the doctor what madmen the Nazis were to continue this war when the skies over Germany were in the complete command of their enemies. Then, remembering the SS men I had been living with, I said, "Are they really insane, Doctor? Are they really insane or am I just using words that mean nothing?"

"Are they insane?"

The doctor said this and was silent for nearly a minute. Then he said, "That's a question I've asked myself thousands of times. Insanity is not a word to be used carelessly. The human mind is infinitely suggestible."

Driving the car, irritable and feeling put upon by Hanna, I said, "Doctor, I have asked you a direct question."

"Yes, Conrad, you have, and it's a legitimate question. You may not like my answer. In my opinion very few of Hitler's henchmen are true psychotics. But even before he came to power I realized that he was creating what we call in my profession a *folie à deux*. Are you familiar with the term?"

"No."

"Among individuals this happens frequently. A man – or a woman – gets another person under control and makes his partner believe that he is not only right but a benefactor. Quite often this person is sincere, though in such a case sincerity is another meaningless word. I'm not talking about confidence men. They know what they're doing. You asked me a question, Conrad, and I'll try to answer it.

"Hitler in my belief has created a *folie à deux* – a duet of folly – with a nation of ninety million people. Others have done it in the past and the great men of your profession have called them men of destiny. The great men of the earth! This is understandable, that they call them great, considering what they have accomplished. Napoleon psychotic? He was a gambler, but he was seldom out of touch with reality. But Hitler is an out-and-out psychotic and the generals and politicians are helpless before him because they can't understand what a psychotic can do. Your colleagues, your historians, they used to talk of 'the dignity of history.' To me the evolution of mankind is utterly marvellous. But there is no dignity in the history Hitler has made, just as there is none to be found in the psyche of a sadistic maniac. Unfortunately, there is some of that in us all and Hitler has found his path to it."

"Professor Rosenthal used almost the same words to me."

I was frightened again. Why was I here? Why was I driving along this road with a woman I loved who distrusted me and shut me out? Why, for God's sake? Had Hanna created a *folie à deux* with me because of her family? Was her father indirectly trying to tell me that? But of course she hadn't and he wasn't.

We passed another column of troops, this time infantry huddled close together in army trucks with motorcycle men on their flanks. Another transfer from Russia? If the British and the Americans killed them their troubles would be over. But when I took a quick glance at their faces I knew they would fight in anguish to the last word of command from above.

Soon afterwards we reached the Danube at Ulm, that beautiful city where Einstein was born. Its ancient heart had been blasted to rubble but the famous spire of the cathedral was still a finger pointing to eternity. It was uncanny how the bombers, even the British who bombed by night, were able to blast the hearts out of city after city and yet leave their cathedrals standing. Did they spare the cathedrals because they needed their spires as markers?

Uncanny also was the peacefulness of the German countryside where farmers were working as usual in their fields, though night after night they had heard the thunder of the bomber streams and seen the flames of burning cities flaring around their horizons. We passed still another troop column moving very slowly because of the *ersatz* fuel it was using. Some thirty kilometers later I saw the burnt-out wreckage of a large bombing plane in a field near the road. On an impulse I stopped the car, got out, and walked over to it and there was a single corpse inside the wreckage. It was the pilot, who must have stayed at his controls while his crew parachuted. There was little left of him but on his only remaining shoulder I made out the scorched word "Canada" and it gave me a feeling of awe. What was the mystical power of England that had enabled her to draw these distant people across the ocean to fight for her? Now, of course, I have become one of them.

As we neared Freiburg an American long-distance fighter plane dipped its nose and made for us. I stopped the car, Hanna and I leaped out and helped Dr. Erlich, and we hurried him across a ditch into a clump of trees and lay down with our faces pressed against the grass. It smelled sweetly of clover and I heard a thrush singing in the branches. We waited and nothing happened. The noise of the plane's engine diminished and I got up and saw it climbing into the sky in the west. Was it on reconnaissance, and if so, for what? Anyway, the pilot had not wasted his ammunition on a Volkswagen.

We reached Freiburg in the evening and the Minster spire was outlined by a sinking sun.

THREE

*T*HE HOUSE WHERE MOTHER LIVED had once belonged to a wealthy Jewish manufacturer who had left Germany shortly after Hitler had taken charge of the country. Afterwards it had been broken up into five separate apartments. There was no *Blockwart* and Mother lived on the ground floor. When she saw me standing in the doorway in my Gestapo uniform she blanched. When I entered and told her why I was wearing it, she trembled so much I thought she might faint. There was no need for me to tell her what danger I was in because of this uniform. But she had always had the strength of the gentle ones who seem able to accept anything. When I beckoned to Hanna and her father to come in, her eyes met Hanna's and she smiled.

"So you are Hanna at last!"

Hanna looked at her and also smiled, "And you are Maman!"

They embraced each other. I introduced Dr. Erlich and when he kissed her on both cheeks I had to turn away because tears of thankfulness were in my eyes. It might still be worth while. Hanna had not turned on me after all.

With Hanna helping, I unpacked the car, and after the suitcases were inside the apartment I left to make my report to the local Gestapo headquarters. It was a small establishment compared to the one in Munich and the commanding officer had once served under

Krafft. I presented the paper signed by Krafft and explained why I was in Freiburg and how long I expected to stay. The officer offered me any assistance I might require but I told him I needed none. It was simply a family matter, I said. He nodded and did not even ask Mother's address.

When I returned to the apartment Mother was cooking supper with Hanna helping her. I was too restless to sit down and stood by the window looking out at the Minster and remembering my grandfather when I was a child.

Behind me I heard the doctor say, "This is truly a lovely city."

"I have never felt at home anywhere else," I said and sat down. I had not realized how tired I was. My eyelids felt as though they had weights on them like a doll's.

There was a calmness in the doctor's prematurely aged face. I was aware of him observing me, probably wondering what kind of man I really was or would become; wondering also how well or how little I understood what manner of woman his daughter was. I felt a sudden happiness and realized that ever since leaving England I had almost forgotten what happiness feels like.

While we were eating supper I asked Mother if the city had been attacked.

"There have been a few warnings. Single planes have flown over us, but they dropped no bombs."

But they certainly took photographs, I thought. There was no need to mention this to Mother. She knew why the planes had come.

"We still hope to escape the bombing," she said. "There are now almost thirty hospitals in the city, each of them with a Red Cross painted on the roof."

"They must be military hospitals. Are many wounded in them now?"

"So far very few."

"More may arrive unless the war ends soon."

I asked her if there was any news from the front in Normandy.

"The radio tells us the British and Americans are being held there."

For how much longer, I thought, and at what cost? The Red Crosses on the hospitals? I did not have to tell Mother they would be more of an invitation than a protection. Hitler had taught his enemies to be as merciless as himself, and some of them must certainly be relishing it. They were human, after all, and Hitler had given them a perfect excuse to do what they could do.

I asked Mother about her health and she admitted to the occasional heart palpitation, but said that the arthritis was the only thing that troubled her. We were sipping coffee (I had brought a small tin I had taken from the kitchen of the barracks) when I asked her if she had news from my father. She told me it was more than a month since she had heard from him.

"Are you worried on account of the bombing in Berlin?"

"The Admiralty has deep shelters."

"I suppose you know what it's been like in Berlin?"

"Naturally."

Neither of us said anything more about my father for several minutes. Hanna and her father ate quietly and both understood what we were talking about.

Finally I said, "Admiral Canaris told me he has had several conversations with Father. He likes and respects him, but my impression is that he considers Father too rash. I don't think they will permit him to be one of them."

She nodded imperceptibly and changed the subject.

We spent the night in Mother's little apartment with Dr. Erlich sleeping in the spare bed, Hanna on a couch in the living room, and me in an armchair. I heard Hanna's voice coming out of the darkness.

"I'm sorry about this morning. Some time perhaps you will tell me what it was like for you in the Gestapo barracks."

"It was Gestapo routine."

"Try to forgive me."

"For what?"

"For what you had to do there."

I felt a wave of peace come over me because she had understood, but I was still bruised and my pride would not let me thank her.

I was almost asleep when I heard her once more: "When all this is over, perhaps I can be good for you again."

FOUR

AT DAWN THE NEXT MORNING I put on a sweater and an old pair of pants and drove into the Black Forest. I found the old forester sitting in the sun sucking an empty pipe. At first he did not seem to recognize me, but when I gave him a tin of tobacco and spoke to him in the Schwarzwald dialect he suddenly smiled.

"You're the young naval officer. And you thought I'd forgotten you! I have a very good memory. I have not forgotten you."

We smoked our pipes for five minutes in silence and he told me it was good tobacco, the best he had ever had. It was; I had made sure that it would be the best. Finally I asked him if he would accept three people in his cottage until the war ended. Myself, a young lady, and an elderly man who was her father. For what may have been three minutes he did not speak and I wondered if he was deaf or had not understood.

"I will pay you, of course," I said. "I will pay you very well. And I will bring rations."

He smiled with a sublime insouciance. "But I also have rations. Hares and pheasants. Eggs from a few chickens. Soon I will have potatoes and turnips. My beans are ripe already." He looked at me with an ancient smile. "The last time you were here you wore a naval uniform."

"I'm on leave now."

He smiled again. "Why do you and these people want to come to my house?"

"Air attacks," I said. "My fiancée and her father. He is old and he has not been well."

"You don't have to tell me a story."

"Will you accept us?"

"I have nobody to talk to here."

I opened my wallet and began counting out paper marks. Seeing them, the old man laughed like an amused child, but what he said was not childish.

"What's the use of that money?"

"Money is always useful."

"Soon all that money of yours won't buy a box of matches. We've lost the war."

"How do you know that?"

The old man's face deployed in a crafty smile. "I have a little radio. I have two batteries for it. At night I put up my antennae. I hear our radio." He smiled again. "But also I hear the English radio."

I asked the forester if I could bring my people up that evening.

"I told you that," he said.

I left him and went back to the city. When I reached Mother's apartment only Dr. Erlich was there. He told me that Hanna and Mother had gone out to buy some necessities. Owing to my father's naval rank, Mother had a telephone, so I called the office of her doctor. I introduced myself to his secretary, who told me the doctor was too busy to see another patient for at least three weeks. I explained that I was an officer on leave, that my mother was already his patient, and asked if the doctor could speak to me for a few moments on the phone. When he came onto the line his voice was brusque and he seemed annoyed, but when I asked him if cancer had been found in Mother, his tone altered.

"Is she in hearing now?" he said.

"No, Herr Doktor."

"Why did you ask such a question?"

I tightened, for I had asked the question only as a cover-up in case the police should check with the doctor to make sure I had told them the truth.

"My mother is no longer young," I said. "Naturally one thinks of these possibilities."

He hesitated. "Are you returning to the front?"

"To my duties, certainly."

He hesitated, then said, "Well, yes, there is cancer. I refrained from telling your respected mother. She should be able to live with it for a few more years. Cancer with older people is slower than with the young. And in the meantime, Herr Leutnant" – I could almost see his shoulders shrug – "who knows what may happen?"

"Who knows," I said, and it was a statement, not a question. "Thank you for telling me the truth."

I hung up and sat silently looking out the window. Dr. Erlich had left the room when I went to the telephone to make the call. Probably he had lain down for a rest. I changed into my uniform and went out to buy some supplies. Bedrolls we all needed and I had told Hanna to leave that to me. I went to four different stores before I found one that had them. Then I went to a grocery and bought a quantity of powdered milk, a few kilograms of rice, and a sack of flour. There was no serious lack of food in Germany because the Nazis had looted the continent of most of the food they needed.

When I returned to the apartment Mother and Hanna were there and it was evening. I packed the car and was giving my instructions when Hanna interrupted me.

"You should have been an actor instead of a scholar. Two months in the Gestapo and you're to the manner born."

I was angry until I saw she was smiling.

"It's good, Conrad. I never thought you had it in you."

"God damn you!" I said, but I also smiled and for an instant I was proud.

"All right," I said, still smiling, "these are the orders and they're necessary. Dr. Erlich, will you and Hanna leave here and walk slowly to the corner of the Kaiserstrasse and the Salzstrasse. I'll pick you up there in the car. Meanwhile, I want to be seen leaving here."

They left and I had a few more words with Mother. Then we both went outside and talked a little longer. We kissed one another and I got into the car. My last words were spoken loudly through the open window of the car. "I wish I didn't have to go to Munich but I must."

My departure had been witnessed. Mother went back to her home and I drove off.

It was twilight when we entered the forest. On the verge of it we passed a few pedestrians and one of them looked at us curiously until he recognized my uniform and turned his eyes away. The Volkswagen bumped over the corduroy and reached the forester's cottage just before dark. We settled in by the light of two lanterns, spread our bedrolls on the floor, and one after the other we fell asleep.

FIVE

*E*ARLY THE NEXT MORNING I removed the licence plates from the car and buried them. Then I tried to conceal the car in thick underbrush near the cottage. It was a very small car but its top was just high enough to be visible above the bushes. I took off the wheels and the car jerked down out of sight. It wasn't much of a precaution but it was better than nothing.

Several days passed with nothing happening and no news. Dr. Erlich and Hanna had brought along a few books in their suitcases and were reading in the sun with their backs propped against a log. The forester smoked and seemed happy to have us with him. Once he pointed the stem of his pipe towards Hanna and Dr. Erlich and remarked, "Vornehme Leute. Es freut mich sehr solche Leute zu beschützen."

Yes, I thought, he was just the kind of man who would be happy to protect them, but if the police came it would be the end of him. I told him I hoped we would not cause him trouble and he spat carefully.

"My wife is dead. My sons were put into the army and killed. What is trouble? Don't worry, Herr Leutnant. I know what I know and I do what I do."

But I could not stop worrying about nearly everything and particularly about my mother. I had toyed with the idea of asking her to join us in the forest but I knew she would never have done so. She had to be home in her apartment if my father called her. Also, if Krafft had his men question her, she would be able to say that I had left for Munich on schedule and the neighbors would corroborate her. When I failed to turn up in Munich, they might believe I had been shot up on the roads or killed in the bombing of a city, but if Mother disappeared they would be sure I had deserted and the hunt would be up. As for Hanna and her father, I still relied on Canaris's assurance that the police knew nothing of my connection with them.

Two nights later the forester's radio was tuned in to London and the BBC informed Europe that American planes had delivered a mass raid on Munich. It was a daylight raid and it struck the city at just about the time I would have been due to arrive in it. God knows how many innocent Bavarians had been slaughtered, but all I could think about was ourselves. This might be my alibi.

"I think we're going to make it," I said.

Hanna and I walked out into the forest. It was a warm night with a gibbous moon in a clear sky and no aircraft within hearing. The moonlight filtered down through the branches and the earth was fragrant. We lay on a patch of soft, dry moss and looked up at the Gothic intricacy of the branches with the moonlight shimmering through them. She was wearing a blouse and a dirndl skirt and with swift movements she opened her blouse, took off her skirt, and embraced me.

"Come into me, darling. Come into me!"

If tenderness can unite with ferocity it did so then for both of us. I had never known anything like it before and neither had she. After it was over she rolled on her side still holding me and in the silence of the forest we heard the stealthy movements of small animals. An owl hooted and we lay together until I became potent again and time vanished. The moon was behind a cloud and it was so dark I could not see her but I saw all of her in my mind. We said nothing because no words were necessary. But these words I have written are necessary because this was the last time Hanna and I made love.

The next night the news on the forester's radio was different. Marvellous, we thought, when we heard the first two sentences; terrible we knew, when we heard the rest:

"An unthinkable thing has happened. An attempt has been made on the life of the Führer. The criminals failed, as they were sure to fail. The police already have some of them. The identities of the others are known and they will be hunted down relentlessly."

We were then informed that the hand of God had been over Hitler and that Hitler had taken command of all Germany including the armies. This meant that victory was now certain. "Deutschland über Alles" crashed out and when it ended the radio was silent.

The forester said cheerfully, "Now let's hear what the English say."

The radio crackled with static while he turned the key and soon we heard a voice speaking such meticulous German it could only have come from a foreigner. The English broadcaster made no mention of the plot to kill Hitler. Instead, he told us that the German armies in France were being annihilated in a climactic battle and that the end of Hitler was in sight.

Time, I thought, time! From now on time is going to be the only thing that matters to us. I looked at Dr. Erlich enquiringly and his face in the lamplight was somber.

"This is terrible," he said. "It will make him totally ferocious. He will drive the people to the bitter end."

"He would have done that anyway. I'm wondering about Admiral Canaris."

"So am I."

"Do you think he was involved in it?"

"You would know that better than I."

I shook my head, for I knew nothing. "I'm also thinking about my father."

That night I may have dozed for half an hour, but no real sleep came. I heard Hanna breathing peacefully, but when I got dressed two hours before dawn she came awake.

"I have to go into town to speak with Mother," I whispered. "I'm not wearing my uniform."

"I understand."

I kissed her, she clung to me and guided my hand to her breast. "It's still dark," I whispered. "It will probably be safe enough. But I have to find out what she knows."

Following the path in the darkness I came out of the forest and arrived at Mother's apartment just as the Minster spire was emerging into the first light. The streets were void and I did not see a living thing, not even an alley cat. It was two minutes after my ring before Mother opened the door. She had been asleep and was in her dressing gown. I went in and closed the door silently.

"Have you heard the news?" I asked her.

"You heard it on the radio up there, I suppose?"

"Yes."

"Your father telephoned me last night from Berlin."

"Was he involved?"

"No."

"Did he dare tell you that over the phone?"

"Not in actual words, but he was able to let me know it."

"So he'd discussed something like this with you before?"

"All he told me was that there were officers who were planning something. He never told me what it was. I don't think he knew."

"Is he absolutely safe? Were any of his friends involved?"

"All I know is that he made it clear that he had nothing to do with it."

"What of Canaris?"

"He did not mention Canaris."

I sat down and breathed deeply. "Thank God! Even if those officers did fail, the war can't go on much longer. The British and Americans will break through at any time now. We heard the radio from London."

"You must leave now, Conrad."

"Yes, I know."

"Don't worry about me."

"And don't you worry about me."

I left unnoticed and met nobody on my way into the forest. When I reached the forest I smelled coffee brewing.

"It's all right," I said. "Now there's nothing for us to do but wait."

SIX

*B*UT IT WAS NOT ALL RIGHT. They came for Mother about a week after I left, though I did not know it until much later. Had she told me the truth about my father? I still don't know whether she had or not. Had Father told the truth to her? I don't know that, either. Long after the war was over, when I was safe in America, I read that seven thousand people were executed after the plot against Hitler, and that the families of all the suspects disappeared into what Hitler called *Nacht und Nebel* – night and fog. Every trace of them was obliterated.

A few nights after I saw Mother, we heard from the London radio that the front had broken in France and that British, American, and Canadian tanks were streaming eastward toward Germany with their infantry following in thousands of army trucks. All the German troops that had not been killed or captured in France fell back to defend the frontiers. I thought the war was sure to end within a few weeks at the most, but it dragged on for eight more months during which several million more people died. Once again Dr. Erlich had been right. Hitler drove his people to the bitter end, and Europe with them.

SEVEN

*T*HE PLANES FINALLY CAME TO FREIBURG. In the forest we heard them approaching from the west like the noise of a vast orchestra tuning up before a concert. Then we heard the reverberation of bombs, we felt tremors in the earth, and from the verge of the forest we saw the smoke and flames with the Minster now hidden, now emerging. This was one of the most merciless raids of the entire war. Apart from a few retreating soldiers and the wounded in the hospitals, the total population of Freiburg was less than a hundred thousand souls. After the war I was told that more than twenty-five thousand died in this single attack. Whether it was actually this bad I still don't know, for there was always a tendency to exaggerate the number of casualties in these extermination attacks.

Wave after wave of planes came in over the city, dropped their bombs, and wheeled away. There was no defence at all. Not a fighter plane, not an anti-aircraft gun.

I looked at Hanna and realized I was sobbing.

"I must go down there. I must go down."

Whatever the others may have thought of the possibilities of my finding my mother in all that carnage, they realized that I had to go. On the edge of the city I moved through clusters of men, women, and children who had escaped. Some of them were in tears, all of them seemed in shock. For most, this was the first experience of a mass air attack.

The smoke became so dense that I did not know where I was. The heat seared my skin. Firemen were working but seemed unable to do anything. The city's heart looked impassable. Suddenly I realized that I was in the Schillerstrasse beside the little Dreisam stream only fifty meters from our old home. Its windows were shattered, and when I touched the wall of the house it was hot. I crossed the bridge to the Schwabentor and stumbled through rubble toward the Minster and Mother's house. A hand came down on my shoulder and it was a policeman.

"My mother," I shouted. "I'm trying to find my mother!"

"If she lived where you're going, you'll never find her until the fires are out. I can't let you enter. Orders."

He turned away but I stepped after him and caught his arm.

"I'm a naval officer on leave. My father is Admiral Dehmel."

He turned around abruptly. "Did you say Admiral Dehmel? Is Frau Dehmel your mother?"

"Yes, now will you let me go."

He looked at me strangely. "Frau Dehmel isn't here. She left the city a short time ago."

"Are you sure? Did you know her?"

"Yes," he said, "I'm sure." And he added, "I'm very sorry about it."

I was in too much of a daze to ask him why he was sorry. I felt only relief because my mother had not been there when the planes struck. But I also felt a terrible grief because this was my city, this was my home, and it had been destroyed. As usual, the bombers had spared the cathedral.

I struggled back through the wreckage, passed through the Schwabentor, and crossed the bridge away from the fires. The clusters of refugees had now become a swarm, and police and troops were trying to make some order out of them. I worked my way through intending to return to the forest and suddenly I found myself a few meters away from a face I had almost forgotten. She was in some kind of uniform and was standing beside a big Gestapo officer of a much higher rank than Krafft's. With him was a small clutch of NCOs.

She saw me at the same instant that I saw her. She pointed at me and screamed, "That's him! Grab him!"

It was Eva Schmidt after all these years. A pair of sergeants closed in and I was arrested. I saw Eva speaking to the officer with hatred in her face and saw his eyebrows rise. He came close and looked me over appraisingly.

"So you are Herr Doktor Dehmel! This is very interesting."

He lifted the riding whip he was carrying and slashed me twice across each side of my face.

"Take him away," he said to the sergeants. And to me he added, "I'm occupied at present but we shall soon meet again."

I don't know where they took me, but it was certainly a long distance from Freiburg. I was lying with my hands and ankles manacled in a closed truck and could see nothing. It was dark when they dragged me out and kicked me forward into a prison. I was locked up in a cell and lay there with my back in a partial spasm for many days. I was given enough soup and bread to keep me alive and I lay there and thought about my parents and about Hanna and her father, and about that terrible expression of Hitler's, "Nacht und Nebel." Was that where Mother was? Had my father been arrested? The Gestapo chief had told me we would meet again. Torture followed by death? I assumed it was certain and tried to prepare myself for it.

The day came when the door of my cell was opened with a crash and two Gestapo goons came in. They kicked me down a corridor into a room with the table and the whips and the instruments. Eva's man was standing there in his uniform and high polished boots. He looked at me without speaking and ordered the goons out of the room and closed the door. Then he sat down on the only chair and looked me over again.

"Your training with us seems to have improved you a little," he said. "You're not as soft as you used to be."

I stood in front of him and said nothing.

"I have decided to introduce myself. I am Obersturmbannführer

Heinrich. You have possibly heard of my reputation?"

"Naturally, sir."

He lit a cigarette, drew on it, held it away, and looked studiously at the burning tip of it.

"There is said to be a common bond between two men who have had the same woman," he said coolly. "Would you agree?"

I said nothing and he smiled slightly.

"If you had been a man like myself, you would have found her remarkably responsive. But you were not a man like myself."

I said nothing.

"When I first saw you," he said, "I realized something that does not seem to have occurred to you, Herr Doktor. Our features are quite similar. Our expressions, of course, are not. And fortunately that is the great difference."

I looked at him and realized that he was right. The bone structure of our faces was remarkably alike, but his mouth was wider and in repose it was a hard, straight line. His eyes were a hard, cold gray.

"You know, Professor, I'm beginning to have a slight respect for you. You almost got away with it. You can thank your father for your failure. If he hadn't joined those imbecile generals who tried to kill the Führer, we'd never have caught you. Did you know what he was up to?"

"I knew nothing of it."

"If I'd believed you had, I wouldn't have asked you the question. Well, they bungled it. Fools and snobs." He stared at me calmly. "Your father was hanged two days ago. Slowly. Do you know what happens to the sphincter muscle when a man is hanged?"

"I received instruction in the SS."

"Their braces and belts were removed from their pants and their pants fell down to their ankles. Their pants caught it. Do you wish to know about your mother?"

I kept my mouth shut and he smiled slightly once more.

"She has been put away," he said quietly, his eyes steady on mine.

"Is she dead?"

"Not yet."

"I'm sure Mother knew nothing."

"As you've already told me that you knew nothing about it yourself, how dare you tell me your mother knew nothing?"

"If my father was involved – and I can't believe he was, though some of his friends may have been – he would never have told my mother."

"A matter of no importance. The Führer has ordered the disappearance of every man, woman, and child connected with those fools!"

I made my last play for Mother. "Herr Obersturmbannführer, there is – or was – my brother Siegfried. You must know of his service to the nation and the Führer. Can't that be considered in my mother's case?"

"You underwent training with us and you ask such a stupid question?" He suddenly barked, "Strip!"

I stood there stupidly.

"Take off your clothes!" he shouted. "All of them!"

I stumbled when I took off my first shoe, but finally I stood naked before him. He rose from his chair, looked over my body, felt the muscles of my shoulders and arms, and flicked my penis lightly with his whip.

"In *that*, at least, there is no resemblance between us. You didn't even know Eva well enough to know she only responds when she is being hurt." He sat down again and crossed his legs, the overhead light shining on his polished jackboots. "Now you will tell me where is the Jew Erlich and his daughter."

"I don't know what you mean."

"Don't insult your own intelligence, to say nothing of mine."

His body seemed to spring from the chair in a single piece and he slashed my face with his whip. My nakedness shuddered.

"Do you deny that you knew this Jewess, Hanna Erlich?"

"I knew her in London before the war, but I left London after the Führer took power."

"We know that, of course. When did you next meet her?"

He sat down again and once more crossed his legs, though his whip kept flicking nervously against his boots.

"I never saw her again."

"This becomes tiresome. Permit me to move the enquiry more quickly. An SS lieutenant was seen driving Erlich and his daughter from that village where they were living. They went in the direction of Munich. The local people thought he was arresting them. A few days later two genuine officers came for them and were told about what you did there. Sturmbannführer Krafft told me the rest. He also told me the story you trumped up about your mother's illness."

"She did have cancer," I said. "You can prove it by speaking with the doctor who treated her. I can give you his name. I can—" I stopped, because I knew it was hopeless to continue.

"I've no more time to waste," Heinrich said. "Where are Erlich and his daughter?"

"In Switzerland."

"Can't you think of a better lie than that? We know about that banker-brother of this Dr. Erlich. They're not in Switzerland. They're some place near Freiburg. Where?"

"I don't know."

"You fool. Now we must waste more of our time with you."

EIGHT

*T*HE TORTURE SESSIONS went on for the rest of the day. During them I fainted several times. The tortures were resumed after I came to. I still marvel that I lasted as long as I did. I didn't know day from night so I can't tell at what time I finally broke. But I did break in the end and told them where Hanna and her father were and told them also that if they found an old man with them he was innocent and knew nothing. Then I became unconscious again. I came to in my cell and the only realities were the pain and the horror and the shame. I expected to be taken out and shot and remembered that during the tortures I had begged them to kill me, just as had hundreds of thousands of others in those years.

How much time passed while I was in the cell I don't know, but a day came when I was dragged out once more and found myself in a room with Heinrich and two of his assistants. My brain was functioning badly. Hanna and her father were also in the room but at first I was not sure whether they were real or images in my mind.

They were real. Heinrich smiled in their direction and pointed to me with his whip.

"He's the one who told us where you were hiding. What do you think of him now?"

Hanna saw the condition I was in and suddenly she screamed, "It doesn't matter, Conrad, it doesn't matter! They arrested us two days after the attack on the city. They killed the forester. So it doesn't matter what you said."

The whip slashed across her face. They were both taken away and I never saw them again. Heinrich looked at me and said in an indifferent voice, "It won't be necessary to torture you again. However, you will not die quickly."

I was shipped to the Belsen camp, where I was to be starved and worked to death along with the other inmates. If the British had been a week later I don't believe I would have survived, for in the end we had nothing to eat at all.

I never told you any of these details, Stephanie. I just couldn't do it. Now that I have written all this down, I don't think I should ever show it to you. What happened to me happened to hundreds of thousands of others and many of them were much braver than I was.

The whole world knows in a general way what happened in those years, but even now, who can really understand *why* it happened? Modern medicine has easily explained the Black Death and Dr. Erlich explained why Hitler became a psychotic. But as time passes I'm not sure that even he explained how it was possible for a man like Hitler to become our master.

So why have I written this? To sound a warning? To suggest that if such things happened in one civilized country, they may happen in others? But thousands have sounded the same warning before me.

Those years seem an eternity ago except when I have nightmares. The Hanna I loved so greatly has become unreal, though the Hanna I saw for a few minutes in the presence of Heinrich will never leave me. Since then I have studied and worked and have known what contentment and happiness are, and nearly all of it I owe to you, dear Stephanie. But what should have been the prime of my life was blighted by the place and the time where I spent it. It was the same for nearly all Germans of my age, and for hundreds of millions of others. We were robbed of our youth, of the best years of our lives, and this may explain why so many of us have failed the youth of today.

Now the storm signals are flying again and the world may easily go out of control once more. Some psychopaths are sure to come to power because no age has ever been immune to them. But if a breakup comes, and quite possibly it won't, the cause of it will at least be more impressive than a miserable little creature like Adolf Hitler.

It will come out of the vastest explosion of human energy this little planet has ever known. It will come because our political habits and institutions will prove incapable of controlling this energy. The entire world is screaming for freedom and is sincere about it, but they don't understand what freedom is. The most violent screamers are really screaming for release from freedom's discipline, which means they are screaming for somebody to return them to slavery.

Is even this correct? Will men ever understand the meaning of the things they do, or why they do them?

PART NINE

Timothy Wellfleet's Story
as told by
John Wellfleet

I BEGAN WITH MY COUSIN TIMOTHY and now the time has come to end
with him. But first I must summarize a long period in the life of
Conrad Dehmel.

After his release from Belsen, he spent several months in what was
called a Displaced Persons' Camp before he was restored to health.
He was entirely alone in the postwar world, as were millions of
others whose lives had been uprooted by the war. Almost every city
in Germany had had its heart blasted into rubble and the survivors
were living like cavemen in holes in the ruins.

A British officer in the occupation army happened to recognize
Conrad during a tour of inspection and Conrad recognized him.
They had met several times during Conrad's London days and this
officer wished to recruit him into the rehabilitation program. But
Conrad could not endure the prospect of working in a land where
everyone he had known and loved was dead, so he wrote to Professor
Rosenthal in America. Nine years had passed since their brief meeting in Berlin, but Rosenthal remembered him. An American visa was
arranged and Conrad sailed to the New World. He spent a week in
Princeton as Rosenthal's guest and was introduced to Einstein. Later,
he was offered a post in the History department of another American
university.

He returned to his historical studies and though his old dream of
creating a grand design of History, Anthropology, and Philosophy
had not vanished, it had been greatly modified. He did a prodigious
amount of research and published many articles in learned journals.
Rapidly he acquired a modest international reputation in the university world. About his personal life during these years I know nothing
whatever. Were there other women in his life? More important, was
there a single woman? I don't know, for there is no record. But he

was not an anchorite and he was certainly a man who needed and appreciated women.

After more than fifteen years in this American university, Conrad resigned on account of some stupid academic squabble and came to us. In his third year in Montreal he met my mother and a year later he married her.

For Mother, alone with two so-called illegitimate children and with her father dead, this marriage was certainly a release from a frightful insecurity, but financial security could have had nothing to do with her decision to marry him. My mother was truly a lovely person, rarer than I ever guessed when she was alive and I was very young. She was so honest she was often bewildering. On the whole, Conrad's last years were happy ones, though like everyone else with experiences like his, there was an underlying sadness in him that in bad moments came close to despair. He and Mother probably had some stormy times, but there is no doubt of their devotion to each other. He made many friends in our city among both our own people and the many European scientists and professional men who had come to live among us. When I myself went to the university he had been dead for some time, but one of my professors told me that he had been regarded as a great teacher as well as an international scholar. Valuable people had respected him. He was several times consulted by one prime minister and was a personal friend of his successor.

But he was nervous. Who could have been otherwise than nervous with his knowledge and experience in what he always called an innocent country? The differences between our country and the Germany of his youth were very great, but there were resemblances that were alarming to all the Europeans who had elected to live among us. Chiefly, that a young generation had lost all confidence in the very meaning of our civilization and had begun to run amok, with foreign influences stirring the revolts. In his old-fashioned way, Conrad felt it his duty to speak out, just as he did on Timothy's show, and as there was an open season on any public man over fifty, he became a target for the neo-Marxists and the separatists.

It was soon discovered that none of them had anything to do with his death, but Timothy certainly did, though unwittingly. The death remained a mystery, though if Conrad had told Mother about his experience with the Gestapo there would have been no mystery at all. As I have said several times, and forgive me if I repeat it, the time of my youth was bewildering to everyone who lived in it. We were in the grip of enormous forces we could not understand. I was accurate when I told André that for ordinary people this was the most exciting time in the history of the world. That was the trouble with it. The prosperity was incredible, even though anyone who thought about it knew it could not last indefinitely. So many exciting things happened that we lived from one crisis to another and our brains were so battered by them that we could not grasp what they meant.

So now I will return to that rare symptom, my cousin Timothy. His story begins in the immediate aftermath of his television performance with Conrad Dehmel.

TWO

WHEN TIMOTHY CAME TO HIMSELF, he knew that Esther Stahr had been right when she told him the government would never surrender to the kind of demands the terrorists were making. The very next morning, in the small hours when he was asleep, troops moved into the city and the police began arresting a number of people under some legislation that was supposed to be applicable only in wartime. Timothy was one of the few journalists who attacked the government for this: "Everything I hated in authority, armies, police, establishments, and my father's generation surfaced when I saw those soldiers and heard about the arrests."

He studied the first lists of the names of arrested people. There was Emile Chalifour, just as Chalifour had expected. Timothy imagined Chalifour in a prison cell raging at him. However, the police soon discovered that he was insignificant and released him before the week was over. But Timothy was still upset about Esther Stahr and the next morning he telephoned her.

"Just who was right and who was wrong?" he shouted at her over the telephone. "Didn't I tell you that war is the health of the state? Look at what they've done now. They've declared war on the kids. They've turned this country into a police state."

There was silence on the other end of the line.

"Did you hear what I said?" he shouted at her.

"You and I can't go on like this," she answered and hung up on him.

Two days after Timothy's performance with Conrad, just as Esther had predicted, the kidnapped cabinet minster was strangled and the news of it went around the world. A few years later the murder of hostages became so frequent that it was hardly newsworthy, but this one was the first to happen in what we used to call a civilized country. The night following, Timothy's Pentagon show appeared and this is Timothy's note on it:

"According to my standards it was a minor masterpiece. General Sprott played a beautiful obbligato to the horror clips Réjean and Jacques had spliced together, but the whole show was wasted. Barely a tenth of my usual audience looked at it. They were glued to the radio and the other TV stations for news about the kidnappings and the manhunts."

Immediately letters and phone calls had poured into the studio protesting Timothy's behavior to Conrad Dehmel and his general treatment of the news. For the first time they began to worry him. A day came when he was sitting in his office planning the next program with Réjean Roy when the telephone sounded. He picked it up and heard a hard male voice.

"Are you Wellfleet?"

"Yes."

He heard heavy breathing before the voice came on again.

"I'm just letting you know that you're not going to live much longer. We've had enough from bastards like you."

He heard the caller's phone click down and told Réjean what the man had said.

Réjean shrugged, "Like I said, things are bad around here."

"Anyway, you and Jacques did a beautiful job. That show was just about perfect."

Once more Réjean shrugged. Timothy recorded that he felt totally alone, that there was nobody he could talk to any more.

THREE

*T*HE ATTACKS ON Timothy's style of journalism grew more numerous and he became even more resentful. "It was all very well for Esther Stahr to tell me I was debasing the profession by making the news a part of the entertainment business, but what else could anyone do? What real news did the pols and the power men give to any of us? What else could we do but guess and be indignant? All you box-watchers who tuned in to The National, just what did *you* expect to get? Now under the emergency legislation they gave us nothing. My private opinion was that they had nothing to give, but we were supposed to fill our columns and air spaces, so we jabbered in a vacuum for weeks. Quite a few columnists and media men jabbered against me, and one of them virtually accused me of being responsible for political kidnappings and murders. He listed twenty-seven shows of mine over a period of three years in which he said that I had invited terrorists onto my programs. I thought of suing him for libel, until I checked back and realized that it wasn't worth while. He had exaggerated, of course; I had not had twenty-seven terrorists on twenty-seven occasions, but I had certainly had them on seven."

The evening after this attack was published, he was sitting at his desk in the studio when a messenger handed him a sealed envelope. It was marked "Personal" and when he recognized the handwriting he was pretty sure what was inside the envelope. It was Esther's formal resignation from the program. "And when I read those cold, official words, the walls of the room began to shake as though in an earthquake. Truly I had never believed she would go as far as this or do it in this way."

He phoned her apartment but there was no answer. He went out and walked the streets and felt the high-strung tension in the few people he passed. He made calls in one phone booth after another until at 23:00 hours he finally found her home. He begged her to come back but at first all he could hear was her heavy breathing at the other end of the wire.

"Esther, I'm forlorn. Please come back. Please speak to me, anyway."

He heard her say, "I'm sorry, Timmie."

"Say something, Esther. Anything."

"Some of it has been my fault," she said.

"Then you'll speak to me again?"

He had always known there was power in her, but now he sensed something deeper than ordinary power – "Thousands of years of experience built into the genes of this woman's ancestors – a cataract of images that once had been facts – the lustful faces of the barbarian goys of the Middle Ages, the lustful faces of the Cossacks and the priests, the lustful faces of some of their own Jewish employers."

Still she remained silent and the two of them listened to each other's breathing translated over the wire.

Finally she said, "You're in danger, Timmie. I have to tell you that."

"In danger from what?"

Again all he heard was her breathing and he thought that the armor was built into her while he had no armor at all.

"From *what* am I in danger?"

"A lot of this – not all but some of it – it's been my fault."

"Answer me, for God's sake! What am I in danger from?"

"Yourself," she said.

"Isn't everybody?"

"No, not everybody."

"Then tell me who I am, for I don't know any more who I am."

Another silence.

"For Christ's sake, do I really deserve this? I didn't manufacture this crazy world."

"I said I was sorry, Timmie."

Then he begged her to let him send her air tickets to Nassau or Antigua. He told her that she was simply tired out and needed a change. He was not suggesting that he accompany her. She could take anyone she wished for a companion. He stopped talking when he realized that he might be sounding like a newly rich husband talking to a neglected wife.

Then she spoke to him. "I'll always think of you. How can I not? I loved you and I still do. Probably you're the only man I'll ever love. It's not all your fault, what happened. What I told you at the beginning about not being able to marry a gentile. If I hadn't said that, perhaps – but I did say it. All along I knew it couldn't be permanent and I didn't believe you wanted it to be permanent. You don't want it now, not really." She paused, then said quietly, "Please understand that what I'm feeling is much worse than sadness."

Timothy recorded that when she told him this a coolness came over him and he felt something a little like peace. He told her quietly that perhaps he understood her at last. He told her that he had truly loved her.

"You tried to," she said gently. "So did I try to help you love me."

"I'm not hanging up on you," he said, "but now I'll say good night."

"Is it good-bye?"

"If you've decided to live with it. Yes, Esther – good-bye."

He hung up and realized that he was standing in a phone booth on the corner of Crescent and St. Catherine; also that it might just as well have been any street corner in any city in the world.

He knew he would be unable to sleep if he went home and began to walk the streets and he recorded that it was uncanny. A few cars whirred softly along empty pavements though it was close to the heart of the city, and this city was not one where everyone went to bed early. Occasionally he heard the screams of distant police sirens. They were still searching and finding nothing. There were supposed to be sixteen different cells but how did anyone know that? So far only two had struck. While he was standing on a corner a prowl car slowed down and the policeman who was not driving rolled down his window and stuck his head out to look Timothy over. Timothy guessed he had been recognized because the cop half turned and said something to his mate behind the wheel. Then he turned back and stared "with the kind of expression cops mobilize when they don't like you." Timothy turned away and continued to walk, it having occurred to him that if he continued to stand he might be arrested for loitering. The car drove past him, then picked up speed, and he heard the whir of its tires diminish in the distance.

"This town is like a herd of zebras smelling leopards," he said aloud to nobody and walked slowly home.

FOUR

I𝑇 WAS FOUR IN THE MORNING before Timothy finally fell asleep and four hours later he woke with the phone ringing. When he picked it up the voice on the other end was his father's.

"Yes," he said, "what is it?"

"What *is* it? What the hell do you think it is?"

Of all the many people he did not wish to talk to at that moment, including the police, his father came first on the list. Half asleep and half awake, he hung up on him. Not in the three years since his program began had his father spoken to him or written a word to him.

"That poor little thing I had done – he had never acknowledged its existence. In those three years only one member of my proliferous family had ever spoken to me and even that occasion was accidental. A year ago I had collided physically with my second cousin Eunice in the nether parts of the Ritz, I coming out of the men's room and she on her way to the Maritime Bar. We had stopped, stared, and laughed. Eunice was a cool little piece, conventional even in her discreet sleeping around with older men, and the last thing she wanted was to have her cosy little world blown apart by political nationalists. I invited her to a drink and she told me she was on her way to lunch with somebody else.

"Would you be interested to know who dined with us last night?" she said.

"Should I be?"

"I think so. Your father and stepmother, no less. When I mentioned your name he turned the color of a turkey cock after his seventh double Scotch."

"You should have told him not to do that. He might get a heart attack."

"What a funny boy you are, Timmie. Apparently you don't know that he's already had one."

I forced a smile and asked her if it was serious.

"Apparently not very, but his doctor's made him slow down."

"So Father watches my show?"

"We all do. It's very clever. Your father says it won't last much longer. Will it?"

"The ratings say so."

"But can't they change very quickly?"

"I'm afraid they can." I looked at her: a neat figure, a neat face, cool eyes, a sensual mouth. "Why don't you go out with one of our *concitoyens*, for a change? That's where the real action is these days. Or haven't you learned to speak French yet?"

"I speak French quite nicely, thank you. And since you're so interested, I'm having lunch with one of them now."

"Will you be speaking French or English?"

"English, of course."

"Is he rich?"

"Much richer than your father, I believe. And is it necessary for you to be as objectionable in private as you are in public?"

Timothy was still remembering this incident when the phone rang again, and he let it ring three times before he picked it up. It was his father back at him and he lay there with his father not talking to him, but at him. "He did not know that I had rigged a tape recorder to my phone which I suspected (rightly, as I later discovered) was tapped by the police. It is to this tape that I, as well as the police, am indebted for a recorded conversation that did credit to neither of us."

And I, more than sixty years later, am indebted to the same recording.

"If I've taken the initiative in making contact with you," his father began, "you may be sure it's important. But first of all let me tell you something – " and for several minutes Timothy listened to his father telling him a lot of things, with particular emphasis on his performance with General Sprott, for which Colonel Wellfleet said he had apologized in a personal call to Washington. While Timothy reflected that his father was like a dinosaur haranguing a baby lizard that had learned to grow his claws into embryo wings, the Colonel ended, "Why don't you answer my question?"

"How can I, when you haven't asked me a question?"

The Colonel had to stop because of a coughing fit and after a final sputter he cleared his throat.

"This is awful," he said, and another cough checked him. Then his voice steadied. "Do you – or do you not – know what happened last night?"

"I suppose a lot of things happened. Why don't you get down to it, Father?"

"What happened to Conrad Dehmel – do you know it?"

"What happened to who?"

Timothy's reply must have been purely defensive, for there was a quaver in his voice. His father let out a roar, then spoke in that lethally quiet voice Timothy had always hated.

"Are you under drugs?"

"Is it really essential for people like you to believe that everyone you dislike is under drugs?"

"Dislike you? I'm your father. I despise what you've been doing and you make me ashamed to show my face, but I don't dislike you. Haven't you taken in the name I just gave you?"

"Of course I know who Dehmel is, but what's he got to do with last night?"

"Oh, I see. So you don't know what happened last night. Well, you'd better brace yourself." Another pause. "Dr. Conrad Dehmel was murdered last night. He was shot and killed and I'm almost certain this would never have happened if it hadn't been for that show of yours. A crazy man did it. You're vicious pretty often, but I never saw you as vicious as you were with him. You were out-of-this-world horrifying with him. I couldn't believe it, what you accused him of. Poor Stephanie was with him last night. She loved you when you were a child and she was with him when he was murdered."

"Stephanie?" Timothy was dazed. "What's she got to do with Dehmel?"

His father gasped. "You – you really mean what you've just said?"

"I don't know what you're talking about."

"My God, for once I have to believe you. You didn't know!"

"Didn't know what?"

"That Stephanie was Conrad Dehmel's wife. The man you've almost certainly destroyed was Stephanie's husband. The country is full of crazy people these days and you zeroed this maniac right in on him."

Timothy recorded that this hit him with the shock of a bullet. His mouth and throat were dry and he stammered.

"How could I know that? I haven't seen Stephanie for years. I never knew she was married to anyone."

The colonel-businessman's voice went cold, factual, and very unpleasant.

"Now I know this world is completely out of control if an irresponsible fool like you is allowed to perform on a national network. You – the great authority and judge of the nations – you didn't know that the only human being you ever really cared for in your entire life had at last found some security and happiness. Conrad Dehmel was a splendid man. Indeed, I thought him a wonderful man – which was just enough to entice a jealous little viper like you to strike your fangs into him. He came onto your program trusting that you'd be decent because of Stephanie. He had a note from her that he gave you and still you did it. I'm partly responsible myself, for when Dr. Dehmel asked me about accepting your so-called invitation, I told him that if Stephanie told you who he was, you'd behave yourself."

Timothy was reeling and almost sobbing with grief and shame. "Note? What note?"

"You mean you didn't receive a letter from him?"

Then he remembered. "Wait a minute, let me look."

He had not worn the suit he used that night since he returned home from the studio. When he urinated against the door of the garage in the alley he had wet his pants and had thrown his suit aside and forgotten it. He found the suit, reached into its pockets, and discovered the letter, unopened. He recognized my mother's precise handwriting. He had not even looked at the envelope when Conrad gave it to him before the program. He returned to the telephone.

I have mentioned several times that there was a kind of desperate endurance in Timothy and it held him together now. He did not collapse and sob with his father on the line. Instead, he controlled himself and said quietly, "Tell me exactly what happened."

His father did tell him exactly what happened. As the whole country was informed by the press *what* happened, I knew this much myself. But in all this time, I never knew until I translated Conrad's final narrative *why* it happened. Here is the cold, factual story, which I myself read as a boy in the newspapers.

FIVE

ABOUT A WEEK AFTER Timothy's program, Conrad appeared in a public debate on the moral issues of the current crisis in our city and province. He had agreed to this debate several weeks previously, and as I later discovered, my mother was so appalled by what Timothy had done, and so fearful that a demonstration would be made against him, that she begged him to cancel the engagement. Of course he refused to do this, because if he had cancelled, it would have been equal to an admission that Timothy had been right in naming him as a war criminal. There were three other speakers on the platform, two of them separatists. One of the separatists spoke first, but when Conrad rose the demonstration against him was deafening.

The student activist Jason Ross, the one who had given Timothy the paper implicating Conrad as a Nazi and a member of the Gestapo, was there with a large claque of neo-Marxists, and they made such an uproar insulting him that he could not speak. After five minutes of this, the chairman shouted over the loudspeaker that the meeting was dismissed. Mother was sitting in the front row and she joined Conrad when he left the platform. They went out the back door of the building escorted by the chairman, for if he had gone down into the audience he would have been mobbed. When they reached the street the situation was still ugly, but a car was there ready to take them home, and then it happened.

Out of the crowd came a white-haired man with a pistol in his hand. He reached Conrad in five steps, stared at him, and screamed.

"Heinrich! You killed my wife and my children and you tortured me. I thought you were dead and then I saw you."

He pulled the trigger and shot Conrad through the heart. Conrad fell on his back and Stephanie went down on her knees beside him. The killer also went down on his knees, pushed Stephanie aside, and stared closely into Conrad's face. Then he leaped to his feet and people who saw him said that his face revealed not insanity but horror.

"My God!" he screamed in Yiddish. "You're not Heinrich! My God, I've made a terrible mistake."

The shock was great, there were no police to take over, and nobody moved. The man looked down at Mother cradling Conrad's head and she later told the police that he bent down and cried at her with such heartbreak in his voice that she pitied him.

"Kind lady – kind lady – forgive me!"

Then he put the pistol into his mouth and pressed the trigger a second time.

I will continue to be factual. Conrad's murder sent a shock through the whole country and was reported in many other countries besides ours. It caused a violent reaction against the popular baiting of public men and it brought an abrupt end to Timothy's program. The letter he received from the network cancelling his program crossed his own letter of resignation.

A memorial service for Conrad was held in the university chapel and the Prime Minister himself, who was a personal friend of Conrad, attended it. The police arrested Jason Ross, who denied Timothy's statement that it was he who had given the information that Conrad was a member of the Gestapo, so it was his word against Timothy's. Ross was released, but his hour in the sun was extinguished and soon everyone forgot about him.

Meanwhile, Timothy's father had gone into action. Immediately after speaking to his son, he and Stephanie went to Conrad's office in the university and collected all his papers and files and placed them in the Colonel's house. Mother would never have thought of this, but the Colonel had once served in Intelligence and he was taking no chances that some document might be found by the wrong people. So it was he who secured most of Conrad's papers, which he later turned over to Mother.

The record of the assassin was searched and there was no mystery in it. He was a Polish Jew whose family had been murdered by the Gestapo and had himself been tortured and put into a camp. After the war he emigrated to Canada and had been living for years in a small town on the British Columbia coast. His name was Dobrovsky and by trade he was a master carpenter. He had told the local people his story and that he was waiting for the gas chambers when the Russians liberated him. They simply let him go along with the others and he walked away. He entered Czechoslovakia and from there he contacted Jewish friends in America. An international organization furnished him with enough funds to emigrate to the New World, and he had gone as far away from Europe as he could.

Dobrovsky lived the rest of his life as a widower and had been highly respected. Everyone said he was a very quiet man. After his suicide, one of the townsmen told the police that on the night of Timothy's show, Dobrovsky had been in his house and they had watched it together. Suddenly, when Conrad was being harassed by Timothy—when he was accused of being a member of the Gestapo—Dobrovsky had turned pale and leaped to his feet and pointed.

"That's Heinrich!" he had shouted. "That's Heinrich! They told me he was dead!"

This, of course, happened at the moment when Timothy had signalled his floor crew to alter the lighting and the camera angles.

Without telling anyone what was in his mind, Dobrovsky then flew to Montreal to kill Conrad.

Timothy, his balance almost destroyed, had tried to discover what the man had meant when he shouted "Heinrich!" He soon found out that Heinrich had been an exceptionally villainous man, but he never found a picture of him. Everyone knew what Himmler, Heydrich, and Kaltenbrunner had looked like, but there were no pictures of Heinrich. The Jewish organization that had tracked down some of the worst war criminals had found no postwar traces of this man. They assumed that he either had been killed in the fighting in Berlin at the end of the war, or had deserted to the Russians and been given a job in their own secret police.

These are the facts as we knew them and it was not from Mother that I learned that Timothy really had been responsible for Conrad's death. I had to outlive my own civilization by three-quarters of my life span before I learned it by inference from Conrad's own narrative.

Anyway, I have little difficulty in reconstructing the immediate aftermath of the assassination. To Mother, Timothy was almost like her own child. She could be very firm with children, but I never knew anyone who had such easy love for them and joy in them. So those words of hers – "All our lives were in those boxes" – they tell me all I need to know.

All the newspapers in the country intimated that if Timothy had not treated Conrad as he had done, the obsessed man Dobrovsky would never have killed him. Now she feared that Timothy might commit suicide from shame and guilt; perhaps believed that if he became a pariah he might commit a slower suicide with alcohol and drugs. She wished Conrad's value to be established by his autobiography, and at the same time she wanted to give Timothy a chance to make an atonement. So he agreed to help her, though as it turned out, not in the way she had hoped. For Timothy had a genuine creative instinct and soon he was telling his own story and weaving it into Conrad's. He never finished it because the boxes were lost.

So that leaves me with one more problem – why were *all* the papers stored in those iron boxes and left in Mother's basement when she went to England a year after Conrad's death?

The only possible explanation is that Timothy also took off after a year's work on the project. His restlessness was insatiable and he would never have found it easy to stay for a long time in one place, any more than I could myself until travel was closed down by the Second Bureaucracy.

Here, then, is the story that André Gervais asked me to put together with the idea that it would be a record from the world I lived in when I was very young. As time passes and more books and records are found, the whole period is sure to be reconstructed and come to light. I will never see this happen, of course, because I realize with some incredulity that I am now in my seventy-ninth year.

PART TEN

John Wellfleet's Story
concluded by
André Gervais

WHEN JOHN WELLFLEET began this story he doubted if he would live long enough to finish it. He wondered at first whether any kind of coherence could be made out of such a jumble of material. He was also troubled about some of the dates in the past and was not always sure that his memory was accurate. He used to say to me that once a man reaches the age of fifty, time passes in a blur; that two years in the life of a man in his twenties can seem longer than twenty years in the life of a man in his seventies. But one thing he was sure of: he remembered the time of his youth much better than he remembered the years between the Destructions and the present. What troubled him most was his belief that none of us would be able to identify with the characters in his book, or have any sympathy with them. And finally there was the glossary; it took us more than a month, working together, to complete it.

For me it was wonderful to watch this strange old man appear to grow young again as he lived with these papers. It angered me also to realize how heartless the Bureaucracy was to have branded survivors like John Wellfleet as inoperatives and put them into those compounds isolated from everyone else. Long before he finished the work, I begged him to leave the compound but he said that he was used to it, that his books were there, and that he did not want to lose any time from his work by moving. However, once he had delivered the book to me, he agreed to come out.

I was living at the time in a small hamlet on the transporter line not far from Metro and I found an empty cottage for him. He often visited us and we visited him and in his last winter I even persuaded him to live with us during the cold months because I was afraid that he lacked the strength to keep himself warm. We had a large stone hearth in our principal room and burned wood from our own trees, which were red oaks. The logs were heavy and made a very hot fire, and in the evenings after work, when the children were in bed and some of our friends came in for conversation, John's chair was always beside the hearth. By this time he limped badly from arthritis and if he had been left alone he would have suffered that winter, which was one of the coldest I can remember.

There was still another thing he did for us which may put him into the debt of future generations. He had a large collection of disks that he called records and an old instrument he called a record-player. It had ceased to function years before I knew him, but one of my friends, who is an electrician, studied it and decided that he might be able to repair it. He did repair it and then music came into our lives.

All of us knew old songs, even some new ones, and there were a few people who could play violins, trumpets, drums, guitars, and even pianos, but music of the kind which requires orchestras had been absolutely forbidden by the Bureaucracy. At first this music was strange to me, very difficult to understand, but it reached my feelings as nothing had ever reached them before. I had never heard the names of the composers until John told me them, and said they had been the glory of civilization even in the terrible days when he was young – Scarlatti, Corelli, Handel, Bach, Mozart, Beethoven, and many more. He also had some records he called "Jazz" and a few he called "Rock." The Jazz I rather liked, but after hearing a few records of the Rock I told him that at least it helped me to understand a little better why his cousin Timothy had been the kind of man he was.

When the warm weather came, he went back to his own little cottage and spent much time sitting in the sun and listening to the birds singing. It was full summer of that year before we finally finished printing the book and I was able to give him a copy. He glanced through a few pages, laid it down, and said that it no longer belonged to him; that it seemed now as though somebody else had written it. When he asked how many copies had been printed, I told him that we had a total of fifty and that we intended to circulate them among our friends who would lend them to others. He smiled quietly and asked if the Bureaucracy would ban it if they knew it had been published. Yes, I had to tell him, if the book were given to the general public the Bureaucracy would confiscate it and burn it. I had done my best with them, but could not make them change their decision. But I also assured him that within ten years, perhaps even sooner, the younger men of my generation would have control of the Bureaucracy and thousands of people would be able to read his book. His expression was strange when he said that this kind of thing had often happened to books before.

A few weeks later, in the late afternoon of a very hot day when I had expected him to visit us, he did not come. I walked over to his cottage to see if he was all right. He was leaning back in his chair with his face toward the sky and even before I touched him I knew he had died, and I remembered an old phrase my mother had used. Literally, he seemed to have passed away from us, yet I had the sensation that though his body was dead, his mind was alive. There was a table beside his chair and a piece of paper on it, a pen lying across the paper. Apparently he had intended to write a letter, but had got no further than the single introductory word "Dear..." Was it his Mother? Was it the girl he called Joanne? I would never know, but I am sure that in this last instant of his life he was remembering someone he had loved.